P9-CBQ-650

CHECK POINTS FOR DANGER

A Leipzig hotel bedroom, where a man and woman came together aflame with desire and chilled by peril... *an East German prison chamber,* where a captive could only outwit his captors so long... *a posh Berlin bar,* where an international body-snatching organization demanded blood money for live goods ... *a vast Communist computer center,* where millions of people were turned into puppets... *a U.S. Army post on the edge of East-West confrontation,* where a young officer faced a decision he dared not make... *the floor of the U.N. and the corridors of power in Washington,* where time was running out...

CROSSING IN BERLIN

"Suspense and intrigue!"
—CHARLESTON POST

"High drama!"
—PUBLISHERS WEEKLY

"As good as *Seven Days in May* ... the best!"
— ABILENE REPORTER

FLETCHER KNEBEL

CROSSING IN BERLIN

CHARTER BOOKS, NEW YORK

This Charter Book contains the complete
text of the original hardcover edition.

CROSSING IN BERLIN

A Charter Book / published by arrangement with
Doubleday and Co., Inc.

PRINTING HISTORY
Doubleday edition / 1981
Charter edition / March 1984

ISBN: 0-441-12290-6

Charter Books are published by The Berkley Publishing Group,
200 Madison Avenue, New York, N.Y. 10016.
PRINTED IN THE UNITED STATES OF AMERICA

For Those Behind Walls

I can only love
        what I am also free
                to leave:
this country
this city
this woman
this life

And that's the reason why
so few love a country
some love a city
many love a woman
but all love life

      . . . . Wolf Biermann
      Expelled from
      East Germany 1976

1

He huddled in his sheepskin coat, shelter from the night wind that whipped across the Platz der Republik and whistled with icy tongues through columns of the cavernous railroad station.

Leipzig's gritty, late November air held the threat of snow flurries. People bent to the wind as they plodded past, homeward bound after a day's work in the publishing houses, metalworking sheds, and fur marts of East Germany's second largest city. They gathered in clumps at the streetcar stops, frosty breath rising like steam in the reflected glow of the running electric sign atop the sooty, old Park-Hotel that flashed news of the world, Communist brand, to an unconcerned populace.

Few people so much as glanced at the bulletins which unrolled precisely, a letter at a time, as if some global judge of the day's calamities were setting type for his own decisions. In contrast to the people of Leipzig, Mike doted on the news. Some evenings he would stand for a quarter of an hour, pocket German-English dictionary in hand, trying to puzzle out, not so much the news of the day as the mind of the government journalist who had strung together such an odd assortment of happenings, imagings, proclamations, and prefabricated events.

Tonight, despite the piercing cold, Mike stood near a trolley stop and watched the recapitulation of the day's developments according to East Germany's Marxist theoreticians: ADDIS ABABA: ETHIOPIA THUNDERS WELCOME TO DDR HEAD OF STATE . . . RIO DE JANEIRO: 20,000 CROCODILES MASSACRED IN TWO MONTHS . . . BERLIN: IRMA REICHENBACH, DDR BACKSTROKE CHAMPION, TRAINS FOR ASSAULT ON 100 METER MARK . . . WASHINGTON: USA PRESIDENT MCCULLOUGH CEMENTS MILITARY-INDUSTRIAL AGGRESSION PACT. Mike had his own version of the last item. A paragraph in yesterday's *International Herald Tribune,* brought from the West by one of the Swedish contractors working on a new hotel, noted that McDonnell Douglas had won a Pentagon missile contract.

He pushed aside the long woolen drape, a kind of giant's apron, that hung in the doorway of the Astoria and served to shield the hotel's foyer from the damp, sooty chill of the emptying streets. At once the lobby's warmth embraced him. He unbuttoned his coat and shoved his fur hat in a side pocket. A clutter of voices, thick East European accents for the most part, filled the lobby and the adjoining dining room and cocktail lounge. The evening hour drew men and women to East Germany's second most popular pastime, eating and drinking. The No. 1 avocation consisted of tramping through the stores with string bags, searching for the battery, the winter coat, the carpet, the shoes, the olives, or the toothpaste that just might have appeared on the shelves since the last hunt.

At the reception desk he was handed his room key by the least amenable of the three women clerks. Stout, matronly, and in unfaltering command, she invariably inquired whether everything remained in order and to his satisfaction. She seldom smiled, rebuffing mildly flirtatious remarks and even standard pleasantries by the guests. Frau Gotsche gave the impression of a woman bravely shouldering immense, if patently unjust, responsibilities.

The Astoria, on the other hand, buzzed with conviviality tonight, serving as headquarters for a convention of East Bloc printers and publishers whose self-assurance stamped them as among the Communist élite. Here the customary course of formal East German socializing—a swing through the nation's athletic and industrial triumphs while tiptoeing around the time bombs of politics and civil liberties—gave way to the easy-humored cynicism that was as prevalent among Communists of high status as among politicians and businessmen of the West.

Pressing through the crowded lobby, Mike saw but one person he recognized, a woman with whom he'd traded banalities about the weather at adjoining breakfast tables. A tall, blond East German with a soft, diffident air, she stood out in this drably, if serviceably, dressed convention throng because of the fashionable cut of her sweater, a bright orange creation with a loose, cowl-like neck. Mike caught her eye for an instant as she approached the dining salon. She smiled and nodded. He waved, resolving to look her up later.

In his room, with its beige wallpaper, cheap lacquered cabinet, and varnished wood furniture, Michael Ralph Simmons washed beside the chain-pull toilet in the bathroom, then changed from his work clothes to a white shirt, tie, and jacket. Not a bad day, he thought as he knotted his tie. The Swedes who had awarded a subcontract to his company, Todd Elevator, Inc., were highly competent, friendly, and smooth to work with. In another three days he would complete installation of a bank of passenger lifts and two large service elevators in the eight-story hotel the Swedes were building to house yet more visiting Communist delegations to Leipzig.

As for East Germany, officially the Deutsche Demokratische Republik or DDR, Mike was ready to leave. A month was enough in this muted country that held its inhabitants captive behind the Wall and the mined frontier. He longed for the turbulence and discords of the West, for the excesses, for shops and ticket booths without interminable queues, for the strident colors and absurdities of what, on the other side, they called freedom. He hoped for another look at the new woman, Ann, whom he'd met just a week before leaving New York. He thought of his daughter, Sally, a student at Cornell. Would she show up at his New York apartment or would she spend the whole Christmas season with her mother? And his son, Dave, an Army helicopter pilot, stationed at Fulda in West Germany, little more than a hundred miles from here. Mike envied Dave his fierce convictions and passions, his thirst for adventure, and wished that he could share them.

Yes, only three more nights to go. Mike Simmons always kept track of time through nights rather than days. Like his hidden self, the night seemed fragile, vulnerable, so in need of company. Days matched the Simmons public self, quietly competent, inspiring confidence, capable and coping, unblustery, normal as it were, a proper shell for a member of an unchanging species inhabiting a quite familiar globe. Nights, on the other hand, cloaked ill-omened fires, erratic acts of violence, eerie explosions, mythic dreams, and the stony tread of terror. By day he sold and installed elevators, earning merit badges for his composure and reliability. By night he knew the howl of the werewolf and once had awakened with a start to hear his own scream of fright dying in his throat.

But this night was still young, far from the mutters of midnight, and as he walked the long corridor toward the elevators—unfortunately not smooth-riding Todds—his thoughts ran to the familiar. Food, for one thing. The veal Schnitzel again or the reliable Röstbrätl? Perhaps venison for a change? One ate quite well in the showpiece Astoria dining salon, seldom encountering the freak shortages that upset restaurant and store managers. The pot roast? Yes, pot roast and salad and a red wine from Bulgaria.

The dining room was packed. Tobacco smoke fogged the air and voices merged like a distant hum of traffic. People were in a good mood. They laughed, chattered, and clinked beer steins. Mike Simmons stood uncertainly, scanning the hall for the German woman and waiting to be seated by one of the waitresses who wore trim blue vests and white shirts.

"Mike!"

Sven Alsten, chief of the Swedish team building the new Inter hotel, was waving at him. "Come join us," Alsten called. Mike caught a flash of orange next to him. A lucky night? He walked to the table, target of appraising glances from Alsten's dinner companions and a private smile from the uncommonly attractive East German woman.

The Swede, a partying bachelor, had surrounded himself with comrades from the printers' convention. They were seated in a booth under a cluster of amber lamps and a mural depicting a snarling white overseer on horseback whipping black workers on a tropical banana plantation. Mike was introduced to a Russian named Yuri something, an agreeable, slim, female bureaucrat of an East Berlin ministry, and the tall German woman with that appealing softness. Her name was Gisela Steinbrecher and she edited publications at the Technical University in Dresden.

Alsten swept up a chair and Mike squeezed in at the end of the table between the Swede and Frau Steinbrecher. She wore, he noted, a wedding ring.

"Prost!" Yuri, the Russian, poured half of his beer into Mike's glass and brandished his stein. He was a huge man,

built like a pro-football tackle, with a balding crew cut. Mike clinked and drank.

"A thirsty capitalist," said Yuri approvingly. "And smart enough to sit beside beauty." He held out his stein toward Gisela. "Prost!" This time they all toasted.

They were speaking German, but now in deference to Mike—everyone knew that linguistically impoverished Americans could speak but one language—they switched to English.

"What news from the West, Mr. Simmons?" asked the slender East Berlin bureaucrat. She was, it turned out, a high official in the Ministry of Culture and she wore the button of the ruling Socialist Unity Party (SED), clasped hands against a red flag, on the collar of her dress.

"Don't ask me. I've been over here almost a month now."

Alsten described Mike's job of supervising the final stages of elevator installation.

"So the American is here to raise all good Socialists to the stars." The Russian managed to mangle the English language almost beyond recognition.

"And help bring the American dollar back to the upper floors," said Alsten. They all laughed. In the hierarchy of values in the international fraternity of conventioneers, Marxist or otherwise, few things outranked money of whatever species. Traveled, sophisticated Communists, Mike had found, adhered to the maxim coined by a bartender at P. J. Clarke's in Manhattan: Money isn't everything, but it's way ahead of whatever's in second place.

While group tours from the United States were not uncommon in East Germany, few people had the opportunity to converse with an individual American in an informal setting. So, for the moment, Mike starred as the table's attraction.

"As bad off as the dollar may be"—Mike couldn't resist

the temptation—"it still brings ten East marks anywhere in Leipzig."

"You are also a currency trader?" The subminister of Culture smiled pleasantly enough, but her voice had an edge of challenge.

Mike back-pedaled. "Of course not. I haven't dealt in money myself. I'm just talking about what's common knowledge in the street." Common knowledge also noted that a foreigner arrested for black market currency dealing might be let off with a warning and fine or he might be slapped into jail, depending on the vagaries of DDR politics and the shape of *détente*.

"Have you been to the opera here?" asked Gisela Steinbrecher in a bid for safer ground. Her blond hair curved to her shoulders; she had an engaging way of holding his glance with hers just a fraction longer than the custom and he sensed a budding of mutual interest.

"Yes, last night. They did *Salome*, not one of my favorites, but beautifully sung and staged. As a production, tops, absolutely."

"Better than your Metropolitan in New York?" Gisela blushed slightly as she labored through the English.

"As good, certainly. A fine performance, even though I never cared for all that agonizing by Salome when she holds John the Baptist's head on a platter."

"I never did either," agreed the bureaucrat from the capital.

"Well, you know," said Alsten in his fluent if sibilant English, "when you've seen one bloody head on a platter, you've seen them all."

They ordered dinner from the crisply efficient waitress, ate while Alsten and Yuri debated the merits and shortcomings of Leipzig, and then drank more beer. Later they were joined by a friend of Yuri's, a tipsy Russian with a gleaming gold tooth, and two drinking companions from the convention—an enormous, steamy woman who published textbooks in Bulgaria and a hearty Romanian trencherman, editor and printer of party tracts in Bucharest.

The Romanian, whose speech flowered with bouquets, complimented the woman from the East Berlin Ministry of Culture on her splendid aroma. Pleased, the lady functionary said she always bought her perfumes in the hotel Inter shops. There the East German authorities, in a fine display of contempt for their own system, permitted Western goods to be sold to any customer who offered hard Western currencies in payment. DDR marks were no good in the state's own luxury shops.

Yuri, remarking that both he and his companion had attended several printing conventions in the West, confessed he liked the German beer "over there" better than the brands available east of the frontier. His young comrade added that capitalist women had a sexual sheen that he failed to spot among females of the Socialist Bloc. He looked about him somewhat belligerently.

"You do not know what you have not been privileged to sample," retorted the Bulgarian textbook publisher. She was furious. Mike surmised that the Soviet printer would find her open sexuality and peasant dimensions a challenging combination.

They all slipped into a good-humored, if wary, exchange that centered on the material defects of the systems they lived under—the shortages, the frequently poor quality of imports from partners in the Communist camp, long lines for goods and services, cramped housing, niggardly pensions. Like Americans complaining about long gasoline lines or inflation, they vied in telling stories of how they beat the system. Yuri said that he and his comrade had a steady supply of Western goods because their boss had as good connections as anyone in the Soviet Union. Gisela told of her aunt in Stuttgart, on the other side, who sent her packages of clothes.

"Including this Pierre Cardin?" asked the East Berlin subminister of Culture, fingering the Dresden woman's modish orange sweater.

"Yes." Gisela saw Mike admiring her. She blushed, a soft pinking that intrigued him. He became acutely aware of the warmth of her body beside him.

The Bulgarian publisher said that she abided by her country's rules, but that every person had the right to an occasional transgression just to avoid the monotony of perfection. She had a friend high in officialdom who brought her perfumes and clothing accessories from his numerous trips to Paris.

The Berlin bureaucrat's father drew an old-age pension and was thus allowed, like all East German men past sixty-five, to visit the West or, if he wished, to leave for good, thus freeing the state of its financial obligation to him. But this father always returned and from his trips he brought little luxuries for his daughter. The jovial Romanian had a lady friend, clerk in a clothing store, who alerted him whenever good men's-wear imports arrived.

Slowly they forged bonds as their investment in mutual culpability mounted tale by tale. They ordered more beer, laughed, and gossiped. They were successful Communists, secure in their profession, and they enjoyed this odd circle of peers where they could build friendships with the mortar of a common cynicism. After all, weren't most self-respecting citizens smugglers at heart, no matter what system they lived under?

"You all tell jokes about us Russians behind our backs," said the comrade whose mouth shone with a small fortune in gold, "but you are afraid to tell them here. So, I will tell a joke against the Soviet Union."

Side conversations subsided. They all looked at him with

9

wondering expectation. Ever since the Polish labor confrontation startled the world the previous year, new anxieties complicated the usual tension between the Soviet Union and the small countries it had corralled for Communism at the close of World War II. People who feared that the benefactor's tanks might come calling in their neighborhoods were hardly in a mood to laugh at Moscow's foibles, whether behind the back or not. Just what was this gold-toothed Russian up to?

"You know why so many comrades get in line to see Lenin in his glass coffin at the Kremlin?"

"No. Why?" Alsten, the Swede, obliged.

"Because they know it's one line where the goods won't be exhausted before they reach the counter." The Russian stumbled through the wilderness of English, telegraphing the punch line as he went, and was applauded and cheered with vast relief upon his safe arrival. Some of the party were getting drunk.

The Romanian bon vivant said that he always joined any queue that he happened upon. There was always the chance, he said, that some line would lead to the laces which failed to come with the shoes he bought in a blind queue two years ago.

"I have the latest from Radio Erehwon," said the Bulgarian publisher. An imaginary station invented by cynics and supposedly located somewhere in Eastern Europe, Radio Erehwon broadcast satire almost exclusively.

"The radio asked its listeners: 'Can the human male get pregnant in the DDR?'" Beaming, the lady publisher waited for the hecklers to quiet down. "Radio Erehwon gave this answer: 'In principle, no, but if it brings in West German marks, anything is possible.'"

Emboldened by the welcome accorded such stories, Mike decided to float one of his own. Risky, perhaps, but what to lose now? He had only three nights to go.

"Two DDR soldiers were patrolling along the Berlin Wall," he ventured, "when one soldier asked, 'What would you do if the Wall suddenly collapsed?'"

At the mention of the Wall, the face of the East German cultural bureaucrat tightened and the Romanian dropped his eyelids like blinds. Mike ignored the warning signals. He had gone this far.

"The second soldier said, 'Why, if the Wall collapsed, I'd run climb a tree.' 'Climb a tree?' asked the first border guard. 'Why would you do that?' Replied his partner: 'To avoid being crushed in the stampede.'"

No one laughed. The lone smile soon faded from Mike's own lips. Alsten made an awkward business of clearing his throat. Time in the little group stretched like rubber. In the ensuing silence, Mike felt a leg against his. Gisela rapped his ankle, then slowly rubbed the spot with her foot as if to assure him of the friendly source of the rebuke. He pressed back gently, provoking, to his surprise, another leg massage. He glanced at her, but Frau Steinbrecher, coloring faintly, stared without expression at the Romanian across the table.

"That's a propaganda story manufactured by the reactionaries in Bonn," chided the normally agreeable female functionary of the Ministry of Culture, "or perhaps by your radio cold warriors in Munich."

"That story's offensive to our brothers and sisters of the DDR," said the Bulgarian, her handsome bosom quivering. "Besides, it's an old joke."

The senior Russian joined the attack, but somewhat judiciously with the air of a superior officer who wishes to place an infringement of good taste in perspective.

"Our friend may be excused, as someone from another hemisphere, from knowing that the Wall was built to prevent willful imperialists from sabotaging our fraternity of Socialism. Not you, of course." He shook his finger. "But your government and its lackeys in Paris, London, and Rome."

The American had trespassed on forbidden ground and until the consequences, if any, could be assessed, they would fall back to accredited Communist positions.

"Well, the Wall has been a fact of life for two decades now." Alsten apparently hoped that a strong dose of fact could take the sting out of Mike's fiction. "It was just twenty years ago in August that they began building the Wall near the Brandenburg Gate."

"Yes," said the Russian of the gleaming tooth, "my father commanded one of the tanks that faced American armor that month. He's retired now."

Now Mike had been outdone in tactlessness. He decided the young Russian must be drunk.

"We needed the show of arms to keep Western provocateurs from causing trouble." The functionary of Culture offered this swiftly lest the thought of Russians in tanks prove too bellicose for a supplier of peaceful elevators.

"The Wall—" Mike intended a neutral observation to the effect that the Wall had lasted for a generation and the divided Germany it symbolized for almost two. A sharp warning rap at the ankle dissuaded him. "I've only seen the Wall twice," he concluded lamely.

But south of the Berlin Wall he had seen forty miles of the armed, mined, raked, fenced, electrified, gunned, trapped, patrolled, and dog-guarded frontier from a U. S. Army helicopter piloted by his son, First Lieutenant Dave Simmons. Six weeks ago, on an overcast October day when mist rolled over the Rhön hills near Fulda, he saw the rich fields and pastures scarred by a gash a hundred meters wide as if some crazed god had run amok and slashed the ordered countryside with a giant scythe. He saw the watchtowers, spaced only a few kilometers apart like derricks in an oil field; the runs where German police dogs, barking and snarling, raced back and forth on leashes along the twelve-foot-high fence; the strip of bare ground raked or harrowed regularly to provide fresh turf for footprints; concrete slabs slanted inward to halt autos careening toward the chain link fence from the east; and the sinister mines, fixed to alternate posts, which fired laterally whenever a hand grasped a wire strand and which, just a month earlier, had shredded a teenage boy bent on flight to the West. And all this, not to keep some real or imagined enemy out, but to keep the citizens of East Germany in.

The scalped terrain of the death strip might have bordered a Nazi extermination center of haunted memory, a prison camp in Siberia, or some quarantined wasteland poisoned by radiation. Mike Simmons understood why Dave, who flew a sector of the frontier almost daily, despised the Wall and its 850-mile chain link counterpart along the entire boundary between the two Germanies.

"The Wall has served us well by permitting us to build a Socialist society in peace." East Berlin's slim administrator of Culture seemed content to fall back on the comforting vacuity of state-certified buzz phrases, abandoning the tempting, but ever perilous, field of badinage.

"The Wall satisfies both sides," proclaimed Yuri, peering at Mike as if in challenge to debate.

But Mike let the moment pass and soon the talk turned to less flammable topics. They chatted of sports and travel, of men and women, children and families, yet without the easy humor and warming bond of shared transgression of a few minutes earlier. The Wall had thrown its shadow. In this Germany, the one east of the frontier, people rarely spoke of the Wall in public. On this side one spoke of the Wall among friends, seldom with strangers. Even within a family, people sometimes hesitated to discuss the Wall when pictures of it appeared on West German television, which most

East Germans watched despite state disapproval. The Wall bred its own customs, its own fears, its own subterfuges.

Conversation fell into several groupings and Mike found himself groping about in fractured German and English with Gisela. He and the Dresden woman already had staked a claim to a special relationship, an intimacy of strangers, via their wordless dialogue beneath the table. So now they suffered willingly enough through the briers of language.

But at last Frau Steinbrecher reached linguistic limits. Failing several times to decipher one of his sentences, she asked haltingly whether he spoke another language.

"I get by in street Spanish," he said, "enough to understand and to unload most of what I want to say."

"Español!" She let out a little cry of joy. *"Lo hablo, yo. Estudié el español cinco años en la escuela."*

So, she had studied it five years in school. Her voice had a fetching throaty timbre and he liked the faint freckles splashed along her cheekbones.

"Tell me something about your work and how you live," Mike said in Spanish. "I've been here a month, but I've only been in a few offices and just one home."

"I'm in charge of editing university publications," she said in her German-accented Spanish. "I got a doctorate in chemistry at the university. I have a nice office, and the ten people who work for me treat me with great respect just as if I deserved it." Her laugh had a light, self-deprecating touch. "I make twelve hundred marks a month, which isn't great, but with my husband's salary, a thousand a month, we live comfortably in our three-room apartment."

Mike felt an unexpected twinge of jealousy at her mention of a husband, even though he'd already noted her wedding ring and had speculated that such an attractive woman in her thirties must certainly have, at the minimum, a husband and perhaps a lover as well.

Her husband, Karl, an assistant professor of physics,

taught at Technical University in the same building where she worked. They paid less than a tenth of their income for rent, but a quarter for food. They were saving for a Trabant or a Wartburg, the East German cars, but they might settle for a motorcycle. They owned a television set and a little cottage, or shack, with garden in the country.

She liked swimming, music, computers, and the television news from West Germany, although they could not receive West German TV in the Dresden area and she saw it only in other cities. She also liked the month of May, Camus, the Chilean poetry of Pablo Neruda, orderliness—she was, after all, German, she said—and, sometimes, daydreaming. She would love to visit the West whenever the state cleared her to attend a publishing convention, but meanwhile her travels had been limited to a week's "very Socialist vacation" on a Bulgarian Black Sea beach and a brief trip to Russia.

She asked about his life in America. Did he have a wife, family, and what did he like to see, read, hear, enjoy? As he talked about himself, Mike became aware that they were communicating simultaneously on a number of levels. He could feel their thighs touching, the rhythm of their breathing, a meshing of unspoken thoughts, frequent locking of eyes, and beneath it all a strong, compelling sexual current in which they moved together as naturally as fish in a river.

So it came as a disappointment later, when he suggested that she come up to his room for a nightcap, that Gisela gave him a flat "no," albeit with a fetching smile.

"No, señor," she added in swift if heavy Spanish, *"no vengo a su cuarto."*

"Oh?" Lights dimmed.

"Instead you come to mine, *dos cuatro nueve.* It is hidden, *digamos,* off the main corridor near the stairs." She repeated. "Two four nine."

"Enough Spanish, you two." Yuri raised his beer stein.

"Join the crowd." He rapped his glass mug against Mike's, slopping beer on a platter of pastries.

The other Russian had his arm around the ample waist of the Bulgarian publisher, a woman twice his age, and was extolling her charms in an atrocious mixture of German and English. The lusty Romanian debated the accommodations at the luxury hotel, the Metropol, in East Berlin with the friendly female bureaucrat from that cheerless city. Both were quite drunk and repeatedly misunderstood each other's English which they stuffed, like popcorn, with extra consonants.

"Yes, we all switched to English out of politeness to you, Mike," said Alsten in a tone of mock reproof, "and then you desert us for a private chat in Spanish."

"Excuse us," said Gisela, again with faint roses in her cheeks. "I will speak English if it kills me."

"And it will," roared Yuri. "A terrible language, English." He pounded the table, causing the steins to jiggle. "Not fit for the lips of such a beauty."

"No one has spoken proper English since Shakespeare," said Alsten.

"Hear! Hear!" The Romanian rapped the table in imitation of Yuri who slapped him on the back and summoned the waitress for yet another round of beer. They talked on, inhibitions dissolved by alcohol.

Gisela at last pleaded fatigue—she had been up since 6 A.M., she said—and made her adieus despite a chorus of soggy male protests. It was another half hour, after more beery salutes and increasingly blue jokes, before the two other women said good night and Mike felt free to leave.

"See you at the shack tomorrow noon," said Alsten.

As he walked away, Mike could hear the young Russian proposing a toast to international amity and the clinking of steins as the men raised yet another salute.

Riding the elevator to his floor, the third, Mike recalled

the parting words of Mark Jacoby, vice president for Todd's overseas division, after Simmons volunteered to take over final stages of the Leipzig job from the supervisor who'd come down with pneumonia.

"One last thing, Mike," Jacoby had said. "Take it from an old hand who's spent a lot of lonely nights in the Communist countries. If you think you've got something going with an East German woman there in Leipzig, forget it. Five to one she'll be a security agent or informer of some kind and you'll wind up in deep trouble. You don't need that, Mike. And Todd sure doesn't need it. Not worth the risk, old buddy."

Gisela an agent? Did East Germany train its secret operatives in the delicate art of blushing? He stood on his floor for a moment, pondering. Ah, the hell with Jacoby's advice. Mike Simmons could take care of himself. He headed for the stairs and trotted down to the second floor. He peered into the short hallway that cornered on the main corridor. Empty.

He was about to knock on the door of No. 249 when he noticed that it stood slightly ajar, cracked perhaps a half inch. He rapped softly and entered.

The door clicked behind him. Mike stood quietly, adjusting his eyes to the darkness. Like his own room, this one had a foyer with the bath off to one side and the main room beyond.

"Gisela?"

"*Buenas noches, señor.*"

He took a few tentative steps toward the low voice. In a downpour of thoughts, he again recalled Mark Jacoby's admonition. Mark would call him a fool. Perhaps, but after a month of continence, he hungered for a desirable woman.

Yet, along with his urge, he felt a familiar tremor, less physical than mental. The night neared those hours of silent alarms when nameless fears and sometimes terror loitered in the recesses of the mind.

Lights from the street filtered through the drawn mesh curtains, casting pale, shifting geometries on the wall. Gisela came toward him, holding a finger to her lips in a signal for silence. She wore a frayed, blue cotton bathrobe and her hair hung loosely about her shoulders.

She bent her head slightly, her chin tucked in, suggesting both entreaty and vulnerability. Her coasting smile had a trace of shyness. Mike was beguiled. She might as well have worn a tag: "Human female. Affectionate mood. Handle with care."

When he kissed her, she responded willingly but briefly, then brought her lips close to his ear.

"We must speak softly like this," she whispered in Spanish. "While there's only the smallest chance that this room is monitored, I cannot take that chance. Neither can you."

"Whatever you say." He embraced her and felt her body mold itself to his. He hardened almost at once. Gisela kissed him, this time with fervor. They stood locked together, sampling lips as they might a new wine.

"Let's get into bed," he said. "It's chilly out here."

She laughed quietly. "You don't need such excuses. There are so few secluded places for lovers here that one learns to be terribly candid about such things." She sighed. "Very unladylike, no?"

"I like it." He moved her gently toward the bed.

Gisela threw off her bathrobe and Mike caught a flash of her long, naked body as she slid beneath one of the down-bloated quilts, buttoned into a sheet, which cover German beds, East or West. She squirmed about, tunneling a warm groove beneath the *Federbett*.

He undressed quickly, conscious that she was watching, threw his clothes over a chair, and snuggled in beside her.

They heated each other, rubbing playfully. Then, as the bed gradually took on a nestlike coziness, she nuzzled to him, entwining her limbs with his. They sipped at each other's lips and Gisela traced fingers like feathers along his spine. They lay together, subtly questing and tempting.

Mike became aware of Gisela's distinctive odor, a compelling compound of body heat, slightly acrid breath, and a lingering fragrance of foam bath, the latter thanks to the small gift packages found in Inter hotel bathrooms.

Instant lovers through some enigmatic collision of chemistries, they lay in each other's arms, vulnerable, testing, offering and receiving, wondering, alternately greedy and languid, trust growing with each wavelet of passion. Folded snugly in the cocoon of love, they became ready acolytes of pleasure. Mike kissed her shoulders and breasts, venting a surge of gratitude, then explored with his tongue the long, smooth reaches of her body. She arched toward him and he could feel her pulse of desire. When at last he kissed between her thighs, she gasped and seized his head with both hands. Soon Gisela ventured with her lips, brushing Mike's belly and limbs with her long hair, skimming light kisses over his skin, and then feasting as he did.

Even as he claimed and yielded, Mike wondered anew at the power of ecstasy. A torment of the senses not unlike a blast of pain, a fury to devour along with an urge to surrender, a passion to merge with this woman, all women, all nations. And the wonder of this incredible intimacy, so deeply commanding, a communion beyond understanding with a woman he knew so slightly and so obliquely that they had to converse in a borrowed language which fit them as randomly as secondhand clothes. He marveled at his need, far stronger than he had suspected, and at his wish to treat this unknown bedmate, this blushing editor turned partner in lust, with a tenderness bordering on worship.

But as the mind marveled, the body groped and fumbled

in awkward throes of passion, more sweaty than sublime, less hallowed than gymnastic. At times they lost themselves in mindless frenzy, addicts of the senses, blind to all but their mutual craving, the world beyond the creaking bed obliterated. And as the minutes fled in a kind of drugged delirium, Mike became aware that they were moving in near-perfect harmony. Never before had he known a woman so subtly tuned to his own nuances of passion. Whether this rare blending of two into one devolved from his own long-pent needs, from some unknown urge of Gisela, or from a fortuitous melding of two kindred spirits, he did not know. What he did know was that never before in his life had he achieved such total union with a woman.

When they began the final rite of love with a slow, measured cadence, quite unlike the rapid beating of their hearts, he held her firmly, seeking to assure her through strength of arms of his wish to protect, cherish, and fulfill. Again now that rush of exquisite tenderness, an upheaval of formless emotion, and a feeling akin to adoration. Had it been a time for words, he might have whispered, "I love you," and meant it for this hour and this night. Instead a torrent of feeling overwhelmed him as their ardor came in long rushes. And at last, that unsought convulsion of two bodies locked in a conspiracy of immolation.

When their moans and sharp cries finally faded and they had spent their passion, they lay together, damp with the juices of love, lax and sated, head pillowed against head, holding hands like children.

Thoughts tumbled slowly as Mike felt the soft touch of Gisela's hair on his shoulder. How strange to be seized by such utter felicity and extravagant pleasure in this ambiguous city where long, exhortatory propaganda banners flapped in the chill winds and graceless modern buildings abutted medieval taverns and shops that had survived the garlands of Allied bombs, falling like sullen prayers, that had demolished Leipzig during his long-ago adolescent years.

She put her lips to his ear and he anticipated a loving kiss or whisper of affection.

"I must get out of this country," she said slowly and distinctly. She gripped his hand. "You will help me, Miguel."

Abruptly his mood changed. Tenderness fled. His body tensed as Mark Jacoby's warning echoed in the suddenly chilled room.

2

Gisela's words were Spanish, but the insistence and the imperative tone quite German, rupturing at once the web of love that he had woven around this accomplice in passion. His spirits sank. Of course. She had toyed with him, after all, feeding his fantasies with a deception of the senses. He felt used. It was not he whom she wanted, but an escape channel to the West. He could hear Mark Jacoby chiding him, "So what did you expect, an instant lay with no demands?"

Mike withdrew his hand from Gisela's and refortified himself with the wariness and caution that he had exercised sporadically since crossing at Checkpoint Charlie a month ago.

"I don't know if that's possible," he began in a normal voice, Gisela clapped a hand over his mouth.

"No. You must speak low into my ear like this," she whispered. Her moist breath stirred him sexually, but now he resented her for it.

"Oh, come on."

"No, no." She tapped his lips. "Believe me, it is best to be prudent."

"I forgot." This time he went through the business of edging closer so that he might whisper to her.

"Here one does not forget." Between her whispering and the German-accented Spanish, Mike had to strain to catch each word. "Over there, on the sunny side, yes. Here, no. It is not paranoia that makes us act as we do, letting down our guard completely only in our own home . . . and sometimes not even there."

"Okay, we'll keep it low." He'd play it her way, but he too would maintain vigilance.

"I feel tension in your muscles. Your mood has changed." Her breath, stroking him like a tropic breeze, seemed at odds with her words. "I can't blame you. So soon after our love-making, I ask a dangerous favor. Wrong time, no? But I can't help myself. I'm filled to bursting with this thing for many weeks now. I have learned something that leaders of the West must be told."

Mike boosted his defenses a notch higher. Of course. She had faked her ardor and now would come the spurious appeal. The time-worn scenario lacked only the specifics: beautiful female agent enmeshes foreigner in escape plot for which, when she turns him in with a poignant smile signaling a tremor of remorse, he would be tried and sentenced to prison.

Well, on with the act, artful Gisela of the sham moans and quivers, you blushing and freckled operative of the SSD, East Germany's secret security police. Whatever you plan, you will not hook Michael Simmons.

A loud knock split the room's silence like a cleaver.

Mike froze. My God, what was that? Gisela clutched him beneath the Federbett. . . . Act Two? Now police would burst through the door. . . . He caught his breath, awaiting the crash. He could feel Gisela's heart racing and he heard her whimper. With fright? Lady Agent acting? If so, she was superb, for her fear enveloped him like a cold fog.

Another knock on the door, peremptory this time. Mike began to shiver. Not in years had he felt such disabling fear.

"Wer ist da?" she called. Mike was certain he detected near-panic in her voice.

The muffled reply carried a name that sounded familiar.

"Oh, one of those Russians." Relief flooded her speech. "I'll handle this."

She flipped out of bed, snatched up her bathrobe, and wrapped herself in it. When she opened the door, a shaft of light knifed the entryway.

"Nein, nein. I am married woman," she said sternly in German. "You go to your bed."

Mike saw a bulky form lurch against the doorjamb. It was Yuri, the older of the two Russians and the heaviest drinker. He said something in muddled German.

"You go to your room," Gisela commanded. "You're drunk. You sleep it off and tomorrow we'll all gather for lunch after the morning session."

The Russian appealed in florid, garbled German. He loved her, it seemed, with limitless ardor.

"I'm flattered. However, it is very late. I would dislike to have to call the front desk, but I must have my sleep."

"A kiss," the Russian implored. Gisela placed her cheek in the crack of the door and let him kiss her, a loud, wet mouthing. Apparently appeased, he staggered off down the hall.

Discarding her bathrobe, Gisela slid back into bed. She huddled close and asked Mike to rub her back and shoulders. "It's cold out there." She covered his face with kisses. "I'm so tired of those Russians. Since I'm two years old, they're camped here in my country."

"What did you think when you heard the knock?" Mike's fear had evaporated.

"I was terrified. I had no idea who it could be. And you?"

"I was sure it was the police, so I assumed that you'd trapped me."

"Ssh. Not so loud," she whispered. "What do you mean, 'trapped'? . . . Oh, you thought I worked with the police?"

"And why not?"

"How awful! You thought I made love with you as part of my job? To trick you?"

"Yes."

"How painful for you, Miguel. And now?"

He hesitated. "I think you made love—well—as a favor to me so I'd help you get out of the DDR."

She framed his face in her hands and gazed deep into his eyes. She smiled, indulgently, he thought, as one might with a child.

"I am very honest with you." She brought her lips to his ear and resumed whispering. "I want desperately to get out to the West. I must. I have urgent news for your leaders that is being suppressed here. But also I wanted to do the love with you. Do you understand?"

"Tell me more."

"Perhaps you are impossible, after all." She sighed. "First, you're an American, naive about world politics and about what it means to be a prisoner in one's own country. Second, you're a man and so without appreciation for the ambivalent feelings of a woman."

"Meaning?" He kept the sentries posted.

"Look, I wanted to have the love with you, but also, more important, I imagined you as a possible helper to get me over there." She paused. "Now what do you think?"

Mike said nothing. The thought that she still might entrap him, while diminished, had not entirely faded.

"Do I hurt your feelings?"

"Yes, but I'm more worried that . . ."

"That I'm not what I say I am? That I'm an officer sent to catch you? So now you too have mixed feelings." She

25

laughed softly and nibbled at his ear. "Consider, Miguel. Why would the state bother with an installer of elevators when it has much more important people to watch? You have such a large ego? Or so many military secrets? . . . And anyway, I would make a ridiculous agent because I can't hide my emotions. For instance, Karl says that when I think of sex, I blush."

Karl? Oh yes, her husband, the professor of physics.

"Did I blush tonight?"

"Yes, you did. Several times."

"So, you see." She kissed and hugged him roughly. He sensed that the display of affection was not feigned and he responded with slowly mounting passion. When the long kiss ended, they smiled at each other.

"No mixed feelings there," said Mike.

"It would be wonderful to share and trust with a man in all things as you and I have learned so quickly to do in our love-making."

"You don't trust Karl?"

"In most things, but not the deepest. We both belong to SED, but he believes. Or does fear mold his opinions? He is more cautious than I am. I take chances. Karl never. If he knew that I planned escape, he would be shocked. In the end, he might betray me. I'm not sure, but I feel he might."

"You wouldn't risk telling him?"

"Never. . . . And yet, you know, even though his love for me has cooled, I am still fond of Karl."

"But you take chances with me, a stranger you've never seen before."

"I see very few people from the West and none in the informal atmosphere at the table tonight. You know, we in the DDR like Americans. I felt I could take a chance with you. If you think I used sex, well, I'm sorry, Miguel. Maybe I did in a way. And yet I wanted you, too. . . . Oh, I don't know." She clung to him. "How can I sort out such strong feelings? Many things are true. . . . I must get out, I tell you. I have urgent news. Every day that passes increases the danger."

"What is this big news?"

Outside the wind moaned thinly at the window ledge. A loose metal fixture slapped against a building and a late train groaned and huffed as it pulled into the mammoth terminal. The time, Mike guessed, must be nearing two o'clock.

"Can you reach the most influential scientists in your country?"

"Some, I'm sure." He could make connections through his old school, MIT.

"You must listen carefully." Gisela's continued use of the imperative annoyed him. In Spanish the Teutonic commands sounded discourteous, overbearing. "Did you ever hear about what scientists in the West call—I say this in English—'the greenhouse effect'?"

"Greenhouse. Hmm. Yeah, I think so. Isn't that a theory that increased burning of fuels puts more carbon dioxide in the atmosphere? Something about changing the climate in some God-awful way?"

"Yes, yes." She squeezed his hand. "At the Technical University in Dresden, I had a brilliant friend, a chemist, Otto, whose hobby for some years has been doing computer calculations on the rising level of carbon dioxide in the atmosphere. This year he came up with numbers, far worse than those coming from Western research, which frightened him—and me too."

The tempo of Gisela's speech accelerated and Mike could sense her feeling of urgency. At the same time the constant whispering between the two naked lovers lent an air of unreality to the scene. Her alarm seemed more frivolous than not. At this hour in this hotel in this country, all seemed dreamlike, tenuous.

But her whispering poured the story into his ear. Scientists in the West calculated that with ever-mounting burning of fossil fuels—oil, coal, gas—the world would face a crisis of climate early in the next century. With far more carbon dioxide in the atmosphere, global temperatures would creep upward, melting polar ice caps, raising the level of oceans, endangering coastal cities, and shifting great deserts northward.

But Gisela's friend, Professor Otto Kleist, had concluded that the world faced catastrophic climatic changes many years earlier. If the industrial nations did not drastically curtail the burning of fossil fuels at once, deserts would soon spread toward higher altitudes, turning the world's most abundant bread basket—the corn, wheat, and soybean states of the American Midwest—into an arid waste and dessicating such fertile regions as the Argentine Pampas and the plains of Northern Europe. Famine and disease would stalk the continents. By 1990, he predicted, salt water two to ten meters deep would flood many of the great seaports, inundate such low-lying areas as Florida and the Netherlands, and ruin millions of acres of coastal crop lands.

"Last summer," she said, "Professor Kleist wrote a long paper, fully documented, that warned of world disaster within ten years. He took it to the Ministry of Science and Technology in Berlin and urged that it be disseminated to scientists, most of them in the West, working on the CO_2 problem. Instead, a week later, authorities ordered him to cease all research on the matter and destroy copies of his report.

"When he protested, he was warned to desist. He refused, stating that he would take his case to the head of state. So the SSD ransacked his office at night and stole his tapes and notes. Not a trace left of the intricate calculations he had amassed over the years. Otto, beside himself with rage and frustration, didn't know where to turn. He had never joined the party. Finally, he appealed for help to a high university official, a friend, he thought.

"That did bring prompt results." Gisela's voice took on a bitterness Mike had not heard before. "The state ordered him out of the university and confined him to his flat in Weisser Hirsch, the old residential suburb overlooking the Elbe. It used to be a beautiful place, they say, but now it's shabby and gloomy, all the mansions broken up into two- and three-room flats. Otto's kept to his place alone, not allowed out of his yard, no visitors permitted, no telephone. People who write him get no reply. Men in gray raincoats pace up and down his block."

Far away a siren screamed. Down the corridor a door banged and a male voice cursed thickly. The small hours tiptoed amid random terrors.

"But why?" asked Mike. "I don't understand. Why would the state silence a man who thinks the world's in trouble for consuming too much fuel?"

Gisela sighed. "You would have to live here to understand fully. Although it's small, the DDR ranks eighth in industrial output among nations of the world, and the SED and its Politburo want ever more production. Nothing must stand in the way of bigger and better output.

"And our major fuel is brown coal, lignite, which is mined around here. Brown coal's a leading export too. The trouble is it releases heavy amounts of carbon dioxide. If we had to cut way back on brown coal, it would ruin the DDR, believe me. Then, of course, since the trouble in next-door Poland, our government is harder on anyone who disobeys its orders."

She thought for a moment. "So in Berlin they turned their backs on unpleasant facts, I suppose. Or perhaps they didn't believe Otto's figures and decided to rid themselves of a possible nuisance, a man who resisted them. Here it is very easy to disbelieve. For some, disbelief is a way of life."

"And you? How do you fit into this?"

He felt unhinged, disconnected. The story unrolled so swiftly, bits and pieces flying about like scraps in a high wind. Truth? Semitruth? Fiction? While he had all but dismissed the idea of Gisela Steinbrecher as a government agent, he wondered if she had concocted the account, appealing to his sense of responsibility as a resident of the planet, in order to persuade him to help her escape.

"I carry all of Otto's conclusions in my head," she answered, "as well as his methodology, most of the important steps and some supporting calculations. In short, I know enough so that any CO_2 expert in the West would appreciate and understand the data within a matter of hours."

"If you know so much, I'm surprised the security people didn't implicate you along with the professor."

She moved away from him. "You're still suspicious of me, aren't you?" Now she was irritated.

"Reverse the roles. Put yourself in a strange hotel room in, say, Romania, and how would you feel?"

"I'm not sure. . . . I thought we had become so close and *simpático* during the loving."

"I thought so too, but now . . . Look, Gisela, if I'm to help you, I've got to trust you completely and so I have to question you to clear away doubts."

"So you will help me?" she asked with a quick leap of spirit.

"I didn't say that. I haven't decided." He tried to study her face in the thin, wavering light. "Please, can't you understand?"

She brushed his throat with a kiss. "Yes, yes. Oh, Miguel, I must get out. I need your help so badly. . . . What else do you want to know?"

"Well, for one thing, did the SSD question you?"

"Oh yes, but only a few minutes. They quizzed all of Otto's friends, some for many hours. But you see, with me, they had no real suspicions. I am well connected in the party, I say all the right things, and my record is clean for them. I was a leader of Freie Deutsche Jugend, the Communist youth organization. Karl is diligent in party affairs and my sister is a relative by marriage of the head of state and the party."

"How come Professor Kleist disclosed all his research to you?"

"Until the ministry ordered him to stop, he made no effort to hide his studies. He didn't broadcast his work, but a lot of people knew of it, at least vaguely." She paused, rubbed her feet against his as if in the act of reflecting. "I'd been calling on Otto for some years in my job as editor of technical papers. We grew to like and trust each other— these things are so subtle and yet so obvious here to those who think alike. So I helped him write and polish the long account he took to Berlin."

"Oh." Mike frowned. "Didn't they question you about editing his stuff?"

"The *Staatssicherheitsdienst?*" The name for the secret security police slid off her tongue like sand down a chute. "Yes."

"Certainly. I told them that of course I edited all university technical reports. But I pretended the material was too complicated for me and that I was solely concerned with framing it in proper language. . . . The same replies from a person with a poor party record might have provoked more questions, but with me, one of the privileged who are above suspicion, almost, the answers were satisfactory. The *Stasi* checked back only once. Had I ever noted anything odd about the Herr Professor's behavior? Apparently they wanted to build some mental case against him should liberals abroad get hold of the story. I said no, nothing unusual."

Mike could feel her tense momentarily. He remained silent, waiting for her to continue.

"I"—she gripped his arm—"I have a confession. I was tempted to tell them that sometimes he did act queerly. Isn't that disgusting?" She choked off a bitter laugh. "I almost lied about dear Otto to make it easier for myself. Unless you live here, you can't possibly know how this system poisons people."

Her admission had the resonance of truth. Only an accomplished actress could have fabricated the incident with such fine nuances of self-criticism. His wariness eased.

"When did you decide to escape?" He kissed her shoulder and a responsive tremor passed over her.

"The day they put Otto under house arrest. From that moment on, life here became unbearable. But I'd often thought of it over the years. Not that I don't approve of Socialism, because I do. I think Socialism, without the ugly repressions we have here, is the most humane of systems, the most satisfying for the future."

She paused. "Remember your story tonight about the stampede? That's an old joke that used to reflect the truth. Today, no. If the Wall came down tomorrow, while almost everyone would take the opportunity to visit over there, only a few thousands, I think, would leave permanently. For the material things, life is not bad here. Did you know our per capita income now surpasses that of Great Britain? We have food, shelter, and security until we die. Nobody has to claw his way as in the West, yet our standard of living is getting closer and closer to that in Hamburg or West Berlin."

"Now you sound like an SED official addressing a factory brigade meeting."

"You must understand me. This country is my home," she said with feeling. "I was born here and have lived here thirty-eight years, nowhere else. We have made tremendous progress since the war when this land was heaped with rubble, and hordes of poor, starving, shivering people wandered about. My own family . . ."

She took his hand. "May I tell you about a German family, Miguel, one of millions, but mine?"

"Of course. I want to hear." He felt her intensity like another presence.

Her family, she said, never recovered from deep wounds of that Second World War which shattered untold numbers of German households, East and West. Hitler's manic drive into Russia took the life of one grandfather, a *Wehrmacht* captain. Both maternal grandparents perished in a British bomber raid on Hamburg. Her father was wounded during the invasion of France, never regained his health, and died before she entered the university. The massive Anglo-American bombing assault near the end of the war that turned Dresden into an inferno and consumed more than a hundred thousand lives left her, a two-year-old, with only a broken leg. Her mother, however, came out of it grotesquely scarred and demoralized. Frail in health, she nevertheless managed to live into her sixties. She died last year. Now only Gisela and her sister, Frauke, survived. Frauke lived in Kaltennordheim in the border zone and could be visited only with a pass.

"I tell you all this so you can appreciate my background and why I feel as I do about this land that has suffered so much. I could talk all night and maybe sometime I will with you. Right now something that Frauke said recently will explain us. 'We are,' she said of the DDR to my aunt on the other side, 'a clean, decent, orderly, hard-working, prospering, sports-proud, cultural people—and we're in jail.' For me, that says it all."

Mike savored the stillness for a moment, then asked: "If it hadn't been for the professor and his findings, would you have planned to leave anyway?"

"I think so. But you know, Miguel, it is difficult. Hundreds have been killed trying to cross the frontier—in the minefields, on the fence, or the Wall." She reflected, tracing a finger along his arm. "I might have waited for an opportunity to go to the West on editorial business, then defected. But my travel chances are not great."

"Don't you have children?"

"My little boy died after a delicate throat operation when he was only four. That was a year of terrible sorrow for us, but time has healed the wounds somewhat."

"You don't mind leaving your husband forever?"

"Of course I do. I told you that I love Karl." Gisela fell silent. With the warmth of the bed and her gentle, measured breathing, he began to lose the sense of intensity with which she'd infused her talk.

"But," she resumed after a time, "everything is relative, isn't it? It isn't that I don't want Karl, but that I want the life of the West more. But you see how intricate everything is! I don't dare tell Karl my thoughts about escape. Perhaps I do him an injustice, but I can't risk finding out. And so my suspicion that ultimately he would betray me; that suspicion festers and spoils our marriage.

"For that, thank the Deutsche Demokratische Republik. Our leaders boast that they liberated the people from the tyranny of wealth and the squalor of poverty. They did indeed, but they also liberated many marriages from the old safety and joy."

A clear picture of the husband eluded him. "Tell me more about Karl."

"He's a big man, strong, slow-moving. He is not so concerned with his—with me anymore. The old love has wilted. Now he has his physics and his stamp collection."

"Jesus. A stamp collector!"

"Yes, you could make fun of Karl, I suppose." She sounded hurt as if an article of her clothing had been criticized. "He's a good, steady husband, reliable and generous. We've had political arguments but actually, while he mouths the government's line, I don't think he cares much. Just so the authorities leave his physics and his stamps alone."

After a long pause, she said firmly: "I might be shot trying to get across, but I'll risk it."

Mike pondered. "Why not call on your aunt in Stuttgart to help you?"

Gisela shook her head. "No, Frieda is too old, almost eighty now. She gets confused."

"No other relatives in West Germany?"

"None."

"I admire your courage. You'll need it all to get across."

"I'm tough, Miguel, very tough inside."

"I believe it. Steinbrecher, breaker of stones. It takes tough people to smash rocks."

"So. You see? You would not be helping a weak, timid female."

"And just how would I be able to help you?" Mike pictured the death strip as he had seen it from the air, guard towers and searchlights, savage dogs, barbed wire, land mines that would blow a person to bloody shards of bone and flesh. What could he do against such barriers?

"In a very direct way." She hesitated. "But it would be foolish to waste time talking about it unless you are going to help me. Will you, Miguel?"

"I want to, Gisela, but I must consider a number of things—myself, my family, the company. I'll have to think it over. How long will you stay in Leipzig?"

"The conference ends day after tomorrow. I'll be in the hotel one more night."

"Then I'll give you my answer tomorrow night. I must think about it. If I decide to help, I'll want to go all out with no changes of mind."

"I understand. It would mean commitment and many hours of your time."

Commitment, sacrifice—and risk. For a woman he'd only known a few hours. "Okay, tomorrow night. Your room again?"

"All right. And, Miguel, you must say yes. You must." She kissed him fiercely.

"You're an extraordinary woman."

"So," she whispered breathlessly, "we must not be seen together except in a crowd. . . . And I could not bear to be with you in bed tomorrow night if you said no."

"I wouldn't like that either."

"So why not give me a signal of some kind tomorrow night at dinner?"

"Okay. Let's see. If I wear a brown turtleneck sweater, that means, yes, I'll help. If I wear a shirt and tie, then the answer, sadly, is no."

"Clear. Oh, Miguel."

They sealed the agreement with another kiss, prolonged yet laden with uncertainty and restraint. Doubt had sabotaged passion.

"I'll be wearing the same orange sweater," she said. "Here we have not the luxury of many wardrobe changes."

"Don't worry. You look elegant in it."

He dressed in the dim, shifting abstractions of light filtering through the drawn curtains, conscious that Gisela was watching him in silence. Before departing, he leaned over the bed and kissed her chastely on the forehead.

"I'm Lutheran, you know, so I pray," she said. "Tomorrow I shall pray for a brown sweater."

Upstairs in his own room, he stood for many minutes gazing out the window. Fatigue dulled his thoughts, yet he sifted through recent hours, trying to evoke Gisela's gestures, intonations, the aura and feel of her plea. So much depended on unuttered nuances.

The wind picked and sighed at crevices of the massive railroad station across an arm of the Platz der Republik. A long red-and-white banner, "BUILD THE FUTURE THROUGH SOCIALISM," tugged aimlessly at its cords. In the distance a train wailed beneath the starless overcast. The streets were deserted. Mike felt stabs of the old loneliness and despair. These were the black hours, the alleys cf the night.

3

Mike hung his yellow hard hat on a peg, took off his rain jacket, and stepped over to the kettlelike iron stove. A brown-coal fire, belching smoke out the stack toward sodden skies, warmed the board hut that served as construction headquarters for Sven Alsten and his Swedish crew.

"Another bitch of a day," said Mike.

A driving rain pelted the drafty shack. Through one misted window he could see the raw hulk of the unfinished Inter hotel where he'd spent most of the last month. Through another loomed the scalloped tower of Karl Marx University, tallest structure in the city and known for centuries as Leipzig University where such notables as Goethe, Robert Schumann, and Edward Teller, chief architect of the H-bomb, had schooled. Now the skyscraper was the world's only institution of higher learning boasting a posh nightclub on its twenty-seventh floor, with a special vomiting basin in the men's room. A city of six hundred thousand, Leipzig, ancient home of medieval fairs and Johann Sebastian Bach, had undergone fateful changes since American troops seized the bomb-gutted city in 1945 and then relinquished it to the Soviet Army.

"How are you coming with those door locks?" Bland but solid, Alsten. A fine engineer from Stockholm with a prodigious appetite for work and play, he seldom showed bloodshot eyes from the night before.

"We're not. Goddam it, Sven, you ought to dock the pay of anybody who fools around with those elevators." Mike slapped the rough planked table that rested on sawhorses. "I mean it. That's the third time some playful bastard has pried open the doors at one of the floors. Like I told you before, you force those doors and we got trouble." He blew on his hands, rubbed them for warmth. Late rising after only a few hours' sleep, Mike Simmons felt edgy today anyway, without the added frustration of broken contacts and contact arms. "How about some coffee, pal?"

"Coming up." Alsten filled two mugs with some of the Costa Rican coffee an assistant had brought through customs in his luggage.

"Let me show you what we're up against." Mike set his mug on the planked table, then sketched outlines of the elevator shaft on the back of an invoice. "Look, every floor has a door-lock assembly for each shaft. . . . About like so. . . . Okay, if this contact arm breaks, the elevator stops dead. We want that. Our safety guarantee, right? But prying open the doors has got to bust the contacts. It's not the $75 American cost of the set that bothers me, it's the lost time."

"How much time?" Alsten blew on his hot coffee.

"Well, I only had two spare assemblies and I used them on those other breaks. I figure maybe two-three weeks to get some in."

"Three weeks!"

"I might do better if I bring them myself. Look, don't blame Todd for the delay. My men have strict orders not to force the doors. One of your people must have done it last night. If you don't take some disciplinary action, this is liable to keep on happening."

Alsten heaved a sigh. "You know that means dealing with Lanz?" Werner Lanz was the brigade leader on the job, charged by the party with insuring political rectitude, raising the Socialist consciousness of hard-hats, and looking after the welfare of some one hundred union members building the hotel.

"I know. I'll do it, much as I hate to get into a hassle with that slippery character." Mike held out his hands to the big-bellied stove. "Just so I can do it in here where it's warm. Will you do the interpreting?"

"I suppose I'll have to." Alsten shrugged. "Let's get this over with." He leaned out the door, summoned a nearby workman, and asked him to fetch Herr Brigade Leader Lanz.

Werner Lanz made his headquarters on the opposite side of the hotel skeleton in another shack dubbed "SED Haus" by the workers. Accordingly, he arrived but little dampened by the rain. A short, wiry, intense politician with swift, birdlike mannerisms and a gift for liquid phrases, not unlike the trilling notes of birdsong, Werner Lanz held his job in far more esteem than did the workmen whose welfare he tended.

"Herr Alsten. Herr Simmons." He bowed slightly after taking off his raincoat. "You wished to speak with me?" He wore the clasped-hands SED party button on his leather jacket.

"Yes. We have a problem, Herr Brigade Leader. I'll let Herr Simmons explain it to you." Alsten kept the formality on the high plateau where Werner Lanz dwelled during working hours.

"*Bitte.*" Lanz gave Mike his full, earnestly respectful attention.

With Alsten translating, Mike first complimented the intelligence and know-how of DDR workers, praise only slightly exaggerated, then eased into the matter of the broken contacts. Explaining the mechanism and the rupture, he said the East Germans assigned specifically to elevator installation had brought the matter to his attention. Lanz should know that Mike was urging Alsten to impose penalties on any unauthorized person riding in, or tampering with, the elevators.

Listening raptly, Lanz shot glances back and forth at the two foreigners like a wary bird on a limb. Then he delivered a long, singsong reply, or perhaps proclamation, in which he extolled the devotion of his construction craftsmen to Socialism, to solidarity, and to the advancement of the DDR through superior buildings, specifically hotels. Amid such lofty commitment, it was unthinkable that members of his union should interfere, either intentionally or accidentally, with elevated progress.

Nevertheless, Mike replied after Alsten's extensive translation, somebody had forced open the doors on the third floor of No. 4 shaft, cracking the contact arm and rendering the elevator immobile. This was the third such incident and it must not be repeated or else completion of the building would be greatly delayed, *nicht wahr?*

Ah, but the brigade leader had conducted personal investigations of the two previous incidents, without demand by the Herren Engineers, as it were, and he had found to his satisfaction that no one forced hall doors. On the contrary, the malfunction occurred because of defective material.

"Defective material!" Mike was astounded. "Are you implying that Todd Elevator is guilty of poor workmanship in these door-lock assemblies?"

Nein. Lanz made no allegation about the skills of Todd's work force. He merely wished to point out the definite probability that these particular parts failed to meet the specifications for stress.

Mike's temper spurted. How could the brigade leader have tested the broken parts since Mike himself had taken them out in the process of replacement?

No, replied Lanz, he had not tested the parts. But since his comrades had not forced open the doors, how else to explain the malfunction save through defective material?

"Goddam it, what kind of specious reasoning is that?" Mike was boiling now. In twenty-five years' working with door-lock assemblies, he had never known a contact arm to break without heavy pressure on the hallway doors.

"I'm not going to translate that," said Alsten quietly. "Cool it, Mike."

Mike got himself under control with an effort. Spacing his words, he told Lanz of his career-long experience with the assemblies.

Ah, but Lanz had read, not in *Neues Deutschland* or other East German organs, but in the Western press itself, of massive recalls of American automobiles because of part failures. Also, as the Western press pointed out, cars coming off the Detroit assembly lines on Mondays often broke down because workers, hung over from weekend whiskey or drugs, either turned out poor work or failed to keep pace with the bosses' demand for more speed. This was quite unlike the DDR where workers always met the reasonable norms set by the planners. Werner Lanz offered the indictment in happy, skittering style, darting glances from one agent of the exploitive West to the other.

Mike readily granted the sins of humbled Detroit, but said that Todd Elevator's percentage of defective parts had never exceeded a fraction of a percent. "And to my knowledge," he added, "no contact arm ever broke except when it was supposed to—through the forced opening of doors."

The combatants lofted their arguments back and forth

while Alsten sought to moderate and modulate. In the end, Mike paid homage to the honor and integrity of the Herr Brigade Leader's construction comrades, and Lanz withdrew his allegation of possibly shoddy workmanship at Todd plants. He promised to post a notice which, without reference to past misfortunes, would insure the future inviolability of Herr Simmons' well-crafted elevators.

They bowed to each other amid a flourish of adieus, and Werner Lanz walked into the rain, glancing sharply about him like a bird about to pluck a worm.

"That guy's nobody's fool despite his mincing ways," said Mike. "Sorry I blew my stack. I don't know what got into me. My God, I started defending Todd like I owned the company."

"Suppressed American chauvinism," Alsten bantered.

"Could be. I've got to watch myself around Werner."

A workman arrived with the daily hot lunch from the Mitropa restaurant in the railroad station. Alsten sniffed at the containers.

"Hmm. Bockwurst, potatoes, and carrots. Honey biscuits for dessert. How does that strike you?"

"Let me at it." Mike had skipped breakfast.

Alsten pulled a battered chair up to the table. "What did you think of that crowd last night, Mike?"

"Man, you can sure round up the characters. Talk about your expense accounts, those Communists know how to run up the tab when they're away at conventions."

"People are people the world over." Alsten cut off a chunk of Bockwurst. "I got some good laughs last night."

"I did too, but not my wall story."

Alsten shook his head. "I'm surprised you told that one."

"I knew I shouldn't, but something goaded me. . . . It's because they're ashamed of the Wall, I guess."

"More than shame," Alsten reflected. "They're prosperous here in East Germany now, but they're still prisoners

43

and resentment over the confinement runs deep. Probably not many would leave permanently, but they'd sure break out for travels to the West if they could."

"Plenty tough to escape, right?" Mike, with Gisela occupying his thoughts, welcomed the opening.

"Less than a couple hundred a year make it now, some of them weird efforts like the two families who crossed to Bavaria at night in a homemade balloon."

They finished lunch, traded views on the Bockwurst and honey biscuits and refilled their coffee mugs.

"You and I haven't talked much politics, Sven." Mike leaned forward on the makeshift table, glad that the dispute with Lanz had opened the subject. "You've been here over a year now and you speak the language. Tell me, what's to escape from? I'm curious. Oh sure, shortages, fairly dull life, not much fun, lots of slogans and marches, Werner Lanzes, and Communist hype. On the other hand, the state guarantees womb-to-grave security, showers workers with prizes, and treats their world-champion athletes like royalty. Also, no unemployment at all. No going on relief and scratching around for a job like we have to do in the West in bad times. Hell, the people here are better off than two-thirds of the world."

"But they're in jail, Mike. This state has fifty thousand *Grenztruppen* patrolling the border with the other Germany, to make sure nobody gets out. That's a lot of guards for a country no bigger than your state of Virginia."

Mike agreed with a nod.

"And lots of smaller prisons inside the main one." Alsten's brief laugh was sardonic. "Things look placid on the surface here, but don't be fooled. A fellow who strays too far from the party line runs the risk of being put away." The Swede pushed away the remains of his food and lit a cigarette. "Just a few months ago over in Dresden, a respected university chemist came up with some research data the regime didn't like, so they kicked him out of his office and put him under house arrest. He'll be lucky if he ever gets out."

Mike hid his surprise. "Was there any public discussion of it?"

"You can't be serious, Mike." Alsten snorted. "No, not a word on TV, radio, or in the papers. They pulled it off in secret."

"So how did you find out about it?"

Alsten wagged a finger. "Here you don't disclose your sources. It came over the grapevine, the *Flüsterpropaganda* they call it. You can bet Otto Kleist wishes now he'd tried for the other side while he had the chance. Rotten break for an old man."

"Old?" The adjective lightened a dreary day. Mike had assumed Gisela's dear friend to be young and handsome. Once again he'd forgotten his foster father's chief piece of valuable advice: Never assume anything. "How old is he?"

"Seventy-four, I think. Actually, he was retired, just using an office at the university."

"The Technical? Our friend, Frau Steinbrecher, edits publications, you know, at the Technical University in Dresden."

Alsten nodded. "Same place. I'm sure your lady editor knew him, but you'd never hear a peep out of her about it." He inhaled deeply, finishing off the butt of his cigarette. "Say, you two became very friendly, skipping along in Spanish. Where did you learn it?"

"South America." Rain lashed the windows and drops from the shanty's leaky roof hissed on the stove. "I've done a fair amount of work for Todd down there. Frankly, I could use some of that climate right now." Mike stretched, then asked casually: "Anybody ever approach you to help with an escape?"

"Yes. A young fellow who works on this job. He came to me about switching to stonework, then began dropping hints about getting out." Alsten lifted his hard hat and plastic raincoat from the wall pegs. "I had to turn him off despite my personal feelings. I can't afford to take a chance. We figure to bid on a lot more work here—worth millions."

Alsten waited while Mike fastened the hooks of his rain jacket. "We Swedes manage to stay on the sidelines of your big East-West slugging match." The two men walked together into the cold rain.

Mike worked through the spongy afternoon with his mixed crew of Swedes and East Germans. Final phases of the installation—checking, adjusting, testing—went slowly. Although the hard rain eased off to a drizzle and then stopped, fittings and tools remained damp, girders and floors slick, and spirits low. He tried to shut Gisela and her troublesome plea out of his mind, concentrating on work, but conflicting images kept flickering—Gisela molding her body to his at first kiss; gray watchtowers with gun slits commanding stretches of raked, red turf; feverish whispers; a stylish, bright orange sweater; the frenzied barking and lunging of German shepherds on a dog run; his son, Dave, peering down from his helicopter.

Darkness had fallen by the time Mike made his way across the Platz der Republik with its homegoing crowds queuing up for streetcars and its electric sign totting up humanity's daily accounts: "BERLIN: DDR CHAIRMAN HEINRICH VOLPE AND FEDERAL REPUBLIC CHANCELLOR KURT RAUSCHNIG TO CONFER IN WEIMAR IN MARCH . . . LUANDA: MILLION ANGOLANS HAIL DDR CHAIRMAN VOLPE . . . NEW DELHI: USA EMBASSY UNMASKED AS SPY NEST . . . BERLIN: IRMA REICHENBACH BREAKS WORLD RECORD IN PRACTICE SWIM." In front of the columned rail terminal, largest in Europe, he passed a squad of Soviet soldiers, engulfed in brown greatcoats, marching toward a train. Mike had seen uniformed Soviets infrequently. Few of the four hundred thousand troops that Russia maintained in East Germany were permitted to mingle with the native population, but occasionally they left Soviet bases and airfields in uniformed groups.

Delegates of the printing convention milled about the Astoria lobby. Mike looked for a flash of orange but failed to see the woman who had burst into his life like a new symphony, all novel harmonies and perturbing dissonances.

In his room he took his time showering, shaving for the second time that day, slapping on lotion, and inspecting himself in the mirror. A bit fleshy, that one hundred eighty pounds on a five-eleven frame. A few more strands of gray in the black hair worn full in the back in a stylistic compromise between the longhairs and the scalpheads. Hair, so they said, made a statement. Well, okay, that's where he stood, somewhere in the broad middle. Not a bad profile. Some women still thought him attractive. Gisela, too?

Sloshing and padding about the small bathroom, toweling with unusual vigor, resolving to renew daily workouts soon, Mike Simmons realized what it was he was doing. He was postponing the moment of decision. An old gambit, followed since boyhood, but one that he seldom fretted over. For him it worked more than half the time, a passing percentage in the long battle for survival.

Instead of sitting down with pad and pencil and adding up pros and cons like an accountant of the psyche, he pushed toward the deadline without method or guide. He let his thoughts swarm, his impressions flit about, and his emotions tumble in an indiscriminate wave of feeling that broke over him like surf.

When this haphazard mix of fact, fancy, prejudice, hearsay knowledge, and feeling receded on the shores of his mind, Mike usually knew what to do. Some people called it intuition. He called it decision.

Briskly now he put on his shorts, undershirt, trousers,

FLETCHER KNEBEL

and shoes. Pulling open the top drawer of a dresser, he
looked down on his clothing. To the left rested two turtleneck sweaters, one gray, one brown. To the right lay a half
dozen shirts with button-down collars. He hesitated only
momentarily. Reaching down, he picked up the brown
sweater.

So, he had decided. Energy coursed through him. He felt
new, fresh, recharged, ready for any challenge. He whistled
a few bars of an old favorite, title forgotten, and stepped
jauntily to the door.

On the floor, just inside the doorsill, lay a plain, white envelope. Inside he found a sheet of paper with a single English sentence written in a neat, flowing script. No signature.

"I pray two times today for brown sweater."

Lutheran prayers answered, Gisela Steinbrecher, Lady
Stone Breaker. Apparently she had tucked the note under
his door while he showered.

On the way to the lobby he pondered the sources of his
decision. A stranger, scratching among motives, might con-
clude that Mike had acted out of fancy for a woman and
antipathy for a regime that imprisoned its own population.
Only half right, he knew. The fancy for a woman, yes. But
also a strange presentiment about the Wall and its ugly appendages, those guard towers and deadly fences severing
the old Germany. He hated the Wall, not alone as a symbol
of mass oppression, but as a private enemy, a forbidding
presence that evoked dark terrors of childhood.

Ever since his early Omaha days with Mac and Dolly,
those pious despots of the nursery, Mike had detested walls,
especially unadorned, blank walls. His father, an itinerant
plumber, had disappeared when Mike was but two years old
and he retained no memory whatsoever of the man. A year
later his mother died of pneumonia, leaving the responsibility for little Michael's rearing to half a dozen relatives,
none of whom evinced great eagerness for the task. The

child wound up with Dolly Peck, a cousin of his mother, and Dolly's husband, Mac, an anguished, Bible-quoting, dogmatic fundamentalist.

Childless themselves, Mac and Dolly believed that the essence of education lay in putting the fear of God into the young. They harried little Michael with admonitions to love, admire, worship, pray to and fear the Holy God, with emphasis on the fearing. Mike's knee-pants days were laced with lengthy evening prayers, stories of gory battles from the Old Testament, and memory sessions in which Mac recited passages of Scriptures and forced Mike to learn them word for word. Dolly and Mac constantly enjoined him to welcome "God's manifestation," and from his first hours with the Pecks, Mike pictured God as that "man at the station," a huge, brawling vagrant who hung around the Omaha railroad yards, striking fear into the hearts of boys like himself.

Mike took an early loathing to this strenuous faith of Dolly and Mac Peck and soon rebelled. He squirmed on a high-backed parlor chair, kicking the rungs, during prayers. He refused to memorize the more incendiary of the apocalyptic verses favored by Mac. He formed a special hate for Isaiah 24:1—"Behold the Lord maketh the earth empty and maketh it waste and turneth it upside down and scattereth abroad the inhabitants thereof." Only an unwashed, smelly, bearded vagrant from the railroad station, Mike concluded, would treat people in such a frightening manner, and more than once he hinted as much to Mac.

For his mutinies against the Master and the Word, as well as for the ordinary behavior lapses of boyhood, Mike was exiled to a dank, dark room in the basement of the old frame house in Omaha. Mac or Dolly would place the child on a stool in the middle of the bare-walled room, previously used only for storage, shut the door, and warn him not to emerge until called. Usually his sentence lasted half an hour, but in cases deemed to involve wicked sacrilege or serious infractions of the conduct code, the couple forced Mike to remain on the stool for an hour. Once they went off to Wednesday-night prayer meeting and forgot him. When released several hours later, Mike had fallen into hysteria and had to be carried, whimpering and shuddering, to bed. Hours passed before the shivers and sobs ceased to convulse the small thin body. Mike dreaded "the dungeon," as he knew it, and came to hate every crack and splotch on the four plastered walls. Fear struck with regularity, reducing him to a quivering bundle atop the stool. He cried a great deal and occasionally he screamed with terror when his imagination conjured up predators poised for attack. He knew that the Pecks could hear his screams, but not once did they shorten the period of punishment.

Fortunately for Mike, this ordeal lasted only a few years. While he was still in second grade at school, a half sister of his long-vanished father moved back to Omaha and prevailed upon the Pecks to let Mike live with her and her husband. Laura and Roger Murray were decent, kindly people who reacquainted the boy with the solace of love, home, and friendship. He lived with the Murrays through high school and accepted their offer to pay for a college education. For years, until their deaths within a few months of each other, Mike paid an annual visit to the Murray home in Omaha and exchanged affectionate letters with the couple every few months.

But the brands of a fierce, vengeful God and of walled imprisonment were upon him. For years, he could not pass a church without flinching. The aversion to organized religion faded in time, but the curse of those basement walls remained deeply embedded, flailing his unconscious and tormenting his nights. The nightmares, peopled by phantoms and monsters, almost always involved walls: high walls, dark walls, walls that moved in to crush him, walls that toppled on him, brooding walls, sinister walls, walls that haunted, pursued, and tracked, walls that grew abominably deformed arms and legs. And now he faced an actual wall that might be battled and conquered through the person of an immensely intriguing woman who had so suddenly and passionately entered his life. Could the unconscious be cleansed through struggle in the outer world? If so, what better vehicle than helping Gisela Steinbrecher to escape across the Wall? Perhaps by fighting the death strip, he might somehow exorcise, or at least come to terms with, these private terrors that burst through walls and pillaged his sleep. Just how this might occur, he did not know. It was not a thing that he knew, but something sensed or divined.

The Wall, stark and eyeless, beckoned with unseen hands to his own walled alleys of the night.

Only once since his college days at MIT had he known a season undisturbed by demons. They had left him for an entire summer after graduation when he and a friend tramped ancient Inca trails in the high, gaunt Andes, ending at Machu Picchu in sleeping bags amid curling mists. But they returned, those looming walls and those masked companions of the night, when he went to work for Todd, and they hovered in the shadows through his marriage, the childhood days of Dave and Sally on Long Island, the promotion escalator at Todd, his divorce, and the bachelor years that followed. They receded during his assignments in Latin America, then prowled his nights once more when he came back to New York and a desk in Todd's executive offices.

So when Red Fleming came down with pneumonia and had to leave Leipzig a month before completion of the job, Mike volunteered as his replacement. A Communist country, his first, at least would offer change from New York's suffocating paperwork. At most, it might waylay those hooded couriers of alarm. No such luck, of course. Some nights he had awakened with clammy hands, and once had bolted upright in bed only to see his shapeless foes float through a crumbling wall and fade like smoke from a dying fire.

But not tonight. Now he rode the crest of resolution. He sailed out of the elevator and through the lobby toward the dining room, his whole body alive.

Bright orange flared in his path.

Gisela stood alone, riffling the pages of a magazine. When she looked up, she saw him. Instantly her glance told her what she wanted to know. She flashed a radiant smile. His mind flicked back unbidden to a bubbly girl named Polly, earthy smells of early spring, first love . . .

"What a heavenly color you're wearing." She said it in Spanish, her voice low and seductive.

"Will you join me and the others for dinner, Frau Doktor?"

"No. We must stay apart." She spoke rapidly. "Just in case you wore brown tonight, I arranged for an apartment where we may talk normally."

Confidence in prayer or in her own charms?

"Miguel, you must go there at nine-thirty prompt. Number 10 Hainstrasse, a block behind the Information Zentrum. You know the Zentrum?"

"Yes."

"I will arrive several minutes earlier and will leave the building door unlocked. Number 10 opens to a courtyard. You turn right in the court and enter the building with the wide stairs. It is next to the Wilhelmshöhe Café."

"Oh, I know that café. It's closed at night."

"Good. Then you walk up three flights to Apartment 31. Three, one. You must repeat all that, Miguel."

"Orders, orders." He grinned, repeated the directions.

"Now I go to dine with the others from last night. You must eat somewhere else. Nine-thirty exact, please."

As Mike turned away, he saw one of the reception clerks

studying him. Quickly she averted her eyes. It was not one of the comely, crisply pleasant, polished young women, but Frau Gotsche, the matronly votary of order and formality.

He dined at Auerbachs Keller, a restaurant tracing its lineage to Goethe and an ancient wine vault of Faustian legend, then queued up for a ticket to an East German-made movie, *The Engaged Couple,* a prizewinner at the 1980 Czechoslovakian film festival. Brilliantly acted, directed, and photographed, the motion picture depicted the trauma of life in a female prison under the Nazis. In the denouement, the lover, who remained true to his betrothed during the decade she spent behind bars, managed to meet and embrace her just as he himself was carted off to a concentration camp. While East German film-makers were free to explore every aspect of Germany's Nazi past, a movie about conditions in contemporary DDR prisons, especially one focusing on political prisoners, remained unthinkable in the country's film colony. Mike and the Leipzig audience left *The Engaged Couple* silently and wet-eyed.

With a few minutes to spare, he sauntered along darkened streets, past the old town hall with its enormous blue-and-gold clock, and through the twelfth-century marketplace to Hainstrasse. The end of the rain had left a damp, penetrating chill. The downtown streets were almost empty. East Germans, overly supplied with collective activities throughout the day, sought the privacy of home and the anonymity of the television screen at an early hour.

The opening to No. 10 was indeed a courtyard between a confectionery shop and a luggage store, both of which had long lines of customers during the day. He made his way to the apartment entrance next to the café. The door opened as promised. Mike clicked the lock behind him and mounted the wide, curving stairway. Gisela answered his soft knock at the apartment door.

They moved into each other's arms as eagerly as two lovers who had not met for weeks.

"When I saw the color of your sweater, Miguel . . ."

"I loved the look on your face."

After the first rush, Gisela kissed slowly, savoring without demanding, and he welcomed the familiar pressure of her lips and that distinctive, compelling scent that he now associated with her, a mélange of breath, body warmth, and foam-bath fragrance. No matter what happened between himself and this suddenly important woman, he knew he would never forget that unique aroma.

"Here is the apartment of my friend Ulli." Gisela swept her arm about. "One room with little kitchen and shower, toilet down the hall. Ours for two hours. Ulli comes back from her mother's about midnight."

One end of the large room served as a parlor, holding several finely crafted hardwood chairs with brocaded seats, a towering elderly armoire, a thick-tufted carpet, a cheap, modern coffee table, large television set, small radio, and brand-new floor lamp, the shade still in a paper wrapping. At the opposite end stood a low, wide bed without headboard, the fat Federbett lying swathed in fresh sheeting like a pregnant woman in a newly laundered nightgown.

Gisela arranged a pair of the hand-tooled chairs near the flimsy coffee table—two aristocrats moving into a tacky neighborhood—and tuned the radio to the government-run Berliner Rundfunk. A happy symphony, as light as childhood, filled the room.

"Oh, Mahler's Fourth."

"You know music, Miguel?"

"More or less. But that's too loud, isn't it, if we're going to talk?"

"We set the radio over here like this." She placed it on the floor near the door, stretching the wire cord to its limit.

"But we leave the volume up. Who knows? The walls may be thinner than we think."

Gisela took his hands in hers for a moment after they seated themselves, then smoothed her skirt and sat back with an air of expectation.

"So, Miguel, how do I get over there?"

"How's that?"

"What should I do to get out of the DDR?"

He had heard her correctly the first time and he was astounded. This unsettling woman seldom lacked surprises.

"I haven't the vaguest idea, love." The Spanish *mi amor* slipped out unsummoned.

She sat there patiently, hands folded in her lap, like a wayside madonna awaiting deliverance from flood, fire, or quake.

He found the request as irritating as her posture. The German insistence sounded harsh in Spanish, that sunny vehicle of conciliation and evasion. Also he felt manipulated. He had agreed, at unknown risks to himself, to help. Not to lead, initiate, or shoulder the lead.

"Look, Gisela, you've got me wrong. I don't know the first thing about arranging an escape. That's your end. I'm willing to help, but you'll have to tell me what to do."

"But I know nothing. You're the widely traveled man from the West. You know many people over there."

Her approach was plaintive and again he wondered about her innocence as he had originally when he noted her blushes. Could she, after all . . . ? No, no, the SSD could never tune an actress to such perfection. He had committed himself. No more subversive doubts.

"Sure, I know people, but none in the escape racket. . . . Really, Gisela, you stop me cold. I never expected this. I have no idea how to start."

"Then we must find out together, no?" She made it sound as easy as a phone call.

"Well, yes. I suppose so." He felt carried along by this singularly determined woman, yet lost, too. The romantic strings and winds of the Mahler broke for a long, guttural, officious announcement and he suddenly felt not eighty miles from the nearest exit to the West, but eight thousand.

"I will tell you what they say on the Flüsterpropaganda." Not at all disheartened by his response, Gisela shed her aura of patient innocence as easily as a molting bird sheds feathers. She gripped the wooden arms of her chair and proceeded in businesslike fashion to cover the options. "First, there's the Baltic route."

But that, she said, was impossible in winter. And it required great endurance and stamina which, although a weekend swimmer, she did not possess. Also, unless one lived in the seacoast towns, one could become suspect during the weeks of preparation. Those who fled by water had to procure wet suits and fins, no easy matter, and study tides, sun and moon tables, beaches, patrols of the National Volksarmee, routes of the gunboats, underwater obstructions, and a host of minor details.

If one elected to swim across the Elbe where it formed a natural border with the Federal Republic, the defector faced almost certain death by machine-gun fire from swift river patrols.

Then there was the flee-for-fee network, once almost shattered by the SSD but now again returning to operations. These shadowy organizations spirited East Germans across by a variety of means, in freighted crates, beneath automobile seats, via false passports and forged papers, even in Allied military vehicles which, under the old Berlin agreements, passed through Checkpoint Charlie without inspection.

"But the latest price quoted is fifty thousand marks," said Gisela, "and I have less than three thousand."

She understood why the fee was so high. Just last month

a trucker from the Federal Republic drove a load of furniture across DDR territory from Helmstedt, in West Germany, to West Berlin. He pulled off the Autobahn for only a minute at a prearranged spot east of Magdeburg. A DDR defector climbed into the sealed trailer through a sliding panel at the bottom. Before the truck could start again, the NVA seized both men. Convicted, they each got eight years in prison. The luckless defector already had paid twenty thousand marks out of the fifty thousand total charge.

Tunneling, a favorite method of escape in the early years of the Wall, had been all but abandoned, she said. In Berlin, constant patrols, informers, and sophisticated detection devices made tunneling a lethal venture. A few escapers managed to scale the Wall with grappling hooks, but they were those who worked or lived near the capital's concrete barrier and knew the minefields and patrol times by heart.

In the country, border guards had demolished all structures within several hundred meters of the wide, mined frontier, and all persons living in the border belt had to submit to regular screening procedures. Except in rare places, such as a gorge or along a stream bed, defectors had to burrow and dig about a quarter of a mile, a task requiring months of effort in view of the close surveillance of inhabitants, terrains, and tools.

"If only Mother had emigrated to Stuttgart when she reached the women's pension age of sixty," said Gisela ruefully, "then when she died last year, I could have been cleared to attend her funeral. . . . An uncaring thought? Perhaps, but practical. . . . Of course, I'm not sure I was ready last year. I might have come back to be with Karl."

"Oh, surely Karl would have attended your mother's funeral with you."

"The Politburo is too clever for that." Her laugh had a caustic ring. "If a husband or wife gets permission to go to the other side for the death of a close relative, the spouse must stay here—hostage of the state."

She talked of other escape routes, a visa for Yugoslavia and then across the lightly guarded frontier into Greece; a boat crossing of the northern Elbe during a heavy, nighttime snowfall; walking out with a forged West German passport; knowing an Interflug pilot and persuading him to transform a regular domestic flight, with her aboard, into a dive for a West German airfield.

All of this seemed remote and highly improbable to Mike. He could neither picture Gisela fleeing across the Elbe like a modern-day Eliza nor visualize just how and where he could help. Mahler's Fourth moved into its dreamlike passages as the orchestra's strings crafted a gossamer setting for fantasies of daring flights to freedom.

"They say the best route now is at places where they're replacing the fences." Gisela's voice brought him back to the reality of her unflagging will. "You know they've been 'modernizing' the frontier, as they call it, for many years, meaning that they're forever making it more deadly to escape. But I'm told that at the places where they do this work, it is sometimes possible to cross."

"How's that?"

"In places the fences are actually down for a week or so and the mines have been cleared away so the work crews don't get killed. This leaves unfortified gaps several hundred meters long."

Oh, yes. His thoughts skimmed back to that day in October when his son, Dave, flew the chopper through billows of mist along the border near Fulda. At one point Dave had pointed down, then explained with a metallic growl of his throat microphone that guards had been exploding and removing mines for several days, preparatory to dismantling the old fence and erecting the newest, escape-proof model.

"Now I remember," he said. "Yes, I've heard that too."

Gisela's mood lightened. "Maybe we should concentrate on that way." She thought for a moment. "You leave in two days, Miguel?"

"That's right."

"Then over there, where you can ask questions freely, you must find out the places where the fence is down."

"That might take weeks, Gisela."

"You will find out." She was stubbornly confident.

"But how would you ever get near such places?" Mike frowned. "You need a pass to be anywhere near the frontier, don't you?"

"Yes, for five kilometers back. But I have some relatives and friends in the frontier zone. My sister, Frauke, lives in Kaltennordheim near the border and I have a permit that hasn't expired yet. It helps to be a good SED activist."

"And how am I to get word to you?"

"Why," she said brightly, "we will meet right here two weeks from tonight. Ulli adores affairs of the heart and she'll let us have the apartment for all night, maybe two. I'll come from Dresden."

"Is this an affair of the heart, Gisela?"

"I think so." She said it seriously, again with a splash of color in her cheeks. She gazed into his eyes as if an answer were hidden there. "I wonder, Miguel. Do I feel these stirrings because of love or because you've agreed to help me? I'm not sure." She might have been pondering a problem in mathematics, so solemn she seemed. "But I do have great warmth for you."

"And I for you, mi amor." Again that phrase, not consciously spoken.

She leaned forward for a kiss and immediately Mike wanted her. She traced the dips and rises of his face with soft fingertips.

"Can you return in two weeks, Miguel?"

In his years of working with elevators, Mike had dealt

with perhaps fifty cases of broken door-lock contacts and shunt bars. Now, for the first time, he looked back upon a break as one of good luck.

"It just happens that an accident on the job makes it necessary for me to come back here again. So, yes, sure, two weeks from tonight right here."

"Oh, Miguel." Her eyes danced. "I know I'll get out. I know it."

For an hour they talked ways and means. If ever he needed her, he should contact Ulli Beitz at the theater and concert ticket counter in Information Zentrum. Gisela showed him a framed photo of Ulli and he saw a pleasant woman of thirty-odd years with a great mass of hair. Ulli's apartment had no phone, but he might come here in a dire emergency. Gisela also gave him her home address and her phone number at the university, but again these should be used only when other channels failed and then only through a third party.

Mike gave her Sven Alsten's working phone number and his room at the Astoria. Sven, he knew, would relish intrigue in the cause of romance. Mike also supplied her with two numbers in West Berlin, that of the Alsterhof, a hotel where he had stayed, and that of Walter Delaney on Wildpfad in the leafy Grunewald residential section. Delaney ran Todd's European operation through his Berlin office.

They devised a simple code, based on elevator parts, to cover elementary situations. They tried to translate such terms as overhead, hatch, sling, platform, door lock, counterweight rails, hoist machine, shunt bars, selectors, pivot points, pits, and safety switches into Spanish, but in a few cases fell back on the English word. They wrote down the code and equivalents, but Gisela vowed to destroy the paper after she committed the meanings to memory.

She also made up a brief, coded exchange in German for Mike's use at the ticket counter with Ulli Beitz. Her friend, happy to speed the pursuit of love, would understand that Mike wanted her to contact Gisela for him.

Mahler's Fourth had given way to a string quartet playing chamber music that Mike did not recognize. Light, nippy, often fluttering like a long-tailed kite on a summer breeze, the melody evoked children playing and lovers strolling in meadows far from watchtowers, walls, and armed guards.

Mike glanced at his watch. Eleven-twenty.

"Yes," said Gisela. "Ulli returns at twelve." She pointed to the bed with its clean, unwrinkled sheets and pillowcases. "We can't leave the bed like that. Ulli thinks we're here for love." She tucked her chin at that downward angle and glanced at him with the small, shy, vulnerable smile.

Peacocks rustle trains. Swans preen. Frogs croak. Scorpions dance with locked claws. Spiders vibrate their webs. Gisela Steinbrecher tucked her chin and Mike Simmons, captivated, swept her into his arms.

Their lips had barely touched when he found himself thrown to the side. Gisela, with slim but firm swimmer's muscles, toppled him to the bed, shoved him under the fat quilt, and with muted cries and laughter began yanking at his sweater. Mike joined the game. They tusseled and clutched, snatched at each other's clothing, fought a sham battle of hands, feet, and elbows. When they finally lay naked and panting beneath the Federbett, Mike's shoes rested at the foot of the old armoire, Gisela's brassiere dangled from the floor lamp, and Mike's sweater hung limply on a chair like the pennant of an ambushed scouting party.

With only a moment's respite, they claimed each other hungrily, buccaneers of passion, and moved with only cursory preliminaries into the strong cadence of love. This time their urge mounted in a steady, powerful rhythm which swept them out to seas of pure sensation. And when they expired together on the sands of the little death, they lay unspeaking for a long time while the chamber music, entering the senses once more, tinkled along, all chimes and murmurs, as incongruous as a parasol in the wake of a hurricane.

"My God," he said.

"We have many ways yet to make love, Miguel." She kissed him and he could sense her deep satisfaction. "Yes, many ways, I think."

And then she flew about the room, retrieving her clothes, pulling on the orange sweater and a black cotton skirt, straightening the rug, replacing the radio. Together they arranged and smoothed the bed.

"You must go now, Miguel." She brushed him with a parting kiss. "I'll wait for Ulli. Remember, two weeks from tonight here, eight o'clock. . . . Or twenty safety switches, yes?"

"I don't like you walking back to the hotel alone at this hour."

"Here is little fear. The streets are usually safe. . . . This is a well-run prison."

They hurriedly reviewed their contacts, Ulli Beitz, Sven Alsten, Walter Delaney in Berlin, and then he was out the door and stepping cautiously down the unlighted stairs.

He walked swiftly through shadowed downtown Leipzig, up Hainstrasse to Brühl where Konsument, the big department store, stood on the spot where Richard Wagner once lived. Locked and dark now, Konsument by day was filled with people who choked its aisles and escalators in endless quest of that East German consumer miracle: an ample supply of the exact item one wanted. Mike walked past the visitor information center where the unseen Ulli worked, along Hallischen, and through the pedestrian walkway under the Platz der Republik. He passed but one couple, booted and wrapped, hurrying arm in arm, and several men in woolen caps apparently leaving some late work. The

62

gritty air had dried, but the chill clung to the shadows like a bony hag. The blackened sky, blotting out moon and stars, pressed down on the city.

At the Astoria reception desk Frau Gotsche, curdled with care, handed him his room key. "All in order, Herr Simmons?"

"Ja, ja. Too bad you have the late duty tonight." He tried to make contact in his halting German. Sometime, he hoped, he might fetch a smile from her.

"I take my turn." Reliability, that least lively of the virtues, saddled her brow like a sculpted German war hero astride his horse of bronze. "May I offer a word of caution, Herr Simmons?"

"Of course, Frau Gotsche."

"Do not succumb to those who offer illegal rates for your Western currency." She lectured like a schoolmistress. "It is all strongly forbidden. Not in order."

"Thank you, but I haven't exchanged a single mark." What the hell was this, the old hatchet face? "I heed all instructions. I am disappointed that you think I need reminding."

She drew back, her mouth prim. "I'm sorry. I wanted to be helpful." Her self-righteousness galled him and he struggled for a retort. Then he thought of Gisela. "So I am obliged to you, Frau Gotsche." He bowed and forced a smile.

Tomorrow there would be only one more night to go.

4

Mike fidgeted. He paced about. He scratched at his shirt. He studied the weather outside—cold and dry with a large, blurred sun struggling to shine through its ragged shroud. He looked at his wrist watch. He cursed softly. He paced once more.

Around him, in this waiting room with its dreary beige walls, stood a dozen people in that state of nervous suspense endemic to airports, dental suites, and border-control stations. One woman with intimations of the Middle East about her—Syrian? Lebanese? Turk?—moved inside endless folds of gloomy cloth that rustled and sighed like a field of wind-whipped grain. A chattering French couple called up that repertoire of shrugs, clucks, pursed lips, and wrinkled brows with which French travelers customarily register their disapproval of inferior populations and landscapes. A young man with russet beard and Birkenstock sandals sank to the floor, drew his legs into the Lotus position, closed his eyes, and presumably consigned the Self to meditation. Everyone else kept glancing at the slot, half hidden behind the counter, through which the passports disappeared on a curious little conveyor belt seemingly made of marbles.

The transients were caught in the toils of Checkpoint Charlie, that aging corridor of passage between the two Berlins, the two Germanies, two peoples with a common heritage and language, two fractions of freedom, two visions, two political pantheons and, above all, two allies of the military superpowers in Moscow and Washington, each deformed by myopic leadership and each supplied with enough savage medicine to cremate humanity and scald the planet into a lifeless moonscape.

Checkpoint Charlie, a cluster of prefabricated shacks akin to the Quonset huts of the Second World War, presented a temporary visage like that of an actor whose greasepaint might be removed at any moment. This look of impermanence was, however, at worst a hoax and at best an instance of bureaucratic sloth. The control station, after all, had stood here for almost four decades and showed no signs of disappearing any time soon.

Now on this raw November day, as Michael Ralph Simmons awaited return of his American passport, Checkpoint Charlie offered a narrow aperture in the high, thick concrete Wall that ringed West Berlin for a hundred miles. Not far away stretched the bald expanse of Potsdamer Platz, its East Berlin turf pocked with vehicle traps, spiked with searchlight towers, hemmed by ruins of World War II, and haunted by the nearby bunker where Adolf Hitler took his own life in 1945 as Russian troops stormed the burning city.

Two structures dominated the divided sky of Checkpoint Charlie and vied for the allegiance of those who passed from one Germany to another. To the northeast the DDR's twelve-hundred-foot television tower pierced the overcast like a buried lance, the great bulb of its upper shaft as distracting as a goiter. Only a block away from the control point, on West Berlin soil, towering over the death strip, stood the nineteen-story headquarters of the Axel Springer publishing empire whose owner placed the building smack against the Wall as much in confidence in the West as in defiance of the East.

"Sharlief . . . Finster . . . Herr and Frau Dubois . . . Giovanni . . . Ahman." The gray-uniformed control officer had begun handing out passports as they bobbed into view on the conveyor from the hidden den of occult security rites. One by one the travelers grasped the booklets as they might a lifeline thrown into churning seas. They clattered out of the metal shack, heading for the next level of decompression. Mike stood alone, his name uncalled.

"Simmons?" he asked.

"Noch nicht fertig." The official vanished into the security den, dropping chunks of German as he went.

Mike resumed his pacing. He had now passed half an hour in this bare, chill room that smelled of disinfectant, musty clothes, and stale tobacco smoke. Several new people arrived, including a man who wore a swirling black cape and cursed magnificently in Italian.

Mike closed his eyes, leaned against the wall, and resorted to an old routine in times of stressful immobility: picturing each of the women with whom he'd slept and for whom he still harbored affection. Long ago he had ruthlessly exiled from memory several females who, he decided, had failed to meet the most charitable standards of behavior, hygiene, or taste. Today, as usual, he ran through the remaining list beginning with sweet Polly, first love, a high school pom-pom girl who took quiet pride in her bust, acclaimed as the neatest pair in the junior class, and who tasted of Juicy Fruit chewing gum. Then Charlotte, the Radcliffe freshman who liked to do it outdoors, and Stacey who brought him little gifts, tie clasps and fingernail clippers, and then through Germaine, Helen, and Virginia. Oh yes, he had loved them all, still loved them indeed, had been loved in turn by most, fiercely by some. He had just arrived at Susan, on whose unslakable lusts he dwelled more lovingly in memory than he had in fact, when he heard his name called.

Gray uniform stood behind his counter, holding out the blue booklet embossed with the haughty golden eagle. "Why did it take so long?" Mike wanted to ask, but of course the inquiry would merely compound futility. Few states deployed agents who answered to foreigners and some, like this one, rarely bothered to respond to their own countrymen. Mike took his passport, checked inside to make sure it belonged to him, and moved along a planked walkway to the next examination by customs. The officer, barely glancing at Mike, approved the single piece of luggage without looking inside.

Farther on, at the window of currency concerns, a head protruded into the frosty air and a voice asked for his passport and the copy of his currency declaration. Upon entering a month earlier, Mike had signed a paper stating the amount of money he brought into the country. The head disappeared. Minutes passed. Mike pulled on his fur-lined gloves and stamped his feet. The head reappeared and the voice asked that he step inside, please.

Now what?

The small room held a wooden table, a desk lamp, and two chairs. On the walls hung a photograph of the chief of state, Chairman Volpe, wearing glasses and looking benignly professorial, several proclamations or perhaps regulations, and a lengthy slogan, something about education and production promoting Socialism's new world.

"*Sprechen Sie Deutsch, Herr Simmons?*" The officer in his gray uniform held Mike's passport and currency statement.

"Nein."

The officer passed into an adjoining room, shutting the door behind him. Through a small window Mike could see about fifty yards away the white line that here separated the two worlds. It crossed Friedrichstrasse, binding the pavement like a bandage. On this side, red-and-white barriers and posts cut a zigzag pattern, making it impossible for vehicles, as in the early days, to slam across the border at top speed. On the other side stood the prefab huts where Allied military men monitored entering cars.

"Good afternoon, Mr. Simmons." This time it was a woman with a pleasant demeanor, ingratiating voice, and neatly pressed uniform. "A few questions, if you don't mind, sir." She spoke English with a British accent. "You brought in quite a lot of money, did you not?"

"Yes." With no idea where this headed, Mike decided to offer no more information than necessary.

"Let's see. You declared 523 West marks, $27, and $3,000 in American Express checks."

Mike nodded.

"And you stayed here twenty-nine days, all in Leipzig, with no travels except between Leipzig and Berlin?"

"Yes."

"You came to Berlin today?"

"Yes."

"By car?"

"No, by train."

"Isn't that a great deal of money for twenty-nine days, Mr. Simmons?"

"Not for a businessman."

"Ah, yes. You worked on the new Inter hotel in Leipzig?"

"Yes."

She frowned. "I thought a Swedish firm was building that hotel?"

"That's right. My company had a subcontract for the elevators."

"Yes, yes." She drew a slip of paper from his passport

and consulted it. Mike became alarmed. Just what was all this? "Oh, now I see. Todd Elevator, Inc. Is that correct?"

"That's right."

"Now how much did you spend in the DDR, sir?"

"Oh, about twelve hundred dollars American, mostly for food. A few bottles of vodka in the Inter shop."

She needed to know exactly how much money he had left. Mike was not alarmed. He knew that this or similar scenes were repeated many times a week at border-crossing stations. East Germany had a ravenous hunger for the hard money of the West, that of the Federal Republic in particular, and it exacted fourteen-dollars-a-day tribute from the millions of West Germans who came across to visit relatives in the DDR.

While the woman looked on, Mike counted his remaining West German marks, traveler's checks, East German marks, and odd change. He produced receipts from the Aussenhandelsbank for traveler's checks cashed in Leipzig. His company, he noted, had paid his hotel in advance for a month. He still had a day's credit left. With the customs official checking his calculations, Mike could account for all but seventeen marks.

"Seventeen marks missing. How regrettable." Another pleasant smile. "But not a major difficulty perhaps. You traded no Western money to individuals?"

"No."

"Then I think we may consider you in order." She handed him his passport. "By the way, did you entertain anyone, Mr. Simmons?"

"A few for dinner. Perhaps four or five people all told."

She folded the slip she'd taken from his passport into precise quarters. "Including a Frau Steinbrecher of Dresden?"

A jab of a needle could not have startled him more. He tried to steel himself, hoping his face did not betray him.

69

"Entertain a Frau Steinbrecher?" He rapped the question back like a badminton bird.

"Come now, Mr. Simmons. Didn't you meet Frau Steinbrecher at the printers' convention in Leipzig?"

"Why yes, I did." He would proceed with utmost caution. Suddenly the cramped room felt cold.

The customs woman smiled thinly. "You needn't get— what's your American word—uptight? Frau Steinbrecher is held in high regard here. She was honored with the Star of People's Friendship for her editorial work and there's talk of her being proposed as a candidate for the People's Chamber."

"Oh." Mike felt some response was called for. He did not relax.

"I knew Gisela Steinbrecher, Gisela Helmich then, in the FDJ during our school days. A hard worker and active party member. You were fortunate to meet her, Mr. Simmons. We wish more people from the West could talk with such an excellent example of the modern Socialist woman."

No words, however disarming, could mask the chilling implication of Gisela's name being mentioned here.

"And what is your name, please?" he asked.

"Frau Müller."

He held out his hand. "A pleasure, Frau Müller." He felt disrobed somehow.

She arose after shaking hands. "So, a safe journey home, Mr. Simmons. Will you be returning soon?"

"Yes, in a few weeks. We've had some problems and I must bring back some spare parts for the elevators."

"Perhaps we shall meet again then. As for now, all is in order. Good day."

He walked swiftly from the hut and along the planked walk, carrying his single handbag. At the exit, he showed his passport a final time to a young soldier who then pressed a button to open the last gate in the East German security complex. The iron gate clanged behind him and Mike walked the fifty yards to the white dividing line. He crossed into West Berlin with only subliminal awareness and neglected to wave, as intended, to the U.S. soldiers on duty inside the shack from which the American flag flew. He had also planned to stop at the Haus Am Checkpoint Charlie, a museum of the Wall, its history, its outrages, its corpses, but he passed the bright yellow shop with scarcely a glance.

Who was the informer? That affable assistant subminister of Culture or whatever her title was? The desk clerk, Frau Gotsche? Perhaps. Frau Gotsche had seen him talking to Gisela and had offered gratuitous advice about money-changing. But then it could have been anyone. What did this mean for the escape plans? Would Gisela too be examined? Questions swarmed like threatening wasps. He felt bare, unprotected.

But West Berlin, that enclave of democracy which peace jugglers of World War II left stranded one hundred miles inside Communist lands, soon ignited fires of rejoicing in Michael Simmons. His senses flamed with sights, sounds, and smells of the turbulent city that he recalled visiting some time in the distant past, although in truth he had passed through here only a month ago. He felt a nervous elation as he hailed a cab and taxied several miles to the Alsterhof on Augsburger Strasse. The hotel stood just a few blocks off Kurfürstendamm, West Berlin's chief boulevard where flocks of tourists surged past theaters, shops, sidewalk cafés, movies, restaurants, and nightclubs and gaped at museumlike sidewalk display cases filled with samples of expensive clothing, jewelry, and accessories.

Although it might hover amid the nations of Europe in freakish isolation, an Eiffel Tower without legs, a shining lake without a shore, West Berlin throbbed with life this afternoon of late November. Fashionable women, leather-coated young men, jeans-clad adolescents thronged the

streets, and everywhere amid the bustling crowds Mike saw
that Berlin phenomenon: short, squat, elderly women, all
dressed in sexless beige hues and all wearing little wool
hats. Along with its surface glitter and often raucous vitality, Berlin held an abnormally high proportion of pen-
sioners and thus beneath its skin claimed demographic kinship with East Germany, one of the world record-holders in
numbers of old people.

What struck Mike Simmons, only a few minutes away
from the queues of the East, was not so much the contrast
in abundance—show windows laden with luxuries, a splurge
of cars, clothes, and cafés, the staggering consumer overkill
of Ka-De-We, an immense downtown department store—but
the difference in color and rhythm.

East Germany was a nation of monotones, its houses,
buildings, and cities the color of earth. It was as though the
Politburo had outlawed visual stimulation, hidden all the
color charts, and repealed paint. Aside from bold shades in
the dress of a few young women, some neon signs, and the
red-and-white propaganda posters, almost everything man-
made ranged from somber brown to the hue of ashes. The
overall impression was drab and, for color-conscious people, depressing. While West Berlin might not rate as a riot
of reds, blues, and greens, it glowed by contrast with its
eastern sister. It offered shimmering advertisements, like the
Mercedes-Benz logo slowly revolving atop the Europa Center, giant flashing signs, entertainment posters and displays,
splashy clothes of every style and cut, and the rainbow
dance of cars and motorcycles.

West Berlin had a special sound unheard east of the
Wall. The city pulsed with exhilaration, clamored with life.
Horns blew. Barkers cried. Traffic hummed. Construction
crews hammered. Pedestrians laughed and gossiped. Young
people shouted. Jet planes whined as they lowered with full

flaps toward Tegel Airport. West Berlin had its own distinct music, even as Paris or New York.

The sound of East Berlin, Dresden, and Leipzig, the major East German cities, was by contrast curiously muted. It was not that these urban centers lacked noise. Traffic growled, streetcars, trains, and buses got underway early in the morning and great crowds pressed ceaselessly through the stores in search of goods. But a certain vivacity, a certain heedless chatter was missing. The tone and rhythm spelled caution. People were subdued. Several times in Leipzig, Mike had marveled at the hush as throngs with string bags tramped through the stores on their shopping rounds. He heard the shuffle of feet, the movement of bodies, but very few of the brisk, spirited, disputatious, raucous voices of West Berlin. The sound of the other Germany was more somber than animated. Only in the soccer stadiums did East German crowds roar without restraint.

Ordinarily Mike would have immersed himself in West Berlin's fresh delights of sound and abundance, promenaded along Ku'damm, ogled the women, seen an afternoon movie, or drunk himself into a happy mood at any one of a thousand bars. But today Gisela held his thoughts in leash. No matter where he looked or turned, he felt the tug of his promise.

Checking in at the Alsterhof with only half a mind tuned to the formal exchange with the reception clerk, he first cursed himself for giving Gisela his word, then promptly repented and resolved to get down to work to find her an escape route. After settling in his room he called Walter Delaney at his Berlin office and arranged to meet in late afternoon.

He placed a call to Lieutenant David Simmons in the helicopter pilots' ready room of the 11th Armored Cavalry Regiment in Fulda, but had scant hopes of reaching him before nightfall. His son might be flying, engaged elsewhere, or off duty. Luckily, Mike reached him at once. Dave was serving his tour as duty officer.

They traded the usual health and welfare inquiries. They had not talked since the night before Mike crossed into the DDR.

"Remember the day we went over your regular route and you showed me where repairs were being made?" In speaking over the microwave links across East Germany, Mike thought it prudent to avoid specifics.

"My regular route? . . . Oh yeah, yeah. Sure. What's up, Pop?"

"I can't go into it now, Dave, but I have a friend over there who wants to take a look."

"At the repairs?"

"Yes, wherever they might be right now. Do you follow me?"

"Yeah, I think so." Dave's voice took on a note of eagerness. "Take a look in passing, we might say?"

"Right. Dave, I'd like to come to Fulda and have a long talk with you. How soon are you free for dinner?"

"I have a friend from Bremen staying with me a couple of days, Pop, but she leaves Friday. How about Friday night?"

"Okay. I've got a couple of days' business here anyway. See you Friday evening then. I'll come by train."

Mike napped briefly, then met Walter Delaney at the Roma, a smoky Italian bar and pasta house on Marburger Strasse two blocks off Ku'damm. Delaney ordered small beers which in Berlin meant glasses only slightly smaller than ski boots.

"Prost! Glad you made it back from the land of shitty slogans and kiddies' bedtime hours. If you're not off the streets by 9 P.M. over there, you're liable to get a busted ass when they roll up the sidewalks."

Delaney was a rough, burly sort with full jowls, dark

pouches under his cynic's eyes, and a ragged, smoker's voice. A non-company man who held Todd Elevator in the same contempt he had for governments, churches, hospitals, and most other institutions, he was also a phenomenal sales-man, champion of the worldwide elevator and escalator in-dustry. Rival salesmen regarded him with awe, the only man known to have called his chairman of the board "a dumb bastard" to his face without losing his job. Mike liked Walt Delaney for his raunchy candor, but also because they shared the same pessimistic world view. The difference was that Delaney's black outlook on the world seemed to buoy his spirits, infusing him with a perverse joy, while the same view meshed with Mike's night hours of ghouls and brutes.

"Walt, I need some door-lock assemblies for the Leipzig job. How soon can I get them?"

"We can have them here from the Frankfurt warehouse in twenty-four hours." He reached in his pocket. "Want me to call from here?"

"No, no. Tomorrow's okay. I guess I ought to have half a dozen. Some idiot's forever forcing our doors."

They talked about spare parts, progress on the Leipzig job, and Delaney's recent sales. Mike calculated that in the last month alone, Walt's commissions amounted to more than thirty thousand dollars. Then he broached the subject that so engrossed him.

"Walt, I met a woman I like over there." He trusted Delaney. "She wants to get out and I want to help her. But Christ, I haven't a clue where to start. I need some help."

"Cock trouble, huh? Didn't Jacoby give you his company lecture about keeping hands off that Communist pussy?"

"He did." Mike grinned. "And I didn't."

"Tell me about her. I don't mean her name or where she works or any of that shit." He waved his beer glass. "I just want to get a feel of her, no pun intended."

Mike launched into the story, glad of someone to listen as

75

he unburdened himself. He had just begun to describe Gisela, without naming her, when someone addressed Walter in German.

"Herr Delaney. . . . What a surprise!"

They looked up to see the speaker standing by their table. Heavy-set with a comfortable paunch and somewhat formal smile, the man was scrubbed and curried. The fit of his suit and vest hinted at personal tailoring.

"What an unexpected pleasure, Herr Lerchbacher." Walter got to his feet with a slight bow. Then a flurry of handshaking accompanied the introduction of Mike. Delaney changed within seconds from mordant vulgarian to polished cosmopolite.

No, Herr Lerchbacher could not join them. He and his business friends were just leaving. Yes, he would return to Frankfurt tonight after a brief business trip to Berlin. Of course, he looked forward eagerly to his next opportunity to entertain Herr Delaney at dinner in Frankfurt. Another spray of parting handshakes.

"Just who was that?" asked Mike when they settled back in their chairs.

"A guy who has a lot of clout in Europe. Rudolf Lerchbacher is a senior official at Deutsche Bank, the biggest of the West German commercial banks. He handles all of Todd's financing over here."

"You sure changed your act in a hurry."

"And how. I always believe in keeping on the good side of bankers and over here you do it the formal way. Actually, Rudi's lively enough when you get a few drinks in him. And financially, I'm like that with him." He held up two entwined fingers. "I've steered a couple of good American accounts his way. He owes me one, ol' Rudi does. . . . So, back to your story."

Mike ran through the whole script, including the recent incident at Checkpoint Charlie. Why he trusted Delaney implicitly, he did not quite know. Perhaps for the same reason that customers bought so many of his elevators. A man who jeered at his own company, class, and country— with the obvious exception of bankers—seemed to invite confidence from those who also suffered the world's idiocies and duplicities. And along with his skepticism and blunt talk, Delaney had a natural warmth that disarmed people.

"No," he said when Mike finished. "Your woman doesn't sound like Stasi. You say she didn't mention that carbon dioxide-hunting chemist the second night?"

"Not a word. Although I didn't realize it until this morning coming up to East Berlin on the train."

"That makes her look less like an agent. An SSD woman would have made sure she harped on that theme again. Keep her story straight." Delaney took a long swallow of beer. "I hope that story's a fake, though. With cancer in everything from bacon to beer, that's all we need right now—a lot of carbon dioxide to choke to death on." He lit his second cigarette since arriving. "Your deal with the woman's dicey, Mike. You must know that.

"Shit, man, these two Germanies are crawling with spies, informers, agents. At the same time they have millions of open contacts, visits, trade, negotiations. . . . Why they even have two lawyers, a guy named Mertz in West Berlin and the other attorney named Reschke in East Berlin, who get together every few weeks and set a price for the Federal Republic's purchase of East German political prisoners. Can you believe it? Fixing the price of prisoner flesh, just like brokers set the price for gold in London. . . . So, with all that yakking back and forth across the Wall, the security crap is a real waste of the people's money, if you ask me, but of course if governments don't waste it one way, they'll do it another."

"Actually dangerous for me?"

"Probably not, but could be. Let's say on a scale of one

to ten; with one being happy fucking ever after and ten being Hauptstrasse prison in East Berlin, you're playing somewhere around four or five."

"How do you read that little business with Frau Müller at the checkpoint?" Mike grimaced. "I don't mind saying that scared the hell out of me."

"Sure it did. And Müller's not the broad's name. You can bet on that." Delaney blew a long stream of smoke that broke over the edge of their booth. "I see that one of two possible ways. One, your woman is suspect and they'll nail her for something. Two, she is indeed a sterling party type and Frau Not-Müller's praise can be taken at face value. But either way, you're on notice that they've got you in their dirty little sights and you'd better walk the straight and narrow."

"You don't think I ought to keep that apartment date in Leipzig?"

"Whoa, Mike. I don't tell anybody what to do."

"But if it were you," Mike insisted, "would you keep the date?"

"No way. Listen, I've had a few lays in the Jolly Red Giant countries, but believe me, they were one-night stands. I intend to sell a lot more elevators behind the Wall and I'm not going to jeopardize that business for a steady piece of tail, no matter how juicy."

Like Sven Alsten, like Walt Delaney. Business first.

"And if you were in love?"

"Love!" Delaney gulped on his beer. He wiped his mouth. "I won't insult you by asking whether you're in love after only two nights with the dame. Anyhow, I don't believe in the stuff." He eyed Mike critically. "Let me ask you a question instead."

"Shoot."

"Suppose this gorgeous creature said to you: 'Mike, let's face it, we're desperately in love, a love unique in this sorrowed land since the days of Goethe. However, I like it here and do not intend to leave. Therefore I want you to live with me in the DDR. I'll divorce my husband who's grown so cold toward me and we'll settle down in my beloved Communist homeland where we'll love and fuck each other forever more.' Would you stay?"

"No." Mike laughed. "Of course not."

"So much for love." Delaney sat quietly for a time, rubbing his glass in small circles. "I don't mean to be rough on you, Mike, but it helps to cut to the guts of the deal, right? If a man's feeling for a woman can't survive a difference in customs and systems, it may be the hots, but it ain't love. . . . So, if you're going ahead to help the lady escape, you'd better have another reason."

Another reason? There was his feeling, swelling like a swiftly germinating seed ever since Gisela, only three nights ago, confided so abruptly and fiercely her vow to flee to the West. He could not quite isolate and tag the feeling, but he could sense that it was beginning to dominate his thoughts. Last night, alone in Leipzig after Gisela's return to Dresden, he had dreamed of the Berlin Wall ripped apart by lightning and a dozen Giselas with streaming hair racing down the jagged bolts and diving through a gap in the Wall. The long, raw strip that split the two Germanies had become allied with his own tortured images of walls and with those grisly phantoms that plagued his nights and sometimes brought him sharply awake to find himself drenched in sweat. The exact links eluded him, but that the DDR's death strip and his own furies sprang from the same human dementia, he had no doubt. He hated and feared them both and somehow one might have the power to obliterate the other.

"Walt, I hate that Wall." His vehemence surprised them both.

"Yeah. Well, don't we all?" Delaney eyed his associate in

business—he often called it "licensed white-collar crime"—
with new interest. "You telling me that's why you're going
to help this broad bust out? Because you hate the Wall?"

"In part, yes. I think the goddam thing is an abomination
in a fairly civilized continent."

"Civilized!" Delaney hooted. "Shit, man, you're in the
country that only yesterday, as time goes, cremated
6,000,000 Jews. Oh, pardon me, make it only 4,193,000
Jews—that's according to one German authority who supposedly added up all the cattle-car shipments, got the lower
figure, and decided his countrymen had been maligned. Can
you believe it?

"Jesus, Mike, Germany's supposed to lead the world in
culture. Some culture! Richard Wagner's daughter-in-law
goes on the tube a few years back and says Hitler was a fine
friend, and if he could come back, she'd sit down near his
favorite visiting chair and have a nice chat with him. Hell,
everybody who's over fifty years old knew at the time of the
wholesale gassing of the Jews, but you can't find one in a
hundred today who'll admit it. They showed *Holocaust* on
West German TV a couple of years ago and half the country wandered around, looking pitiful and saying, 'Who, us?
Oh, say it isn't so.' The fact is that most Germans have conveniently blocked from memory everything that happened
here before 1945."

Delaney lit his third cigarette and blew smoke that leaped
like a spear at the basketed wine bottles hanging above the
Roma's bar.

"Not that the Germans are much worse than the rest of
our great and noble human race." He boosted his volume.
"I got an Argentine friend who had all his nails pulled out
by the fucking security inquisitors down there. Look at
Cambodia, half the population rousted from home, burned,
slaughtered, or sent out on the roads to starve. Or look at

Brazil, Russia, Chile, South Africa, even some prisons in the U.S.

"They got about a hundred countries on this globe where they'll deball you just for making fun of the top guy. Why, another friend of mine criticized the PRI, the ruling party in Mexico, and they threw him in a prison tank with a lot of foul, smelly fags who gang-raped him forty times before morning. Then the smirking guards let him out, claiming it was all a mistake.

"And you're worried about the Wall!" Delaney shook his head. The pouches beneath his eyes looked as creased and weathered as a crocodile's hide.

"The Wall's a symbol of all those atrocities, for one thing." Mike spoke slowly, trying to formulate his thoughts. "I can't do anything about your Argentine friend's fingernails, but maybe I can get one person across the Wall. One person."

He could not tell Walt about the other reason—the night terrors and his need to banish them somehow. One could confide the externals to Delaney, but not the shapeless fears and longings that lay deep within. Walt picked up the drumbeats that men marched to, but very little of the flute music or the tremors of the strings.

"Well, what the hell, you've decided. And you're not here to listen to me complain about the human race." Delaney blew another column of smoke in a long, whistling sigh. "What you want from me is leads on where to find help."

"Right. I don't know where to start."

"Okay, there are some refugee organizations that'll have some tips. I know a couple of guys, for instance, at the Working Group for Human Rights here in Berlin. I can put you in touch with some people who came across earlier this year. Of course, you have the flesh traders who'll deal for money. Oh yeah, there's a guy named Spider Butler in

Helmstedt on the border. Spider's a member of the British Frontier Service which used to be a big outfit patrolling the frontier. Now they're down to a token handful, just enough to keep a British presence. You can call Butler at British headquarters in Helmstedt. Like you, he hates the Wall and he'll do his best for anybody trying to breach it."

—"Do you know any of the professional escape people?"

"No, but I can line up some names with a few phone calls." Delaney raised a pointed finger. "But it costs dough, Mike. The rate's up around thirty thousand dollars a head. You want to spend that kind of money on the lady? I'm talking dollars."

"No, but I'd like to hear the propositions."

"Okay, I'll make some calls from home and phone you at the hotel tomorrow." Delaney summoned the waiter for the check. "I'd better be getting home now. I promised Sue I'd make it on time. We have people coming for dinner."

"I'd appreciate it if you didn't mention this to anybody back in the New York office." Mike helped Delaney with his fashionable fur-collared overcoat.

"You kidding? I tell the home office fuck-all about my private business—or anybody else's."

Mike accompanied Delaney to the nearby subway station, then walked briskly back to the Alsterhof. As he crossed the street in front of the hotel, he saw a man in a trim, gray overcoat moving away from him down Augsburger Strasse. Something about the carriage, a sway of the shoulders, the gait, the swing of the arms perhaps, triggered a message from the brain cells where memory dwells. The message spelled familiarity. But where and when? The man disappeared in a crowd.

Herr Kunze, the epitome of formality and service at the Alsterhof's front desk, handed him a folded slip of paper. "This arrived by telephone just a few minutes ago, Herr Simmons."

Mike read it in the elevator—a late-model Todd Classic—ascending to his room.

"Pop: New switch on your project. It's urgent you get here tomorrow. Call me soonest. Dave."

5

Disco music thundered in the concrete guardhouse like runaway trucks. Private Vicky Washington, trim and busty in her tight-fitting olive uniform, struggled with the telephone while Private Spencer Young, his white UP belt and scarf vying with the high gloss of his black combat boots, dashed in and out of the banging door to fling salutes at vehicles entering and leaving the *Kaserne*.

The compound housed regimental headquarters and two squadrons of the U. S. 11th Armored Cavalry on the outskirts of Fulda, a hilly, bustling city of sixty thousand Germans, baroque architecture, and a massive, twin-towered cathedral. A few miles to the east, knifing sharp angles through the foothills of the Rhön hills like lines of a jigsaw puzzle, stretched the denuded strip of earth and lethal fence that severed the two Germanies. The élite and history-proud Blackhorse Regiment, its mounts long since buried beneath the tread of tanks, armored vehicles, and rolling 155-mm. howitzers, patrolled a section of the armed frontier. It trained for war in a time of peace, always a duty dusted with ennui and bickering and marked by the escalation of petty concerns, such as spotless sidewalks and gleaming footwear, to a level of geopolitical strategy.

This afternoon a foremost concern of the occupants of the guardhouse where Mike Simmons awaited authorized contact with his son, First Lieutenant David Simmons, was to keep warm. The single room, its walls matted with well-thumbed orders, lists, announcements, and decrees of USAREUR, or the U. S. Army in Europe, held a toasty warmth thanks to an electric heater that glowed white-hot with the throb of ravished kilowatts. Between futile efforts to make phone connections with Lieutenant Simmons or other helicopter pilots, Private Washington sniped at Private Young for permitting gusts of icy air to enter each time he bolted outside to snap salutes at passing vehicles.

"Spencer," she complained once more, "don't keep the door open so long."

"You're telling me for the zillionth time." Private Young took the rebuke in equable temper. "Ain't you got this civilian his man yet?"

"Nobody knows no Simmons on this base, not that I can find." She again inspected a sheaf of mimeographed telephone numbers.

"I can go back to the hotel. I have his number there," Mike offered.

"Hey, wait a minute." Vicky Washington waved a pencil. "Here's a D. Simmons under the 'P's.' Spencer! What's an 'S' doing along in the 'P's'?"

"Now how would I know that, doll?" Private Young bopped about the room, snapping his fingers to the disco beat. "She only been here a week," he explained to Mike.

"Fut! You been here five months and you don't even know the number for the big colonel."

Young aimed a man-to-man wink at Mike behind Private Washington's back. "She still think the Army supposed to make sense."

"Well, one thing," said Mike, "if the Russians ever invade, they'll never get far if they have to give orders over our Army's phone system."

The two soldiers gave the remark a bigger laugh than it deserved and Private Young began to improvise lyrics for the driving music. Both Unit Police were black. After Mike's work in the all-white DDR, it was good to pick up again with that special black style, easy, supple, with a touch of flamboyance.

Vicky Washington at last reached Lieutenant Simmons who said he'd come right over to get his father.

"Your son, huh?" she asked. "Did you ever put in Army time over here?"

Mike shook his head. "Nope. I was lucky. I did two years in the Army, but in the States, just before the Korean mess."

"My old man was stationed in Germany in the late fifties," said Private Washington.

"Mine, too. At Heidelberg." Young half-shouted to make himself heard over a new blast from the portable stereo set.

"You're a second-generation Army here," said Mike. "What was supposed to be temporary is becoming permanent."

"You can say that again." Young jumped out, leaving the door wide open, saluted a major leaving in a jeep, and popped back in again. A shaft of cold air shot across the room as Vicky Washington aimed an equally frigid glance at the offender.

"Some of the dudes here grew up in Germany," said Young, "and lots went to school here a year or two. I did my fifth grade in Heidelberg."

First Lieutenant David Michael Simmons arrived, capturing the small guardhouse like a booted invader. At six-foot-three he towered above the three occupants, and his husky frame, swelled by a padded winter combat jacket, all but obscured the window through which Young monitored approaching traffic. Though the family resemblance was unmistakable, Dave had green eyes in place of his father's brown and a broad, firm jaw that dominated his profile, giving him a look of resolution and tenacity. Rugged and strong, at twenty-five he still exuded the zest that had characterized him since he had toddled about a playpen.

Father and son embraced fondly, but with that certain awkwardness and restraint marking men who had not shed the memory of parent and child roles.

The two men left the guardhouse and walked through the thin, fading light of a cold German afternoon on the eve of winter.

"I came as soon as I could, Dave." Mike had to stretch to keep up with his son's stride. "Your message rang bells. What's up?"

"A new gap in the border. But it'll only last a few days. We'll have to work fast."

"I thought you had a woman visitor from Bremen?"

"I do. But tonight she'll look after herself. You and I are going to case that border opening."

They headed toward one of the long, white, oblong buildings that stamped the Kaserne grounds with that bleak, institutional look worn by Army posts the world over. Home of Wehrmacht training units during the Nazi years, the compound had fallen to American troops grinding through Fulda as the Third Reich collapsed in ruins. Now the sons and even some grandsons of that triumphant U.S. force rode new tanks, planes, and troop carriers alongside another German army, this time against a common enemy, one more choreographed switch of partners in the age-old ballet of warfare.

Instructors in the dance of death and school for human killing always masked their sepulchral profession behind flags, uniforms, medals, brass bands, and the righteous yammering of nations. And every new generation offered strong, clean young men—and now women—who failed to see the corpse behind the mask and who studied arms as their brothers and sisters studied medicine, law, or commerce.

With such thoughts in mind, Mike felt a moment of sadness as he saw the dimensions of his son's pride in the uniform. Actually, Mike's delight whenever he saw Dave anew was often streaked with a pale melancholy and sometimes in his fatherly love he ached for his son, for his son's inevitable loss of youth and for the fragility of life. And perhaps Dave's heedless strength reminded Mike of his own shrinking powers and coming death. Whatever the source of the sadness, it touched their meetings with a poignancy that could be evoked weeks later by a picture, a post card, or a passing young man who reminded him of Dave.

And now this military thing. Lieutenant David Simmons obviously thrived in the role of command. He walked with a long, confident stride, the least hint of a swagger to his gait. He returned salutes with flair, greeted enlisted men he knew with a proper mix of friendly interest and the restraint of rank. He pointed out the tank park, a mess hall, the building that housed regimental headquarters, all with the verve of a realtor showing prime property. Mike had forgotten Dave's appetite for Army garrison life after almost two years of it.

They had dispensed with their greetings and family news by the time they reached the building that housed Air Troop to which Dave and his Cobra helicopter were attached.

"You still like military life, don't you, Dave?"

"It's okay. Good duty here. The 11th Cav is one sharp outfit." Dave spoke with his usual animation. "Comfortable room in town. Almost enough women for a bachelor. Can't complain, Pop."

"Do you think you'll stay in?"

"Doubt it." Dave owed the Army four years after his

ROTC contract at Cornell. "Big world out there. Still, I like it here. The Cav's doing a real job."

The solid, old stone building teemed with soldiers in working green fatigues. They clumped along the dim corridors, turned in and out of doorways, carried file folders, juggled mugs of coffee, and managed amid the scatteration of errands to look slightly mystified as if not entirely sure of what they were doing. Images of forts Benning, Hood, and Bragg of thirty years ago flashed across Mike's mind. Weapons might change, but armies went on in the same old fumbling ways.

Dave excused himself briefly to complete an assignment, leaving Mike in the care of a Sergeant Fuller, a career soldier with the tale of two decades of NCO clubs' booze and beer written in the bulge of his waistline. His chin had abdicated some time ago and was now sliding slowly downhill to join his neck. A monument of resignation, Fuller sat behind a bare desk with his hands folded on his belly.

"Hey, Sarge!" A young black soldier stood in the doorway. "Am I supposed to take this to S-4 or what?"

"No!" Fuller glowered. "To Major Riley in S-2. I told you twice."

"Okay to split now?" A voice of guile from the doorway.

"Did you scrub the deck of Baker room?"

"No, I . . ."

"Listen, Monk, I want every goddam inch of that floor scrubbed down until it shines—or I'll have your ass." Sergeant Fuller spoke with weary disgust. "The colonel's bringing his inspection party through here at seventeen-thirty and I don't plan to take any shit just because you want to bug out early."

After rejecting several more appeals, Fuller turned to Mike, his face heavy with futility. "We got a real goat fuck going here today, Mr. Simmons. Trouble is, we have a new major, a transfer from the Third Infantry in Würzburg, and he don't know fuck-all about Cav procedure. To say nothing of a bunch of newbies just over from Stateside."

"My memory of the Army," said Mike, "is that whatever has to be done, the guy who knows how to do it has just been transferred or else he hasn't arrived for duty yet."

"That's the Army." The Sergeant sighed. "In the field this outfit ain't bad, but handling the paperwork around here is like shoveling shit in a blizzard."

Dave returned and escorted his father down the corridor to a small room that held a battered desk, two chairs, and several metal lockers. Maps covered the walls and a radiator hissed quietly.

"Let's wait here until the captain of Air Troop can see us. Routine courtesy call. Just tell him you're visiting. No details, okay?" Dave, his father noted, had picked up a habit of staccato speech, somewhat like a gun firing. "After that, let's do our talking in your room at the Europa. Then tonight we take a ride in the Opel. I'll show you the place where the fence is down."

"You sure it's all right, Dave?"

"No problem. We give plenty of VIPs a night briefing at the border." He hoisted himself to the desktop and swung his shiny black boots. "Pop, I'm glad you came right away. This particular gap in the border will only last a week to ten days, no more. Who's coming across?"

Mike quickly ran through Gisela Steinbrecher's story, omitting her name and the scenes of their intimacy. "She claims she already has a pass for the border zone."

"Is this woman, ah, important to you, Pop?"

"I . . . I'm not sure, Dave. I think so."

"I have a reason for asking." Dave rushed ahead, eager to flee the delicate subject of his father and "other" women. Since his parents' divorce when he was a teenager, Dave Simmons, maneuvering for love and self-interest, found it easier to visualize them both as sexless. "It's dangerous to cross even when the mines are blown and the fence is down. People can get killed."

"We know that. She says she's ready to run the risk. Of course, I'd like some handle on the odds."

"Sure, that's why we're here. I want you to get the whole picture. . . . Come over here."

They stepped to a wall map which depicted the border area patrolled by the 11th Cavalry via helicopters and armored trucks. The regiment also manned observation posts and rotated tank crews to forward bases within a few yards of the border.

"Okay, we're here." Dave pointed with a pencil. "This jagged green line is the border in a section we call the 'Parrot's Beak.' Now the open place in the fence is right here, not far from the town of Melpers. See it?"

Mike slipped on his glasses. "Yep. About how wide is the gap?"

"Call it three hundred yards. They blew the mines the day before yesterday. Helluva fuckin' noise, according to the guys in Fox troop. Now today they were trucking up fencing material and digging new postholes."

Dave carried on with his briefing. Observation of the East German replacement teams enabled 11th Cav intelligence to estimate that the Grenztruppen would take from a week to ten days to erect the new wire-mesh fence with improved S-70 mines affixed to alternate fence posts. These mines exploded laterally whenever someone touched a wire strand, firing TNT and shrapnel along the fence. Right now, however, the three-hundred-yard stretch stood open. Fortunately, the nearest dog run was a mile north, so that a person might cross without provoking a volley of barks. Also, this area stood midway between watchtowers, about a mile in either direction. The night before last, searchlights raked the area every half hour from 7 P.M. to 5 A.M., times exactly duplicated last night. The lights would be timed again tonight. An East German foot patrol of two border guards passed through the open area once every ninety minutes, an armored truck every four hours. Watchtower guards could order troops to the area within seconds.

"You add it all up, Pop," concluded Dave, "and I figure a defector from the DDR has about a fifty-fifty chance of making it."

An enlisted man knocked, brought word that the captain was ready to see them.

Captain Orville McCutcheon of Air Troop liked to emphasize informality of command, "free" staff brainstorming, and combat readiness. He stressed all three in the first several minutes with Lieutenant Dave Simmons' father. His door bore the self-mocking legend, "Sanctum Sanctorum," and his wall held a placard that enjoined: "Speak Up Now! After I Decide, It's Too Late."

They chatted about the Army's need to have parents and dependents understand the soldier's duties, about Mike's trip to East Germany, and the mission of Air Troop of the 11th ACR.

"We're here to keep a sharp eye on Heinz across the border and to absorb the first shock when and if Ivan attacks." Except for the twin silver bars glinting on his shirt collar and his closely trimmed hair, Captain McCutcheon might have been a young college professor. He wore spectacles and tempered the firmness of command with a judicious puckering of the brows. "Of course, we're alert at any moment to handle problems arising from IBCs. My men . . ."

"What're IBCs?"

"Pardon me, Mr. Simmons. Army terminology. Illegal Border Crosser, anyone coming over to our side at other than control stations."

"Illegal by the DDR's definition or by ours?"

"Illegal, even deadly on the other side," said the captain. "They shoot to kill, you know. Over here it's a bit more complicated. Technically we're supposed to let the West German border patrols—they have three outfits doing the job—handle any IBC problem unless they're not on hand, in which case we take over. Eleventh Cav people on border duty do not become involved in the schemes and plans of DDR defectors. Basically all that is a matter between the two Germanies.

"But, of course, once an IBC is across the border on West German soil, we give them all the aid and assistance we can. That includes returning the fire if DDR troops shoot across the line. That's happened, not often, but Heinz is jumpy ever since the Polish labor strikes. We have to be ready."

"I'm sure you do." Through the window Mike could see a row of mobile howitzers lined up side by side, their long barrels as close and snug as soldiers on parade, a perfect target for a single enemy missile. Whatever this command anticipated, it wasn't war.

"If a soldier wants to relax, the 11th Cav is no place for him. Right, Dave?"

"Absolutely not, sir. The men understand that."

Captain McCutcheon came around his desk to shake hands. "Good to have you here, Mr. Simmons. I'd like to spend more time with you, but we're standing the colonel's inspection at seventeen-thirty."

The Simmonses said their good-byes, walked through the Kaserne, past the guardhouse where Private Young flicked them a smart salute, and across the highway to the Europa, a small, neat, very German hotel catering to the friends and relatives of the American military. Mike and his son continued their talk in Mike's cramped, second-floor room and at dinner over Kohlroulade—mixed meat in cabbage leaves—a salad, and a rich, creamy cake with the coffee.

"I gather you don't like the Wall any better than I do,

or you wouldn't be here." Dave toyed with his demitasse of coffee.

"I'm beginning to hate that Wall, Dave. It's getting to be an obsession with me."

"Welcome to the club. It's not an obsession with me, but I sure hate the fucker." Dave's sudden laugh was harsh. "Every time I look down on death alley, I think of what one of the tankers in Gator Troop said once. I'm walking through the tank park in a downpour, sucking up mud. I see this sergeant I know pulling maintenance on his M-60. He's standing with his body sticking out the tank hatch and this miserable look on his face. Rain's streaming down his face. 'What's the matter, Urken?' I ask him. Urken shakes his head. 'Lieutenant,' he says, 'this fuckin' fucker's fucked.' And that, Pop, is exactly what I feel about the world whenever I see the goddam Wall or any extension thereof. So, until somebody threatens me with a court-martial, I'm going to do what I can to crack it. . . . Only, just to be on the safe side, let's keep this try between us, huh?"

"Sold." Mike eased back in the armchair. "You'd think our policy would be to help as many people as possible to get out of East Germany."

"Not really. The West likes to make propaganda out of the Wall, but governments on both sides are satisfied with the status quo. I do a lot of rapping on this with a Brit named Spider Butler who—"

"Oh. A friend gave me his name as a possible man to help. British Frontier Service in Helmstedt?"

"That's the guy. He's famous on both sides. Worked the border for almost thirty years. He's convinced everybody's secretly happy with the Wall. For one thing, it's good insurance against a reunited Germany with eighty million efficient Krauts scaring the be-Jesus out of the world. Maybe we can tip Butler off on this operation. We can use him." Dave pushed away from the table. "Well, let's take a look at the border where our IBC will come through . . . we hope."

Dave drove his dark blue, secondhand Opel cautiously in the moonless night. Patches of thin ice clung to the highway that looped through German villages—clusters of white, cement-block houses with red tile roofs—past bare fields divided by farm fences and strips of woodland. Even in the darkness compressed beneath the low overcast, the rolling farmland showed the owners' concern for order and neatness. Farm implements were stowed in compact stacks near the houses, many of which were already dark by eight-thirty o'clock. For a stretch, the highway ran through a gap in the forested Rhön hills, then sprang into rolling farmland again.

After a drive of perhaps twenty miles, Dave pulled off on a dirt road, halted the car, and switched off the headlights. Ahead of them stretched a narrow valley between low, sloping hills. Stubbled acreage and a patch of woods flanked the winding dirt road.

"Okay," said Dave, "we've got about a quarter-mile walk to the border."

The cold air, apparently below freezing, nipped at their faces and hands. Mike drew on his gloves and pulled the sheepskin collar about his ears. They walked along the road in silence, Dave carrying a bulky instrument of some kind. Several lights shimmered in the distance.

"That's Melpers. East German village of a dozen houses," said Dave in a low voice. "Only screened party people allowed to live there."

Several hundred yards from the car they came to the debris of an abandoned farmhouse. Timbers of the second floor had collapsed and lay tumbled about the thick stone foundation. Dave plucked at his father's sleeve and led him behind the ruins.

"This will be our station the night she comes across." Dave took the instrument out of its case. "Here's an ambient light scope. On a dark night, you can make out a human figure at five hundred meters. Here, try it."

Mike stood at the corner of the stone foundation and peered to the east through the scope. At first he saw only a muddy mix of yellow and black, but soon began to distinguish features of the landscape. In ghostly perspective, he saw the blurred outline of the fence to the right and to the left with a long gap between. Some distance to the east, he could make out a secondary fence, also with a large opening. As he searched with the scope that turned darkness into a kind of witches' twilight, he saw movement. Two figures. He handed the scope to Dave.

"Yeah, that's a West German patrol, the *Bundesgrenzschutz*. The BGS covers our side of the border even closer than we do. . . . No, wait a second. That's the American patrol from Post Alpha. Two guys. They walk three miles south, then back again. Cold duty on a night like this."

After the patrol disappeared behind a low hill, Dave led his father forward another hundred yards or so. The dirt road ended abruptly at a signpost. A few feet beyond a brook bubbled over rocks and made little sucking noises as it flowed between banks of brown, matted grass. Mike failed to make out the words on the signpost.

"*Achtung! Bachmitte Grenze*," said Dave. "Attention, the middle of the creek is the frontier." He placed one foot on the grassy bank and straddled the gurgling stream. "Our first violation. If this were daytime, you might see a Whiskey Fifty truck pull up pretty soon over there and a bunch of border guards pile out of it. You see, they built the fence about fifty yards back of the brook, so sometimes careless people go over the border without knowing it. The *Grepos* love that. . . . Well, this is your crossing. We shouldn't hang around here. Let's get back to the car."

In the warmth of the Opel, with the heater going full blast, Dave talked steadily as they drove back to Fulda. The overcast parted to expose a few stars and occasionally a sliver of moon.

"We may have cloud cover, but we can't count on it." Dave had taken full command of the operation. "I looked up the moon tables. No moon next Tuesday night. Can you get word to your IBC in time for her to cross Tuesday night?"

"I'll try. It's awkward to reach her, you know."

"Yeah, well Wednesday and Thursday are alternates, but no later. By Friday they'll start wiring those new S-70s that can blow you as full of holes as Swiss cheese."

Dave outlined his escape plan with military precision as he steered the Opel over the winding highway to Fulda. He'd schedule the actual crossing for 7:15 P.M., midway between searchlight sweeps. Vigilance of border guards hit its lowest level in the hour after their evening meal. The IBC should hide in the woods that covered a ravine on the East German side. The lower part of the gulley, which extended about ten meters into the scalped strip, had been shaved of all foliage, but the depressed terrain afforded protection. Emerging from the ravine, the IBC should flop to her stomach and crawl the rest of the way to the stream that marked the border.

"Please, Dave, that 'IBC' sounds as inhuman as the Wall." He turned to his son. "Her name's Gisela."

"Sorry, Pop. I use that Army lingo without thinking." The glow of the instrument panel tinted his face a greenish gold. "I don't like to use her real name. Let's call her Polly."

"My God! How'd you happen on that name?"

"My only American woman since I've been here. I met her last summer in Berlin."

"Did she taste of Juicy Fruit?"

"Come again?"

97

"My first love was a high school cheerleader named Polly. She chewed Juicy Fruit gum."

"Oh." Dave glanced at his father. "Then let's call her Peggy or something."

Mike touched his son's arm. "That's okay, Dave. It was a long time ago." So much was a long time ago now. "Actually, Polly will do fine."

"Whatever you say." Dave, glad to retire from awkward emotional ground, resumed his military-style briefing, the officer in command. On the appointed night he and Mike would drive to the same field, arriving at the tumble-down farmhouse at seven-o-five. If nothing untoward happened, Dave would signal twice with a flashlight at exactly seven-fifteen. As soon as she saw the signal, P. would begin moving down the ravine, commencing her crawl on the flat ground. Dave would hurry forward, bending to present a low profile. He would cover her with an automatic rifle. P. should crawl toward the *Achtung!* marker and not get to her feet until she was well past the boundary brook. Safely into West Germany territory, she would run with Dave for the protection of the farmhouse foundation.

Under no conditions should P. leave the shelter of the wooded part of the ravine until she saw the flashlight signal. Something might go wrong on the last day, such as an early completion of the fence or the stationing of permanent guards. In the event a mishap occurred during her crossing, P. should use her judgment. If only a few meters out, she should crawl back; if more than a third into "death alley," as Dave called it, she should either continue to creep forward or stand up and make a run for it.

Dave would give his father, for transmission to P., a map showing a one-hundred-mile section of the border, plus a detailed topographical map of a five-kilometer square surrounding the spot where crews were replacing the fence.

"The big question mark," said Dave, "is how she's going to get herself to that ravine. That's fairly open farm country over there, much like this side. From what we hear, anybody moving within five kilometers of the border, even with a pass, gets questioned frequently." Dave shook his head. "Jesus, that's going to be tough, if indeed it's possible at all."

Dave came up to his father's room in the Europa to continue the planning. He wanted everything precisely clear, nothing left vague or subject to chance. Mike would fly to Berlin tomorrow, cross to East Germany with his boxful of elevator parts, and try to contact P. at once. As soon as she committed herself to a night, preferably Tuesday, Mike should return to Fulda. Dave would try to contact Spider Butler for help on the operation.

Mike grinned. "Sounds fine to me. You're the commander. I take my orders from you."

Dave handed his father a small, flat package. "These are the maps in a watertight wrapper. Don't get caught with them, Pop. Or P. either. They'd put her away for years."

"Okay, IBO. I'll be careful."

"What's this IBO?"

"Illegal Border Operator."

"Oh, well, all right." Dave shook his father's hand. "Until Tuesday, Pop, or sooner if you're ready. And listen. I'm awful glad we're in this together. Really."

Dave pulled the door closed as he left, but his shy smile, so at odds with that firm military jawline, seemed to hover diffidently in the room. Mike's thoughts of his son were warm and tender as he undressed and eased into bed.

Three hours later he awoke with a start, his heart pounding, his forehead damp with sweat. An inky blackness held the small room like a vise. Somewhere behind brooding walls he heard the methodical tread of terror, those hollow steps that stalked his nights. Not until the window took on the first pallor of dawn did the old walled trauma from childhood disappear and permit him to fall into a fitful sleep.

6

Early the next day Michael Simmons joined the quiet, orderly line at the "cultural events" counter in Leipzig's Information Zentrum, a structure with tall, sun-splashed glass panels. The morning sunlight glinted on the terrazzo floors and the marble counter where Ulli Beitz sold tickets for the theater, concerts, and special attractions.

Fräulein Beitz, as seen past a dozen heads of the queue, appeared to be a pawn of her hair, a lush, black nest that tumbled and wandered about. She swept away strands with the back of her hand or blew sharply upward to clear her eyes. As he drew nearer, Mike saw that Gisela's friend was a somewhat harried woman of perhaps thirty with a drifting smile and an engaging way of treating each person as a special individual, a rare trait in a country where the tempers of ticket-sellers were often as short as queues were long.

Mike reflected on the ease of his re-entry into East Germany. He had flown from Frankfurt to West Berlin yesterday noon, collected his door-lock assemblies from Walt Delaney, and crossed in the late afternoon at Checkpoint Charlie. With military maps and a magnifying glass in his side pocket and thoughts of Gisela's flight uppermost in mind, he felt edgy and apprehensive as he handed his passport to an impassive border guard. But the officer in the field-gray uniform apparently had his thoughts elsewhere, perhaps on East Germany's runaway victory at a European indoor track meet the night before, for he stamped a visa after a cursory examination of the letter from the Ministry of State Security about the elevator installation. Mike took an evening train to Leipzig. The Astoria found him a room with bath despite his lack of reservation and Frau Gotsche actually waited on him out of turn, her way of honoring a familiar, respected guest. He considered going to Ulli Beitz's apartment at once, but had ruled it out as far too risky.

Now at the head of the line he again rehearsed his German-code phrases while Fräulein Beitz squared away her working supplies in neat little stacks.

She brushed at a flying pennant of hair as she looked up.

"Have you tickets for Herr Simmons?" he asked in German, stressing his name.

"Herr Simmons?" Her drifting smile lingered as she appraised him with new awareness. "Interhotel Astoria?"

"Yes. Simmons or Steinbrecher. Room three-eight-four."

"Three hundred eighty-four?"

"Yes."

"Einen Moment, bitte."

She left her counter, disappeared to the rear. Several minutes passed. Feet shuffled in the line behind him. When Ulli returned, she handed him a slip of paper and fixed his eyes with a look of deep intensity. He had seen that look several times in the DDR, the effort to attain precise understanding without the hazard of incriminating speech.

Mike walked rapidly several blocks to the hotel construction site, found Alsten's shack empty, and opened the envelope. Ulli's message read: "I will try to reach her. Be in your room 384 at the Astoria at 1400 today."

That gave him four hours in which to handle replacement of the door-lock assembly. He rounded up two men of his special elevator crew and settled down to work on No. 4 shaft. Manfred, who spoke some English, pointed to the spot on the third-floor doors where an instrument of some kind had chipped the paint and scarred the metal.

"I show to Werner Lanz." He grinned. "I tell him man bust doors. He say, No, bad American parts."

"But he posted a notice, I see, ordering people not to touch the elevator doors."

"Ja. Werner talk two ways. So is job of brigade leader."

Mike continued work after his crew knocked off for lunch and succeeded in completing the assembly replacement. He visited briefly with Sven Alsten, told him the entire installation lacked only finishing touches, and that he would return in a week or so for final trials of the equipment. He reached his room with time to spare.

The phone rang a few seconds after two o'clock.

"Herr Simmons?" Ulli's voice.

"Speaking."

"Your theater party will meet tonight at the same place," she said in slow, measured German. "Eight o'clock."

"Same place . . ." But Ulli had hung up.

The hours dragged despite the sunny weather and a temperature that reached almost springtime levels. He changed into his exercise suit, sweat socks, and running shoes and ran under the Platz der Republik, past the park on Goethe Strasse, and around the Opera House. After a shower and another change of clothes, he took the streetcar to Gohlis, a district of gaslights, cobblestone streets, and dingy apartment houses, and visited the house-museum where Friedrich Schiller, the poet, wrote of joy and freedom, commodities in chronically short supply in this dolorous land for centuries, thanks to the arrogant rule of the Junker landed aristocracy, savage disciplines of Hitler's Third Reich, brutish reprisals of Russian occupation forces, and finally to the crude repressions and authoritarian measures of the DDR's own Socialist Unity Party.

Later Mike toured the Zoo where keepers bred lions, tigers, and other wild beasts for the export market. He finished off his tourist's afternoon with a stroll around the Volkerschlachtdenkmal. This monument, from whose brooding heights one could see the poisonous industrial haze hanging over Leipzig, was a landscape-crusher as cumbersome as its name. Together with its stagnant memorial pool, it commemorated the Leipzig defeat of Napoleon in 1813 and provided a caricature of all massive shrines to the always flourishing industry of human butchery.

Mike followed this weighty afternoon with a light supper, then spent an hour going over the topographical maps Dave had provided. The minutes crept forward and at last, shortly before eight, he set out for Ulli's flat. An acid breeze stirred the evening air and a few couples sauntered about the normally deserted downtown streets. As he prepared to turn from Brühl into Hainstrasse, Mike noticed a man in a pullover sweater loitering before a display window of Konsument. The man's carriage, a certain roll of the shoulders, touched a memory button. Where had he seen that moving silhouette before? West Berlin? On Augsburger Strasse three nights ago, wasn't it? And somewhere else before that? Mike looked across the street for a better view and, as he did so, the man turned his back, ostensibly to inspect the show window.

Instead of rounding into Ulli's street, Mike walked a few steps farther to Fleischer-gasse, turned left, and made his way to the Kleines Joachimathal, an ancient, moldering passageway that cut through the block back to Hainstrasse. There he glanced about and, seeing no one, hurried to the No. 10 courtyard entrance. The door to the apartment building was unlocked. He closed it behind him and heard the lock click. Now he noticed the beating of his heart and his unusual tautness. As he mounted the winding stairway, he thought the old steps creaked far more than during his first visit. He rapped softly at No. 31.

Almost at once the door cracked open a few inches, then swung wide. In the shaft of light from the small apartment, Gisela looked as radiant as she had in the Astoria lobby the night he appeared in this same brown turtleneck.

They hurried into each other's arms, leaning against the door which Gisela closed with a flick of her heel. Their kiss had the fever of urgency. Gisela's body folded itself to his as naturally as a lover of years' standing, and her aura enveloped him with a seductive familiarity. He savored that compelling odor that was uniquely Gisela's. Desire flared, but they snuffed the flame almost at once and drew back, both breathing deeply. They broke into simultaneous laughter over their mutual response.

"I missed you, mi amor," he said.

"I haven't slept soundly since we made love here. Oh, Miguel, I wanted you so much."

They doted on each other's endearments which soon, however, tangled with the night's logistics. She smelled delicious and could she stay all night? It made her so happy just to see him, and yes, she could stay until morning since Karl luckily was working all weekend with friends on university matters. Mike loved it when she ducked her chin and Ulli was a doll to let them have the apartment. Yes, Ulli had gone to sleep with *her* man and wasn't Miguel sweet to wear the brown turtleneck again; she would always love that sweater, and fortunately this was only their second night here, so she wouldn't have to register.

"What do you mean, register?" He probed beneath her gaiety.

"Oh, nothing to worry about." She touched his cheek

with a kiss. "If you stay overnight at someone's place more than twice, you're supposed to register in the *Hausbuch.*"

"You're kidding."

"No, no, Miguel. Every large apartment building and most city blocks have such registers and also 'house trustees,' informers really, who report all unusual doings to the police. But the *Vopos* don't enforce registration unless you make trouble for the system. If you do, they use it as a club. Have no fear."

But the idea alone alerted them. An escape business loaded with danger must seize the hour and shunt aside a languorous affair of lovers. He suddenly became aware of the portable radio, resting near the door. It bristled with martial music. Somewhere men marched.

"You have good news for me." She took his hand and led him to the brocaded chairs by the flimsy coffee table. "I can feel it."

She wore a blouse the color of jonquils and a gray skirt, slit above the knee in the style that had swept Western countries several years earlier. Her hair, carefully combed, hung to her shoulders with a single broad curl at the bottom. He loved the splash of freckles along her cheekbones and he found himself brimming with affection.

"Were you questioned by anyone?" He must know at once.

"No. Why do you ask?" She frowned.

He sketched the scene in the currency control room at Checkpoint Charlie with a "Frau Müller."

"Oh, but I know her. Yes, yes. Lotte Müller and I were schoolmates in Dresden and friends in the Freie Deutsche Jugend. I saw her last year in Berlin and we talked of old times in the youth group. I like Lotte."

"She told me you hold an important decoration by the state, the Star of People's Friendship. You didn't tell me, modest one."

"Yes, for being a nice, tame editor. You see what a good Communist I am, Miguel?" She scowled. "But it's very, very bad that they know you and I are friends."

"I've tried to guess who reported on us. Frau Gotsche at the Astoria desk, the older woman there, saw us talking."

"Perhaps. Or that Culture ministry woman at dinner. Or anyone at that table for that matter. You see now how it is here, Miguel? . . . But tell me the good news."

"Yes, I do have good news. But first, as they say in the jokes, some more bad news." He told her in less than nimble Spanish of the man who, he thought, had followed him tonight and maybe twice earlier.

"You must be very careful, Miguel." She insisted that he describe every detail and movement that he could remember. When he finished, she sat for a time immersed in thought. "I doubt it would be the same man on both sides of the border. That would be difficult to arrange. If it is the Stasi, that is disgraceful and you'd have every right as a foreign businessman to complain. Except now, of course, because of me, you can say nothing."

She stood up and paced about, her modishly tapered high heels tapping a dissonant beat. Mike suspected that this new woman in his life yearned, among other things, for fashion and elegance.

"Are you sure he didn't see you come in here?" Gisela switched off the floor lamp. At the window she lifted the edge of the full-drawn blind and peered into the dimly lit street.

"I think I ducked him, but I can't be positive."

Several minutes passed before she switched on the light and seated herself again. "We must not be seen together again until we meet on the sunny side. . . . We must act fast. I feel there isn't much time left."

Fear flowed like a dark river, lapping about them and

eroding their hopes. In his mind, black eddies threatened to flood a narrow escape channel near Fulda.

"Is Tuesday night fast enough?" he asked.

She brightened at once. Gisela had an extraordinary way of transmitting her moods and Mike's spirits lifted in the wake of hers. Yet nothing, in fact, had changed. Except that he wanted her. Now. He felt confused. Was he falling in love?

"Miguel, tell me. Where? How?"

"They're repairing the fence about a hundred fifty kilometers southwest of here." He pulled out the large topographical map. "Look. It's a little south of a direct line between Meiningen on this side and Fulda on the other."

He spread the map on the floor and they knelt beside it. She traced her finger from Leipzig southwest through Weimar, which gave its name to the short-lived republic in the years before Hitler, through the Thuringian Forest to Meiningen, a few miles from the frontier.

"Now we spot the repairs exactly with this." He placed the smaller map on top and they compared the two until they found the area southeast of Fulda.

"Now see the red dot?" asked Mike. "That marks the gap." He described the location and his nighttime inspection, but omitted any mention of Dave.

Gisela used the magnifying glass to study the maps, twisting them about to get better light from the floor lamp.

"I'm not sure my pass extends that far," she said. "My sister, Frauke, lives here in Kaltennordheim." She measured on the map. "That's a few kilometers. But I'll manage somehow." In the stubborn set of her jaw, she reminded him of Dave. "I can always plead being lost if I'm caught. . . . I hope."

Mike supplied her with details of the operation. She must be in the woods of the sloping ravine, which they located on the topographical border map, a few minutes after seven o'clock Tuesday night. The flashlight across the border would wink twice precisely at seven-fifteen if nothing appeared to interfere with a crossing. On that signal she should walk down the ravine and begin crawling as soon as she reached flat, unshielded ground. If something then went wrong, she should use her own judgment, either making a dash for it or crawling back to the cover of the ravine. He briefed her on the stream, the border signpost, the tumble-down farmhouse, and the location of watchtowers and dog runs.

"My expert believes you have a fifty-fifty chance to make it. But you could be killed or seized, you know."

"I've already decided to do it." She did not hesitate. "Let's go through it all again."

They went over and over the plan, drilling Gisela until the ten-minute span Tuesday night illumined her mind like a thin, green diagram on a computer screen. By a flick of will she could retrieve the instructions or send them back to the memory bank.

"My big problem will be to reach the ravine," she said when they finished the drill. "Don't be surprised if two of us show up.

"Frauke would dearly love to live over there, but she lacks my determination. She and Dieter Augstein, her husband, own a Trabant. Dr. Augstein is a specialist in tropical medicine and he travels a great deal on government missions. Right now he's in Cuba for a month, so maybe Frauke will drive me. Or perhaps she'll let me 'steal' the car. . . . Oh, there's so much to figure out."

They talked escape until they were weary. At last Gisela folded the maps back into the small, waterproof cover. "If I'm caught, the English names on these will add years to my sentence." Fear hovered like a cloud, but almost at once she brightened again. "But of course I'll never be caught. Never."

The oddly appointed room, half valuable heirlooms and half cheap, styleless furniture, seemed to take on Gisela's glow. Mike felt warmed as by a companionable fire.

Gisela fetched two glasses of vodka from Ulli's closet-sized kitchen and they toasted the venture ahead. They sat on the floor, nuzzling, sipping at the strong liquor and listening to the music which had swung from martial airs into the deep enchantments of Bach. Then before they knew it, they were talking about themselves.

"I had you almost constantly in mind these last few days," she said, "and I felt that you were a strong, loving man, dependable, too. A woman, I think, could live happily with you. But then, perhaps it's my fantasy at work and you're not like that at all. Sometimes, Miguel, I want things so powerfully that my imagination makes them so. Do you understand?"

"Sure. My fantasies have been at work on you, too. Would you like to know what they've built you into?"

"Please." She leaned on his shoulder.

"You're strong and determined. You called yourself tough. I believe it."

"Clear. I won't argue with that."

"Very sexual. Female passionate."

"Yes, yes. That you know."

"A taste for elegance. In the West you would wear the latest fashions if they fit your own style."

"Agreed again."

"You're lovely. You can charm. Quite seductive when you wish."

"That I wouldn't know. That's subjective, Miguel, but I'm flattered."

"Beautiful. . . . And I love the way you smell." He sniffed at her throat. They laughed.

"Smart, sensitive, intelligent, daring, too."

"Oh my." She glowed. "No negative qualities?"

"Germanic ones. I think you can be demanding, commanding, brusque at times, superorderly."

"Oh, much worse than that. Do you wish to hear the bad parts of this Gisela you've promised to help?"

"All right."

"My mother told me I'm selfish. I believe it." She took a swallow of vodka. "Remember I almost betrayed dear Otto Kleist to improve my standing with the party? I have this fear within me that I might sacrifice others to get what I want. Do you like such a quality?"

"No. But maybe you overstate. For instance, you didn't betray the professor. You merely thought of it."

"Sometimes I lie when I'm afraid the truth would spoil my plans."

"So you're an honest liar." He laughed.

"At times I have terribly ambiguous feelings. I either want everything or am torn between two desires."

"You can't count that as negative, Gisela. That's just being human."

"So there you have the bad Gisela." She looked into his eyes. "And now you."

She pictured him, she said, as a skilled engineer, a man who had known many women, but loved few. He went along smoothly, not wanting to hurt people's feelings, but he probably erupted now and then. He had a temper, she guessed. He had some fresh, boyish qualities. Perhaps he was naive, actually. He would be strong in crises, a man people could depend on. She thought him very lovable. Handsome, too. About forty-seven years old.

"No," he corrected. "Fifty-three."

"Oh, you started life so long before me." She cocked her head, reflecting. "Okay. That will be all right."

He leaned over and kissed her forehead, still wrinkled in concentration. "For your honesty," he said. But also because her remark, for the first time, implied a future.

111

"I have a dark side, Gisela."

"I don't believe it. What could it be?"

"Sometimes I'm terrified at night. I wake up with the shakes." He began hesitantly, reluctant to expose what he regarded as a critical flaw in an otherwise acceptable, if unremarkable, character. He had never confided his night terrors to close friends or family. Why he now wanted to tell Gisela, he was not sure. Perhaps her candor impelled him, perhaps a recognition that only the baring of mutual vulnerability could open the door to true intimacy. At any rate, he now talked along without restraint, depicting those hours of dread in the basement of the old Peck house in Omaha. He told of the punishments for shirking his religious chores, of the bare walls, the high stool, and the imagined fanged predators that prowled the walls. He told of the nightmares with which he had lived ever since, of the demons, the formless evil shapes and the fears that ravaged his sleep. Gisela listened without interrupting, her chin cupped in her hands and her elbows propped upon her legs. Her long hair shaped a hood of silence.

"And now you know what none of my friends do," he finished. He felt embarrassed and wary. While women often appealed to their men to drop masculine defenses and expose personal shortcomings, they nevertheless admired strength and shied from weakness. Would Gisela think the less of him now?

"How awful, Miguel." Her sympathy carried no overtones of diminished esteem. "Did you ever speak to a doctor about it?"

"Oh yes." He felt easier. "I went to a psychiatrist in New York for a long time. He had no trouble tracing the source of my nighttime torments and he made me relive many of those hours when I had to perch on that goddam stool, shivering and shaking with fright. The re-creation of those early scenes was supposed to cure my nightmares, but it didn't. The psychiatrist finally came up with the theory that being imprisoned as a kid inside those four basement walls had made me more sensitive than the average person to the perils of everyday life. He figured that the nightmares and alarms that woke me up at night provided a safety valve for the very real hazards that we all face but manage to suppress or edit out of our brains."

"What real hazards? I don't understand."

"Like jet planes. They crash and explode, you know. Automobiles kill tens of thousands of people every year and put millions in the hospitals. Every day in the advanced countries, so-called, we miss death in fast cars by inches. All the hazards of machine civilization, you know, on top of the old natural disasters, earthquakes, floods, hurricanes, avalanches. Then add on the institutional horrors, armies, navies, wars, rebellions, invasions. And torture, terrorist attack, kidnapping, murder, you name it. . . . The Wall and your risk in getting across. . . . Actually, Gisela, it's a hell of a dangerous world as you must remember from everything that happened to you and your family in the war." He paused, essayed a smile. "Hardly anybody gets out of this thing alive."

"But most of us face those perils, Miguel, and yet we sleep soundly at night." She reached out and stroked his face. "I feel sorry for you. You need your rest, mi amor." It was the first time she had used the Spanish endearment.

"I guess I'd sleep even more restlessly in the DDR. I don't think I could stand living with a heritage that included the cremation of millions of Jews."

"Oh, now you're talking about the other side." She waved her hand. "It's the Federal Republic that must live with that awful guilt."

"Both parts of Germany participated in the crime," he said. "You had plenty of death camps on what's now East

German soil, Buchenwald, Sachsenhausen, Ravensbruck; God knows how many."

"But here we resisted." She nodded her head for emphasis. "And here right after the war, we purged our government of all Nazis. By contrast, over there they let the old Nazis stay in power. Judges, deputies, administrators. On this side we have shed our guilt, Miguel."

It was an old East German claim, he knew. Equally responsible for the horrors of genocide, from the cattle cars to the gas chambers to the sweet, sickly odor of burning human flesh, the DDR had outlawed the past by decree, then tossed its guilt over the Wall for the West Germans to shoulder.

"Oh, come on, Gisela. You're too smart for that. You can't repeal what happened just by saying so. Today the DDR merely ignores what its older citizens did here forty years ago."

"We do not ignore." She raised her voice. "School children are taken to Buchenwald regularly. We teach that this must never happen again."

"But you blame it on the West Germans. I heard one of those talks. You'd think that not a single person who lived east of the Elbe had anything to do with the Holocaust."

"The DDR has many sins," she said testily, "but the killing of the Jews is not one of them. We had nothing to do with that."

Her jaw had a stubborn tilt again and suddenly, with a shock, Mike realized that he faced a woman whose childhood and adolescence had been shaped by a state that repealed, rewrote, and retooled history at will. His own combative juices had commenced to flow and he wanted to continue the argument, but he decided to drop the subject. This was not the time. And yet the impact of the shock lingered. Despite her dissent and her resolve to flee her homeland, Gisela carried the stamp of the DDR upon her. He must try to understand, to make allowances.

"Is there more vodka?" He twirled the empty glass.

She fetched the Russian bottle from the kitchen and poured liberally into the cut-glass tumblers. Their brief wrangle had clearly unsettled her. She downed half her vodka in one swallow.

"You know I might not make it across, Miguel." Gisela reached into a wide pocket of her modish skirt and withdrew a small but bulging envelope. "I've written down all I can remember of Otto Kleist's calculations." She handed him the envelope and he turned it over, examining it. "You must carry that on your person, not in your luggage."

"What do I do with it?"

"If anything happens to me, you must deliver it to people at this place." She handed him a slip of paper. "I cannot say this in Spanish, let alone English."

The slip read: "Geophysical Fluid Dynamics Laboratory, Princeton, New Jersey, USA."

"And," she added, "you must make a copy of the contents and deliver that to the ecosystems people at the Marine Biological Laboratory."

"Where's that?"

"Woods Hole. In Massachusetts." She struggled with the old Indian name. "On the Atlantic Ocean, I think. No?"

He nodded. "You'll get across, Gisela." He shoved the envelope into a side pocket of his pants. "But if something goes wrong, you have my word. I'll get this to the right people."

"Whether Professor Kleist's fears are justified, I don't know," she said, "but I trust him. When he says that heavy burning of fossil fuels may alter our climate drastically within ten years, I pay attention. I think your scientists in the West will too."

How contradictory. The very government whose crude

reconstruction of history she accepted without challenge she would now defy by smuggling out data which it sought to bury.

Once more they rehearsed the drill for Tuesday night. She went through it without a mistake. Then they talked more of themselves. They traded their little flatteries, their confidences, and their avowals of affection. They did all but declare their love and when they climbed into bed past midnight, they folded into each other's arms with sighs of relief. Now they could compliment without words, anoint with the soundless senses, and feel the luxury of total surrender. They made love slowly and gratefully but also confidently, for now, the third night together, they stroked familiar limbs and fanned familiar fires. Their caresses carried them through an hour of pleasure, at times silky and at times as rough as sandpaper, before their passion crested. They fell asleep soon after.

And then, after what seemed like hours later, Mike came abruptly awake. "Ah. Oh. What?" Gisela was shaking him. "Oh, did I have a nightmare?"

"No, no." Her lips slipped along his shoulder like a warm, moist breeze. "You slept quietly, Miguel, I think. But it's almost daylight and you should leave here before people start moving around."

He dressed in silence, then leaned over the bed for a good-bye kiss. She clung to him, suddenly so fierce in her embrace that his neck ached.

"Until Tuesday night, mi amor."

"Yes, mi amor." Slowly her arms fell away. "Until Tuesday."

In his last glimpse of her as he turned at the door, she looked like a schoolgirl in her bed with only a saddened face and corn-colored hair showing. He fixed the picture in memory, then closed the door behind him and hurried down the old, creaky steps.

7

Dirty weather blew up early Tuesday, twirling scraps of paper in dizzy spirals about the streets of Fulda and moaning at the tower bells of the old cathedral. The chill December norther brought a rainstorm in the afternoon. At first the rain lashed at quivering windows and overflowed the gutters of the hilly city. Then the violence spent itself and, as daylight began to fade, a slow drizzle fell from the steely overcast like water from a leaky roof. Forecast: Intermittent rain throughout the night, temperature a few degrees above freezing, no break in the cloud cover until Thursday at best.

First Lieutenant Dave Simmons welcomed the first gusts from the north like old friends. The worse the weather grew, the more buoyant his spirits became. By evening, when he and his father settled down to an early dinner in a small town near the border, Dave fairly rattled with good cheer. Also, as Mike was discovering, Dave had installed himself as the commander of the night's mission despite the presence of Malcolm (Spider) Butler of the British Frontier Service, a veteran of border surveillance and a man who knew more about the lethal frontier than anyone else in the

West. Dave had lured Butler down from Helmstedt, one hundred thirty miles to the north, with a veiled telephone call about the night's "adventure" as he had styled it and as indeed he regarded it.

They gathered over rib steak, potatoes, and a crisp salad in an old inn of the medieval town that had escaped bomb damage in World War II because of its insignificance in the global struggle. Several of the eighteenth-century houses, with their crossed beams and stuccoed exteriors, had been holed by shells fired from American tanks, but for the most part the hamlet came through unscathed. The three men ate at a planked table beneath low, smoky beams while the proprietor shuttled to the kitchen where his wife did the cooking. Between runs, he sat in a corner and smoked and gossiped with cronies.

Dave had selected Fladungen for the early evening meal because it lay between Fulda and their border target. He had selected the Goldner Adler because he knew the owner and because the place was seldom crowded. They could discuss their plans in a tranquil setting.

Mike liked the legendary Spider Butler the moment they met. Thin, knobby, with rodlike arms and legs, all spidery straight lines and angles, he spoke bluntly in a rich London accent that borrowed liberally from the public schools while grounded in Cockney. A gregarious type, at core a showman, the Spider had joined an institution, the British Frontier Service, in its youth, but had long since outgrown it. Now he was the institution and the slowly dwindling BFS lived in his rakish shadow.

"You're perhaps thinking they call me Spider because I look like one, Michael," he said soon after Dave made the introduction. "But no. I'm the Spider because I live at the Wall, spinning my web and watching every crack and crevice. Like the spider, I know my habitat. Do you believe me, Michael?"

"Of course." Mike laughed. "What's to doubt? You're a friend of Dave's. That's enough for me."

"Come, Michael, test me. Test the Spider. Ask me something about my Wall."

"Okay. How do you feel about it?"

"How do I feel? Are you one of those feelers from California then, Michael?" Butler, who boasted he never forgot a name, trained his memory through endless repetition. "I hate the Wall, Michael. But since it provides me with my victuals, I also love it. In admitting that love-hatery, I am far less hypocritical than our slippery statesmen of the West, all of whom boast of their hatred for the Wall, but fail to mention their secret fondness for the same abomination."

He raised a bony finger for emphasis. "Our politicians and businessmen love the Wall because it keeps the mighty Germans divided. The Jews of the world love it because they think it's at least some small punishment for the gassing of six million Jews by Hitler's Reich. The West Germans love it because it proves the superiority of their system. Military officers love it because it makes good propaganda for bigger armies and more weapons spending. Travel agencies love it because they can send thousands to Berlin to stand on the platforms that overlook the Wall. There, our well-fed tourists can shake their heads and mumble about man's inhumanity to man. Artists, writers, and entertainers love the sheer theater of the Wall. And the mass of voters in the Western democracies love it unconsciously because it hides the complexities of international politics and makes everything quite simple, Michael. It's a prison wall, what, and over there are all the bad prisoners and their keepers, and over here are all we good chaps."

The Spider paused for intake of steak and beer. He licked his lips and darted a swift glance at Mike to gauge the impact of his declamation. Mike had the impression that Butler delivered his sermon on the Wall to anyone willing to lis-

119

ten. Mike's thoughts veered to Gisela. Where was she this moment? Driving with her sister near the border, walking through the Thuringian Forest, or sitting in some police station trying to explain her movements to skeptical Vopos?

"Of course, on the other side," the Spider resumed, "the Russians love the Wall because it keeps seventeen million Germans at home working as only Germans will for the glory of dialectical materialism. Several hundred thousand East Germans, the party nobility, love the Wall for the same bloody reason. In fact, the only people on earth who hate the Wall unreservedly are the poor working buggers of the DDR who have to live behind it, Michael, with no chance to come over here and listen to me run off at the mouth about it."

Lieutenant Dave Simmons saw his opening. "Which brings us, Spider, to tonight's IBC. Our woman will come across, if she comes at all, just"—he studied his wrist watch— "just an hour and fifty minutes from now."

Butler inclined his head. "Pardon me, Dave. We do have work tonight, illegal work, for which we could both draw a reprimand or worse. I outrank you, you bastard, but for this operation I left my beautiful blue uniform at home." The British Frontier Service wore uniforms modeled on those of the Royal Navy. "So I report to you, sir. You're in command."

"Okay." Dave smiled but set his jaw. Like the Spider, he wore civilian clothes, two sweaters and a leather jacket to keep him warm inside his rain gear. He looked like a commander. Even sitting down, he easily topped the other men.

"Pop, Spider thinks the dog-run diversion is a good idea." Dave bent his head and lowered his voice, although the nearest diners were several tables away. "We cased the area yesterday afternoon."

"From a distance," Butler interpolated. "I've had my picture in every rag in the DDR. So they know me, thanks to those bloody Grenztruppen cameras. Remind me, Michael, to tell you at tonight's celebration how the sods snapped me pissing on a haymow one day and slapped the picture in the criminal news sections to show the depravity of the West.

"That picture drew a laugh from no less a personage than Kurt Rauschnig, chancellor of West Germany. I gave him a VIP frontier briefing last spring along the fence near Helmstedt. Decent bloke, Rauschnig. Maybe he hates the Wall privately, but his political moves . . ."

Dave's cough made a point of order.

"Sorry, old boy. My last interruption, I swear."

"So Spider will drive his own car to the meadow near the dog run," said Dave, "and then walk about a half mile to the border. He'll start his racket, setting off the dogs, at seven-fourteen. Right, Spider?"

"That's it, Davey. Foul night for all of us, too, but fine for our lady of the crossing."

Michael wanted to know the distance between Spider Butler's post and the gap in the fence, where he and Dave would take their station.

"Just about a mile." Dave took a pencil from his jacket and sketched a section of the border on the back of a beer coaster. "We're down here to the south, Pop. That hill near the old farmhouse foundation stands between us and Spider." He went through the night's scenario a final time. He ticked off the schedule, made certain all watches jibed to the second, and said they'd meet back in this same inn after P. came safely across. Spider would go unarmed, but Dave had two weapons in his Opel: an Army M-16 for himself and a German hunter's shotgun for his father. They would not shoot, however, unless fired upon from across the border. They shook hands around before leaving the table.

Outside the inn, Dave gave Spider Butler a case enclosing an ambient light scope. "But keep your head down," he reminded. "They've got these things too, you know. . . . See you in a couple of hours."

The two automobiles, each with an easy run to the border, rolled out of Fladungen at 6:30 P.M.

Rain pattered on the Opel's roof as Dave headed out of town and onto the winding macadam road. Tires sang a sibilant monotone on the wet pavement. The headlights picked out road signs like sudden sentries, and the car rocked under occasional gusts of wind. The night was black, unrelieved by those pale, gray shadows that etched the countryside under moon or starlight. The sky shuddered ominously, great black billows tumbling to the east before the gusts that sprang across the furrowed fields and whistled through the wooden fences.

"I let Spider have the old scope," said Dave. "We're going to use the new thermal imagery device. It'll show people and objects like noontime. . . . You know, the Spider gets up in his pulpit to preach to new guys but, man, he delivers. That old boy knows this frontier like the back of his hand."

"I liked him," said Mike. "Good guy."

They drove on in silence and then, before Mike had prepared himself mentally, Dave had turned off the highway, switched off his lights, and rolled a few blind yards on the dirt road. Mike could distinguish familiar hills on each side and he recalled how stubbled fields ran down the valley toward the stream that marked the border. Dave held a flashlight under the dashboard and tested it once. He slipped it into a pocket and then tested a second flashlight in a similar fashion. His son, Mike noted, believed in doubled precautions.

A light rain fell on their rain gear as they stepped from the car to the muddy road. The dampness accentuated the chill. Mike drew on his gloves. Dave handed him the shotgun.

"You got to show me how to use it," said Mike. "I haven't fired a gun in ten years."

"Here." Dave gave instructions in a low voice and demonstrated by aiming up at the tumbling clouds. Then he hung the Army M-16 across his back by a sling, picked up the thermal imagery sight, and set off down the road with his father at his side.

They made their way carefully, trying to avoid puddles and the low, muddy stretches. They could see but little. Darkness blanketed the valley and swallowed the hills save for a few yellowed spots that hung from distant black clouds like lights of a ship at sea. These, Mike remembered, marked the East German village of Melpers, a mile or so to the left near the place where Spider Butler would disturb the peace. Mike could feel a tightening in his chest and throat, and he sensed that if he tried to speak to Dave, the sound might come out as a croak. But speech was to be banned. Dave put his finger to his lips.

Mike peered ahead, trying to pierce the night and locate the wooded ravine behind the opening in the frontier fence. It seemed highly improbable that Gisela would actually be over there now, crouched in the darkness, ready in a few minutes to crawl on her belly like a lizard. Had she indeed managed to reach the rain-washed gulley? Had her pass proved good for this area of the border zone? Was she alone or with her sister- and where? Perhaps she had been seized by guards and even now was undergoing interrogation in some military outpost.

And then a contrary thought occurred. If Gisela did come across, bolting out of the night like a wild animal fleeing predators, his life would change dramatically in ways he could not foresee. In flashes he imagined himself walking the streets of West German cities with her, buying her clothes while her eyes danced with pleasure, seeing her stand in a crowded theater lobby among other chicly dressed women, snuggling together beneath fat Federbetten, introducing her to friends, traveling in the sleek Intercity trains that sped from Munich to Hamburg or curved along the Rhine past gabled villages that seemed plucked from the pages of fairy tales. But what then? Would they go home to the States? Deliver Professor Kleist's research to American ecology scientists? Remain together as lovers? Marry? He could not know. Staring ahead, trying to distinguish looming shapes in the night, he could only surmise that in a few minutes—fewer and fewer now—his life would either alter radically or suffer an immense sense of loss.

Dave pulled at his sleeve and they moved off the road, walking through matted weeds and grass and over stretches where mud sucked at their boots. A structure bulked in the dark. They had reached the stone foundation and the tangled beams of the collapsed farmhouse. They crouched behind the stonework. Mike leaned his shotgun against the wall. Dave took the thermal imagery instrument from its case, knelt at the corner of the house, and sighted to the east. The rain fell lightly but steadily. It dripped from Mike's chin and funneled off his rain jacket. The damp cold penetrated his padded clothing. If the temperature fell another few degrees, the rain would certainly turn to snow.

Dave, after sighting, pointed to the luminous dial of his wrist watch. Seven-o-seven. Right on time. He handed the sighting instrument to his father and they changed places at the corner of the ruined building.

Placing the cupped rubber shield against his right eye, Mike sighted across the border, about a hundred yards distant, to the wide, plowed strip where the mines had been exploded a few days ago. He could see the jagged ends of the wire-mesh fence to the left and to the right, some heavy road equipment, a ditch, slanting concrete slabs, and a gradually rising slope to another broken fence beyond. If not quite illuminated by the noonday clarity Dave had promised, the scene certainly stood out in silhouetted shapes as sharply as if bathed by the ivory light of a full moon. Mike centered the device on the wooded ravine behind the denuded strip. He gasped.

"My God!" His amazement demanded to be vented. The exclamation, if not loud, was audible to Dave.

Partially hidden by a tree trunk, low to the ground, rested a rounded shape. There was no mistaking the outline and pattern of a human figure, apparently in the act of crouching or kneeling. As his eye adjusted to the distance and the eerie light, he could distinguish clothing and the white blur of a face, misted by the falling rain. There was only one person.

He was sure that the figure was Gisela and a wave of feeling, admiration blended with tenderness, swept over him. Yes, she was tough, as she had said. She had courage and grit. Perhaps she was indomitable and no state, however relentless, would ever crush her. His feeling of tenderness had a rare, ethereal cast, as sexless as mist, unlike anything he had felt before. He wanted to hold and comfort her, to wipe the rain from her face, to rush her to shelter, to wait upon her.

Dave motioned for the night-sighting instrument, changed places with his father again. He held out his wrist watch. Seven-eleven. He propped the scope against the corner of the foundation with his left shoulder, pulled a flashlight from his pocket and laid it on the ground. He fished out the second flashlight, palmed it, moved his thumb toward the switch. Dave had become an exceedingly thorough man.

They waited several minutes in silence, then Dave lifted his arm so that his father could see the luminous hands and numbers on his wrist watch. Mike watched, fascinated, as the greenish second hand swept around the dial. Seven-fourteen. In the distance, a dog barked faintly and almost at once a great yapping and howling began. Muffled by rain, the sound seemed to come from far to the north. It ebbed and swelled, flowing down the scalped frontier like a wild, ghostly lament.

Then, far to their left, they saw the shaft of a searchlight moving mechanically, sweeping back and forth in the direction of the clamoring dogs. The watchtower, Mike knew, was about a mile distant. The area before them, where no fences sealed the border, remained in darkness.

"Now," whispered Dave.

He stepped from behind the crumbling foundation, aimed his flashlight toward the ground and blinked it twice, precisely two seconds between flashes.

Then, as he had briefed his father several times, First Lieutenant Simmons handed him the sighting device and started walking rapidly toward the stream that marked the border. He crouched low, his automatic rifle unstrapped and held in both hands as he glided through the rain.

Mike clamped the sight on the ravine, immediately spotted the figure he assumed to be Gisela. She had moved to the base of the wooded gulley, still shielded from the view of anyone not positioned directly ahead of her. Now she flopped to her belly and began squirming to the west. The border lay perhaps a hundred yards from her. As she crawled, Mike measured the remaining distance, counting silently. On the fringe of his sighting device, bathed in that peculiar ivory light, Dave approached the border signpost. He held his gun before him.

Gisela seemed to crawl as slowly as a snail. Her pace exasperated Mike. She had moved not more than five yards. For God's sake, woman, hurry. Faster, please, faster, faster, pacing the beat of his heart. In the distance, the dogs howled like a wild pack. Dave reached the stream, dropped prone on the soaked ground. In Mike's scope, rain fogged the ivory scene, lending it a surreal cast.

And then, in the fraction of a second, the world suddenly blazed like noonday. Intense light, stronger than the rays of the sun, seized the frontier strip. Millions of units of candle power flooded the entire area of repairs, throwing every rock, furrow, machine, concrete slab, and pile of fencing into bold relief. Three searchlights from the concrete watchtower drilled the ground.

Mike dropped the useless sighting instrument without thinking. He stared toward the woman with sickening fear. She reared up like some startled amphibian creature trapped on land. In the spectral brilliance he recognized her. It was indeed Gisela. For a moment panic ravaged her, instantaneously carving deep lines in her face and sapping it of strength. She wore, oddly, a stocking cap and beneath it her features seemed to freeze in a look of utter hopelessness. In the garish light, she could have been a mime with a face painted white as eggshells.

Her sculpted immobility lasted only an instant. She whipped around and began crawling through mud back to the shelter of the ravine.

"Back!" Mike's needless shout leaped involuntarily from his throat as he jumped up and ran toward the border. The shotgun, forgotten in the turmoil, lay on the ground behind him.

Then came a sound of horror, an efficient, rhythmic clatter of steel like a pneumatic drill exploding against rock. Mud spurted across the width of the strip, scores of miniature geysers erupting from the soaked earth in ragged lines that advanced swiftly to the south. A lament of bullets whined through the rain.

Had Gisela been hit? Mike could not tell. She reached the protection of the ravine on her belly, then struggled to her feet, slowly, Mike thought. She appeared to clutch at her lower leg. She ran upward, half staggering past rocks and trees. A second figure seemed to materialize from the woods. Had another person joined her? Mike could not be sure. Almost at once Gisela was lost to sight, swallowed by the dark mouth of the night.

"Bastards!" Dave spotted the source of the machine-gun fire the moment his father did.

Some distance north of the break in the fence, an East German armored troop carrier rolled toward the gap on the paved roadway which ran the length of the frontier. A soldier in the shielded crown of the car fired the gun as the carrier came into view. Machine-gun bullets sprayed a wide swath on the East German side, but did not veer across the border.

Dave Simmons swung his M-16 automatic rifle to the left, lined up the carrier, and pulled off a burst that splattered the armored vehicle like a clanging of dishpans.

"No! Dave, don't!" Mike ran to his son and grabbed at his rain jacket.

The firing in the carrier stopped. The border guard dropped below the protecting shield. From a slit in the vehicle, a smaller searchlight swept across the border and probed the valley. Father and son dropped to the ground a few yards west of the brook that divided the two Germanies. Dave began crawling swiftly away. Mike followed. His belly hugged the mud and matted grass.

A rifle burst from the carrier chopped at the path near the signpost. Another winged into the nearby furrowed field. By the time the probing light neared the two Americans, they had squirmed behind a mound some fifteen or twenty yards back of the border.

The trio of powerful searchlights from the watchtower maintained their dazzling hold on the frontier's no-man's land, bathing its macabre appointments in the brutal light that once attended the sleepless nights of Nazi death camps. The small light from the armored vehicle flicked over the West German valley, picking here, holding there. The carrier did not move. Nothing stirred in this brilliant artificial light. The high illumination continued for perhaps five minutes that seemed to Mike, lying prone behind the mound, like an hour. Then all lights went off and the rain-drenched darkness engulfed the frontier once more.

But now a medley of noises filled the night. Far off the angry dogs still barked. Nearer could be heard shouted commands, the grinding of gears, and the wet hum of tires. Close at hand, on this side of the border, Mike heard several people running toward them.

"West Germans. The BGS patrol," said Dave. He sat up and brushed mud from his rain gear. "Did she get away? I couldn't see."

"I think so." But how far? Could she possibly elude the busy DDR guards?

"That's good."

The two-man West German patrol had slowed to a walk. The soldiers were only a few yards away.

"As for us, Pop, believe me," said Dave, "we're in trouble."

Mike realized that his collar was soaked and that cold rain had cut a channel down his back.

8

Feeble morning sunlight scratched at the frosty window-panes of Air Troop's Sanctum Sanctorum as Mike Simmons, arraigned with his son before the tidy desk of Captain Orville McCutcheon, seethed with suppressed anger. This whole proceeding, with its bloodless military judgments and its cool, factual review of last night's "incident," seemed ridiculously divorced from the demonic reality: Men employed to track and kill other human beings had fired volleys of high-velocity bullets at an unarmed woman merely because she wanted to move across a few yards of the earth's surface.

One might forgive Captain McCutcheon his lack of concern for the woman's fate. He had not, after all, known Gisela Steinbrecher, just one of millions of humans who faced violent death every month. What Mike could not overlook was the captain's assumption that the Simmonses, father and son, had somehow transgressed the canons of common sense and seemly behavior by taking up positions at the rain-soaked border where they had witnessed the assault by a Goryunov heavy machine gun.

"What we want to avoid is a written reprimand going

130

into Dave's record." Captain McCutcheon met this new day freshly shaved and scented. "Your son, Mr. Simmons, is one of our finest young officers and we want to keep him clean for promotion."

Mike listened with but one ear. At this moment, while McCutcheon spoke in laundered phrases, Gisela might be lying somewhere gravely wounded. Had she escaped the Grepos and their raking fire? That single question had haunted his sleep and dominated his waking moments since the apprehension by West German border troops last night. The BGS patrol, after learning of Dave's military status, had "escorted" the Simmonses to Alpha, the American observation post, for interrogation by an S-2 officer.

"You see, Mr. Simmons," McCutcheon continued, "I'm placed in an awkward position here. . . ."

Mike suddenly recalled the warning of an overweight psychologist who once tutored Todd Elevator executives in the intricacies of "stress management" for an exorbitant fee.

"All conflict generates stress," said the heartily aggressive academic, "much of it beneficial to a healthy organism. But beware of the situation where your own objectives are clearly defined while those of your antagonist are cloudy or unknown. The stress arising from that mismatch can tear you apart."

Right now the U. S. Army's objectives seemed as cloudy as those of the Simmonses were clear. Father and son had wanted to help Gisela Steinbrecher pass safely and secretly through a dangerous frontier. What did the Army want? The longer this professorial captain talked, the less certain Mike became of the answer and the more the stress tugged and strained.

"Mr. Simmons," asked McCutcheon, "when you visited the Cav last week, were you here to make plans for your IBC?"

The hated initials lit a fast fuse. "Damn it, Captain, do

we have to call her an IBC?" Mike could hear the anger in his voice. "She's an East German woman, a human being, who put her life on the line last night. She might be dead or dying right now, for all we know."

The explosion shook both Army officers. McCutcheon shifted uneasily in his chair, a puzzled look on his face. Dave Simmons glanced at his father as he might at a flawed weapon. In the military's grand traffic in human lives, individual death in combat zones rarely surfaced as a matter for communal grief.

"I know how you must feel. We're all sorry the lady failed to make it across." The captain's consolation had a dutiful cast, reminding Mike of the funeral director who attended him and his foster mother, Laura Murray, when they picked out a casket for Roger. "But unfortunately we must put our feelings aside and deal with the situation as it exists on this side of the border. I'm going to have to report particulars of this IB—pardon—crossing incident to the colonel. He in turn will have to report to Fifth Corps headquarters." Captain McCutcheon climbed the chain of command, hand over hand, until he reached such lofty heights as the U. S. European Command in Stuttgart, the American ambassador in Bonn, and President Frank McCullough and the Pentagon in far-off Washington.

"Now I don't want that report to involve Lieutenant Simmons in some American civilian attempt to bring an East German national across the border." McCutcheon tapped a pencil on his desk blotter. "That wouldn't look good on his record."

"Is it against regulations for an officer to help someone defect to our side?" Mike tried, not with complete success, to cap the depths of his anger.

"Specific regulations? Well, it's certainly against policy. I don't have to tell a well-informed businessman like yourself, Mr. Simmons, that the two Germanies live in very delicate balance. That's been true ever since the 1971 agreements that stopped Communist harassment of auto and rail traffic into West Berlin. Now if West Germany wants to disturb that close balance by assisting East Germans to break out of the DDR, why that's the business of the West Germans."

McCutcheon removed his black-framed eyeglasses, blew on the lenses, and polished them vigorously with a tissue. "But it's not our business. The mission of this regiment is to help defend Western Europe's freedom and keep the Warsaw Pact forces on their side of the border. We are decidedly not in the business of spiriting people across the frontier."

Mike wanted to retort that the best way to defend freedom was to encourage it in all places, including frontiers, but a glance at Dave reminded him that his own mission this morning was to help get his son off the Army's hook.

McCutcheon fingered a sheet of paper on his desk. "Read one way, this S-2 report from Post Alpha might indicate to some people that an officer plotted with his civilian father to bring an East German national across to West German soil. One might also deduce that the two men armed themselves and went to the border in a downpour to accomplish that purpose."

The captain eyed the pair sitting in front of him. "But I don't think that's the way it happened at all. I think that Lieutenant Simmons escorted his father to the Parrot's Beak sector to show him how the death strip's elaborate weaponry operates at night. While there, they witnessed the attempted shooting of a possible I—defector. When part of the volley sprayed West German territory, Lieutenant Simmons returned the fire with his M-16 rifle which he'd taken along as a routine precaution." McCutcheon pushed the Post Alpha report aside. "You two men were understandably upset when interrogated last night. In broad daylight, after a good night's sleep, I think we can all get a better perspective on the facts. . . . I take it you don't disagree with any of that, Dave?"

"Thank you, sir," said Dave obliquely. "I appreciate it."

"The fact that another BGS patrol encountered Spider Butler of the Brits' Frontier Service only a mile away . . ." McCutcheon paused for dramatic effect. Butler's name had not been mentioned previously by any one. "I take it that's just another coincidence in a rather unusual night."

"Thanks again, sir." Dave looked quite solemn.

The captain referred to other border episodes, chatted about the Kaserne, Fulda, and the 11th Armored Cavalry Regiment, then drifted into a discussion of the Army as a career. Among other matters, he opined that "smart young Rotzi officers" like Lieutenant Simmons had as much chance for advancement as West Point graduates.

As father and son left, McCutcheon walked them to the door and laid his hand on Mike's arm. "I'm really sorry, sir. Let's hope she's alive and well and not under detention. Believe me, if she'd made it, I'd have brought champagne to the celebration."

The Simmonses reviewed their case as they walked through the compound, Mike stretching to keep pace with his son's long stride.

"You suppose that's the end of it, Dave?" Mike inquired with only a fraction of his mind. The remainder already raced ahead to Leipzig where it probed for news about Gisela.

"That's it, I think. Unless the colonel hears something and bugs McCutcheon. Mac's okay. He could have made it rough for me."

Father and son parted at the Kaserne's gateway guardhouse where Private Young threw them a flashy salute.

"I don't know what to say, Pop. I know the shooting was an awful thing for you." Dave hesitated. Emotional intimacy was an unmapped battlefield for him. "I hope she gets home safely and that she'll try again someday. . . . I'd like to meet her."

"I must get back to the DDR right away. I have to know what happened to her."

"Hey." Dave made a fist and struck it lightly against his father's arm. "Take it easy over there, will you?"

They shook hands as they said good-bye, their gloves insulating them from the warmth of flesh and their breath misting a subtle barrier between them. Mike could feel moisture in his eyes as he turned away. Forever barriers, frontiers, walls.

He caught the Hispania express to Frankfurt, only an hour from Fulda, and flew to West Berlin, arriving in late afternoon. He spent the travel time trying to devise alternate routes to news of Gisela should the Ulli Beitz channel fail. Mike realized that this time he would have to proceed with great caution. If the authorities held Gisela, if she were wounded, or—yes, face it—dead, then her friends and acquaintances already had become suspect. She might, of course, be at her sister's place in Kaltennordheim, perhaps sound of body, perhaps badly wounded and in need of medical care. If hurt, could she risk contacting a doctor? Alien questions of this type proliferated and plagued him. The nearer he came to East German soil, the more he realized that finding out about Gisela might become a long, tricky, and risky task. Unless, of course, she had managed to return safely and unharmed to her Dresden apartment, a possibility he regarded as slim.

Amid his speculation he became aware of the strength of his feeling for her, a feeling beyond and apart from what he customarily thought of as love. For Gisela he wanted safety, security, and a good life, just as he did for Dave or for Sally. He could not long entertain the thought of Gisela suffering, maybe paralyzed, perhaps undergoing an operation. He knew that for the rest of his life he would carry in his mind a painful image, as sharply delineated as a strand of hair under microphotography, of a crawling Gisela caught in the brutal glare of searchlights and rearing up, her rain-streaked face frozen in panic, like some trapped wild creature. He could see the silhouette of fear, as fixed as sculpture, topped by that blue stocking cap that looked so poignantly childlike. The image had flashed in his mind just before he fell asleep last night, again this morning in the haze of awakening, and he knew that it would recur many times. He could tolerate the memory if Gisela survived un-injured, but if she should die or live on severely crippled, her look of terror under that sudden lash of searchlights would dwell indefinitely in his museum of fears, one more exhibit to torment his nights.

On the other hand, the sharing of that grotesque frontier scene—he in relative safety and she in mortal danger—forged a link that no lovers' moonlit bay, festive ball, or romantic island interlude could ever match. They had conspired to bring her through the world's only real iron curtain, they had failed, and for many years, if she lived, that failure would bond them in special ways. While it might not unite them permanently, the whole episode, and in particular that scene on a death strip as bathed in artificial light as the Houston Astrodome, would live forever in their common memory.

Now Mike wanted to touch her, feel the throb of life in her, hold and caress her. These minutes of travel dragged feverishly.

In West Berlin he placed some belongings in the extra suitcase which he now kept at the Alsterhof. He also left papers that he did not wish to take to East Germany. These included Gisela's letter to the American scientists and a copy of the elevator code. A second copy he carried in his wallet.

Mike called Walter Delaney, ostensibly to tell Todd's European chief of his need to give the Leipzig elevators a final inspection, but actually to let Delaney know that once again he would pass behind the Wall. The inspection gambit did not deceive the star salesman for an instant.

"Still hot for that East Bloc pussy, huh?" A sharp intake of breath cut Delaney's husky growl and Mike could imagine the glow of the cigarette. Ordinarily Delaney's sexual slang fell easy on the ears, but in today's circumstances, the vulgarism had an offensive sound. "What are you doing on this side? I thought you were in Leipzig."

"I came over to see my son in Fulda. Remember? He's the big guy who flies an Army helicopter."

"Yeah. Say, I just heard something on the radio about Fulda. Some kind of shoot-out at the border near there last night. What was that all about?"

"You got me. Everything was quiet around the regiment's headquarters this morning. . . . Say, Walt, I only figure to stay a few days this time. If I'm not back in a week, send out a search party, will you?"

"No problem. I'll just tell the SSD to watch out for a sex-crazed American on the prowl for decent Communist married women." Delaney paused, then resumed without banter. "How you coming on the project, Mike? Did you ever contact those flesh merchants whose names I gave you?"

"No. We're trying another route."

"Not Fulda again, huh?" Delaney threw the bait casually. It snagged on silence. The two men waited each other out.

"Look, Walt, I'd like to level with you," said Mike at last, "but a phone line's not the place."

"No need, lover man. I think I get the picture. If you're not back in seven days, I'll flash the American embassy over there."

"Thanks. And keep the New York office off my back."

"Those bastards. I'll tell 'em you've gone to Siberia to

sew up a prison camp exclusive on deep-mine elevators.
. . . Hey, maybe I should try that on my next trip to
Moscow. . . . *Ciao.*"

The letter from the East German Ministry of State Security about the Todd installation again sufficed to fetch Mike
a visa after only a few minutes' delay at Checkpoint Charlie, and the evening train for Leipzig pulled out of the Ostbahnhof a few minutes before dark. He shared a second-class compartment, never as stodgy as first, with a frail little
widow who quickly corrected him when, opening the conversation, he described Leipzig as "pretty." She wagged her
forefinger like a semaphore. "Nein. Interesting maybe," she
said, making a sour face, "but pretty, never." As soon as she
learned he came from America, she unloaded complaints
against the regime as readily as a U.S. taxpayer grumbling
over federal spending. She faulted her skimpy pension, one-party rule, nosy police, shortages of fruits and hand lotion,
the dreary press, untrustworthy neighbors, dull DDR television, propaganda in the schools, and the obstacles to travel
to the West. She dismissed each defect with a word or two,
relying on an artful repertoire of vinegary, waspish, and
mordant facial expressions to convey her message. "As for
the Wall, I suppose people in America can't even imagine
that horrible thing." The minute the conductor appeared to
punch tickets, her gloom vanished and a beatific smile
blessed the task of that puzzled functionary.

Mike's return to Leipzig was less than auspicious despite
starry skies and unusually mild weather for December. A
tall, very correct reception clerk, with crimson nails and
brooding eye shadow, informed him that five hundred sixty
guests filled the Astoria to capacity and that the first accommodations would not become available until midnight when
some circus performers from Budapest would check out to
return to Hungary. Unfortunately, Mike would have to re-

make the bed himself from emergency linen supplies because the chambermaids had gone home for the night.

He tried to find Sven Alsten, but the Swede, so said the deeply shadowed clerk, had left town and would not return until the next day. Mike dawdled over dinner, near the same hotel mural of a white overseer lashing black plantation workers, then wandered the empty streets, and had a drink at the bar. When he finally reached bed near one o'clock, he found himself exhausted but sleepless. He dozed fitfully through the night, flinching when searchlights flailed a stricken Gisela or the methodical stutter of machine guns tore his ragged dreams.

In the morning, after retrieving his passport from the reception desk, following the customary nightlong police inspection accorded papers of new registrants, he reached Ulli Beitz's spot at the Information Zentrum counter only a few seconds after opening. She masked her surprise by fussing with her hair, transferring hairpins from her mouth to rebellious puffs and streamers of that great black thundercloud.

Mike spoke his prescribed code piece about tickets for Herr Simmons, gave his Astoria room number, and managed to add an extra phrase denoting urgency. Ulli said she would call his room at 1 P.M. Mike, noting that he was the lone customer at this early hour, took time in his halting German to ask if Ulli could inquire and report much earlier. All right, said Ulli, with that faint smile that fled like a wild thing, she would call his room as soon as she learned.

Mike grabbed at his room phone when it rang an hour later.

"Herr Simmons?" Ulli's tone forecast bad news. She was sorry, she said, but the theater would be impossible. The other party had gone on vacation to visit a sister. When would she return? Ulli did not know. When Mike pressed, she pleaded lack of time, many customers in line, you know. Mike insisted. Ulli sighed in sympathy, but said she must go now. The click of the phone told him that she had hung up.

Unwilling to lose his only firm line to Gisela, Mike threw on his sheepskin coat, left the hotel, hurried the two blocks to the Information Zentrum, and took his place, seventh in line in front of Ulli's station. When he moved up to the counter after a long wait, Ulli was decidedly displeased to see him again. She averted her eyes, showed no evidence of the drifting smile, and fussed with a theater ticket while he spoke his rehearsed piece in plodding German at a level just above a whisper. Please, he pleaded, let him come by Ulli's Hainstrasse flat this evening to discuss his thwarted love. Certainly Gisela could be contacted somehow. He might have to leave the country any day and he must see his sweetheart. All right, she said hurriedly, seven o'clock at the apartment. Building door open. Leave now, quickly, bitte. She cast wary glances at the lobby.

Mike walked through sharp morning sunlight to the nearby hotel construction site. He found Sven Alsten working over a sheaf of papers in the headquarters shack where a fire of brown-coal briquettes burned in the iron stove.

"Michael Simmons himself." The Swede shook his head in mock wonderment. "Do you know I'm stuck with one of these endless official forms because of you and your elevator doors? I have to wade through a couple of kilometers of questions before I even approach the point of the thing."

"What is the point?"

"Werner Lanz reported your little debate, shall we call it, to his superiors, so now the Ministry of State Security wants a full account of the door-lock assembly situation."

"Jesus. . . . Why?"

Alsten hunched his shoulders and spread his palms in a gesture of futility. "Who knows?" Rays of sunlight danced on the tip of his ball-point pen. "Bureaucratic overkill, the curse of the working classes. What is my age, weight, height, and nationality? What is yours? What is estimated cost of the building? How long to build? How many workers employed on project? How many on the subcontract in dispute? My passport number and expiration date? Same for you. And I'm still two pages away from the broken door locks."

"How long will it take, do you suppose?"

"Two hours at least. A man from the Ministry says he'll stop by at noon to pick up the filled-out form." Alsten yawned and stretched. "But what brings you back? I thought we'd seen the last of you for several months."

"Company paperwork, Sven. Corporations have their own bureaucracies, you know."

"Well, make yourself at home. No more problems with the lifts, as far as I know." Alsten bent over his papers once more.

Mike spent most of the day checking his six elevators, four Todd passenger Supremes and two heavy-duty freight Clydesdales. All operated smoothly, gliding noiselessly up and down their shafts amid a flurry of plastering, flooring, and electrical work. The new Inter hotel neared the final burst of activity before completion.

Manfred, the elevator specialist who spoke rudimentary English, told Mike that Lanz now took a keen interest in the door-lock assembly parts and checked the small units daily.

"I think he wants to find American parts *kaputt*." Manfred nodded knowingly.

"Well, keep an eye out, will you? I don't want anyone messing with the doors."

"Ja, ja. No man touch while I work here."

Leaving the construction site in late afternoon, Mike felt at once that he was being followed, this time by a man in a clay-colored raincoat whose shape struck no familiar chord. When he tested his hunch by stepping into the recessed entrance to a bakery, he saw that the man halted to study a shop window.

Mike walked on to his hotel, noting as he ducked under the great flapping curtain in the doorway that his follower also headed toward the Astoria.

He spent an hour in his room, passing the time by using his German-English dictionary to decipher stories in *Neues Deutschland,* the ruling party's official organ. The central committee of the Socialist Unity Party took a half column to send "warmest wishes" to Heinz Klopfer, secretary of the National Planning Commission, on his sixtieth birthday. He had, it appeared, used all his "strength for the reconstruction and stabilization of the DDR after liberation of our people from Hitler's Fascism by the glorious Soviet Army." An interviewer quoted Renate Stecher, once the world's fastest woman and Olympic 100 and 100-meter champion in 1972, as saying her little daughter was "doubly protected"—by the home and by the state. Energy-savings tip? Mike learned he could save 20 percent of his refrigerator bill by defrosting the box as soon as the ice became one centimeter thick. The Ministry for Transport, the administration of the nation's rail system, and various unions and officials announced that they were mourning the death of a former traffic minister, a holder of the Karl Marx Medal, and a "courageous fighter against war and Fascism."

But as Mike plodded through the translations, another part of his mind schemed at a more hazardous game. He must negotiate the few blocks to Ulli's apartment without being followed. Somehow, he vowed, he would outwit the man in the clay-colored raincoat.

When he emerged from the hotel at dusk, Mike noted that his tracker paced the sidewalk near the corner. When he saw Mike, he glanced at his wrist watch, then looked up and down the street as if searching for someone late for an appointment.

A moment later the stakeout specialist stared in confusion. Clad in a dark blue exercise suit and wearing cushion-soled running shoes and a wide grin, his quarry passed him at the speed of a cantering horse, ran across the street against the red light, dodged a truck and a Wartburg sedan, accelerated his pace in front of the ponderous Haupt-bahnhof, and lost himself in a crowd at the far end of the Platz der Republik.

Recovering slowly like a man in shock, Clay Raincoat finally broke into a run himself and headed for a telephone in the Astoria lobby where a clock told him that he had lost his man a few minutes before 5:10 P.M.

Several backward glances assuring Mike that his tracker had abandoned the chase, he slowed to a jog and headed up Goethe Strasse past a park and small lagoon. By the time he reached the imposing opera house, he had changed to a fast-paced walk. Other pedestrians paid scant attention to him. Exercise suits were a common sight in East Germany.

Mike felt fine despite his rapid breathing. He could feel the pulse of blood through his body, the tingle in his limbs, and the air's refreshing chill on his face. Alternating between a walk, a jog, and a loping run, he toured the grounds of Karl Marx University with its scalloped tower. Knots of students strolled about and he saw many young women wearing hip-tight corduroy pants and high heels, another Western style that had recently caught on here. He headed toward the ponderous city hall and then turned to the Georgi Dimitrov museum where, in 1933, the Bulgarian Communist defied Nazi efforts to convict him of arson for the Reichstag fire. Circling this East German shrine, Mike returned to Leipzig's mid-city area, settled into a steady walk, regained his natural breathing rhythm, and stopped at a sidewalk stand for a long, smoking Bratwurst on a bun.

He turned into Hainstrasse a few minutes before seven, satisfied himself that no one followed him, and reached Ulli's courtyard precisely on time. The building door, as she promised, stood unlocked.

Ulli, apparently waiting for the sound of footsteps on the stairs, opened her door before he had a chance to knock. Although she offered him tea, Mike could see that she disliked this visit. She had a strained, apprehensive air, fussed unduly with her great tangle of hair, and forced a smile during the formalities of greeting. The radio throbbed with a big-band number from a long-ago decade.

They sat on the fine antique chairs before the cheap coffee table and waited stiffly until Ulli heard the kettle whistle. She seemed relieved to bustle about the cramped kitchen and reluctant to return. Accepting his tea with thanks, Mike knew he must take no longer than necessary.

"I will hurry," he said in his fumbling German. "I know this is inconvenient for you."

"People misunderstand, you know." She reached to the bookshelf and turned up the radio's volume. Could that be "Smoke Gets in Your Eyes"? It was.

"I must get in touch with Gisela." He leaned close to Ulli. "I miss her so much. And I have to leave soon."

She rushed through a thicket of German and Mike had to ask her to repeat slowly. "Pardon." This time she enunciated at kindergarten tempo. "This afternoon I called Karl. He said that Gisela is at her sister's and will not return until next week."

Gisela alive! That heaviness deep inside him began to dissolve. "She isn't sick, is she?"

"*Nee.* But sad to say, she had an accident that will confine her to her sister's house in Kaltennordheim."

"A bad accident?" He waited as if on knife-edge for the answer.

"I don't think so. A bruise, as I understand it. She stumbled and fell while walking."

With a machine gun spitting metal all about her, he added silently. Again that surrealist scene flashed in his mind and he could almost hear the bizarre accompaniment, a distant, furious clamor of dogs.

"Will it incapacitate her for long?"

"I believe not, Herr Simmons. Next week Karl expects her back."

He sighed. The weight crumbled away and he felt like soaring. Gisela not only had survived, she apparently had not been badly injured. "May I write out a message that you may perhaps read her as soon as you can?"

"Naturally." She scanned his exercise suit and canvas running shoes. "Mr. Simmons, have you been running?"

"Yes. I do it in good weather. For health."

"But without your identity papers, you must not go out. That is no good, for foreigners no less than residents."

"Oh, don't worry." Mike fished in his jacket pockets and withdrew his passport from one and his wallet from the other. "I never go out without both money and passport."

He extracted a piece of paper tucked in a slot behind his wallet's credit cards and consulted the code that he had drawn up with Gisela. Selecting from the elevator terms, he constructed a brief message in Spanish on paper provided by Ulli: "Please contact me as soon as possible through Ulli or, if I've returned to the other side, through Sven Alsten."

He slipped the code back in his wallet and handed the paper to Ulli. "Lovers' secret talk," he explained. He rose to leave. "Please add my love when you read it to her."

"Naturally." Now at last came that fetching smile of hers, a tracing of sweet melancholy that floated by in parting. Ulli, he saw, was relieved to see him leave.

The news about Gisela gave him a powerful psychological lift. Alive, she apparently would be neither invalided nor crippled. Outside he broke into a trot despite the darkness of the streets and soon found himself running at a fast clip, the spongy soles buoying his every step. He gulped at the chill air and pumped his arms in circles. How great to feel the pulse of life and to know that Gisela also lived, apparently outside the clutches of soldiers or agents of the state.

He ran all the way to the Astoria and pulled up, panting happily, in front of the entrance. He reached out to part the curtain which flapped in the doorway.

Hands gripped his arms. Two men emerged from the shadows, one on each side of him.

"Herr Simmons, you are required for questioning." The heavy voice spoke English with a polished British accent.

The hands on his arms turned him firmly toward the street.

"I must go to my room to change clothes." He tried to draw back.

"That will not be necessary." The agent's accent might have been fashioned at Eton or Harrow.

"I demand to be allowed to contact the American embassy." He spoke with a bravura he did not feel.

"That will not be possible." The hands tightened on his arms as they propelled him forward.

A black limousine, a Russian Zil, Mike thought, glided from the corner and halted directly in front of the hotel. A passing couple, arm in arm, gaped for a moment, then hurried away.

9

Silence, East Germany's dark sleeve of enterprise, wrapped the automobile and muffled the swift movements of its occupants. The two abductors, clothed not surprisingly in clay-colored raincoats, half-lifted, half-shoved Mike onto the rear seat. They sandwiched him between them and fitted his eyes with sunglasses, the lenses of which were painted black, allowing him only the narrowest of peripheral vision. The instant he was seated in the center, the limousine rolled away from the curb and accelerated swiftly. Unlike many East Bloc cars, which rattled and wheezed as they aged, this one performed noiselessly. Even the shifting of gears took place as if swathed in cotton.

The man on Mike's left occupied a great deal of room. From the corner of his eye, Mike took in a large body inclined toward flabbiness. The agent breathed heavily from his modest exertions and smelled of beer and cologne. The other guard, the one who had spoken English with an educated British accent, had lean, hawkish features and wore a broad-brimmed felt hat of the kind favored by Chicago gangsters of the Prohibition era. Neither agent, for such Mike assumed them to be, turned toward him and Mike could not see or hear the driver. The only identifiable human sound came from the fat guard who yawned deeply, the exhalation as busy as a leaky balloon. This, apparently, was just another routine snatch.

The limousine rolled north toward the Gohlis district, then angled to the right into a main thoroughfare that Mike took to be the Strasse der Deutsch Sowjetischen Freundschaft which led to the Autobahn to Berlin. Via his slit of side vision, Mike noted that only a few people walked this shadowed street where German-Soviet friendship purportedly thrived. The limousine, moving at about fifty miles an hour, had even fewer cars challenging it for running space.

Mike turned toward the black hat. "Where are you taking me?"

"No questions." He spoke as quietly as the hum of the motor. "You will remain silent."

This abduction must mean, of course, that Gisela too had been or soon would be apprehended. How had agents of the state managed to link both of them to an escape plan? He retraced his movements of the last ten days, weighing those on this side of the frontier to see where he had slipped. Or had he been under constant surveillance in both Germanies? He recalled that male silhouette, a seemingly familiar figure, on Augsburger Strasse in West Berlin.

Mike felt no fear. Instead indignation simmered, then slowly swelled into anger. What an infantile perversion of normal contact between human beings, to scoop a man off the sidewalk at night, shove him into a car, and order him to silence! What clause in the social contract had he breached, what harm done? What deed of Michael R. Simmons had infringed the rights of any person—or animal or plant, for that matter? He assumed he'd be questioned about his part in the attempt of Gisela Steinbrecher to cross from one geographical area to another, an offense only to those with a monstrously distorted view of suitable human conduct. Rage boiled over, the intensity compounded by his visual impotence and by the thought of Gisela's almost certain seizure by anonymous agents like these. Occasionally when lights of the Autobahn flickered, he caught side glimpses of the impassive strangers beside him. They sat like bulky mannequins in this speeding show window, grown men squandering enormous amounts of time, energy, and money on a hollow, if pernicious, mission.

"I demand to be allowed to call the American ambassador!" The words exploded from him.

The thin-boned agent turned slightly. "One more word out of you and you'll be gagged," he said drily.

Again that eerie hush settled on the car, relieved only by a thin moaning of tires, the motor's hum, and the soughing exhalations of the overweight guard. Mike wondered which State Security office or prison in East Berlin awaited him and what kind of inquisitor would question him.

Then he remembered. That code in elevator jargon!

Immediately he shoved his hands into the front pockets of his blue exercise jacket. The wallet rested in the right pocket. He explored with his forefinger the slot behind the folding plastic casing that held his credit cards. He felt the slip of paper, moved it with his fingertip, and slowly maneuvered it up and out of the small leather pocket. Guessing that one or both of the agents might be watching, Mike stiffened his arms as if stretching for relief from the cramped position. At the same time his fingers crumpled the paper and rolled it into a small ball.

The next move came only after considerable thought. He coughed loudly several times, clapped his right hand to his mouth as if to shield his seatmates from contamination, popped in the little paper ball, and gulped in that strangled way that people sometimes do after coughing. He felt the incriminating code slide down his throat, no more and no less awkwardly than a thick vitamin pill.

Through his thin band of sight, Mike saw both agents turn toward him. He coughed again, pointed at his throat, and shook his head apologetically. At the same time he felt a spurt of confidence. In an opening skirmish, he had outwitted the SSD, the vaunted and rudely efficient security forces which spilled no less than fifteen thousand secret police agents, as well as thousands of organized informers and collaborators, over the landscape of this small country.

But his confidence waned as the car rolled through the outlying streets of East Berlin where street lamps cast dim yellow pools, monotonous apartment blocks shouldered the night sky, and the few people on the streets hurried along as if sauntering were a crime. The city had a heavy, brooding mien and his spirits sank accordingly. When they rolled to a stop and his glasses were removed in the courtyard of a massive stone building, the first fingers of fear plucked at him. He assumed he had been brought to SSD headquarters in Berlin-Lichtenberg.

His two companions of the rear seat bundled him, arm in arm, into a dimly lit vestibule. At a caged counter, a phlegmatic clerk in a frayed cardigan wrote down Mike's name, occupation, age, nationality, and home address. He was then ordered to turn his pockets inside out. The agents placed the wallet and passport on the counter and motioned to Mike to unstrap his wrist watch. The clerk methodically counted the money in the pocketbook, logged the three articles in a ledger, and handed Mike a carbon copy of a receipt. Not a word had been spoken.

The guards now turned him over in silence to a dour woman, with a complexion the color of ashes, who wore a dark brown dress and carried a ring of keys. She led Mike down a long corridor that smelled of disinfectant, opened a door, pointed him inward, and then closed the door behind him. He heard no key turn.

The fairly large room had one barred window and totally

bare walls painted a neutral, aging green. An overhead globe gave off a feeble light. The room held exactly four pieces of furniture, a wooden chair in the middle of the room facing a kitchen-sized metal table on which rested a flexible-necked desk lamp. Behind the table stood a worn leather swivel chair.

Mike walked about the room. The bottom half of the single window was painted black. The top half, smudged and dusty, apparently had not been washed for weeks and afforded only a veiled view of the building's upper stories across the courtyard. He seated himself in the straight-backed wooden chair and waited. And waited. And waited. Sharp images, unblurred despite the passage of almost half a century, fastened on his mind. . . . A basement room, a high stool, four bare walls plastered a dingy white, the old feeling of fear, a five-year-old's panic in the dungeon of punishment. . . . And still he waited. He guessed that he had passed an hour here alone. The silence, all but total, unnerved him. The only sounds came from a distance, muffled and indistinguishable. He tried to prepare himself, but found that arming against the unknown proved futile. At last he resorted to his old routine of picturing the women with whom he'd slept. But he got no further than Stacey, the bringer of little gifts, when he abandoned the parade as demeaning to its participants. To evoke the images of lovely women in the relative freedom of park benches, subway cars, passport offices, and dental suites seemed quite fitting, but not a single one of his old loves belonged in an East German interrogation room.

He began to tire and he had just considered the possibility of lying on the floor when the door opened and in walked a slight, dapper man carrying an armload of supplies. He shot a perfunctory yet unmistakable smile, first of the evening, at Mike, stepped to the table, turned on the desk lamp, deposited his supplies, and seated himself.

151

The newcomer was ruddy, sandy-haired, had a trim mustache, and wore a dark blue suit with vest. An SED party button glinted on his lapel. Without looking up, he began arranging his equipment. He carefully placed three ball-point pens, a pad and rubber stamp, several paper clips and a watch to his right, lining them up like the knives and spoons of a table setting. In the center he placed a thick pad of lined paper. To the left he stationed a pocket calculator, a small calendar, and a German-English dictionary. Finally, in front of the pad he put down a tape recorder and Mike's passport and wallet. He spent considerable time positioning these items, realigning some, then pursing his lips and studying the total effect with all the concentration of a Japanese flower arranger.

He switched on the tape recorder. "Well, Herr Simmons, let us begin." He spoke a heavily Germanic English, surveyed Mike in a not unfriendly fashion, and lifted one of the pens.

"I demand my right to call the American ambassador."

"Ah. Wishes to see the U.S.A. ambassador." He spoke syllable by syllable, gearing his speech to the jotting down of the request. Then he took up Mike's passport. "Well, we have here on this ten December Herr Michael Ralph Simmons, U.S.A. passport No. K 259 1258. Is that correct?"

"Yes." Mike tried again. "I demand to see the American ambassador."

The official laid down pen and passport and folded his hands neatly on the pad. "It will not be productive to repeat that request, Herr Simmons. I am here to collect pertinent data preliminary to your interrogation. I am not authorized to grant any request of yours except to accompany you to the toilet in case of need." He smiled, not unpleasantly. "Well then, I shall proceed. Please answer my questions."

He opened the passport again. "Born 5 May 1928?"

"Yes."

"Born Omaha, Nebraska, U.S.A.?"

"Yes. . . . And what's your name, please?" asked Mike.

"That is of no concern here."

"What do I call you then?"

"Well . . ." The word seemed oddly cumbersome. "I suppose 'sir' would be appropriate." He looked like a satisfied employer. "Yes, 'sir' would do rather nicely, I think." He picked up Mike's wallet. "American Express card No. 3719 366148 41001. Correct?"

"I have no idea."

Sir held out the pocketbook and invited Mike to inspect the card.

"Do you verify that number?"

"Yes."

It took half an hour to run through various cards in similar fashion. VISA, EXXON, Social Security, University Club, New York driver's license, New York City public library card, Bloomingdale's, National Elevator Industry, Inc., and the Chemical Bank all had numbers which Sir methodically noted, one institution a line.

"What is this, Herr Simmons?" He held up a slip of paper. "233 East Fifty-fourth. (212) 355 3287."

"The address and phone number of a friend in New York."

"The name, please?"

"I decline."

Sir bit his lower lip. "Ah, subject refuses to identify person with address and phone number, allegedly in New York City." He again paced his speech to his writing, then leaned back as if to view his handiwork in better perspective. What he saw pleased him. Herr Sir appeared to take inordinate satisfaction in these humdrum clerical chores. Mike's memory vaulted back to a cool afternoon on a plateau of the Peruvian Andes where he visited an old colonial monastery. His guide, a slight, mincing monk from Spain who wore a

153

cowled robe, had a queer habit of walking backward, a few paces in front of Mike, while he pointed out niches and paintings of historical interest. He trotted, he danced, he minced, always to the rear, droning through his uninspired singsong lectures. Just as did Herr Sir, the Spanish monk took exquisite pleasure in his routine chore and, as with Herr Sir, he gave off emanations both epicene and malicious.

It took the East German registrar fully two hours to amass required data on Michael Simmons' vital statistics, schooling, career, relatives, religion, as well as his movements within the DDR and names of East Germans he knew. Mike refused to answer only twice, first to give the name of Ann Gilpin whom he'd met recently and whose New York address appeared on the slip in his wallet, second to give the occupation and whereabouts of his daughter, Sally, and his son, David.

At last Herr Sir placed his palms on the table and leaned back with a proud expression. He fairly burst with self-congratulations for a job well done. "Well, I think that completes our assignment." He switched off the desk lamp, bowed to Mike, and gathered up his supplies much as the architect of a new cathedral might take up his drafting board and tools after completion of the prizewinning design.

He had reached the door when Mike protested. "Hey, I need to use the toilet."

"That will be taken care of."

The severe female guard in the shapeless brown dress made good the promise within a few minutes. She led Mike down the long corridor, also painted a dark institutional green, to a closet-sized room which held a toilet bowl. She waited outside, then escorted him silently back to the interrogation chamber.

Again he waited. And waited. He had lost track of time,

but casting backward to his apprehension in front of the Astoria at about 7:30 P.M., he calculated that it was now about one o'clock in the morning. Soon fatigue welled up, demanding surrender. He had slept but sketchily the night before in Leipzig. After nodding off several times in the chair, he lay down on the floor and tried to sleep. But he wore only the cotton exercise suit with no sweat shirt and a cool draft flowing over the worn carpet disturbed him. He coiled into a fetal position for warmth and finally drifted into a troubled slumber.

"Get up!"

Mike came awake with a start, found himself blinking into a strong beam of light. The flexible desk lamp had been twisted so that it shone down on him. He rubbed his eyes, stretched, and slowly raised himself.

"Sit in the chair and face this desk."

When his eyes became accustomed to the light, Mike saw that the owner of the voice rapping out commands was seated in the swivel chair where Herr Sir had spent such pleasantly rewarding hours. The replacement was powerfully built with heavy shoulders, a bull's neck, and brush-cut blond hair. He had sparse eyebrows, fair skin, and pale blue eyes so that the overall impression was one of a washed-out, colorless neutrality allied with great strength, a combination that Mike, not yet fully conscious, found vaguely sinister and threatening.

Like his predecessor, this examiner came equipped with abundant supplies, Mike's passport and wallet among them, which he dumped on the desk like refuse. Then he took a small tape recorder from his pocket and set it up with a microphone adjusted toward Mike. He folded his arms and fixed his eyes on Mike's, locking the two men at once in a visual struggle. Determined not to waver, Mike concentrated on the pupil of his antagonist's right eye, a small black raft afloat on a noonday sea.

The official turned on the tape recorder. "Herr Simmons, I will question you with respect to suspected violation of the laws of the Deutsche Demokratische Republik." He spoke a serviceable if guttural English. Rummaging through the collection on his desk, he was forced to lower his eyes, thus letting Mike win their first skirmish by default.

"The rules of your interrogation are as follows." He referred to a mimeographed sheet in his hand. "One: You will answer all questions. Failure to do so will be taken into account by the Ministry of State Security in disposing of your case. Two: You will not pose questions to the examiner without explicit permission. Three: You will not be permitted to contact anyone outside this building." He ticked off a number of regulations, including those governing toilet trips, medical attention, and personal belongings. "Finally, subject will retain an alert posture at all times during interrogation. . . . Do you wish to make a statement before we begin?"

"Yes." Anger coursed through him again. "I demand my right to telephone the American ambassador."

"Request denied. You have no such right here." The examiner raised his voice. "My notes show that twice previously you made that same demand. You will not do that again. Is that clear?"

"Yes." Mike looked his new adversary in the eyes. "Of what am I accused here?"

"Not in order. If you ask that again, you will be penalized severely."

"What kind of penalty?"

"Not in order!" The sudden shout astonished Mike. The interrogator thrust his huge head forward and glared. "You will not ask questions here. I repeat. No questions." Now his shout became a roar. "Is that understood?"

Mike bobbed his head.

"Answer me!" Red splotches sprang like storm warnings from the pale sea of a face.

"Yes." Mike glared back. What did his adversary remind him of?

"And that kind of belligerent attitude will get you nowhere." The examiner's look was one of contempt. "Believe me, if you do not cooperate here, you are lost."

Then, as if to reassemble his thoughts, he shuffled through his papers and rapped out a series of biographical questions that went over ground already covered by his predecessor. He kept his eyes down and raced through the inquiries, hardly waiting for the responses. Then he stopped.

Silence flooded the bare room. Mike could hear only the ticking of his foe's watch.

"When did you first go to work for the Central Intelligence Agency?" The question came like a shot from ambush.

"What?" Mike was prepared for almost any opening but this.

"No questions!" Another roar. "Answer me. Now."

"I've never worked for the CIA."

"We'll nail that lie before we finish. . . . Do you know Sven Alsten?"

"Yes."

"What does he do?"

"He's headman for the Swedish contractors building an Inter hotel in Leipzig."

"Do you know Inge Herschel?"

"No." Struggling to find the proper image, Mike decided his inquisitor looked like a huge peeled radish.

"Do not lie. We have information that you met Inge Herschel at dinner in the Astoria dining room in Leipzig the night of Thursday, 26 November."

"Oh." The affable bureaucrat from East Berlin? "If she

works for the Ministry of Culture, yes, I did meet her, but I didn't remember her name."

"Do you know Gisela Steinbrecher?"

"Yes." Oh, God. Now it would start. He could feel his heart pound.

"Where and when did you meet her?"

"At the same gathering at dinner at the Astoria."

"What does Frau Steinbrecher do?"

"I understand she's an editor of publications at the Technical University in Dresden."

"Did you ever meet Frau Steinbrecher after that?"

"No." Had he replied too quickly? He felt unsure of himself now. "Well, I chatted with her the next evening in the lobby. That's all."

"What year did you begin work for the Central Intelligence Agency?"

"I've never worked for the CIA." Then he snapped: "I told you that once." Immediately he recognized his mistake. No display of emotion. If he kept it low-key and steady, he wouldn't be tempted into dangerous verbal combat.

"What does Sally Simmons do?"

"I refuse to discuss my daughter."

"How long has she worked for the CIA?"

"Same answer."

"And I remind you of the first regulation. Failure to answer questions will prejudice the authorities against you."

Mike did not respond.

"What does David Simmons do?"

"I refuse to discuss my son."

"Is it not true that David Simmons is a sergeant with the 11th Armored Cavalry Regiment, U.S.A., an offensive strike force stationed in Fulda in the Federal Republic under orders to destroy defense units of the peaceful Socialist nations?"

"I refuse to discuss my son." Mike felt sure that Peeled

Radish's adjectives were chosen for the benefit of the tape recorder. The near-miss on Dave's rank and duty failed to warm the chill he felt when the correct unit designation dropped. How did the SSD know that Dave Simmons served in the U. S. Army at Fulda?

"Why did you visit West Berlin twice within the last week?"

"Damages to our elevator installation. I had to get spare parts quickly."

"For what purpose did you go to the U. S. A. Mission in West Berlin?"

"I never went to the U. S. Mission." Where was it located anyway?

"Do you know Franklin Mott?"

"No."

"You called on him at the Mission. Don't lie."

"I did not."

"And isn't it true that Franklin Mott is a CIA agent working under cover of the Mission?"

"I have no idea."

"Do you know Richard Helms?"

"No."

"You do not know Richard Helms, the former head of the U.S.A. Central Intelligence Agency?" He almost yelled the question. "Don't lie to me."

"Oh, that Helms." Mike throttled his temper. "I've heard of him, of course. I never met or talked to him."

"What was the name of the Eastern Europe CIA unit, supervised by Helms, for which you worked?"

"I don't know. I never worked for any CIA unit."

"Who is Manfred Weisbrod?"

"I don't know."

"You lie." The interrogator pitched his cry in triumph. "Manfred Weisbrod worked with you on elevator installation in Leipzig."

"Oh, that Manfred." He began to hate Peeled Radish. "Yes, of course. I know the Manfred who worked for me. You're trying to trap me."

"You will not comment on State Security procedures." It was a half shout. "This office seeks the truth of the subversive operations directed against it by the reactionary, Fascistic powers of the West. At no time do we attempt to mislead, dupe, or trick those under interrogation." He raced through this little speech, obviously for the benefit of superiors who would listen to the tape. "Do you know Hildegarde Gotsche?"

"I know a Frau Gotsche who works as a reception clerk at the Astoria. I don't know her first name."

"Do you know Werner Lanz?"

"Yes. He's some kind of political brigade leader on the new Inter hotel construction job in Leipzig."

"What do you mean 'political'?"

"I understand he's the SED representative with the workers."

"When did the Todd Elevator cover for your CIA activities begin?"

"I've never had any CIA activities." Did the SSD truly suspect that he worked for the CIA? If so and if that were the thrust of this interrogation, Mike felt confident of emerging unscathed. But he assumed that all these CIA inquiries merely served to throw him off guard and that the Gisela escape questions would soon begin to pelt him like hail. He mentally braced himself.

Peeled Radish pressed forward relentlessly, usually at a bullying level that ranged between loud blustering and a roar. He threw out scores of names, mostly those of East Germans, but some from West Germany, Britain, and the United States. Politicians and others in the news accounted for some, but the majority meant nothing to Mike. Occasionally the interrogator swerved back to the handful of people whom Mike knew in East Germany. Each time Gisela's name came up, Mike's pulse quickened, but Peeled Radish never pursued a line connected to her. Nor did he ever refer to Ulli Beitz, a name Mike feared might be hurled at him at any moment.

Always the quizzing swung back to the CIA. When did he start at CIA headquarters in Langley, Virginia? How soon would he retire from the CIA? When had he spied for Operation Scarab? Was his cover name Gerald Knox when working for the CIA in Vietnam? What were his duties in the Division of Plans? Did he report to Clinton Ryder at the Buenos Aires CIA station while ostensibly representing Todd Elevator in Argentina?

His string of denials, no's, and nevers grew monotonously long, the minutes dragged into hours and he felt his strength waning. Once he actually nodded off and recovered with an upward jerk of the head. At last the bull-necked interrogator flung a final CIA question, sneered at Mike's negation, and swooped up his utensils, pad, and tape recorder. "Your examination will resume at 9 A.M." Peeled Radish walked, or more accurately stomped, to the door.

"What time is it now?"

In answer, the door slammed.

Moments later it opened again and the ashen-faced matron in the brown dress beckoned to him. They marched down the long green corridor.

"What time is it, please?"

She shook her head. *"Ich spreche nicht Englisch."* The keys on her ring clinked like sad chimes.

He tried in German. *"Wie spät ist es?"*

Again the matron shook her head, silently this time. She opened a door, waited until he entered, then locked it behind him.

The room duplicated the one he had just left in size, color, and dismal aspect, but differed in several features. In-

stead of chairs and desk, this room had a lidless toilet bowl
in one corner and an iron cot with a mattress and sheet, but
no blanket. Mike looked about the room, could find neither
closet nor blanket. A powerful, unshielded bulb in the ceiling threw harsh light that illumined the bare room as starkly
as the frontier under searchlights. Mike looked everywhere
for a light switch. There was none. Nor was there a string to
pull to extinguish the light. At least twelve feet separated
the carpetless board floor from the ceiling, and even if he
stood on the cot, Mike knew he could not touch the bulb.
Nevertheless he decided to try. The cot would not budge. It
was bolted to the floor.

Now he became aware that the room was unusually cool
and growing colder. There was but one window, located
near the ceiling. One of those basement-type windows
which swing inward and up, it gaped wide open, fixed by a
metal arm. While the temperature had not dropped radically, the night was, after all, a December one and the air
had cooled to near freezing. Another swift inspection told
Mike that he could not reach the window latch to close it
and that the room held neither radiator nor other heating
unit.

Obviously his abductors and inquisitors did not want him
to sleep in the few remaining hours before they renewed his
examination. This fact became doubly evident when an engine of some kind began pounding somewhere below his
window. It sounded like a pump, for a long gasping sigh
would follow the initial drumming.

While he could perhaps manage a sleepless night, Mike
wondered how long he could survive the cold without falling ill. He had already begun to shiver and he slapped his
arms and legs in an effort to generate some warmth. He had
nothing beneath his flimsy exercise suit save a pair of jockey
shorts. Only his feet, encased in sweat socks and the canvas
running shoes, remained reasonably warm.

Now a prolonged shivering seized him like an attack of palsy and he realized how vulnerable the combination of weariness and cold had made him. What to do? In a warm room the sheeted cot would lure him, but in this cold the thought of lying immobile was unthinkable.

He knocked on the door. When he heard no response, he beat it until it threatened to crack. He experienced the onset of panic and he slammed his fist against the wooden panels again and again.

At last he heard a cry in the corridor and then the rattle of a key in the lock. When the door swung open, the female guard of the sour mien stood facing him. Aside from an eyebrow lifted inquiringly, she regarded him with flat disinterest.

"You must close the window," he said in German. "I am very cold."

"Ja, ja." She unpenned a rush of words while pushing him back with her hand. After she had locked the door, he persuaded himself that she had promised to fetch someone or something that would close the window.

He paced back and forth near the door as far from the window as possible. He felt miserable. The air pouring through the open pane grew colder. The engine outside pounded, groaned, and gasped. The light overhead continued to throw its merciless glare and his eyes began to itch. He could understand that a prisoner subjected to many nights of this treatment might go mad or tell his interrogators anything they wanted to hear if it but gained him heat, darkness, and a properly covered bed.

He walked. He paced. He jogged. He beat his arms and slapped at his legs. Minutes passed, became a half hour, then an hour. He hammered on the door again, waited futilely for an answer. Occasional gusts rattled the window and whipped icy air into the room. He tried to recollect the questioning and concentrate on what it meant or portended, but found sequential, logical thought impossible. Instead, random images flogged his mind: Gisela shivering in an identical room, perhaps in this building. . . . A kid on a high stool, wracked with sobs in the trauma of lonely isolation. . . . Sven Alsten spreading his hands to a glowing brown-coal fire. . . . Peeled Radish yammering for his tape recorder. . . . Dave firing a burst at the Grepos' armored car. . . . Mike himself tunneling under a heated Federbett.

When he glanced toward the window while slowing from a jog to a walk, he saw the gray smudge of a new day. He guessed the time at 6 A.M. Another three hours to go in this insane freezer.

All at once his temper flared. The anger exploded and raced through him until his whole being filled with fury like some primitive animal engorged with blood. The bastards! The vicious, inhuman, sadistic bastards! These sons of the Nazis, schooled in the preludes to torture, had learned their lessons well. Out of the ovens and into the freezer. Grovel before the state. Take orders. Submit. Mike welcomed his rage like an old friend. He could feel it coursing the length of his body, routing his shivers, heating his blood, and firing his will to resist. By God, they would not freeze him into docility or shine him into fright like some mole caught outside his burrow. He quickened his pacing and felt the anger slowly bring him back into equilibrium, his numbing cold and his weariness balanced by the glow of an inner strength.

When hours later a key scratched the lock and the door opened, Mike had neared exhaustion. A deep chill penetrated to the marrow of his bones and his body ached with fatigue. He had trudged back and forth, fifteen feet to a lap, his legs growing as heavy as lead, for what seemed like an endless winter.

An elderly, gray-haired man beckoned him to follow. The instant Mike stepped into the warm air of the corridor, a tremendous shivering convulsed him as if in farewell salute to his night of icy trial. Tears welled into his eyes, and if he'd been alone, he would have surrendered to the urge to weep. Curiously, he felt grateful to his captors for freeing him from the freeze locker, and he realized he must steel himself lest he make some unnecessary concession in a spirit of conciliation. His anger had long faded. Instead, a great torpor overcame him, slowing his walk and padding his brain. His eyes smarted, his skin itched, and he wanted to sleep for a week.

Again Mike's guide ushered him into last night's examination room. He stood still for a moment, relishing the warm, drugged feeling. Then he saw that the table had a tray of food and he responded with Pavlovian sensations of hunger. Pulling up the chair in which he'd sat for hours, he surveyed his breakfast: coffee, a hard-boiled egg, two hard rolls, and a pat of butter. He gulped down the food without complaint. The coffee was bitter and lukewarm, but at least it was liquid. Mike realized he hadn't drunk anything since the tea at Ulli's long, long ago.

His daylight interrogator did not keep him waiting. He arrived only moments after Mike finished eating. The Stasi had sent still a third gunner against its suspect. While this official also toted an armful of supplies, he differed radically from the others. A stout, fatherly sort with a relaxed manner and easy stride, he smiled at Mike upon entering and promptly engaged him in small talk.

"Well, Herr Simmons, you enjoyed your breakfast, I hope." He spoke cordially in English with only a trace of Teutonic accent.

"Sure did. After that God-awful night."

"A bad night? What went wrong?"

"Wrong!" Anger shot upward in the sluggish waters of his torpor. "The room was freezing cold. They refused to close the window. No heat. A bright light in my eyes. No blanket. And for good measure, some darn motor pounded away outside."

"Oh, I'm terribly sorry." He seemed genuinely distressed. "I can't understand what happened. Somebody failed his duty. I hate to say this to a foreigner, but even the Ministry has lapses."

"Come off it. That was all rigged to soften me up for the next round of questioning."

"I beg to differ, Herr Simmons. We have strict rules here. All those detained for questioning must be treated as guests." He frowned sympathetically. This man, Mike decided, was a competent actor with only a thin slice of ham in him.

"If that was guest treatment, I'd just as soon be a prisoner, thanks." Mike tired of the game. Drowsiness lapped at him.

"Again my apologies, Herr Simmons. . . . Well, we must begin our work." He switched on the tape recorder. "Do you wish to make a statement first?"

"I demand to call the American ambassador."

"Yes, I see that's a major concern with you. Perhaps that will be possible after we complete our work. . . . Now, are you comfortable, Herr Simmons?"

Mike sneezed, wiped his nose on the sleeve of his exercise jacket. "Hardly. But I guess I'll manage if your outfit doesn't give me pneumonia."

The interrogator shook his head like a kindly but firm father. "I'm afraid you'll have to curb your bent for sarcasm, Herr Simmons. If you wish to clear yourself of suspicion, you must take this proceeding quite seriously, you know."

"Just what crime am I supposed to have committed?"

Father bestowed a sunny smile. "Well, that's exactly what we're trying to find out here today, isn't it?"

"Oh, go ahead." Who killed logic? Did Cock Robin kill

logic? His thoughts entangled themselves like worms in a bucket.

"All right, Herr Simmons, who is Werner Lanz?"

"I told Peeled—the man last night. Lanz is the SED representative on the Inter construction site in Leipzig where I installed six Todd elevators."

"You had a dispute with Herr Lanz?"

"Yes."

"Would you please describe what happened?"

"Somebody forced the doors on the third floor of our No. 4 shaft. That breaks the door-lock assembly and stops the car. It won't move. Lanz contended that nobody forced the doors, that defective materials caused the break."

"That's a synopsis. I want you to describe everything about that event from start to finish." Father tilted back in his swivel chair and folded his hands behind his head. "Take your time. Just be thorough, please."

Mike talked for ten minutes, happy to be on familiar, technical ground. This segment of his examination arose no doubt from those forms Sven was filling out yesterday. As he spoke of elevators and their parts, Mike's weariness lifted and he felt reasonably normal for a spell. He recounted the scene with Lanz in the construction shack as accurately as he could recall it. "So, it was a draw, I guess. We both took back what we said, but he did post a notice warning workers not to pry open elevator doors."

"Very good. I think I get the picture." Father nodded amiably. "Now please tell me in detail exactly how those door-lock assemblies work?"

Mike obliged with another lengthy explanation.

"I take it, Herr Simmons, that we come down to a case of your word against Herr Lanz's. Isn't that correct?"

"No. Not at all. Those doors were forced."

"What proof do you have of that?"

"The paint was scratched and the metal scarred where somebody used a bar to pry them open."

"Of course, you don't actually know a bar was used. And the scratching could have been coincidental, isn't that right?"

"One chance in a million, maybe. But I know those contact arms never break unless somebody pries open the doors."

"Never? How can you prove that?"

"Let's say that in my twenty-five years' experience, one never broke without forcing."

"So you withdraw your unconditional negative?"

"If you insist." Mike felt fatigue overtaking him again. He wanted to slide into a deep pool of sleep. "Look, what's this all about? What the hell difference does it make? Lanz and I had an argument. If you want him to win it retroactively, go ahead. I couldn't care less."

"Are you now saying that Lanz may have been right about the defective materials?" Father spoke quite gently.

"No, goddam it. I did not say that. But if you want to pretend the parts were bad, be my guest. Jesus, it's idiotic to drag me here and question me for hours about an insignificant incident like that."

Father leaned forward, his attitude somewhat stern now. "We do not permit profanity here, Herr Simmons. As for the incident's degree of significance, that is for the Ministry to decide. Shall we proceed?"

Mike nodded glumly. His head ached.

"Beginning with your first days with the Todd concern, describe your various jobs, including your assignments outside the U.S.A. . . . Just a moment." Father reversed the cassette in the recorder. "All right."

This time Mike spent perhaps half an hour on his career biography, covering his tours in Latin America and his administrative job in New York. He sneezed several times and once had a fit of shivering and felt that he might topple off his chair at any moment from exhaustion. He told of going to Leipzig and his work there. "And that," he concluded, "brings us down to last night when the SSD so ungraciously snatched me off the sidewalk without even allowing me a change of clothes."

"It will not be helpful to your case to continue those sarcastic remarks," Father chided in a low voice. "Now, moving back to South America, you headed the Todd office in Chile during the term of President Allende, did you not?"

"No. I went to Santiago two years after Allende's assassination. I worked there only five months."

"You were in adjacent Argentina during Allende's term?"

"Yes. In Buenos Aires."

"With regular contacts by telephone and Telex to Chile. Is that correct?"

"Regular? No, I doubt I talked more than a dozen times to Santiago in a couple of years."

"Who did you talk to?"

"I can't remember. Businessmen in Santiago mostly, several times to a salesman we had over there."

"What was the salesman's name?"

"Chuck Murphy. Charles F. Murphy."

"And he at the time was an agent of the U.S.A. Central Intelligence Agency, right?"

"Not that I ever heard of." Dear God. This dreary CIA business again.

Father questioned at length on Mike's duties in Latin America and his possible links to U. S. Intelligence agencies, then suddenly swerved back to Werner Lanz and the case of the mysterious broken door-lock fixtures. He covered the same ground all over again, sometimes word for word. Mike knew that Father sought to trap him in contradictions, but since he had nothing to hide in this area, he slugged away without hesitation.

Noon came and slid into gray afternoon and still they talked about Werner Lanz, Manfred Weisbrod, door-lock assemblies, Todd's manufacturing procedures, and the prices of materials. The lack of sleep and the tension irritated his bladder and four times he had to repair to the toilet under escort. And still they talked of halted elevators. The elderly attendant brought cheese, sausage, bread, and water for him—and even while Mike ate his lunch, Father quizzed him quietly about shunt bars and contact arms. By midafternoon, in a haze of fatigue, he began to have wavering images of elevator cars and shafts bending and twisting over the Leipzig skyline. He no longer could tell truth from falsehood or more accurately, he no longer cared. Father's mild questioning and his mumbled, cloudy responses had the texture of fevered dreams. Yet deep down rested the belief that this whole ridiculous elevator sequence was a diversion designed to lure him into a false sense of security. Any moment now the questions about the abortive escape of Gisela Steinbrecher would begin, shattering his dreamlike trance and driving him toward a lengthy prison sentence. He sensed that he had lost, but he was beyond caring. If he did not sleep soon, he would collapse.

Mike was about to tell Father that he had reached the limits of endurance when the interrogator leaned back in his swivel chair, made a chapel of his fingers, and subjected Mike to a long, contemplative study.

"Herr Simmons, I think we've gone about as far as we can go." Again he gazed at Mike for some time. "What are your thoughts about this interrogation?"

"Unless I'm missing something, I can't see the point of all that elevator stuff." His head felt woolly and he wondered if he made sense. "I know one thing. I've told you the truth about everything you brought up."

"Hmm." Father switched off the tape recorder and slowly gathered up the tools of his craft. "I'll be back later. Make yourself as comfortable as you can."

The moment the door closed, Mike slipped to the floor and stretched out. He welcomed the thin, worn carpet as he might a luxurious bed with sheets of satin. At once he drifted into the twilight zone, surrendering to his exhaustion with a feeling of bliss. Even the shapes of monsters, outriders of the terror that swept so many of his nights, could not alarm him now. His muscles yearned for peace and within a minute he had fallen into a pit of sleep.

A voice called from far away, a hand pressed his shoulder, and he came up slowly from the depths. When he opened his eyes, he saw Father bending over him.

"Time to get up." His voice had a soothing quality.

Mike raised himself, straightened up on weakened legs, rubbed his eyes, and looked about. Above the painted half of the window he could see that darkness had come. Father seated himself in the swivel chair and motioned Mike to his old interrogation seat.

"How long did I sleep?"

"Several hours. Are you refreshed?"

"Hardly. I feel drugged. I could sleep for a week."

"You'll have the chance." Father smiled. He seemed pleased. "You are being released."

Mike blinked. "You mean right now? Just like that?" He had expected anything but this. He tried to adjust to the idea of freedom.

"Yes. I'm afraid, Herr Simmons, a mistake has been made. On behalf of the Ministry and the DDR, I wish to apologize to you."

Mike noted that Father had not brought the tape recorder back with him. "Thanks." He sneezed and Father held out a tissue. "Thanks again." Then he thought of his ordeal in the freezer room. "But for what happened last night, no thanks. That iceberg treatment was intentional."

"Another regrettable error. I trust that you won't think too severely of us, Herr Simmons. In all societies, miscalculations are made. We think our system is superior, of course, but we are human and thus not error-proof."

"I don't blame you personally." Whatever happened to Gisela? Had she not been seized after all? Mike wanted to leave at once, yet his curiosity demanded satisfaction, too. "Why did your people pick me up and why these hours and hours of questioning?"

"I'm sorry." Father raised his palms in a gesture that absolved himself of responsibility. "At my level I take orders and do my duty."

"I understand." Mike had no grudge against this man. He had behaved decently. Under other circumstances . . . "May I leave now?"

"You may." Father stood up and extended his hand. Mike shook it. "We will drive you back to Leipzig."

Leipzig? . . . No, no. He had a sudden, overpowering desire to quit East Germany immediately, to break across the border and never come back. "I would rather be taken to Checkpoint Charlie. I finished my elevator work yesterday, as you know from your questioning."

"But your clothes and other belongings in Leipzig, Herr Simmons?"

"I'll have Sven Alsten send them to me. I prefer to leave the DDR tonight." He had a change of clothes in the suitcase at the Alsterhof, but he would cross the border now if not a single article of clothing awaited him. He had an all-consuming need to reach the other side without another hour's delay.

"As you wish. Follow me, please."

Father led him down the long corridor of the flaking green walls that smelled of disinfectant. At the cage, the bored clerk in the faded sweater traded Mike his wallet, passport, and wrist watch for a signed receipt. He insisted that Mike count his money. It was all there, to the Pfennig, but Mike would have signed if all of it had been filched.

In the dimly lit vestibule Father turned Mike over to two broad-shouldered young men. He gripped his hand in parting.

"A pleasant journey, Herr Simmons."

"Thanks." He felt oddly touched to leave Father in this gloomy temple of insecurity. "Good luck to you."

Again two men assisted him into the back seat of an automobile, although more politely than twenty-four hours earlier. This time the guards fitted him with wrap-around painted glasses that sealed off all side vision. They rode for some time, but from the sounds outside the car, Mike had the impression that they were merely driving around East Berlin.

When the car halted after some forty minutes of driving and his glasses were removed, Mike saw that they were on Friedrichstrasse near Checkpoint Charlie, that cluster of temporary metal huts that comprised the famous passage-way between two worlds. One of the agents accompanied Mike through passport, customs, and currency controls and his advices, spoken in low tones to the officials on duty, sped Mike through the complex almost as fast as he could walk.

He glanced at his wrist watch as he crossed the broad white line that split the two Germanies. Nine-thirteen.

A moment later, an American soldier looked away from the closed-circuit television screen that monitored the checkpoint area. "Hey, Sarge," he called to the ranking noncom in the control shack, "get a load of that freak! Walking through here at night in weather that'd freeze your balls—in nothin' but one of them silly jogger suits."

At the corner of Kochstrasse, Mike hailed a taxi. Once inside, a fit of shivering and sneezing laid hold of him. And yet these first moments west of the Wall were, he knew, among the best of his life.

10

Like West Berlin itself, he lived as if by mirrors, remote from home turf, marooned on alien soil, dependent on strangers, a hostage of new obsessions and old torments.

After that first euphoric hour following his latest and, he vowed, last crossing from the other Germany, Mike had slept for fifteen hours. Awakening in midafternoon at the Alsterhof, not far from the city's center, he found himself with a running cold, stiff joints, and a touch of fever. He managed brief calls to Walt Delaney and to his son, Dave, in Fulda before dropping into another fitful sleep. He spent the next three days in bed, nursing his cold and speculating endlessly on the two questions that now absorbed his thoughts. Where, how, and in what danger was Gisela? Why had the Stasi arrested and quizzed him at such length only to free him abruptly without charges?

He went over his speculations once again when Walter Delaney came to visit the evening of the third day, bringing him the latest edition of *Elevator World*, the trade journal. The worst of the cold had passed, but Mike remained propped in bed, with fruit juices, water, aspirin, cold tablets, tea bags, and magazines cluttering the small bedside

table. Outdoors a winter wind whipped at the trees framing
Würzburger Strasse.

"I told New York you had a little brush with the police
over there." The big man spilled over the room's lone easy
chair. His cynic's face had a crafty look, his two-of-us-
against-the-venal-world expression that Mike had seen so
often. "Nothing much, I said. Still, I told Jacoby you probably wouldn't want to go back. They're sending over a replacement to tidy up the last-minute stuff. He'll fly in here
after the holidays so you can brief him on which assholes to
avoid in Leipzig."

"Thanks, Walt. I'm sorry I couldn't level with you when
I came through here from Fulda the other day. I'm leery of
phones."

"With reason. I figured your woman had something to do
with that shoot-out down there. Right?"

"Right." Mike told his fellow Todd executive the entire
story. Trusting Delaney thoroughly, he spared few details
because he valued the canny salesman's appraisal of people in general, Communist variety in particular. Delaney
smoked three cigarettes through the long account.

"Sounds to me like they had you in SSD headquarters in
Berlin-Lichtenberg," he said when Mike finished. The dark
pouches beneath his eyes evoked images of an old, weary
lizard. "That three-way whipsawing they did on you is routine stuff. First, the orderly, Germanic accountant, then
Peeled Radish bully boy, and finally the understanding pa-
ternal type." He laughed harshly. "Those fuckers!"

"But how do you figure it, Walt?" Mike sipped at his orange juice. "The heavy questioning and freezer treatment,
then suddenly, oops, pardon us, all a big mistake."

"Christ knows." Delaney thrust out his legs and shoved
his hands in his pockets. "Maybe they honestly suspected
you might be CIA. Why not? You have a good job for
cover, you hang around Leipzig for a month, then suddenly

make a couple of fast trips West soon after you spend a night with some East Bloc biggies. Also your tail reports you taking suspicious walks at night. Looked at from their viewpoint, it makes sense."

"I suppose so. But what a way to check me out."

"That's the system. Now you know." Delaney fired another cigarette, inhaled, and shot a smoky shaft toward the window. Night had closed in and the wind had died. "But my guess is that you were a pawn in some inside party fight. If that's on target, it explains the Werner Lanz and elevator questions. You're right. That was real horse-shit, nickel-and-dime stuff—unless it involved a fight for power. Suppose a Politburo big shot opposed giving an American company a subcontract on a big hotel with high visibility? And somebody else favored it? So Herr Opposed gets you picked up and passes the word to make you look as bad as possible. . . . But that's just guesswork. Who the hell knows?"

"I figure if they'd connected me to Gisela's escape try, they'd have poured it to me."

"Absolutely. You'd have had a grilling that would rattle your teeth. What's more they'd send you to prison for a long stretch. . . . So, as of now, they have no idea of your real connection with Frau Steinbrecher."

"And you think that means she's safe?"

"I do. If Gisela had been under arrest, they'd have nailed you in a hurry."

They speculated some more, talked company business, family, and health, then returned to the subject of Gisela.

"You'll have a couple of weeks around here, Mike. What do you figure on doing about her?"

"I'm wondering whether to get in touch with the commercial escape people." Mike eased out of bed, went to the closet, and rummaged in the suitcase that held his extra clothes, copy of the elevator code, Gisela's fat letter to the American carbon-dioxide specialists, and a notebook listing, among other items, three *Fluchthelfer* contacts given him by Delaney. Returning to bed, he read off the three names. "Which do you recommend?"

"Wolfgang Dahlem, no question," said Delaney in his raspy, emphatic way. "He's to the escape business what Spider Butler is to the Wall. He's been at it twenty years, ever since the Wall went up. He helped the famous Harry Seidel dig one of the first tunnels and later set up his business for hire."

"How can we be sure the Stasi hasn't infiltrated his outfit?"

"His success. My source tells me Dahlem has had seven straight deliveries without a miss. He's so good, the East Germans have tried twice to assassinate him."

Mike looked at his notes. "What would I do? Just call this number you gave me?"

"Yeah. And be ready to fork over thirty grand to Dahlem and his Fluchthelfer crew. He's the deluxe outfit, you know." Delaney stood up and grinned down at Mike. "Of course, with your winning touch, that's no problem. It must be great to be so shitty rich."

"Look who's talking. You make that much on one commission."

"No more, sonny boy. America's a colony these days, owned jointly by the Arabs, Japanese, Germans, and minor thieves. Our money doesn't talk anymore. It whispers. . . . Well, beat that cold and let me know how you make out with Dahlem."

"If I go that route. I'm just not sure yet."

The next morning, awakened by streaming sunlight, Mike felt immeasurably better. So much so that he started the day with an easy jog around the block, his first exercise since the Leipzig run startled the agent of the clay-colored raincoat. Bright and windless, with a sky that held only small floating clouds, this December day offered moderate temperatures in the forties.

After breakfast he set off for an outing, trusting that by the time he returned, he would know what to do about Gisela, less by purposeful decision than by hunch, osmosis, and absorption as was his custom. First he walked to the huge nearby Ka-De-We department store, pushed through the crowds of Christmas shoppers, and hurriedly bought himself a topcoat to replace the snug sheepskin left behind in Leipzig. Pushing upstream through incoming customers toward the exit, he thought how Gisela, with her yearning for new fashions, would love to lose herself in this consumer maze with its lavish displays and overflowing banks of luxury goods. He thought of how she looked that last night in Leipzig, tucked in Ulli Beitz's bed with her corn-colored hair fanning over the pillow.

He turned toward Kurfürstendamm, threaded through throngs of bustling, well-dressed Berliners, window-shopped in the ground-floor stores of the towering Europa Center, and stared up at the shattered steeple of the Kaiser Wilhelm Memorial Church, one of West Berlin's few remaining reminders of the city's devastation in World War II. He sauntered along Ku'damm, jammed curb to curb with vehicles, past the stores, theaters, and glass-enclosed sidewalk restaurants. Today, under the flooding sunshine, brash Berlin crackled and brayed in its freakish, yet always defiant, isolation.

But Michael Simmons soon realized that his mind kept wandering far from the staccato music of the city. He thought of Gisela and of the Wall that barred her from this thriving island, and before long he found himself boarding a bus and traveling to the Brandenburg Gate where so many of the early confrontations over the Wall took place.

There he mounted the stairs of a tall wooden platform and like tens of thousands of tourists before him, he looked down on the concrete blocks of the Wall. A few yards beyond, in East Berlin territory, stood the massive Brandenburg Gate, its stone columns framing five passageways for Unter den Linden, once one of Europe's most beautiful boulevards. Now the Wall garroted the graceful old avenue like an executioner's collar, draining life from both Berlins and leaving the thoroughfare near the Wall with a seedy, melancholy air. On this side the ruptured boulevard had been renamed Strasse des 17. Juni in memory of the 1953 uprising of East German workers which the Russian Army crushed with tanks and machine guns.

On the other side Unter den Linden now stretched between files of monotonous government buildings, including the blocklong Soviet embassy, that serviced the capital of East Germany. Mike stayed for an hour near the two-century-old gateway monument, looking down on the denuded plaza from several wooden platforms that abutted the Wall. Pairs of Grepos in their stone-gray uniforms, rifles slung from shoulders, patrolled the East German side, reminding Mike that somewhere out there other agents of the state had held him for the longest hours of his life. The recollection went through him like a deep shiver and he knew that no mission, no matter how safe or how lucrative, could ever lure him beyond the Wall again. He did not hate the regime, that miniature clone of the Soviet Union, nor from this vantage point today did he fear it. Rather it filled him with sadness, just as the quiet of many East German crowds had resonated with some somber chamber within him.

Mike strolled along the Wall to the nearby reconstructed Reichstag, home of the old Germany's fire-gutted parliament which Russian shells and Allied bombs had blasted in World War II. He followed the Wall until it leaped across the Spree River where it prevented escape-minded East Germans from diving into the water and swimming to this side.

The Wall, he realized once more, had a powerful if perplexing attraction for him. Though deadly gray, a long, ashen scar on the landscape, the Wall nevertheless taunted him like a living person. In defeating it, besting it, outwitting it, he might somehow disperse those images of childhood walls and overcome his private terrors, those shapeless ghouls that scattered witches' dust through so many nights.

He took a cab to Bernauer Strasse, the most infamous of the Wall-sundered streets, and on the way he began wondering how to raise thirty thousand dollars in cash. Should he sell the lot in Omaha, liquidate his stocks, or close out the two savings accounts? Whatever he did, hiring professional escape specialists would drain a third of the savings he had accumulated since his divorce. He pondered the implication of his thoughts. Had he indeed decided to spend thirty thousand in a second effort to help Gisela flee her homeland? And would he invest the money to free a warm, loving woman or rather to win his private struggle against an opaque, soulless barrier of concrete?

He spent several hours on Bernauer Strasse, the divided street where hundreds of Berliners leaped from apartment windows to freedom in the first days of the Wall back in August 1961. A few also leaped to their death and markers now commemorated them by name. Long ago, East German demolition squads dynamited the building from which the people jumped, leaving only stone facades, complete with bricked-up windows and doorways. Then in the summer of 1980, East German soldiers bulldozed the facades, erasing the last reminders of early heroism, and replaced the building fronts with prefabricated sections of the Wall. Brave young trees softened the street's grim visage on the western side, but to the east, behind the new Wall, lay the inevitable death strip: plowed ground, minefields, light poles, concrete watchtowers with gun slits, patrol runways, slanted cemented slabs that from a distance looked like

gravestones in a military cemetery. For all of its contention
that, of the two Germanies, the Federal Republic remained
more securely shackled to its bestial Nazi past, the DDR
was the one whose lethal barriers offered the world a constant visual reminder of Hitler's extermination camps. Cou-
pled with the goose-stepping troops who paraded along
Unter den Linden on May Day, and other occasions when
East Germany showed its military muscle, the death strip
seemed almost intentionally calculated to fan fading memories of the demonic Nazi era.

Mike climbed the observation platforms, traded small
talk with tourists, brooded, strolled the mean street, thought
of Gisela, reflected on nuances of his interrogation by
Peeled Radish and Father, wondered where Todd Elevator
would send him next, and inspected the markers of those
whom the Wall had killed.

The bright sunlight had faded into dusk when he took a
bus through rush-hour traffic back to the center of the city
and then walked the few blocks to his hotel. He knew that
the matter was settled. Yes, he would spend what it took to
bring Gisela to the West she dreamed about—and to score
his own private victory over the Wall. He would call Wolfgang Dahlem's number.

Herr Kunze, the formal, ever-efficient Alsterhof reception
clerk, had now formed a rapport with Mike that included
smiles and chit-chat.

"You've become quite popular, sir, since your brief
illness." He handed Mike a message from his box. "Three
calls—and all from the same lady."

Mike unfolded the paper in the elevator: "Herr Simmons, please call Ingrid. 891-9055. Important."

When he called as soon as he reached his room, a
woman's voice answered after two rings.

"This is Mike Simmons," he said in German. "Someone
named Ingrid wished to speak to me."

"Oh yes, Mr. Simmons." She spoke slowly in English. "This is Ingrid. I have an important message for you." Her tone was guarded. "I think you will recognize the source. Quote: 'The hoist machine has been repaired and operates again in Dresden. Need new counterweight rails and hope you can lend pivot points through this supplier.'"

Gisela! At once the room filled with music.

"Can you hold the line a second?" He felt a surge of joy.

"Certainly."

He hurried to the closet, opened the suitcase, and found the duplicate of the elevator code, still resting between pages of his address book. Yes, as he'd thought. "Hoist machine" meant Gisela herself, "counterweight rails" signified an escape attempt, and "pivot points" equaled money. Sweet Gisela, breaker of stones, lady indomitable.

He picked up the phone again. "I want to talk to you as soon as possible. Where and when can we meet?"

"The Tano, a small *Kneipe* on Lietzenburger Strasse near Meineke Strasse. Can you come now?"

"Yes, sure."

"I will be in the last booth. I am wearing dark glasses and a black knit dress. My name you know—Ingrid."

"Right away."

He found the Tano after a short walk along Lietzenburger. A small, dark, smoky night spot that, like a hundred others in West Berlin, catered to lonely men with money to spend, the Tano had an intimate, three-sided bar tended by a buxom, vulpine blonde. Three women in skin-hugging gowns lolled at the bar and scrutinized Mike with quick, mercenary glances, then turned back to a stout customer in suit and tie who laughed loudly at his own joke. Full-length photographs of nude women, framed in red, covered the walls. A pornographic film in full color unrolled on a large screen to the accompaniment of grunts, moans, and exaggerated sighs. On a tiny stage in the corner, a young nude dancer practiced an erotic routine with lighted candles. No one paid the slightest attention to her or to the movie.

To reach the last booth, Mike turned a corner that isolated the table from the rest of the establishment. The brown-haired young woman sitting there wore a black dress, sunglasses, and a small, stylish, gold wrist watch.

"Ingrid?"

She inclined her head. "Please sit down." She spoke directly with no sexual overtones. "A drink?"

"Yes. A vodka on the rocks with a twist of lime."

She pressed a buzzer on the wall. One of the gowned hostesses took the order. Mike's swallow of vodka was his first taste of an alcoholic drink in a week. He and Ingrid wasted little time over the amenities.

"I suppose you know why I called you." Ingrid lowered her voice. "My group has been contacted by a person over there who wishes to leave. The person gave your name as one able and willing to pay our fee. Is that correct?"

"First, who is the person?"

Ingrid, toying with her drink, apparently measured him from behind her smoked glasses. After a time, she asked: "May I see your passport, please?"

Mike handed over the blue booklet with the smug golden eagle on its cover. She studied it carefully before returning it. "You work for the Todd Elevator company, is that right?"

"Yes."

"What references in Berlin can you give us?"

Mike could offer only two, Delaney and Herr Kunze at the Alsterhof, and he realized anew the extent of his isolation in this alien city, itself an international symbol of isolation. She questioned him about friends and business contacts in New York, inspected his credit cards, and inquired in some detail about his family.

"Our fees range from fifteen to thirty-five thousand

American dollars per head," she said at last, apparently satisfied. "The exact amount depends on many factors, including the number of people in the party and the difficulty of the job. The message to you spoke of a loan, but of course the principal on the other side has only a few marks now. Can you afford our terms?"

"That depends on the conditions. For instance, how much down?"

"We require five thousand dollars in cash, West German marks, upon agreement, the remainder upon safe arrival of the person on this side. If we fail to deliver, we refund your down payment."

"Fair enough. Then my answer is yes. I can manage it. . . . Now who is the person over there?"

"At this stage we never supply names. It is a woman, aged thirty-eight, blond, well-educated, with an intellectual job in Dresden. She gave us the name of your hotel and entrusted us with the message which, I assume, is in code. Does that satisfy you as to her identity?"

"Yes."

"Are you ready to enter into an agreement with us?"

"First I should check with a friend. I had intended to call a service like yours this evening. My friend recommended one that he said is superior to the others."

"Did he give you a name?"

Mike bobbed his head.

"Was it Wolfgang Dahlem?"

"That's it."

"I represent Herr Dahlem." She smiled broadly. "So, may I tell him you're ready to reach an understanding with us?"

"Please do."

"Wait here, please." She disappeared in the direction of the bar.

Mike sipped at his drink and waited. The inexhaustible

dialogue of grunts and groans, murmurs and moans signaled continuing heavy action in pornoland while a burst of male laughter gave notice that the well-fed businessman still enjoyed his own humor.

"Wolfgang will talk to you now if you're ready." Ingrid stood beside the table. "You walk up Lietzenburger Strasse a block and a half to Fasanenstrasse, turn right to No. 70. Take the elevator to the second floor. Wolfgang's in No. 2-A."

Mike reached for his wallet, but Ingrid put a hand on his sleeve. "No, the drinks are on us. In here I'm the only woman who pays. I'll leave now. You wait several minutes before you go."

A whistling wind vied with the roar of traffic as Mike walked along Lietzenburger. Clear night skies had followed the sunlit day, and the stars strewn so freely across the ebony dome shone with unusual clarity. He thought of strolling with Gisela arm-in-arm through nighttime Berlin, wondered where she was at this moment, and wished he could tell her how much he admired her courage for contacting the Dahlem people only a few days after her harrowing experience at the border.

He turned right into Fasanenstrasse, a quiet, tree-lined block between Lietzenburger and Ku'damm. No. 70 turned out to be a five-story apartment building with a stone facade bearing metal plaques for, among other things, a doctor's office and the Dante Society of Berlin. Mike made his way to No. 2-A. A stocky man with the build of a professional wrestler and wearing a turtleneck sweater answered the knock. Admitting Mike to a foyer of old stained wood, he frisked him thoroughly, then led him into a large room furnished in modern design with splashes of color. Mike had a quick impression of angles, indirect lighting, understated style, expensive craftsmanship, and colorful Mexican imports. Dahlem or someone close to him had sophisticated tastes. The strongman disappeared through a side door and soon the obvious head of the establishment entered and stood for a moment beside a rich brown wall hanging that featured a prowling yellow jaguar.

Tall, lean, marked discreetly with authority and class, the chief wore a sedate green tie and white shirt, green cardigan and neatly pressed trousers, all no doubt from fashionable houses.

"Good evening, Mr. Simmons. I'm Wolfgang Dahlem. Sorry we had to greet you the way we did. I'm sure you appreciate the need for precautions."

"No problem. What surprises me is your command of English. I wish I could reciprocate in German."

"I have four languages, more or less." Dahlem appeared to be in his late forties. "For our business, German would suffice, but I've been a language hobbyist ever since my undergraduate days at the Free University here."

They seated themselves on a couch of white corduroy heaped with brightly colored cushions. Mike declined the offer of a cigarette from an ivory box. Dahlem tapped one on his thumbnail and ignited it with a silver lighter.

"So, to business." Dahlem had not taken his eyes from Mike. They were a deep, probing blue. "A woman over there wants to come to the sunny side, as the East Germans sometimes call our Berlin. She contacted one of our people and indicated that you would underwrite the journey. Ingrid assures me that you're prepared to pay our regrettably substantial fee."

"That's right, subject to agreement with you on the exact terms."

"Of course." Dahlem spoke with cool detachment. "Mr. Simmons, I'm going to ask you a lot of questions. I dislike that, but you must understand that the SSD never quits trying to destroy our organization by infiltration, sabotage, and even murder. In this case, since the initial contact came over there from a party person who's been honored by the state, we have to be especially careful. It would be entirely possible for both you and Frau X in Dresden to be Stasi agents. That may seem fanciful to you, but not to us, believe me."

"It does strike me as ironic right now." Mike's half-laugh was a wry one. "You see, five nights ago the SSD picked me off the street in Leipzig, drove me to East Berlin, and spent about twenty hours grilling me."

"Oh." Dahlem riveted his attention. "I want to hear all about that, what they asked, who questioned, everything."

As he had with Walt Delaney, Mike recounted his hours with the accountant, Peeled Radish, and Father, then answered a spate of pointed questions from Dahlem. In all, they spent more than an hour discussing the episode. Then Dahlem probed at length into Mike's personal and business life and wound up asking him all about elevators, manufacture, sales, and installation. The master of the human escape business did it all dispassionately, with the precision and thoroughness of a surgeon.

When he finished, Dahlem at last took his eyes from Mike and gazed toward the hanging of the yellow jaguar. He reflected at length.

He turned back to Mike. "All right, Mr. Simmons, we'll go ahead. Because we're combining several parties this time, I can reduce your fee. The charge will be twenty-five thousand dollars."

"That's total, no extras?"

"Total. And that includes both, of course."

"Both?"

"Yes. The girl as well."

"What girl?" Had they, after all, been talking about two different Frau Xs in Dresden?

"Hilde, the daughter."

"Wait a minute, Mr. Dahlem, there's been some mistake

here." Mike was confused. "I'm talking about bringing across a woman who edits publications at the Technical University in Dresden."

"So am I." Dahlem smiled faintly. "Frau Gisela Steinbrecher, wife of a Karl Steinbrecher. Correct?"

"Yes, but . . ." Mike faltered. "Gisela has no daughter."

"Oh, but she does." Now Dahlem looked puzzled. "Hilde Steinbrecher, aged sixteen."

"You're positive?" Mike was dumbfounded. His mind raced back over discussions with Gisela about family. Had he missed a vital clue somewhere?

"Oh, yes. In cases like this, we insist on talking to the child as well. Should the daughter suddenly decide to stay with the father, well . . . some of our people might get killed."

"The girl's name is Hilde?" Mike struggled to accommodate himself to this radically altered picture. He felt a flash of resentment against Gisela.

"That's right. And Hilde is even more determined to escape than her mother is. The girl's infatuated with all things Western."

"She doesn't mind leaving her father?" He just could not adjust to the existence of a Hilde.

"Apparently she's not on good terms with him. They've had political disputes." He locked his eyes on Mike's once more. "Mr. Simmons, I've assumed an intimate relationship between you and Frau Steinbrecher. Yet you never heard of a daughter?"

"No." Mike shook his head. "I just don't understand. Gisela never mentioned a girl. She talked about a son who died, but not a word about a daughter."

Dahlem considered. "If this changes your attitude, you're perfectly at liberty to cancel out." The escape merchant's unwavering stare began to unnerve Mike. "I never force these things. Our business is too delicate. It can't withstand doubts and misgivings."

In a flashing image, Mike could see Gisela's look of terror when the border searchlights exposed her. Once again Mike sensed the strength of the bond fused between them in that harshly brilliant instant. He yearned to hold and comfort her, to let her know through voiceless caresses that he too died a little that night. And yet, she had deceived him.

"I'm not sure. I suppose Gisela felt"—he fumbled to explain and resented Gisela for forcing him to equivocate before this cold stranger—"that I might be less inclined to help if a daughter were involved."

"I think that's a fair conclusion. As I say, if you wish to withdraw, you may."

"I have other considerations." Mike had this secret commitment as well. To breach the Wall might exorcise those faceless brutes of the black hours.

"Perhaps you'd like to think it over until tomorrow?"

"Yes, I would."

"All right. But tell me, is there anything else we should know that would help us bring off a smooth passage in the event we decide to go ahead?"

Obviously Gisela had not mentioned to Dahlem's agent her abortive attempt to escape near Fulda. Had Hilde also crouched in the dark ravine that night, ready to follow her mother across? Whatever the case, Mike felt that he could disclose nothing. The unknown tangle of loyalties and fears over there prevented him from talking.

"I guess not. If I decide to proceed, I'll have to get money from New York. What's the schedule for paying?"

"The moment we receive five thousand dollars down, cash in marks, as Ingrid told you, we'll set the operation in motion. The remaining twenty thousand dollars payable upon delivery of the goods." His smile was faint, cool. "We always get prompt payment at the delivery site. You met Hans as you came in, didn't you?"

Mike assented absently, his mind on Gisela's daughter. What did she look like? Would she reject him, be sullen and withdrawn like some teenagers he knew? Pine for her father? Would they live together, all three? Questions teemed. The whole scene had changed.

Dahlem said something that Mike didn't catch. "What?"

"I said your American politics mystify me."

"Oh." Mike was not interested.

"Yes. For instance, I met Sam Wertheimer, the White House counsel to your President McCullough, when he visited Berlin several months ago. Unlike most politicians, he said very little about the Wall after seeing it. What kind of man is he?"

"You got me." Mike shrugged. "I don't know anybody at the White House. Politics is not my bag."

"In my business, politics is everything." The escape merchant arose. "So then, Mr. Simmons, I'll expect your call tomorrow." He escorted Mike to the foyer and held the door open. "Time's important now. I'm trying to combine another delivery with the Steinbrechers."

Steinbrechers? The plural form had a curious, unsettling impact. Suddenly any future with Gisela seemed immensely complicated.

The night air, growing colder, bit through his new topcoat. He longed for the old sheepskin hanging somewhere back in Leipzig.

He could not summon sleep until very late. His thoughts picked and nagged at this new and vexing shape. A pair had become a triangle. What hurt most was Gisela's refusal to trust him with the fact of her daughter, Hilde. Did Gisela assume that he would help her only if she came across alone? He went through a range of emotions as he lay sleepless in his hotel bed, resentment, pity, anger, compassion, dismay, but always he came back to Gisela herself. He might respect her courage and rue her distrust of him. He might sympathize with her contempt of police state methods and deplore her unwillingness to recognize the DDR's part in the slaughter of the Jews. He might admire her daring and dislike her Germanic insistence and force. But the fact was that whatever the character of Gisela Steinbrecher, he loved her.

When he awoke in the morning, his decision awoke with him. Daughter or no daughter, he wanted Gisela to come to the West. She was his woman. Together they would beat the Wall.

Wolfgang Dahlem took Mike's signal to go ahead without comment. He awaited only the down payment to put the escape plan into operation. Mike called his New York bank that afternoon.

11

Now came the flow of excitement as she sat before the beige computer console, watching the printed green lines unroll at the speed of thought. The feeling rose like a tide. Few sensations could surpass this one for pure pleasure. It almost matched that delicious frenzy on the edge of orgasm.

Carola Probst was being carried along on the rush of discovery. At any moment the computer, riffling effortlessly through its prodigious memory, might flip the magic key onto its display screen. She knew the familiar signs, the sudden hunch, the flash decision to link two hitherto seemingly unconnected events, the stroke of intuition that summoned a new image to mind. And she could instantly check out these intimations merely by punching the keyboard in front of her, thus triggering the computer's lightning-swift associations.

Few East Germans had heard of Carola Probst. No foreigners had ever heard of her. She was a soft-mannered brunette of nimble intelligence, mother of two children, devotee of opera and symphony, and a steadfast Lutheran, the faith shared by a majority of her fellow citizens. The central committee of the ruling Socialist Unity Party and the clubby managers of the SSD, the secret security police, knew chestnut-haired Frau Probst as a heroine of the DDR, a recent winner of the coveted Order of Karl Marx with an accompanying prize of twenty-five thousand marks, twice her annual salary.

She had earned the award by fingering Horst Wolgast of Cottbus as the notorious Federal Republic spy who had pierced the upper echelon of the SED and funneled state secrets to Bonn's policy-makers for almost a decade. Wolgast now served a lengthy prison sentence, thanks almost exclusively to the fact that Carola, fascinated by a puzzle with so many missing pieces, had come to the heavily guarded SSD computer room on one of her days off, a Sunday evening, and had played out her hunch on the console keyboard. She guessed that Wolgast had visited Vienna on the same two days that informants reported the secret trip there of Franz Rogge, deputy chief of the Federal Republic's BND intelligence agency. The computer confirmed her guess and that single fact forged the link that chained Wolgast inescapably to a charge of treason.

Just last month her intuition flagged the name of Uwe Wilcke, a middle-drawer bureaucrat in the Ministry of Mining and Metallurgy. When she asked the computer for its cathode-tube display on Wilcke, it showed that the official had been due back the previous day from a mining congress in Budapest. A call to the Ministry revealed that he had not, in fact, appeared at his desk. Nor was he at home. Carola urged her superior to alert the East German embassy in Hungary. He did so and eventually SSD agents apprehended Wilcke at Budapest's Ferihegy Airport, where he stood ready to board a flight to Rome with a forged West German passport.

Like many quick-witted, ambitious women, Carola Probst had enemies among her fellow male workers. Despite her soft, feminine approach and East Germany's constitutional guarantee of sexual equality, Frau Probst experienced unpleasant vibrations from a number of men who worked in the computer center, the most protected and security-conscious suite in SSD headquarters at Normannenstrasse 22 in the Lichtenberg district of East Berlin. The center's entrance, a thick steel door with a combination lock like a bank vault, bore the warning in red letters: NO ADMITTANCE, AUTHORIZED PERSONNEL ONLY. Carola's relationship with Heinz Lungwitz, chief of computer intelligence, was especially prickly. She divined long ago that Lungwitz, a short, bustling, drum-tight official, highly sensitive to political nuances, envied her and feared that she might get his job someday.

Lungwitz actually had forbidden Carola to set foot in the center this Christmas weekend. He had teased her about being a workaholic and had couched his injunction in playful terms, yet Carola knew he meant it. Nevertheless, here she was on Saturday afternoon, the Second Day of Christmas, sitting before No. 4 screen and keyboard with that feeling of exhilaration that she always experienced on the verge of discovery.

What fetched her back to this padded metal chair in the soundproofed, temperature-controlled room was her hunch about File AM-9374, the profile and time-place chart of Michael Ralph Simmons of New York City, as compiled from all official sources—border control, customs, informers, surveillance agents, SSD interrogators—with whom Simmons had knowingly or unknowingly come in contact.

File AM-9374 rested in the computer's taped memory as one of millions of similar biographical sketches and time-place records. No other marriage in history quite equaled in brilliant compatibility that between the totalitarian state and computer technology. They were made for each other. Like two insatiable lovers who harvest all of life to feed the maw of sex, governments and computers devoured entire citizenries in the name of security, a mythical condition that exists no more for nations than it does for individuals.

In East Germany the Staatssicherheitsdienst fed its computers the name of every East German who reached the age of fourteen, a point at which the citizen as a rite of passage acquired an identity card with picture, address, and school or job information. Thereafter, every time the person came in contact with the police, filled out a form, joined the FDJ, went through Youth Consecration ceremonies, graduated from school, took a job, married, had children, or acquired a passport, busy Stasi clerks added the item to his or her computerized file. Or should the person change address, get a pass to a border zone, visit someone more than twice or for more than three days, register in a distant Hausbuch, be reported by a gossipy neighbor or paid informer, draw surveillance or face interrogation, the personal computer file fattened accordingly. Thanks to the wedded harmony of state and computer, a man of fifty could be denied promotion solely because the computer, which had no reason to lie, divulged the bourgeois criticisms he had leveled at the state thirty years earlier while a university student.

Many years had passed since Carola Probst briefly weighed the ethical implications of this intimate alliance between state and computer. She was not, at any rate, a woman to ponder philosophical abstractions. She adored the computer, admiring its thoroughness, speed, infallibility, and its talent for solving the most arcane puzzles. And since on a practical level, she had the technical know-how to erase distressing data from files of self, family, and dear friends and thus felt no fear of the giant memory, she was always quite comfortable in this large, cheerful sanctuary with its year-round steady temperature and its banks of hooded consoles.

Right now she savored the unfolding results of her basic hunch—that the interest in the American, Michael Sim-

mons, lay not in his links to U.S.A. intelligence, if any, nor
in his squabble with Werner Lanz at the hotel construction
site in Leipzig. File AM-9374 showed that Simmons had
been seized at the suggestion of Russia's top KGB agent in
East Berlin, himself a nephew of Nikolai Varentsov, chief
of the Soviet Union, apparently with the sole intent to har-
ass the Americans in retaliation for subterranean U.S. support of rebellious Polish labor unions. Carola assumed that
the KGB man would have been as surprised as anyone had
the interrogation actually pinned a CIA label on Simmons.
No, the New York elevator executive was but a pawn in the
big East-West power game.

Of far more interest to Carola Probst was her guess that
Michael Simmons and Gisela Steinbrecher of Dresden had
more than a casual social acquaintance. Instead, she speculated that their alliance posed a possible threat to the security of the state. Just why and how she came up with that
hunch, Frau Probst could not say, any more than she could
say how she knew when her children were fibbing or how
she could distinguish one person from another. Exactly how
did one pick out a single human face from four billion
others? A matter of signs, hints, gestures, patterns of behavior and movement.

But Carola could trace the computer path that led to her
hunch. First she had noted a number of references to Gisela
Steinbrecher in File AM-9374. The informer, Inge Herschel, reported that she noted an unusual mutual attraction
in the meeting of Simmons with Frau Steinbrecher at dinner
in the Astoria dining salon the night of 26 November. The
two exchanged personal intimacies in Spanish, added the report of the Ministry of Culture official. The next night another informer, Hildegarde Gotsche, observed Simmons and
Steinbrecher in animated conversation in the Astoria lobby.
Several days later Frau Lotte Müller reported from Checkpoint Charlie currency control that the American M. R.

Simmons had appeared frightened and confused when she mentioned the name of Gisela Steinbrecher. Finally the lengthy interrogation of Simmons by SSD Examiner Helmut Muhlendamm included four references to Gisela Steinbrecher. Each time Muhlendamm mentioned the woman, the American's answers came out suspiciously concise, direct, clear. Carola imagined that behind the green lines of interrogation dialogue on the computer screen, she could hear steeled, rehearsed responses by the American.

She spent an hour perusing the long and chiefly laudatory File D-841 260, that of Gisela Steinbrecher, a model Young Pioneer, leader of Freie Deutsche Jugend, an officer of the student wing of the SED party while attending the Technical University at Dresden, doctor of chemistry, holder of the Star of People's Friendship Award, member of SED, prospective candidate for the People's Chamber, the national legislature, wife of Karl Steinbrecher, an SED reliable, and sister of Frauke Augstein, a relative by marriage of the chief of state, Heinrich Volpe.

One section of File D-841 260 piqued Carola's interest. A programmer had stored in the computer's memory the verbatim tape-recorded interview of Gisela Steinbrecher by SSD agents investigating the case of Otto Kleist, Technical University, Dresden, who did unauthorized research on rising levels of carbon dioxide and whom the state now held in house arrest at his home in Weisser Hirsch. Carola thought it naive of the agents and their superiors to accept at face value Frau Steinbrecher's plea that Kleist's calculations and reasoning were too complicated for her to understand and that she polished the professor's manuscript with only cursory attention to the substance of his research. Could a skilled technical editor and doctor of chemistry rework a scientific text without a fairly good comprehension of the contents? Frau Probst thought that highly unlikely and she viewed Gisela Steinbrecher with mounting suspicion.

But it was when Carola compared the recent movements of Steinbrecher and Michael Simmons, as reported by various sources, that her pulse quickened and the excitement began to rise. She saw that Simmons in early December crossed to West Berlin for the second time within a week, according to two informers, Lark and Sparrow. On 8 and 9 December he was reported in Fulda, West Germany, where his son served in a U.S.A. tank regiment on the border. On Sunday, 6 December, Gisela Steinbrecher left her home in Dresden and with her daughter, Hilde, traveled to Kaltennordheim where their border passes were validated by the Grenztruppen. Late Tuesday night, 8 December, an officer of the Kaltennordheim police, calling at the home of Frauke Augstein while investigating a "border incident," reported that both Gisela and Hilde Steinbrecher were in residence and that Gisela was incapacitated with a cold.

Carola mused on the fact that for at least two days in early December, Gisela Steinbrecher and Michael Simmons, those casual intimates, resided only a few miles apart, she in Kaltennordheim in the DDR, he in Fulda in the Federal Republic.

Officer Noske's mention in his report of a "border incident" near Kaltennordheim triggered Carola's memory. Hadn't a shooting of some kind occurred on the frontier near there about that time? She tapped out the numbers 0-8-7-2-0-3 on the keyboard, summoning to the screen all border episodes for the month of December to date. Yes, yes. There it was:

"Kaltennordheim, Tuesday, 8 December, 1917 hours. A few hundred meters from Melpers near here, a female illegal tried to cross frontier at point under construction. Turned back by personnel carrier machine-gun rounds which in turn took enemy rifle fire from across the border. No casualties. Female illegal, thought to be accompanied by female juvenile, escaped. Protest made to Bonn on enemy fire."

Frau Probst erased the border episodes and recalled Gisela Steinbrecher's time-place chart to the screen. Now she noted that Officer Noske had not questioned Frau Steinbrecher. Could that "cold" have been an injury inflicted by machine-gun fire? Strange that the Steinbrecher woman should be "incapacitated" in a home only a few miles from the attempted criminal border crossing.

Carola thought for several minutes, then phoned her superior, Heinz Lungwitz, at home on the classified, scrambled line. After an exchange of holiday greetings, she revealed that she had defied his orders and come to the center on a hunch. He scolded her, more biting than bantering, but she endured it patiently, secure in the knowledge that the party would never discipline a comrade so dedicated that she insisted on working on a holiday weekend.

"Does the name Gisela Steinbrecher mean anything to you, *Herr Direktor?*" she asked when they had exhausted the preliminary sparring.

"Steinbrecher." He thought in silence. "Isn't she an editor in Dresden?"

"That's the one. Received the Star of People's Friendship."

"Yes, now I place her. Top editor at the Technical University, *nicht wahr?*"

"Correct. Herr Lungwitz, I think Frau Steinbrecher should be summoned for interrogation. I have reason to believe that she tried to leave the DDR in a criminal manner with the assistance of an American, Michael R. Simmons, and perhaps with the help of his son who's with an American tank regiment in Fulda." Carola told of her supposition and computer research.

"Read me Steinbrecher's dossier." Lungwitz, who had spent thirty years maneuvering in top party brackets, always proceeded with caution. After listening to the readout, he said: "As I thought. Her sister is related by marriage to the chairman."

"A remote connection," Carola replied with a sniff of disdain. She regarded her superior as a shrewd operator of minuscule courage.

"Still, a matter for consideration."

"I think Steinbrecher's story to our investigators in the Otto Kleist case was highly improbable. If you had the time to read her answers, Herr Direktor, I'm sure you'd reach the same conclusion."

He thought in silence for a time. "You must grant, Frau Probst, that your whole premise rests on little more than coincidence."

"But if my suspicion is correct," she insisted, "one could uncover the weaknesses of the interrogation section. How could Interrogation ever explain its failure to apprehend the executive Simmons as a criminal Fluchthelfer?"

"True." Lungwitz's chuckle of appreciation had an anxious tremor. The thought of humbling his arrogant rival, the chief of interrogation, both titillated and alarmed him.

"I'm firmly convinced that I'm on the right track, Herr Direktor."

Lungwitz stalled. "If only you had more examples to support your theory."

"Actually, we have fewer missing pieces now than we had in the Wolgast case." Carola knew her use of "we" would cater to Lungwitz's belief that he too deserved the Order of Karl Marx for the Wolgast coup. After all, he had risked his future in ordering the arrest of a man so highly placed in the party.

"About that sister of the Steinbrecher woman. Exactly what is her husband's relationship to the chairman?"

"Dr. Augstein is a cousin of Chairman Volpe, which places Gisela Steinbrecher at quite some distance. . . .

Look, Herr Direktor, we both know this is a gamble, but the odds are heavily in our favor. I feel that in my bones. No great advance is made without some risk, to quote Chairman Volpe." Carola operated on the premise that if a man was basically insecure, the best ploy was to challenge his manhood directly.

"I'll give serious consideration to the detention of Frau Steinbrecher. You have my word on that, Frau Probst."

"I advise an early decision."

"Yes. If I decide to act, I'll issue orders for her apprehension tonight."

"A subsidiary matter, Herr Direktor. The interrogation of the American Simmons indicates that Werner Lanz, brigade leader at the new Inter hotel construction in Leipzig, is an avid reader of the contraband Western press. Interrogation failed to follow up this lead. I recommend that you call Werner Lanz for questioning."

"I'll do that Monday. . . . And now, Frau Probst, switch off the computer and leave the center immediately. You are commanded to enjoy the rest of the holiday. And you must not come in after church tomorrow. That's an order."

"Jawohl, Herr Direktor."

Ten minutes later Carola Probst closed the heavy steel doors with the red letters spelling out the room's high-security status. She left with a spring to her stride and a glow that suffused her whole being. Oh, discovery, how enchanting your charms!

About midnight that Second Day of Christmas, the chief SSD duty officer telephoned Heinz Lungwitz at his home in the select Pankow residential neighborhood where so many middle-bracket party officials lived.

The duty officer reported that the two agents called, as ordered, at the Dresden apartment of Karl and Gisela Steinbrecher. The husband, Karl, a party member, said that his wife and daughter, Hilde, had gone to the Film Theater on Prager Strasse for a matinee movie. Karl had expected them home by 6 P.M. and had prepared the evening meal for them as was his custom on Saturday nights. But they had not returned by 9:25 P.M. when the agents called.

With the help of Karl Steinbrecher, the agents searched the apartment and found that Hilde apparently had taken a small, gold-encrusted jewel box, a legacy from her grandmother, from her top bureau drawer and that Gisela probably had taken a silver brooch, also a family heirloom, that ordinarily was attached to a pincushion resting on her dresser. Karl said that his wife never wore the brooch except on occasions requiring formal attire. Neither mother nor daughter had returned to the apartment by the time the agents left at eleven-thirty to make their report.

Soon after midnight, on the orders of Director Heinz Lungwitz, chief of computer intelligence, the SSD duty officer broadcast an alert to all police, military, and SSD units, giving descriptions of the two Steinbrecher women and ordering their arrest for questioning.

12

On the evening of the Second Day of Christmas, just as Carola Probst was telephoning her SSD superior to urge the apprehension of Frau Steinbrecher, Gisela and her daughter, Hilde, walked with special caution along Sidonien Strasse in central Dresden.

Darkness had fallen, blanketing the monuments, plazas, and malls and the square, graceless buildings that had risen from the bomb craters and rubble of World War II. Dresden had managed to restore some of the stately facades that led prewar travelers to call it "Florence on the Elbe." But the city's core, where the two women found themselves, presented for the most part a solemn Communist profile that seemed to tolerate rather than welcome the people who wandered like midgets over the vast stretches of concrete or gazed at meager displays in the store windows.

Mother and daughter walked warily, with that feral tension brought on by the prospect of danger, because at five-thirty o'clock precisely they were to rendezvous with the professional escape guide who would try to spirit them out of East Germany. He had instructed them to meet him in front of an old building on the southwest corner of Leningrader and Sidonien streets. The building bore a red-and-white sign boasting of the ruling SED party's program: SERVICE TO THE PEOPLE. "A whim of mine," said the young escape technician. He always liked to start an operation under one of the regime's propaganda banners.

Now as the minutes clicked toward the appointed time when she and Hilde would leave their homeland forever, Gisela thought back over the tense, anxious days since she fled from the border near Kaltennordheim under the stutter of machine-gun fire. Almost three weeks had passed since that eerie night and now, as she and Hilde paced in front of the housing development on Sidonien Strasse, scene after scene flashed through her mind.

On the night she would never forget, that cold, rain-swept second Tuesday of December, Gisela and her daughter had moved in silence down the ragged ravine near the border hamlet of Melpers. The soft turf, cushioned by pine needles and wet leaves, felt springy underfoot and occasionally their street shoes squished in the mud. Fir boughs brushed damply against them. Water streamed down the trunks of the gaunt hardwoods. In the inky night, great clouds rolled eastward on gusts of wind. Mother and daughter edged forward cautiously, picking their way through shrubs and over scalloped terrain that neither had walked before.

They had reached the ravine after a soggy trek of somewhat more than a mile. Through the complicity of her sister, Frauke, Gisela had "stolen," then "abandoned," the Augstein family Trabant, a cozy arrangement made possible by Dr. Augstein's absence in Cuba. After leaving the car concealed in a grove of chestnuts and birches, Gisela and Hilde had walked along a narrow, wandering gravel road past the furrowed fields of a farm collective, then into the woods that covered flanks of the Rhön hills.

They came to the foot of the ravine a few minutes before the appointed time. Ahead they could see the construction machinery and tools that the border troops used to rebuild and refortify this section of the steel-mesh fence and its deadly accessories that stretched the length of the frontier between the two Germanies. They crouched behind two tree trunks, Hilde a few yards behind Gisela. The girl had wanted to crawl westward alongside her mother, but Gisela insisted that Hilde wait until she first had tested a few yards of no-man's land. Against the drumming of rain, faraway dogs began to bark.

When Gisela saw the Simmons' signal, two blinks of light, she immediately flopped to her belly and began to creep forward through the pouring rain. Hilde would follow after one minute. Gisela wore two old sweaters and a pair of paint-splotched slacks loaned her by Frauke. A torn blue stocking cap protected her head. She felt no fear. Rather a catlike vigilance tuned her body to a fine pitch.

Even when the searchlights lashed her like giant phosphorescent whips, she was not conscious of fear, only an instant of panic when she reared upward with that stricken look. The alarm tapped a tremendous gush of energy, permitting Gisela to act with the spontaneous reflexes of a hunted animal. She whipped around and crawled back toward the ravine just as a burst of sound, not unlike the punching of a pneumatic drill, assailed her. In the instant before she raised up to a standing position at the mouth of the gulley, something hit her left leg. It felt like the rap of a stick, followed by a stinging sensation on her lower calf.

Hilde too had risen to her feet and Gisela seized her daughter's hand. Together they rushed up the slanting gulley. Fir branches slapped at them, their clothes snagged on shrubs, and they tripped over rocks and rotting limbs. Twice they fell and scrambled to their feet. Now Gisela felt a flooding fear, but instead of paralyzing her, the fright buoyed her determination to elude whoever must certainly follow. Below to the west, she heard the sharp coughs of an automatic rifle, more machine-gun fire, some shouts, and a far-off howling of dogs. She and Hilde reached high ground, ran faster through the woods despite the unseen branches that stung their faces and the debris on the forest floor that caused them to stumble and fall once more.

They emerged from the woods after a frantic, staggering run of half a mile. To the left stretched the open fields of the state farm collective. On the right the gravel road meandered eastward to connect with a paved highway another half mile away. A line of poplar trees, tall and ghostly in the night's pelting rain, bordered the graveled surface. Gisela and Hilde hurried along, keeping close to the trees, ready to fling themselves to the ground should anyone appear. They fled in silent terror, the only sounds their heavy panting and the mud sucking at their shoes.

At last they reached the Trabant, partially hidden by the birches and chestnut trees. Gisela snatched open the driver's door and was about to get in when Hilde called in a stage whisper: "Mother, your leg's bleeding."

Gisela looked down. Blood had soaked through the slacks on her left leg a few inches above the ankle. She suddenly became aware of a painful throb. "No time for it now." She swept up a newspaper from the back seat, spread the sheets on the floorboard, fumbled for the ignition key beneath the seat, found it, and started the engine. Hilde climbed in beside her. Gisela eased the Trabant backward, careful not to spin the wheels and mire the car in the mud. After some awkward slippage, she managed to reach the gravel road.

After a short drive they came to the macadam surface. Kaltennordheim lay to the left, but Gisela turned right.

"Mother, where are you going?"

"Kaltennordheim," said Gisela. "But tires leave mud tracks. I'll go this way for a bit until the mud's gone."

She turned around after a few hundred yards and headed back toward the town, accelerating and pushing the old car to its limits. The chassis rattled and the headlights swept up and down as the car took crests and dips of the road like a cutter breasting the waves in a running sea. Gisela glanced repeatedly at the rear-view mirror while Hilde turned in her seat to monitor the road behind them.

"Headlights back of us," she said after a few minutes of travel on the rain-slick road.

"I know."

They drove in silence, Gisela hunched over the wheel with her foot pressing the gas pedal.

"They're gaining, Mother."

At a fork in the road, Gisela swerved right, away from Kaltennordheim, the car skidding dangerously. Several hundred yards farther, she turned into a dirt road, rolled for a distance, then braked the car and switched off lights and ignition. Soon a car rushed past on the macadam road in the direction the Steinbrechers had been traveling.

Gisela drove slowly back without lights and turned onto the surfaced road again. To their right they could see dim taillights growing smaller in the distance. When the red dots vanished, Gisela crawled along without lights until she reached the fork. After turning toward Kaltennordheim, she switched on the lights and pressed down on the accelerator.

"I think we lost them." Hilde broke a long silence in which the women acted as if even words spoken inside an automobile might somehow reach and alert their pursuers.

"When we turn into Aunt Frauke's," said Gisela, "you run into the house and strip off those wet clothes. I'll get rid of this newspaper. There's blood all over it."

The tightness in Gisela's chest failed to dissolve even when she turned into the driveway beside the old stone house with the red-tile roof. The home had belonged to generations of Augsteins reaching back almost two centuries, and even the upheavals of war and the Communist restructuring of society had failed to break the family grip on the property.

Frauke, a dumpling of a woman whose frenetic, disheveled manner hid a very practical intelligence, appeared at the back doorway the moment the car ground to a halt. She promptly sized up the situation.

"Quick, into the house. Get rid of your clothes fast. Are you all right?"

"Hilde is. I've been shot in the leg, but it's not bad." Frauke rushed to her sister's side as Gisela added: "There's some blood. We must burn these newspapers and slacks before the cops or Grepos come by."

A half hour later, in Frauke's firm opinion, not a sign of the abortive escape remained. The bloody newspapers and slacks had been consumed in the main stove where the blaze of a brown-coal fire heated the living room. Frauke had aired the house to rid it of the odor of burning fabric. She had also bundled the remainder of the sopping clothes worn by her two relatives and hidden them behind the coal bin in the basement. Gisela, in pajamas and with her lower left leg bandaged, had crawled into bed with hot tea and a book on the table beside her. Ostensibly she was nursing a cold and indeed after her ordeal in the rain, she found it quite easy to sneeze and snuffle.

Hilde, wearing dry jeans and an old sweater, bivouacked in front of the TV set which she had tuned to a West German musical show. She was a large, awkward girl with close-cropped brown hair who bore the old-fashioned name that the women of Gisela's family had passed down from generation to generation. She had just celebrated her sixteenth birthday, two years beyond her *Jugendweihe,* an East German ceremony in which maturing youth consecrates itself to an adulthood of responsible Communism. Beneath her passive exterior, Hilde seethed with slumbering passions. She loathed the Youth Consecration, the Wall, her membership in the Free German Youth, and her father's adherence to the "tiresome" SED line. She took pride in her country's world champion athletes, its standard of living, and its egalitarian aspirations. She liked her studies, the family's garden plot and shack in the country, her friends and her ripened breasts. She loved the West German TV shows, "Beat Club" and "Rock Pop," as well as Die Distel, East Berlin's cabaret where the regime tolerated mildly satirical skits at its expense. She adored Dresden's annual Dixieland festival when jazz bands from a score of countries, including the U.S.A., played for days along the Elbe. She relished the few contemporary novels from the West that a friend's grandparents managed to bring back from their travels. She doted on the West German film director, Rainer Werner Fassbinder, and the East German play about troubled youth, *The New Sorrows of Young W*. Someday the girl would outshine her mother's beauty, but the alternate spells of brooding and feverish rebellion that wracked her adolescence gave Hilde's features a cloudy, petulant cast.

The three women had rehearsed their lines while they cleansed and bathed Gisela's leg wound. The bullet had torn part of a muscle in the lower left calf, but Frieda thought Gisela might weather through without risking a visit to the doctor. Since it would be madness to consult a physician now anyway, they bandaged the wound and hoped for the best. They agreed on their story. Gisela had been in bed with a cold since her arrival in Kaltennordheim two days earlier. No one had been out of the house since early afternoon. Rather, because of the rain, they had read, gossiped, and watched TV.

"I can't shake my feeling of depression," said Gisela. "We were so close, just a few meters away from that blinking flashlight which probably was held by Michael. We almost made it, Hilde. I hate to face failure."

"Please, don't ever try again," said Frauke. "Next time it might be your life."

Hilde looked at her aunt with surprise. "Of course we'll try again." Her voice had the ring of resolution. "There are lots of ways to get across."

"But no easy one," said Gisela. "However, I'm afraid we have no choice since they're looking for us right now. If we don't escape, they will find us eventually. You know how thorough they are. . . . Still, my old optimism is gone. It will be very hard, I'm afraid."

Later while Frauke and Hilde were undressing for bed, Hilde called from the bathroom.

"Look out your window." Her tone was one of wondering delight. "You won't believe it."

Outside a soft, thick snowfall coated the driveway and covered the Trabant. Lights from the house shimmered on falling flakes. In another few minutes no one could tell when the car had last moved out of the driveway. Furthermore, the snow clinging to the Trabant's hood indicated that the heated engine of an hour earlier had cooled.

Frauke bounced into the spare bedroom and planted a kiss on Gisela's forehead. "Lucky one! You always were, you know."

Too keyed up to sleep, the three women went through the aborted escape once more, speculated on what went wrong, and debated what to do next. The more they talked, the less they felt like resting and so they were wide-awake when the long-expected knocking occurred sometime after midnight.

With an apprehensive glance at her sister and niece, Frauke threw on a bathrobe, hurried downstairs, and opened the front foor.

"*Ach*, Hugo! What a surprise. Do come in." The relief in her voice carried to the women upstairs.

Hugo Noske, long a familiar, not unsympathetic officer of the local *Volkspolizei*, stamped his feet and shook the snow off his cap. He stood diffidently just inside the door as white flakes melted into his green overcoat.

"Please sit down, Hugo. May I offer you coffee? Tea? Maybe a swallow of *schnapps* to warm you on this cold night?" They had known each other since Frauke came here fifteen years ago as Dr. Augstein's bride and Frau Noske had befriended the young stranger from Dresden. The Noskes were Sorbs, the only sizable minority in East Germany, and thus particularly sensitive to the problems of newcomers to a town.

"Nothing, please, Frauke." He squared his shoulders. "I'm here on official business, you understand."

"At this hour, what else? . . . What has happened?" She pumped alarm into her voice.

"An incident, no more . . ." He waved his hand dismissively. "But we must investigate, you know."

"Of course. Do sit down, please." Frauke fluttered about him.

"No, no. I would soil your furniture. . . . Who is in residence here now?" He took out pad and pencil.

"My sister, Gisela Steinbrecher, and her daughter, Hilde, from Dresden. Gisela's sick with a cold and has been in bed ever since she arrived the day before yesterday."

"And Dr. Augstein?"

"He's in Cuba on a health mission as you must know. He notified the police before he left."

"Ach, ja." Officer Noske made notes. "Now, Frauke, please describe to me your movements since three o'clock this afternoon."

"Movements?" She laughed gaily. "We haven't stirred out of the house, any of us, since noon because of the rain and later the snow."

"Your neighbors up the road, the Kellers, thought they saw your Trabant drive by a little after eight tonight."

In bed together upstairs and straining to hear, Gisela and Hilde exchanged anxious looks. Gisela pressed her daughter's hand. "I've always hated those Kellers," Hilde whispered.

"Must have been somebody else," said Frauke in an offhand, distracted manner. "The Trabant has not been moved out of the driveway today. . . . Look at it yourself, Hugo." She led him to the window and parted the curtains. "Does that look like a car that has traveled anywhere today?"

"Frauke!" Snow made a smooth, white mound of the vehicle and covered the yard and driveway like an endless sheet. Flakes still fluttered lazily downward. The officer smiled at his friend in mock reproof. "Who would know whether any car in Kaltennordheim had been moved before the snow?" He looked inquiringly toward the stairs. "Your sister and niece?"

"Both asleep upstairs. But naturally you are welcome to question them. We have nothing to hide here, Hugo."

"I do not suggest that you have." He frowned, looked about uncertainly. In addition to their friendship, Noske never forgot Dr. Dieter Augstein's family ties to the chief of state, Heinrich Volpe. "It won't be necessary to disturb them at this late hour."

"I might be of more help if I knew the nature of the . . ."

"Orders." Noske shook his head. "You understand. . . . So good night then, Frauke. I regret I had to bother you."

"Always a pleasure to see you, Hugo. Even at this hour."

Officer Noske tramped off through the snow, stepping carefully into his own footprints as if fearful of spoiling the great white mantle that sheathed all of Kaltennordheim with the hush of angels.

Gisela and Hilde did not sleep until the first light of

213

dawn plucked at their frosted window. Instead they planned. They resolved to renew their escape efforts as soon as possible. Waiting would only give the authorities time to piece together scraps of information that sooner or later would incriminate them. They must try to act quickly, but how?

"We must contact the Fluchthelfer," said Gisela at last. "I'm reluctant to do it, but that's the only way when one is desperate and in a hurry."

"But, Mother, they want a fortune."

"I know. But there may be a way. My American friend." Gisela had told her daughter about the meeting with Michael Simmons and his pledge to help her escape, but she had skirted the nature of their friendship. "Perhaps on the other side, Michael could put up the money as a loan to us."

"Oh, I'd work years, if need be, to pay him back." Hilde glowed. "Do you think he'd lend us the money?"

"I'm not sure. We can try."

"Does he love you?" Hilde studied her mother.

Gisela colored. "Perhaps, perhaps not. We've only known each other for a few hours."

"He does. I know he does." Hilde beamed. This year she alternately adored and scorned romance.

"Such matters aside, I will ask him through the Fluchthelfer."

"They say Wolfgang Dahlem is the best," said Hilde.

"And the most expensive, I hear."

"True, but the Dahlem people are the only ones I know how to contact."

"Through the woman at the Film Theater?"

"Yes, as I told you."

They had gone through these initial steps several times in joint fantasy after their first intimate talk when they shared a sudden, blinding realization that they both wanted to flee their country. While each had suspected the other's secret yearning, they could not be positive until they had surfaced that forbidden yet thrilling word, "escape." Then they understood, deeply and intuitively, that they both wanted to leave Karl, home, and country for motives so complex that neither could ever fully articulate them to the other. For months now they had been extremely close, a mother and daughter who vowed to flee together whatever the peril.

"We should go back to Dresden right away," said Hilde.

"If I can walk, dear. As soon as I'm able to travel."

Two days later Frauke drove them to Meiningen where they caught an early morning bus. Two transfers, which Gisela negotiated with a painful hobble, brought them to Karl Marx Stadt and then to Dresden where they took a streetcar home.

The Steinbrechers lived in a three-room flat in an apartment building the color of earth in a clean, proper, and very drab neighborhood in northern Dresden. Their fourth-floor apartment overlooked the Platz der Einheit and one of the many Soviet war memorials scattered through East Germany. This one depicted tanks and guns and a Russian soldier, like one of those who seized Dresden in 1945, with grenade rampant. On holidays Hilde and her friends watched as thin, pale, cigarette-smoking young soldiers from the many Russian bases in the area came with booted officers to pay homage to their Red Army predecessors.

The night of her return, Hilde boarded a streetcar in the Platz der Einheit and rode downtown. Just before the evening performance, she entered the deluxe Film Theater on Prager Strasse, the major pedestrian mall. She checked her coat at the counter in the lobby with the frail, gray-haired woman attendant. Hilde leaned close to her.

"I too remember the seventeenth of June."

"So." The woman bent her head, examining a metal check. "Who died that day?" The husky whisper curled with age.

"Freedom."

"Where does Goethe live today?"

"On the sunny side."

The old woman glanced sharply at Hilde after peering about to make sure they were still alone. "Tomorrow at five-thirty prompt, my child, you must go to the Volkspark Grosser Garten." She frowned over the numbered check. "There on Herkules Allee fifteen meters from the entrance to the *Puppentheater* stand two white benches with a stone receptacle between them. You must sit on the right-hand bench facing the greenhouse across the way. You will be addressed from behind an evergreen bush that grows near the bench. Answer, but do not look around. Five-thirty exact, on the bench."

She pressed the metal check into Hilde's hand and turned away. The coat-check matron was slight, faded, and careworn, and Hilde had remarked several times on the gentle, helpful manner with which she treated all patrons of the motion picture theater.

Gisela herself undertook the next day's mission. At five-thirty a fine evening mist screened the great park which lay not far from downtown Dresden and the River Elbe. Gisela entered the broad esplanade past twin statues of Hercules, one of which showed the mighty, legendary Greek clubbing a wild animal to death. The wary editor crossed tracks of the miniature railroad, which in summer carried thousands of children around the park, and walked half a mile along the wide gravel path. Leafless stands of beech, maple, and chestnut trees framed the foggy esplanade. In the dark, with the last glimmer of daylight gone, Gisela found the twin benches near the puppet theater and seated herself on the one that stood before the clump of evergreens. She had to wait only a few moments. When she heard the voice, she resisted the temptation to turn around.

"Where does Goethe live today?" A young voice, male, firm, friendly.

"On the sunny side."

"So, you wish to go over there?"

"Yes." She blurted the word, conscious that if this were a trap, agents of the state would seize her. Gisela waited in the soft mist. She could feel her wound pulsing.

"How many people?"

"Two. My daughter, who's sixteen, and myself."

"Relax. I have many questions to ask."

The inquiries were quite routine and predictable, designed to establish identities and character. Gisela's tension slowly eased. After gathering the biographical information, the voice explored the emotional ties between Karl Steinbrecher and mother and daughter. He said that no flight could be undertaken if there was even a slight chance that either woman would change her mind somewhere en route and demand to return home. Gisela assured the disembodied voice behind the bench that both Hilde and herself stood committed with no possibility of backing out.

"Now to the money," he said, apparently satisfied on the emotional plane. "Many people in this operation take great risks and must be recompensed. For two of you, we need one hundred sixty thousand East marks or forty thousand West marks."

"Our payment comes from my friend over there." Gisela named Michael Simmons and his residence at the Hotel Alsterhof in West Berlin. "But I must give you a message for him in our private code so that he knows it comes from me."

"Make it short, please."

She thought, then dictated from memory a brief message in the elevator code.

"Anything else you need to tell us?"

"Yes, one thing." She found this difficult to say. "Herr Simmons does not know that I have a daughter. You must tell him, nicely please, that two of us will cross. You see, I feared he might . . ."

"I understand, Frau Steinbrecher. So, we expect word in three days possibly. You must return to this bench at five-thirty on the fourteenth."

The next three days went slowly. Ulli Beitz called with a coded message from Michael, obviously written when he wondered whether or not she had been seriously injured. Now, back on the other side, how would he react to the news that she had a daughter who would cross with her? Would Miguel abandon her now because she had lied by omission? Why, indeed, hadn't she risked the truth with him? What was he thinking now? Would he pay the huge fee? On and on went the guilty speculation and the replaying of the mental tapes.

The wound healed slowly but steadily, the chief complication being Gisela's effort to keep the truth from Karl. She explained the bandage by saying she had fallen and bruised her leg while ailing with the flu at Frauke's house. Karl wanted her to see a doctor. She demurred and he did not insist. In fact, absorbed in his own academic work in the physics department and new additions to his stamp collection, Karl paid even less attention than usual to his wife and daughter.

On December 14, Gisela arrived promptly at the bench. The cold, clear air nipped at her as she stamped her feet and clapped her gloved hands. After a few moments the young male voice spoke again: "The operation is on. Your friend agreed to pay."

She hesitated. "For both?" A world hinged on the answer.

"Yes, for Hilde, too. So, we'll contact you when the time comes. It won't be many days now. Always be ready to leave within a few hours."

Mike's willingness to finance the twin escape evoked a new tenderness in Gisela, and she promised herself never to trim the truth with him again. That night she recalled the special moments of their times together at the Astoria and at Ulli's. But the days were charged with pain and anxiety. When Gisela returned to work after a few days, she removed the bandage and made every effort not to limp in order to avoid questions from her associates at the university. Both she and Hilde lived with growing tension, fearful that their thwarted escape at the border might be discovered at any time and afraid that they might let slip some phrase or sentiment that would arouse Karl's suspicion. Whenever the phone rang at home or office, Gisela answered at once only to feel disappointment when she failed to hear the voice of the escape manager.

When alone, mother and daughter often helped pass the time by doing English lessons from Hilde's schoolbook. Hilde had studied the language several years, frequently learned lyrics as sung by such British rock groups as the Vibrators and The Clash. But even as Gisela struggled to learn the difficult new tongue, the hours slowed down until time itself became unbearable. At any moment, she knew, agents of the state might knock at her door.

Then came Christmas, evoking sadness and guilt in both women. Karl gave each a handsome present, a small, portable stereo set for Hilde and a brightly colored shawl for Gisela. The shawl, he said, was an import from Ethiopia, made by "our brothers and sisters, the new Socialist cadres." Throughout Christmas day Karl, a pedantic, humorless man, became caught up in rare flashes of Yule spirit and devoted himself to his wife and daughter with such consideration and love that even Hilde, who rarely touched her father, embraced him with tears in her eyes.

"Has anything changed with you?" Gisela asked her later.

"No, but I will miss him. I can't stand his attitudes, but deep down I love him."

The long-awaited call came early the next morning, the

Second Day of Christmas, when the two women were eating breakfast and Karl still lounged in bed.

"The bench in one hour." Gisela felt an electric charge at the sound of the familiar young voice. "We leave this afternoon."

Gisela pulled on her warm winter coat, said she was going for a walk, and took a nearby streetcar to the Grosser Garten. The day was damp and chilly with a gray overcast. This time, as soon as she reached the bench, a young man appeared, sauntering from the direction of the puppet theater. Pale, with delicate features and a smile like a slashed purse, he wore a turtleneck sweater and black jacket. Pausing in front of the bench, he bent over to tie his shoelaces.

"We leave at five-thirty exactly this evening," he said in a strong, clear voice, but without looking up. "You and Hilde must be at the southwest corner of Leningrader Strasse and Sidonien Strasse at five-thirty. I drive a black Wartburg. When I stop, get into the car quickly. Bring no belongings except what you can carry in a coat pocket. Your ID, of course. Dress warmly. Repeat the time and place, please."

Gisela did so.

"Do you know that corner?" He kept bending over his shoelaces.

"Yes. It's not far from the Hauptbahnhof and Lenin Platz."

"That's it. Under a red-and-white SED sign." He told of his whim. "Until five-thirty then." He straightened up and strolled away.

Gisela and Hilde tried to be casual that afternoon about their departure, but out of sight of Karl they dressed with care: warm slacks, heavy sweaters, hip-length winter coats, gloves. Gisela shoved the old blue stocking cap in a pocket. Then Hilde slipped her grandmother's little gold jewel box into a coat pocket. At her dresser Gisela gazed down sadly at her sole personal possession of value, a century-old silver brooch. She pinned it on her sweater.

They told Karl they were going to the afternoon movie at the Film Theater, and they did go to the circular building that housed the plushly appointed cinema. They saw an excellent Hungarian film about slowly ebbing married love, but left early. Neither of them could concentrate on nuances of character development, and Hilde, very nervous, twice had to visit the women's toilet. After leaving the movie, they walked for an hour under steely skies until the gray day faded and darkness covered the chilled city.

They reached the appointed corner five minutes early, strolled with feigned insouciance a short distance down Sidonien Strasse, and then returned.

The black Wartburg rolled to the curb exactly on schedule. It pulled away promptly with Hilde in the back seat and Gisela beside the pale young man who now wore a fur hat, a thickly padded jacket, and gloves.

"My name's Erich," he said as he accelerated. "I'm going to leave the country myself and so I'll accompany you all the way, right into West Berlin." Mention of the city warmed Gisela like sudden sunshine. "After two years of this work, I'm hot. I constantly look over my shoulder now for fear the Stasi might be right behind me."

He chattered along with the unconcern of a schoolboy, yet with an undercurrent that denoted strength and reliability. Gisela felt a growing confidence in him as he gave a glimpse of the escape route ahead. They were taking the Autobahn north some one hundred miles to the outskirts of East Berlin. If stopped for a police check anywhere, they would say they were headed for the big holiday Lutheran Assembly being held in the capital of the nation that adroitly juggled the conflicting visions of God and Marx. Erich drilled them on aspects of the assembly and on a description of the fictional guesthouse where they would stay during the three-day meeting.

"If we're stopped," he said with his sardonic smile, "act casual, even a little bored."

They drove through the early winter night with the heat on full blast. In the darkness they saw very little of the countryside, only the lights of approaching and passing cars.

"How do you feel about leaving?" asked Hilde. She was experiencing a skirmish of emotions, pangs of regret along with tremendous leaps of elation. "Are there things or people you hate to give up?"

"Sure. I'm a diver. I trained on the same swimming team with Irma Reichenbach. Our outfit could beat any team in the world in a dual meet." Erich spoke with pride. "Also as a sports fan, I hate to leave the best collection of athletes anywhere. Figured per capita, we own the Olympics now. . . . How about you, Hilde?"

"Mostly, I guess, I regret leaving my friends." Her voice had a touch of sadness. "I'll have to find new ones and we don't even know yet where we're going, really. . . . But I'm not sorry to leave. I hate to live in a country where they keep us in like prisoners."

"Same here. If they blasted the Wall, blew up the mines, and bulldozed the fences, I'd never leave."

"Of course," said Gisela, "a government that would pull down the Wall would trust us with other freedoms, making it unnecessary to escape."

"Exactly so," said Erich.

On the outskirts of Berlin, where open fields gave way to the hundreds of gardens, tool sheds, and summer shanties of city residents, who tended vegetable plots in the warm months, Erich turned off the Autobahn and followed several winding roads.

"We're going to a shack where we meet our guide and

where we leave the car. After we've gone, the guide will drive the car into the city and abandon it in the street. Tomorrow the police will pick it up and begin to look for me."

"You mean you just sacrifice this car?" asked Gisela.

"Right. If we sell it or give it away to someone in the organization, it's too easy to trace. Very risky. So every now and then we get rid of equipment. That's what runs our price up, that and the pay of so many people."

"How many people does Dahlem have?" asked Hilde.

"If I knew," said Erich cheerfully, "I wouldn't tell you."

Erich drove with confidence, turning up a sparsely settled street, then branching off on a road that forked with another. Gisela began to feel that this time she and Hilde would make it, and she had just turned back toward Hilde for a word of reassurance when, without notice, a car drew abruptly alongside. A blue flashing light stroked the night. Police.

An officer in the green-and-white sedan motioned Erich to stop. The Vopo strolled over, inspected each person in turn, asked for the car's papers, and examined them at length. Then he scrutinized each ID card. Gisela tensed as she handed hers over. No questions, she implored silently, for her fear might make her croak like a frog.

"You say you're going to Strausberger Platz for the Lutheran Assembly?" Ruddy face above the gray-green tunic, the officer directed the question at Erich.

"That's right, *Herr Wachtmeister.*"

"Then why are you cruising around way out here in the summer gardens?"

"I'm lost."

The Vopo pushed back his Russian-style fur hat and leaned through the open window. "You came from Dresden on the Autobahn?"

"Yes."

"Why did you exit so soon?"

"We intended to pick up another passenger and take him over to the assembly."

"What's the name?"

"Rolf Viertel."

"Address?"

"Bukesweg 18. . . . He wasn't home."

"Wait here."

The officer strode back to his Wartburg sedan where a partner waited in the front seat. He unhooked a microphone from a dashboard fixture and spoke into it.

"Headquarters will confirm the address," said Erich in a low voice, "and we made sure that Viertel would be away until tomorrow."

"You're lucky." Gisela did not feel at all lucky. She watched the Vopo with dismay.

"No, no," said Erich. "I have four or five names like that in this area. Don't worry. When we plan, we plan in detail."

The officer returned. "All right, turn around and head back the other way."

"Herr Wachtmeister, could you please take the time to lead us to a street that heads toward Strausberger Platz? We would appreciate it."

"Follow me." The policeman got back in his car, made a U-turn, and drove down the road.

"Helps build trust in us," said Erich witn that smile that ran off the corner of his mouth.

The officer led them to a thoroughfare, pointed the way, and turned his police car south. Two minutes later Erich veered off on a side gravel road and headed back in the same direction they had traveled earlier. "We circle this time," he said.

"No more police, Erich, please," said Gisela. "My heart won't take it."

After a short distance on the graveled surface, Erich made a right turn onto a dirt road and switched off his headlights. The car moved forward slowly in the dark. Erich wiped the misted windshield, then rolled down his window and thrust his head out for better vision. Cold air washed over them. The temperature had dropped to near freezing. Gisela shivered. They traveled for several hundred yards. Finally, after dipping downward and climbing a small rise, Erich maneuvered the vehicle into a grassy lane, backed up, turned around, and halted.

"Follow me."

He led them along a path that wound through several fenced gardens that reminded Hilde, with sudden longing, of the family country plot near Dresden. The path ended at a wooden shack not unlike the one where Hilde had often played on summer days. Erich reached to a rafter of the overhanging roof, brought out a key, and unlocked the door. The windowless interior, darker than the night outside, gave off a medley of garden odors: manure, oil, chemical fertilizer, damp earth. Erich found some boxes for them and they sat together in total darkness.

"We're in the garden *Laube* of a sympathizer," he said in a low voice. "Soon our guide comes to lead us to the designated spot where we leave the DDR for good. The guide also brings a man who's escaping. So we'll be four people who go.

"Once we leave this place, absolutely no talking. I'll follow the guide, Gisela behind me, Hilde next, and then the new man. You do exactly as I do. When we reach our conveyance, we will have time to talk. . . . If all goes well, we ought to reach West Berlin by midnight. Free, *lieber Gott*. Well, as free as any of us ever gets in this life."

They sat quietly in the black cold, the only sound their own breathing. The damp ground chilled their feet and Gisela felt a sickly ache above the left ankle. She wondered if the wound had become infected.

They waited a full half hour before a rap sounded on the

225

door. A pause. Two more knocks. Erich opened the door and pulled at the women's sleeves, guiding them outside. There they saw two men, heavily bundled against the cold, faces indistinct in the moonless night. One stranger motioned with his head and took a path that led away from the hut. They all fell into line behind him.

They walked silently for a quarter of a mile, passing innumerable small plots, staked vines, fences, and shanties. In spring and summer this whole area would come to life as vegetables flourished and weekend farmers tilled, hoed, and spaded. Now a rising wind sighed at the bare limbs of hardwood trees and once, far away, they heard the hoot of an owl and the deep, distant rumble of a jet plane. Lights of the city glowed on the horizon. Soon Gisela saw a shimmer ahead. They had reached the banks of a waterway.

The guide dropped to a prone position and Erich motioned them to do likewise. They lay abreast on hard, stony ground, protected from view by a slope in front of them and the trunks of several trees to the rear.

Erich whispered to Gisela. "Pass the word. We're waiting for a boat to edge up to the bank. When it does, we must board within seconds. You must follow me exactly." Gisela relayed the message to Hilde who passed it on to the newcomer.

The minutes passed as if on crutches. Never had time seemed to go so slowly for Gisela. Her leg ached, the ground held a cold, harsh dampness, a freezing wind blew off the waterway, and not even the sweaters beneath her coat protected her from the deep chill that settled in her bones. She wanted to stand up, dance about. Instead she lay on her belly and tried to keep her teeth from chattering.

A patrol boat churned past, its engines pumping smoothly, its cabin darkened. Gisela could imagine marine border guards sweeping the shorelines with night-light devices. The patrol vessel vanished downstream around a bend in the waterway.

Soon red and green running lights appeared to the south, then winked off. In a few minutes an unlighted craft loomed near the shore. "Everyone ready," ordered the guide in a low, hoarse voice. The boat swung their way. They could see the stubby bow. The vessel slowed down, brushing the embankment.

Erich got to his feet in a low crouch and as the others copied his stance, he straightened up and leaped to the broad gunwale of the boat. Gisela too made the short jump, Hilde beside her. The stranger followed. They all stepped down, half-falling to the deck from the gunwale just as the shallow-draft boat veered away from the bank. It swung back to midstream and the running lights were switched on once more. Erich took a few steps forward, ducked into a hatch, and led them down a gangway. Gisela's leg throbbed with pain.

Once below decks, Erich switched on a flashlight, but cautioned them to silence with a finger at his lips. The shaft of light swept a few casks, cartons, coils of rope, and a litter of boards and torn bags of cement. Erich, with the others following, picked his way forward, stooping beneath the low overhead and fingering the woodwork above him. He studied several areas, then pressed his hands against one of the panels. It slid to one side, exposing an opening several feet square.

He handed the flashlight to Gisela. "Shine it up through there." He grasped the edges of the decking and pulled himself up. "Now you get a boost from Hilde." When all four had climbed into the compartment, Erich slid the panel back into place and fastened it with thumbscrews.

Looking about, Gisela saw that they were jammed together in what looked like a storage compartment about six feet high and only a few feet across. The four people had room to stand or to sit with knees drawn up, but had no space to move about in. A bucket of gravel stood in a corner.

"My name is Werner," said the stranger, blinking in the light. Short, intense, wary, he had odd, darting mannerisms.

Hilde and Gisela introduced themselves by first names. Erich and Werner apparently already knew each other. They all sank to a sitting position, closely crowded with knees touching.

"We might as well get used to this," said Erich. "It will take about five hours, barring unforeseen seizure or accident, before we leave the boat in West Berlin."

"Are we on the Spree?" asked Gisela.

"Right." Erich nodded. "Let me explain. This is a one-shot effort that can't be repeated for other escapers. This is an old scow, named the *Ernst Thälmann,* but it has a good diesel engine. It's mostly used for short cargo trips inside the city. Tonight we're taking a load of gravel for about forty kilometers, right through the middle of both Berlins, to a lock near the Spandau fortress. The gravel is to be used in repairs to the lock, but instead of dumping the load, all of us, led by the captain, are going to jump ship and bust through the chain link fence to freedom."

"The captain, too?" Hilde had long since lost her brooding look. She was wide-eyed and vigilant.

"The skipper especially. He's been planning this with us for weeks, waiting for just the right voyage, the one with the minimum of risk." Erich pointed overhead. "We've got fifty tons of gravel over us. Look, this storage cabin has steel beams to support the load. The gravel's about two meters deep all around us. When the DDR guards board us, they'll hear the sound of gravel everywhere—including right here."

With that he dumped the bucket. A river of small stones spread over the deck and came to rest around their feet and buttocks.

"Here's our route on the Spree." He pulled a map of the two Berlins from his pocket and spread it over the gravel which slid about with the motion of the boat. "We got aboard here along the Müggelspree."

The River Spree, which rises in the mountains along East Germany's southern border with Czechoslovakia, flows north and west for almost two hundred fifty miles before joining the broad Havel in the western section of West Berlin just below the Spandau lock. Nearby stands the ancient Spandau citadel, a fortress in medieval times. Navigable for ninety miles, including about thirty within the limits of the two Berlins, the Spree traces a serpentine route through the heart of the city. Parkland landscaping beautifies many miles of riverbank. The Spree connects with a number of canals so that in some areas docks and warehouses form the waterfront. Elsewhere the river's edge becomes the frontier between East and West. Here the Wall's brooding presence casts a shadow over the peaceful current, a fitting backdrop for the DDR gunboats that bustle about like snappish hounds.

Under the early Berlin accords, East German authorities gained control over road, rail, and water routes into the city, insuring their ability to choke off all surface access to West Berlin whenever they wished. With waterways and rails, the DDR actually operated facilities inside West Berlin as well. As a result of East German control of the waterways, few people had managed to use them as an escape route since the early days of the Berlin Wall.

Erich needed to sketch but little of this history for his fellow fugitives, all of whom were familiar with the state's painstaking efforts to lock all gateways to westward travel.

"We move into West Berlin waters about twenty-five kilometers from where we boarded," he said. "The frontier crosses the river just a bit this side of the old Reichstag building where the DDR has a control station on pontoons

229

by the Marschall Bridge. Once past that point, we can breathe easier, but it would still be dangerous to try to land anywhere along the West Berlin banks."

"Why?" Hilde frowned. "I don't understand."

"Because, unfortunately for us, at the inspection station the authorities are putting aboard an engineer who'll supervise the repairs at Spandau. He'll be in civilian clothes, but actually, as we've found out, he's an engineering major in the People's Army. He'll be armed, of course. The boat captain and I can handle him at the lock. That's all planned out. But if we surprised the Army officer by nosing into the riverbank somewhere, he might start shooting."

"Do we have any guns?" asked Werner.

Erich patted his jacket pocket. "I've got a revolver. So does the captain."

Gisela could see Hilde's eyes widen. The girl smiled nervously at her mother.

"Don't worry about shooting," said Erich. "We've planned carefully to protect you people. Our real danger will come at the check station. The border guards always put police dogs aboard to sniff out any stowaways like us."

"Dogs!" Once again Gisela could hear the distant, frenzied barking that awful night when searchlights and machine-gun rounds flailed the muddy death strip near Kaltennordheim. "How will we ever . . ."

"Get through?" Erich grinned in his loose, ragged way. "Attack dogs are almost invariably male. The captain has a female German shepherd, a sweetheart of a dog named Andrea. She's in heat and she's been all over the boat, scattering her scent. Those males will go wild. You may even hear them trying to bust into the captain's cabin where he's got Andrea tied."

"You mean this whole trip was planned to coincide with the time when the captain's dog would be in heat?" asked Werner.

Again the crooked grin. "Better than that, Werner. A female dog comes into heat twice a year, each time from sixteen to twenty-one days. A bitch's heat hits its peak on days ten, eleven, and twelve." Erich cocked a finger. "And this Second Day of Christmas is day No. 11 in the current cycle of Andrea's passion." He beamed at his new friends. "How's that for precise planning! Believe me, when you want to escape, call Dahlem."

"Won't the border guards suspect something?" asked Hilde.

"We doubt it. The captain's been through there a hundred times with that dog of his, including a number of times when she was in heat. Also we hope they'll all be in a happy mood on this Christmastime night." Erich paused. "But I won't try to deceive you. There could be bad trouble. If so, the captain will put on full power and try to bust through to West Berlin waters. In that case . . ." He tapped the pocket where the gun bulged.

"Dogs," mused Werner. "It's nice to learn that faced with a choice between war and love, the dogs choose love."

"So, who will still insist that human beings are smarter than animals?" Erich shrugged, then pointed to the map. "I'd say we're about here at this bridge in the Treptow section. This old tub makes good time going with the current."

The small freighter slid downstream with a minimum of engine noise. A low, grating, not unpleasant sound marked the shifting of gravel on rolls of the boat.

"What a way to spend the Second Night of Christmas," said Werner, his eyes darting from one person to another. "On the way to freedom."

"Ideal time to make the run," said Erich. "Everyone's relaxed."

"Isn't this exciting, Mother?" But Hilde's eyes showed more fear than excitement.

Erich refolded his map and they rode in silence as the

vessel slipped down the Spree with quietly pulsing engine. They sat awkwardly, crammed together in the small compartment, and occasionally slapped arms and legs to aid circulation in the cold night.

Gisela dropped into meditation, soundlessly repeating the mantra she had given herself after watching several yoga and meditation programs on West German television the previous year. Although the East German work-and-action-oriented Communist chiefs deplored passive yoga practices, Gisela and her friend Ulli Beitz had performed the exercises together at Ulli's apartment in Leipzig when Gisela spent a few days with her. Since the Dresden area yielded but poor reception of West German TV, Gisela tended to watch far more television when she visited Ulli.

Gisela found meditation relaxing and peaceful and while she did not meditate daily, she did employ the mind-emptying technique whenever she faced prolonged periods of unusual stress. In just such a situation now, she slowly drifted off, sinking deep within herself. Her thoughts melted away. Tension drained off. The occasional conversational exchange of those around her faded until the talk became little more than a gentle hum. Tranquillity lapped at the shores of her mind.

And while Gisela meditated, the loaded freighter slid quietly through the center of East Berlin, past Marx-Engels Platz, past Unter den Linden, the famous old boulevard, and past the bulbous television tower that spiked the heart of the city. Soon the boat slipped under the bridge at Friedrichstrasse. The passengers bent on escape had been traveling almost two hours at a good speed when the boat's engine shifted to reduced power. The change in rhythm fetched Gisela up from her depths and she slowly opened her eyes.

Above decks a horn sounded.

"The control station," said Erich. "From now on, until I

give the signal, no more talking and no squirming about."
He snapped off his flashlight.

The vessel went dead in the water and bumped against an
obstruction of some kind, undoubtedly the heavy pontoons
which floated from bank to bank of the Spree, leaving only
a narrow passage, easily controlled. Through this opening
in the water barrier flowed millions of tons of goods in the
heavy river commerce between the two German states.

Someone threw a line on board. Voices shouted commands. Feet pounded on the decks of the *Ernst Thälmann*
in areas not stacked with gravel. More voices, thick, gruff.

Then came unmistakable sounds. A light, swift pat-
ter, racing about, together with a familiar clicking. Gisela
stiffened in the dark. The dogs. She could hear them panting, picked out the sound of their claws. They seemed to be
running haphazardly around the deck and over the piles of
gravel. Stones slid about with a noise like coal tumbling
down a chute. Gisela felt Hilde's hand searching for hers.
She gripped and the two women sat with tightly clasped
hands. A sound of clawing. Were the dogs at the wheelhouse where the captain kept his female pet, Andrea?
Gisela felt a sudden chill. She began to shiver.

Now she heard the clamor of men's voices, harsh but
somehow less frightening than the voiceless sound of paws
and panting. The men seemed to be arguing. The dispute
went on and on, then suddenly broke on a note as welcome
as springtime—laughter. More low talk, then boisterous
voices, a few shouts. A man called out a command and
the dogs—two? three?—ran across the deck and apparently
leaped off the gunwales to the pontoons.

Gisela's shivering ceased. Her breathing returned to normal. She released Hilde's hand.

But now came a new sound, a loud scraping of metal on
wood and stone. Someone was shoveling gravel. The shoveling continued for several minutes, then stopped.

The hatch cover was pulled open with a rasping noise and shoes clattered down the gangway.

"You search the hold," ordered a voice. "I'll test the overhead."

The tester began thumping the hold's overhead with a pole, apparently knocking panels at random. Each whack rattled stones with a sound like gravel thrown on a wire screen for sifting purposes. Gisela hugged her knees, closed her eyes, and waited as if immobility itself might prevent detection.

At last the pole struck the panel on which the four fugitives sat. The gravel rattled about in a satisfying manner, but to Gisela's sensitive ear, the sound seemed thinner and looser than that produced elsewhere. Silence. Again the pole smacked the panel. Again the stones jumped about. Silence, longer this time. Gisela involuntarily held her breath.

The banging moved to another panel. She exhaled with relief. The hammering went on, thwack, rattle, bang, rattle. The pounding receded and then stopped. Shoes climbed the gangway. The hatch cover slid back in place.

Gisela shifted her position, reached out again for Hilde. Lieber Gott, she prayed swiftly and silently, our thanks.

Another verbal exchange on deck. The footsteps retreated. Soon the lines were cast off, the engine started again, and the freighter moved ahead.

The captain's horn tooted three times.

"We've made it," Erich whispered. "West Berlin. No more searches. But I'm sure the Army major's aboard, so no flashlight and let's keep the talk to a whisper."

"No more party, no more Stasi, no more Wall." Even at a whisper, Werner's voice had a high, piping tone.

"That beautiful Andrea," said Hilde. "I could kiss her to pieces." Instead she kissed her three companions in the dark and hugged her mother as well.

"We're free." Gisela said it with awe.

Werner kissed both women and slapped Erich on the back.

"Too bad we can't see the map," said Erich, "but we're passing behind the old Reichstag now. Soon we'll swing due west and sail past the Tiergarten, then loop our way out to the Spandau lock. A couple of hours more, that's all."

Despite the cold and the tight quarters, the spirit of success crackled like electricity in the boxlike compartment. Hilde hummed a romantic ballad she'd picked up from West German television. Werner sat with eyes closed and with a small, contented smile as if dreaming of untroubled pleasures. Erich kept ramming a fist into his gloved hand, each blow a celebration. Gisela snuggled into her coat and thought of Miguel. Would she see him tonight? Did he know she was on the way? Would they celebrate her escape with love-making? She recalled their last time in bed at Ulli's, and she imagined his arms around her again.

"Let's play cities to pass the time," suggested Hilde. "I name a German city, then Mother has to give a city that begins with the same letter mine ends with. Same with Werner and Erich, then back to me. If you miss, you must drop out. All right? . . . I start. Berlin."

"Nürnberg," said Gisela.

"But that's over there," protested Werner.

"Not anymore, comrade," said Erich. "Over there's over here now."

"Either Germany," Hilde ruled.

"All right. So it's a 'G.'" Werner pondered. "Greiz."

"Zschopau," said Erich.

"U—U. Let's see." Hilde brooded. "Oh, yes, Ulm."

"Magdeburg," said Gisela promptly.

The game filled the better part of an hour. Erich finally won over his last remaining rival, Hilde, via the strategy of naming half a dozen cities that ended with G.

As he accepted whispered congratulations, Erich

snapped on his flashlight, shielded it, and glanced at his wrist watch. "We ought to be just north of the Charlottenburg castle. Maybe another hour to go." He extinguished the light.

Now began the final stretch when the minutes crawled and the little freighter, although rocking gently on its downstream course, seemed mired in molasses. The cold, stagnant air in the boxlike cabin grew stale and fetid, limbs began to ache, and Gisela could feel a fevered throbbing at her wound.

"What about the toilet?" asked Hilde. "I have to go."

"We think of everything." Erich fumbled in the bucket that once held the gravel and produced a bottle and funnel for Hilde.

"I'm so embarrassed," she said.

"Nobody can see anything, Hilde. Better embarrassed than wet pants. We'll keep talking."

Later they essayed jokes and anecdotes, but none took their minds away from the slow ticking of time. Werner recited passages from Schiller. Hilde chanted lines from Wolf Biermann, a DDR poet and ballad singer of biting irony, who was expelled from his native East Germany in 1976. Gisela reeled off more than a hundred chemical elements from the periodic table, faltering only twice, once on Iridium and again on Thulium.

"We're getting close to Spandau lock," said Erich at last. "This could either be the simplest thing in the world or a shooting match where somebody might get killed."

He kept his voice just above a whisper. "Let me describe the lock for you. Try to fix it in your minds. We enter from the south, ready to be raised two meters for unloading the gravel in the morning. As it is, the gunwales will be about even with the pavement. The lockmaster's house and office will be on your right. There'll be a footbridge behind us. It crosses a spillway and leads to the electrically operated gate, the only exit in a chain link fence that's topped by barbed wire all around the lock.

"One way or another, we're going through that gate. The moment we reach the lock, the captain and I will try to disarm the Army major and lock him in the wheelhouse. Then we jump off the starboard side and make for the lockmaster. No trouble expected from him, but if he refuses to push the button that opens the gate, we'll do it. . . . Now the rest of you, led by Werner, must jump off this same side of the boat—the starboard or right side—and run back across the spillway bridge and head for the gate."

"If we're in West Berlin, why all that trouble?" Hilde was baffled. "Why can't we just walk out?"

"No." Erich answered in a low, calm voice. "First, there's the DDR major to be dealt with. Then, although the lock is on West Berlin soil and tended by a West Berliner, he's paid by East Germany. That's the ridiculous way the Berlin agreements left things. Remember last year when the West Berlin S-Bahn workers struck against the East German authorities who paid them? It's truly crazy, all mixed up.

"So we're not sure just how the locktender will respond. He'll probably do nothing, but we can't be sure. . . . Anyway, you all run for that gate that's controlled from the lockhouse. Either we persuade the lockmaster to push the button or we shove him away and do it ourselves.

"Women, you bust through that gate. Werner, you hold it open until the captain and I get there. . . . All clear?"

"What if the gate doesn't open?" asked Gisela.

"Then we'll shoot it open. . . . Now, when I give the order, everybody follow me up on deck, fast. Werner first."

They waited. The freighter slowed, idled for a time, then picked up speed again. Hilde began counting, reached two hundred before she quit. More minutes dragged by. Erich became restless. The cold stabbed at Gisela's wound.

At last the boat's horn blew once, an anxious plaint on the wintry air.

"All right, here we go." Erich unscrewed the panel and dropped into the hold. Werner followed. The men handed the women down into the cluttered stowage space below decks. They heard the captain call out and a muffled reply from the locktender.

"Now." Erich whipped out his pistol and rushed up the gangway, Werner behind him. Gisela cruelly banged her injured leg on a step. But she held Hilde's hand and pulled her daughter with a strength that surprised her. The decks were bathed in light, apparently from flood lamps switched on by the locktender.

"Here!" Werner helped them up to the gunwale which rode only a few inches below the paved deck of the lock. They stepped up, ran a few yards south, turned across the top of the lock behind the boat, and ran over the footbridge that spanned a spillway. The lights illumined their course like noonday. With Werner in the lead, they flung themselves at the wire-link gate. Werner rattled the handle. It did not open.

Gisela, her heart thumping and her left leg quivering, looked back at the *Ernst Thälmann,* now rising slowly in the lock. On the boat's bridge, just outside the wheelhouse, the garish light spilled over a bizarre scene.

A man, apparently the boat's captain, lay sprawled on the deck. The Army major, as Gisela supposed him to be, stood a few feet away, his pistol pointed down at the prone figure. Andrea, the police dog, raged at the end of her chain in the doorway. Her fangs were bared and she barked hysterically at the major while she tugged wildly against her collar.

"Let loose of that gun!" The major, wearing a heavy gray jacket, was a stocky man with an enormous chest and an unruly shock of hair.

Below the bridge, on the main deck of the freighter, stood Erich. As Gisela watched in fascination, almost as if she were seeing a film script enacted, Erich slowly raised his revolver, took careful aim at the major, and fired.

The Army officer cried out in pain. His pistol clattered to the deck. Erich's shot echoed through the cold, still air from surrounding buildings. Andrea went into a frenzy of barking and lunging. The captain, still clutching his pistol, scrambled to his feet. Erich rushed up the five-rung ladder to the bridge. The major saw his gun on the deck, stooped over, grabbed frantically for the weapon, missed, snatched again. Blood streamed down his hand. Apparently he had been shot in the wrist. The major managed to get hold of his gun, but at that moment Erich smashed the butt of his revolver against his foe's head. The major grunted, slumped, then collapsed like an empty sack. His gun again fell to the deck.

The captain swooped up the weapon and plunged down the wheelhouse ladder, a gun in each hand. Erich jumped off the bridge. Both men leaped from the boat and raced to the lockhouse, a stone building with a steeply pitched, red-tiled roof that resembled a small railroad station.

The lockmaster, standing in the doorway, shouted something and then stepped aside, bowing deeply, and making a flowing sweep with his hand that seemed to say: "Be my guest, gentlemen. Just don't shoot." The two men rushed past him. One of them quickly found the proper switch or button, for the gate came alive with buzzing.

Werner threw the gate open for the women, but they stood transfixed, watching the drama unfold under the lights.

"Come on!" He grabbed first Gisela, then Hilde, and shoved them through the gate.

Windows in nearby apartments flew open and heads popped out. "Run for it!" yelled a heavy male voice just as the captain, followed by Erich, broke out of the lockhouse. Erich trotted over the footbridge toward the gate, but the captain climbed back aboard, mounted to the wheelhouse, and unfastened Andrea's chain. The dog lunged at the fallen major, but the captain reined in the leash and pulled the dog off the boat. Once on the ground Andrea joined her master in running toward the gate.

Werner held it open. The two men and the dog ran through. Then Werner walked through himself, slowly, with dignity, while applause broke out from the nearby apartment windows. Werner joined the others who stood in a knot on the sidewalk a few yards beyond the fence. They hugged one another in the brilliant light as Berliners poured into the streets. Pent emotions burst forth. The captain laughed hysterically. Andrea barked. Hilde broke into sobs. Gisela threw her arms skyward. Erich brayed like a mule.

"Freedom!" shouted the heavy voice from the window. "Welcome!"

"Die Sonnenseite!" Werner opened his arms to his comrades of flight. "My friends, we're safe on the sunny side."

13

Mike Simmons took the call shortly after midnight, at about
the same time that Heinz Lungwitz, chief of SSD computer
intelligence on the other side of the severed city, ordered an
all-points alert in East Germany, looking toward the arrest
of Gisela and Hilde Steinbrecher.

The telephone rang three times in Mike's hotel room before he rolled over and fumbled blindly for it. Panic hooted.
Shards of a shattered nightmare rained about.

"Michael Simmons?" A woman's voice, vaguely familiar.

"Yes." Shadowed tormenters still harried him along a
high stone wall.

"This is Ingrid."

He climbed through muffled layers. "Ingrid?" He came
slowly awake. "Oh. Okay now. What is it?"

"I have good news." Her voice soothed. "The expected
delivery has arrived."

"You mean . . ." In the nightmare, weird monsters on a
death strip spat out teeth like rounds from a machine gun.
"Where?"

"Right here in Berlin."

"Is the, er, goods okay?"

"Yes. Both packages in fine condition."

Both? Oh yes, the daughter, too. "Tell me, what do I do?" Now he was fully awake, soaring on the news. "Where do I go?"

Ingrid laughed softly. "First the money, no? You bring the cash to the Tano. Remember on Lietzenburger Strasse? I am in the same rear booth. Then we'll go pick up the delivery."

"Right now?"

"As soon as you can. I'm at the Tano now."

Never before had he dressed so swiftly. He was still pulling on his topcoat as he hurried to the elevator. At the reception desk, he ordered a taxi and withdrew the thick envelope from the hotel safe. Oh, yes. A room for Hilde. Or should it be Hilde and Gisela? Fortunately the hotel had accommodations on his corridor.

The Tano was not quite deserted on this Second Night of Christmas. Not everyone had family in Berlin. A lone man at the three-sided bar watched the predatory blonde polish glasses. A second customer hunched with a female partner over one of the small tables ringing the screen where Nobel laureates of pornography performed with the clamor of mating seals.

Mike found Ingrid in the rear booth, this time seated with the huge bodyguard with the neck like a fire hydrant.

"Good evening, Herr Simmons," said Ingrid. "You remember Hans?"

"Sure." He nodded to the big man, who smiled vacantly. "They're here, both Gisela and Hilde?"

"Here in Berlin, tired but in good health, anxious to see you. . . . You have the money?"

Mike took the bulky envelope from his pocket. "Frankly, I don't intend to hand this over until I meet Gisela and her daughter."

"Oh, you are the suspicious one." Again that soft laugh.

"Just count it for us, please. Then you keep it until we pick up the delivery."

Mike counted through the packet of thousand-mark bills while Ingrid and Hans watched.

"Fine. All is in order." Ingrid beamed at him. "So. Let's go. Our car's outside."

Hans drove the Mercedes-Benz sedan west through the Charlottenburg district, out Spandauer Damm past the stadium of Hitler's 1936 Olympics, and into the Spandau district. It occurred to Mike that the two escape brokers could take him to some lonely spot in the forest that covered much of the city's western flank, then rob and kill him. But he quickly dismissed the thought. After all, the Dahlem organization, whatever its lack of repute among high officials in Bonn, had performed its shadowy services for many years without a touch of the scandals that had destroyed so many rivals. As Ingrid chatted along, Hans drove across the River Havel, turned north, and halted the car on a residential street not far from a brightly lit Kneipe where late beer drinkers sang and caroused as if in celebration. Ingrid led the way to a window opening on a private room at the rear of the establishment.

There, drinking beer at a round table with two men and a girl, sat Gisela. Her clothes looked like she'd been rolling in dirt, but otherwise she appeared quite normal, for Mike an alluring beauty. Had he been twenty years younger, he'd have crawled up and through the window.

"The money before we go in?" Ingrid's smile was urbane. "Less commercial here, no?"

Mike handed over the envelope. She tucked it in her handbag, then guided him through a side door, down a short hallway to the room where Gisela sat beneath an old stained-glass chandelier. Mike stood in the open doorway, his spirits flying.

"Miguel!" Gisela sprang to her feet, as radiant as that

243

evening in the Astoria when his brown sweater warmed her escape hopes.

She came at once into his open arms and he reveled in that compelling aroma, uniquely Gisela's. "Mi amor," she whispered. He held her closely, felt a surge of affection. Oh yes, he had missed her. Only in touching her again did he realize how deeply. The magic of that first night in Leipzig enveloped him anew as she scattered small fervent kisses.

"Thank God, you're alive and safe."

"Miguel, I'm so happy." She laughed on a single, high, plaintive note, then at once began to weep. "No, no. Not that." She choked back the tears, laughed again, then giggled.

"Easy, baby." But tears welled in Mike's eyes and only a solid kiss prevented a mutual downpour.

"I'm a mess." Gisela pushed away, wiped her eyes on her coat sleeve. She blushed faintly.

He loved her.

"And here, Miguel, is Hilde." She took her daughter's hand and drew her toward them.

Mike saw a girl larger than her mother, diffident, a bit awkward, with brown, close-cropped hair, blue eyes, and an uncertain smile. He embraced her, felt her stiffen when he kissed her on both cheeks and once on the forehead for good measure.

"It is a pleasure to meet you," she said in formal, textbook English.

"For me, too. I hope we'll become good friends."

Her face clouded for a moment before she smiled. "I do, too, Mr. Simmons." Hilde offered him her stein of beer. "Here, a toast. Let's both have a swallow."

The two drank, then everyone toasted success, sharing beers, laughing, joking about how they had outwitted the warders of the Wall. After frenetic introductions, Erich gave an excited account of the landing at the lock several blocks away, the shooting and felling of the East German Army major. People had swarmed into the street at the sound of the shot. Police arrived and an ambulance carted the officer to a hospital. Police questioned them all, but had detained only Captain Alex Engelmann of the river freighter for further examination. Unofficial word from the emergency room reported the major in serious condition with a fractured skull. Although police acted humanely in speeding him to a hospital, they fully expected a shrill protest from East Berlin over their armed intrusion into an area that, while it belonged to West Berlin, was treated by both sides as neutral territory.

Ingrid prepared to leave to rejoin the big bodyguard, Hans, who paced the sidewalk outside. She kissed Gisela and Hilde. "Happy sunny side," she said. "So, our job is finished. Erich and I will go now because Erich must still report to the headman tonight."

"Work, work, work," said Erich with his ragged smile.

Gisela shook his hand. "You're a true professional, Erich. I'll never forget what you did for us."

"The rest of you stay and celebrate," said Ingrid. "The drinks are on us. If you need anything further, Herr Simmons, please call."

Only after the escape merchants departed did Mike become fully aware of the other man in the room. Mike studied him in a puzzled way, then burst out: "My God! I don't believe it. Herr Brigade Leader—Werner Lanz!"

"The same." Lanz grinned. Then in his soprano voice and his peculiar, birdlike mannerisms, he delivered a small oration. It bubbled along, made obvious gallant references to the women, and ended with a flourish like a skirl of bagpipes.

Hilde translated. "He planned to escape for years and would have asked your assistance in Leipzig, but he was already under contract to the Fluchthelfer. Since a brother in

Frankfurt financed the trip, he must work to pay him back. Now that he knows so much about elevators, perhaps he could go to work for the Todd Company." She repeated this last in German.

Lanz bobbed his head. "Ja, ja." He grinned again as he piped another round of chatter.

"Now he makes jokes that I can't translate," said Hilde. "He says you were a fine debater while he played the part of the dogmatic politician."

"He sure fooled me," said Mike. "Of all the people I met back there, he seemed least likely to bust out of the place. . . . Tell me, how did you three get out?"

They exchanged glances. Werner shook his head slowly. Gisela said something to her daughter in German.

"You know how we arrived, so you know we came by boat," said Hilde. "But where we started and how we contacted Dahlem's people, we cannot say. We promised we would not talk, to protect those who follow. That's not kind to you, I know. You've been so generous."

"Someday maybe," said Gisela, "many years from now."

"Hey." Mike was surprised. "You're speaking English, Gisela."

"Hilde taught me a little from her schoolbook." She looked proud of her accomplishment. "And now, Miguel, you learn German, no?"

They finished the beer, congratulated themselves once more on beating the Wall, talked excitedly in a tumble of three languages. Mike found it difficult to look away from Gisela. She was buoyant, flushed, feverish with joy. He wanted her as intensely as he had in Leipzig.

When Gisela took Mike's arm to walk to a taxi, he noticed that she limped. When he asked, she put him off. "Later, after Werner leaves."

They dropped Lanz at the Hotel Am Zoo on Kurfürstendamm where post-midnight holiday crowds still promenaded the wide, lighted boulevard. Lanz, who would meet his brother from Frankfurt the next day at the hotel, pressed the Frankfurt address on them and in his twittering way pledged to stay in touch for an eternity of tomorrows. Then, as he was about to turn away, Lanz remembered something.

He opened his coat, carefully unfastened a button attached to the collar of his leather jacket and held it out for them to see. It was the SED party insignia with the clasped hands of German Communists and democrats.

Lanz leaned over the curb, held the button high, and let it fall to the gutter. "So!" He brushed his hands and with a grin for his friends walked into the hotel.

"Quite a guy." Mike felt as if he had parted from an old friend.

At the familiar Alsterhof with its small, sparkling fountain in the lobby, Mike had moments of hesitation and embarrassment over division of the rooms. Hilde quickly settled the matter. "Mother, I'd like to be alone. You stay with Mr. Simmons."

"Okay, Hilde," said Mike. "But it's not Mr. Simmons. It's Mike—or Michael if you wish."

In the corridor before her doorway, Hilde kissed her mother good night, smiled shyly at Mike, hesitated, then brusquely kissed him on the cheek. "Thanks, Mr. Mike." She stood self-consciously, her legs planted apart in a stance of resolve. "I'll work and pay you back every mark I owe."

"Let's talk finances later." He liked the girl. "We've made a good start toward being friends. And, Hilde, I admire your courage."

Inside Mike's room he and Gisela came together for a long, hungry kiss that spoke for a tangle of unvoiced emotions. And since they were still, in part, strangers, the embrace mirrored the urgent questing of their nights in Leipzig, that city that stood only a few miles and yet a lifetime away.

"Mi amor, I want a long, hot bath," she said at last. "Foam, soap, you, too." She spoke a tangle of German, English, and Spanish with that throaty timbre that so beguiled him. "You rub my back, no? I'm so tired. Look at me, Miguel. I'm a sight."

She did look bedraggled in her grimy slacks and the dirty, hip-length coat that smelled of earth, fertilizer, and riverboat cargo. But beneath the coat, pinned to an old sweater, a silver brooch shone like a lone star in a muddy sky.

"It's been in the family for generations." Sadness touched her fleetingly. "Hilde brought her grandmother's jewel box. Otherwise, we have only these old clothes you see."

"The limp? Were you hurt?"

"Yes. A bullet hit my leg that night at the border. But it's not so bad, I think. I get around."

She took off her shoes and Mike peeled back the wool sock.

"Ah, that doesn't look good." A small, round wound on the calf had closed, but it festered with blisters of yellow pus. "We must get you to a doctor."

"But not tonight, Miguel. I'm exhausted."

When the bath filled, she lay back in the tub, closed her eyes, and luxuriated in the hot water and the foam fragrance, a mass of tinted bubbles that glistened like floating gems. Mike scrubbed her back, soaped her body, and then climbed in beside her. They kissed, laughed, fondled, and splashed about as she returned his erotic touch. Then they stood on the tile floor, happily toweling each other dry. When Gisela tucked her chin in that shy, inviting way, Mike felt a rush of desire.

The love-making that followed had a sweetness quite unlike the nights in Leipzig, for now they merged with a kind of reverence. Their caresses gave mute articulation to their thankfulness for Gisela's safety in escape, for Mike's help, for the richness of life in this night, this hour, this moment. They moved delicately, even gravely, into the cadence of love, and if Leipzig provided the incubator and the playground for romance, Berlin this night offered the chapel.

Gisela had assumed that when their love reached its climax, she would fall into a long, deep sleep. Instead she found herself eager to talk. Rather than depletion, she felt refreshed and so she broached the subject on which she had brooded.

"Forgive me, Miguel, for the thing of Hilde. I wanted—"

"It's okay," he cut in. "I think we'll get along fine. Right off, I liked her."

"But I must explain, so you understand me. That first night when you asked if I had children, I lied by my silence. I did not mention Hilde, only Max who died when he was four. I did not know you that first night, Miguel, and I wanted your help so much. I feared you would not help me and a daughter, too. By the last night at Ulli's, I knew you better and I thought you'd welcome us both, but by then I was afraid to correct the lie. And so I let the Fluchthelfer tell you. That was shameful, not brave of me." All this poured out in a trilingual flood. She paused before she asked: "What did you think when you learned the truth?"

"Frankly, I resented the hell out of you." He caressed her shoulder in the darkness. "But then I had a flash image of you at the border when the searchlights suddenly came on. I realized how much you'd been through, how brave you were, and, well, I felt I didn't have the right to judge. Also, I had to make up my mind soon for Dahlem."

She told him all that had happened, including her guilty Christmas with Karl. "To think that was just yesterday and now here tonight, I'm starting a new life, never to go back."

When she fell silent, Mike told of trying to find her, his ordeal with the State Security investigators and the agreement with Dahlem. "We must stay here in Berlin for at least another week until my replacement arrives from New York. He'll finish up the Leipzig job. Never again will I set foot in the DDR."

"Nor I, Miguel. A week here is wonderful while we make up our minds. So much to decide, no? And I want to promenade, see the stores, soak up this West Berlin I've heard and seen so much on TV. We'll eat and dance and make love and not worry for a whole week. Is that in order, Miguel?"

"Sounds terrific. And it'll be fun to show the sights to Hilde."

"Yes, yes." She became excited again. "I have just three duties. First, the doctor. Then some clothes to buy. Third, I must call the ecology people in the U.S.A. about Otto Kleist's material. Can we afford an overseas call, Miguel?"

"Sure. Which reminds me. I have to call my daughter, Sally. I missed her Christmas day when I phoned."

"About the money, Miguel. Hilde and I consider that a loan." Gisela's tone became crisp, businesslike. "We intend to pay you back even if we can afford only small amounts at a time."

"No money talk this week," Mike ruled. "There's a lifetime ahead and none of the three of us knows where or how we'll be a year from now."

"What do you mean, 'how'?"

"Will Hilde be with us, with you only, or off at school somewhere? Will you and I be living together as lovers or apart as friends?"

"As for us, Miguel, I'm quite sure in my heart how it will be." And within moments she had fallen into the rhythm of slumber. Watching her lying there beside him, serene, safe, beautiful in repose, he experienced a flowering of precious, almost worshipful, tenderness. So strong she was, yet so vulnerable. He loved her.

Their first day, a Sunday, sped by in a swirl of exuberance. After a merry champagne breakfast in Hilde's room, they all went to the nearby office of a friend of Walter Delaney, a physician who agreed to treat Gisela's injury on this last day of the long Christmas weekend. The doctor pronounced the wound troublesome but uncritical, applied compresses, bandaged the leg, gave Gisela antibiotic pills, and asked her to return in three days.

They lunched at Delaney's home in the quiet, tree-bowered Grunewald residential section. Mother and daughter demurred because of their soiled, old clothes, but Delaney insisted. The luncheon turned into a festive celebration, thanks in part to Sue Delaney, a warm, sensitive woman who lent Gisela a clean pair of slacks and welcomed the East German mother and daughter as she might old friends from home. The Steinbrechers, accustomed to nourishing but unvaried fare in Dresden, doted on the delicious smoked salmon from Scotland, fruit and vegetables from Florida, cheese from Denmark, and coffee from Costa Rica. Hilde had to know the name, source, and price of everything.

The two émigrées told of their night of terror at the border and of last night's dash for freedom. This brought up the question that intrigued Sue.

"Why did you leave?" Sue was serving coffee in the large living room where the afternoon sun threw soft amber patterns and where the Steinbrechers had examined and remarked on the furniture, most of it of modern Scandinavian design. "I've heard that one lives fairly well over there now."

"True. Of course, there are shortages, but I could put up with them." Gisela, still embarrassed over the condition of her clothes, brushed self-consciously at her ragged sweater. "For me it was the restrictions: on my movements, my conversation, my job, my reading, even my thoughts. The case of Otto Kleist brought everything to a head." She sketched the episode. "But even without Otto, I think I would have decided sometime to escape."

"How about you, Hilde?" asked Sue.

"I hate the Wall," said the girl with a burst of bitterness, "although I've never seen it. I refuse to be a prisoner in my own country. And then there was our trip to Russia."

"Oh, yes." Gisela pondered. "Perhaps that was the real turning point."

"Since we couldn't go to the West," said Hilde, "Mother and I went to Russia last spring. Moscow and Leningrad mostly, but we saw some small towns, too. What was it you said, Mother?"

"When we came back, I told Karl that in Russia we had seen our future and it depressed us."

"A few nights later, Mother and I had our first talk, hinting around to each other that we wanted to get out. What a night! . . . Oh, the life at home is so dull, so dreary, and respectable. I want to have fun, do as I please like kids in the West."

"You may be disappointed," said Sue.

"Oh, I hope not." Her face clouded briefly as if the thought had not occurred before. "I doubt it. Just last night and this morning I've seen more life than we have around Dresden in a month."

Honoring the escape, Walter Delaney for once suppressed his cynical, mordant comments. He would not, he said, tarnish "these first shining hours of our consumer virgins." Instead he took pictures of the Steinbrecher women with Mike so that, after they purchased clothes, they would have these "before" photographs of the dowdy refugees.

The women ached to feel the pulse of city life, and that afternoon Mike took them to join the Sunday crowds pressing along Kurfürstendamm and through the central city. Fascinated by the wares displayed in show windows, the women stopped before every shop, discussed the prices, marveled over the variety of goods, remarked on the abundance of furs, jewels, cosmetics, liquors, books, paintings, antiques, and other luxuries. They gawked at the blaring advertisements of the film theaters, stopped to read every playbill. They spent a good ten minutes before a window heaped high with electrical appliances. They toured the Europa Center, another citadel of consumerism, and admired the sleek displays in the glass rectangles on the sidewalks of Kurfürstendamm.

They sat at a table in the famous old Café Kranzler at the hub of Berlin for late afternoon cakes with chocolate. The weather warmed unseasonably that Sunday afternoon and Ku'damm swarmed with people. Hundreds of lean, dark Turks, from the large community of foreign workers that so bedeviled and perplexed the Germans, mixed with Indians, blacks, Arabs, off-duty soldiers, and throngs of young people in jeans, jackets, and flamboyant T-shirts. The girls wore the day's trendy costume of the West: kinky hair, shirtwaists, beads and jackets, hip-hugging corduroys or jeans, high heels. The boys preferred leather jackets and helmets and they parked their Japanese motorcycles—Hondas, Suzukis, Kawasakis, Yamahas—up and down the sidewalks. Kids swooped about on bright-wheeled roller skates. A man strolled by with a monkey on his shoulder. Another paced a fierce-eyed tiger cub on a leash. Con artists and vendors of trinkets set up their tables near the curbs. Several organ grinders churned out hearty beer-hall ballads.

Gisela was dismayed by the informal, scruffy dress. For every stylish coat or suit, there were a hundred sloppy jeans and rumpled slacks. The people looked as if they had raided dusty closets for their oldest clothes. Mike overheard a French couple at the adjoining table comparing the Ku'damm crowds disparagingly with the fashionable Parisian Sunday promenaders along the Champs-Élysées. West Berlin was not a city of elegance, and Gisela, a woman who fancied style, was disappointed. Television had not prepared her. Hilde, on the other hand, was intoxicated by the crowds, the young especially. She looked so hungry for teenage companionship that Mike imagined she might simply spring from the table and dive like a swimmer into the pool of surging young flesh.

Everything titillated, puzzled, or moved the Steinbrechers: the abundance of restaurants and bars, the lurid signs for tranvestite shows and gay bars, the great theaters and concert halls, the shattered spire of the Kaiser Wilhelm Memorial Church, the gambling casino, the crush of automobiles, buses, and motorcycles.

That night, at Hilde's suggestion, they saw a rerun of a Fassbinder film, *The Marriage of Maria Braun*. The movie gripped and held them, but also sparked an argument.

"It was colorful, very dramatic," said Gisela, "but I can't understand why Chancellor Rauschnig lets West Germans be pictured that way, so gross, money-grubbing. Very unattractive, really."

"What would you have the chancellor do?" asked Mike.

"Tell Herr Fassbinder that the picture gives a distorted view of his country." She was bluntly insistent.

"And when he stood on his right to make the movie anyway?"

"Discourage him." Gisela set her jaw. "That film makes bad propaganda for the Federal Republic."

"You mean, Mother, not let the picture be shown?" asked Hilde.

"Yes, if it came to that!"

"But, Mother!" Sudden storm clouds gathered. "That's censorship like at home."

"Yeah," said Mike, "one of the very restrictions, as you put it at lunch, that made you split from the DDR."

"It's not the same thing," Gisela maintained.

"Oh, but it is. Isn't it, Mr. Mike?"

"Sure looks that way to me."

The dispute faded, borne away on a wave of new impressions, sights, sounds, and smells. Hilde insisted that even the odor of broiling sausages at a sidewalk vendor's shack was tangier than a similar variety of Bockwurst at a similar stand in Dresden.

The next day Berlin went back to work after its three-day Christmas holiday, but for the Steinbrechers the day opened on the same plane of surcharged emotion that had carried them through their first hours in a non-Communist city. Hilde pounded on the door as Mike and Gisela were arising.

"Quick," she called. "We're on television."

Mike switched on the set and the three people watched as a commentator described the Saturday post-midnight escape and shooting at Spandau lock. He said the five people, including Captain Alex Engelmann of the small river freighter, *Ernst Thälmann,* named for the head of Berlin's Communist party in pre-Hitler days, bolted from the lock after one of them had shot and pistol-whipped the armed DDR major who tried to block the escape. The commentator said West Berlin police withheld the names of all those who escaped save the boat captain in order to protect their identities and any families left in East Germany. A camera panned past the lockhouse, chain link fence, and the lock itself with the old scow, still piled high with gravel, riding in the water.

ADN, the official East German news agency, branded the shooting "attempted murder" and declared that the perpetrator and accomplices, when identified, would be charged with treason, criminal border crossing, and conspiracy to commit murder. Closing on an ominous note, the news service said that the DDR would hold West Berlin authorities responsible for harboring "five vicious criminals" and for tolerating gunplay at a lock "through which annually flows tens of thousands of tons of basic supplies needed for West Berlin's survival."

"Do you think the Stasi has pinpointed you and Hilde yet?" asked Mike.

"If they don't know now, they will soon. Not much gets by them."

"Why worry?" asked Hilde. "They can't touch us over here."

"Maybe not," said Gisela, "but I'd just as soon not have our case tossed about on TV and in the newspapers."

After breakfast, Mike accompanied the women to Ka-De-We to outfit them with presentable clothes. The shopping mission turned into a wondering visual feast and then a kind of celebration. Confronted with aisle after aisle of women's apparel of endless sizes, varieties, and modes, mother and daughter at first could do nothing but stare helplessly. Gisela especially seemed undone by the spectacle. She wandered about, fingered price tags, sorted through racked dresses with a look of confusion and occasionally appealed mutely to Mike for help.

When a brisk young salesclerk discovered that the women were refugees from "over there," she summoned a manager. He, in turn, learning that they owned only the dirty, shabby clothes on their backs, offered a "Christmas present" discount of 40 percent on all purchases. He also assigned the young saleswoman to accompany them throughout the store as their personal consultant.

As a result the Steinbrechers left the store at noon burdened with packages. Gisela wore a stylish purple dress, modish boots, and a fur-trimmed winter coat. Hilde wore new blue jeans, denim jacket, beads, and boots. Mike carried additional packages and still more were to be delivered at the hotel later in the week. The manager and half a dozen salespeople lined up at the exit of the women's clothing section to applaud the Steinbrechers and wish them a Happy New Year in the West.

They ate lunch at the fashionable Hotel Kempinski on Ku'damm where mother and daughter drank in the scene of stylish, bejeweled, chattering women and their florid, affluent escorts. When Mike suggested a sightseeing tour for the afternoon, Hilde came up with an unexpected alternative.

"I'd rather see the Wall," she said. "I want to know what we escaped from."

So they toured sections of the Wall, first near the Brandenburg Gate, where they mounted an observation platform and gazed down silently at patrolling East German border troops with Kalashnikov assault rifles slung at the shoulder. They strolled along the concrete barrier toward the Reichstag past another of the omnipresent wooden crosses that memorialized victims of the Wall. This one honored Heinz Sokolowski, shot while trying to escape from East Berlin, November 25, 1965.

They stood behind the Reichstag at a point where the Wall vaulted to the east bank of the Spree and where crosses commemorated six more persons who were killed while swimming to freedom. Mike and the Steinbrechers gazed at the pontoon station, perhaps a quarter of a mile distant, where the little diesel freighter had brought Gisela and Hilde safely through inspection to West Berlin waters, thanks to the impassioned scent of Andrea.

"I'll love that dog all my life," said Hilde.

As they watched, a loaded river tanker from a Baltic port plowed upstream toward the Marschall Bridge and the waiting marine border guards on the pontoons. While many northern waterways would soon close because of winter ice, the Spree, warmed by recycled waters from factories along its banks, remained navigable in the Berlin area throughout the year.

As the pale sun broke through an overcast, Mike and the two women took a bus many miles to the southwest corner of the city where the small enclave of Steinstücken, linked to the rest of West Berlin by a single road, protruded into East Germany like a bandaged thumb. The Wall flanked the road on both sides. Ever-present East German border troops swept binoculars back and forth, monitoring traffic from windows of their gray concrete watchtowers.

From an observation platform, the women got an unobstructed view of the high gray Wall, rounded at the top to foil grasping hands, and its routinely lethal appendages so reminiscent of the perimeters of Nazi death camps: furrowed strip, minefield, roadway, barrier trench, vehicle traps, bunkers, floodlights, watchtowers, chain link fence at the rear.

Hilde gasped. "Lieber Gott. Look." She pointed.

Quite close to the Wall they saw one of those sights that remain forever fastened in memory. On the ground, midway of the mined strip, lay the carcass of a buck deer. The animal apparently had tripped a land mine and the explosion had broken its back and disemboweled it. Now the deer lay with its legs oddly crossed, antlers and head twisted at a grotesque angle and blood from entrails staining the brown earth.

A portly Berliner, standing beside them, shook his head. "Happens often. Deer, rabbits, even dogs sometimes."

Gisela turned away with tears in her eyes. Hilde stared, immobile, then abruptly became nauseated and rushed down from the platform. They conversed but little as they continued their walk into Steinstücken, an old village of paths, gardens, and substantial homes. In the late December afternoon, with its leafless trees and its tight, gray concrete collar, the hamlet had a depressing air, a permanent invalid of the long sickness that afflicted the two German states.

Hilde wanted to ride the subway lines that ran under the

258

central section of East Berlin en route from one district of West Berlin to another. Gisela refused to go, so Mike and Hilde traveled together on the two branches that cut under the Wall in four places. They rode the bright yellow U-Bahn trains that rolled quietly from one shining West Berlin station to another. When they traveled below East Berlin, the train slowed, but did not stop at the dim, grubby stations that had been boarded up and abandoned for many years—Nordbahnhof, Oranienburger Tor, Bernauer Strasse, Heinrich Heine Strasse. Ghostly, a kind of subway catacombs, the dark platforms, eleven in all, held various obstructions and devices to thwart any escape-minded East Germans who managed to break into the closed stations. Occasionally a lone armed guard paced a shadowed platform. There was but one subway stop in East Berlin, the lighted oasis of Friedrichstrasse where people with proper papers boarded or left the cars on their missions between the two halves of the severed city. It was at this stop that Hilde studiously inspected her shoes, fearing to look up at the Vopos on the platform. The train halted only briefly, however, and Hilde later was able to boast that she had defeated the Wall no less than five times, once by water and four times by tunnel.

That evening, at Gisela's request, Mike placed an overseas call to the Geophysical Fluid Dynamics Laboratory, a U.S. government facility in Princeton, New Jersey. After some shuffling, he located the proper official, a Benjamin Garraway, one of some twenty Ph.D.'s heading the lab's research program.

With Gisela and Hilde sitting at his elbow to prompt him, Mike sketched the case of Professor Otto Kleist, his calculations, the suppression of his manuscript, and his ultimate house arrest. Yes, said Garraway, the lab would welcome Frau Steinbrecher's written report on the research. The Princeton group knew of Kleist and his interest, but had not heard from him in some time. Yes, added Garraway, the scientists at the laboratory would also like to talk with and question Frau Steinbrecher as soon as she could travel conveniently to the United States. He also offered to contact Amnesty International with a hope toward applying pressure on East Germany to release Otto Kleist.

The talk with Garraway triggered a discussion of travel plans, and at dinner that night Gisela said that she wanted to call on the Princeton researchers as soon as possible. The idea of flying to New York entranced Hilde. And so it was decided. With Mike's replacement due in Berlin the next week, they would fly to New York on Wednesday, nine days away. Mike made their plane reservations that night.

For Gisela and Mike the days now floated by like a honeymoon, yet richer, deeper, more poignant than either of them had experienced the first time around. Richer because their ordeals in East Germany, especially Gisela's time of terror at the border, fused them in a manner few honeymoon couples experience. Deeper because they had to delve beneath two radically different cultures to find their common humanity. More poignant because they were older and so knew that these hours, as beautiful and as precious as they were, these too would pass.

After a day of pouting and dragging about, Hilde went off by herself Wednesday afternoon and came back to the hotel in an ebullient mood. She had met three young East Germans at a teenage hangout on Bismarckstrasse. Two brothers and their cousin, a girl, had come across at Checkpoint Charlie the previous year in the trunk of a Ford LTD driven by the boys' father, the East German chauffeur for the U.S. embassy in East Berlin. Since diplomatic and military vehicles were not subject to border inspection by either side, the chauffeur merely waited for an opportune time and drove across with his wife under the front seat and the teenagers hidden in the rear.

"I wish we'd known some diplomats," said Gisela. "It's so simple that way. And, Miguel, we could have saved all your money."

"Forget money," said Mike. "This week everyone should think extravagantly. That's an order."

"Ja, Herr Simmons." Gisela ducked her chin and Mike wanted her at once.

Hilde hit it off from the start with the young East German émigrées. They showed her the ropes, coached her in the tribal rites of West Berlin's teenagers, took her to clannish places, and introduced her to a score of their friends. By the end of the week, Hilde was leading a hectic life of her own, once waved to her mother and Mike from the rear of a speeding motorcycle driven by a boy in leather jacket, goggles, and helmet.

Gisela's leg healed nicely and she and Mike strolled miles of the city's bustling streets, tramped paths through the winter woodlands, sauntered along the canals, lakes, and waterways. Even the weather favored them, for the most part sunny with temperatures in the brisk forties. They dined at fine restaurants, Kopenhagen, Maitre, Alexander. They went to the theater, the opera, heard the Berlin Philharmonic play Dvořák's New World Symphony, one of Mike's favorites, in the glittering, multitiered and galleried Philharmonic Hall. They saw several movies, danced to disco music, and caught two post-midnight nude shows. And always, throughout the daylight hours, Gisela window-shopped, fascinated by the range of goods, confused by choices, and dismayed by the abundance.

To his love for Gisela, Mike now added a new and disconcerting element. He fell *in* love with her, a state he'd not known for at least a decade and one which he always associated with high school and Polly, she of the pom-poms and fragrant gum. It was a giddy time, marked by nervous tremors, soaring flights of fancy, indigestion, and a desire to

shower the beloved with gifts. He bought Gisela flowers, a
watch, a sapphire ring, candy, sunglasses, mixed nuts, a
scarf from Spain, a basket of fruit, and several perfumes.
He found himself touching her constantly, disliked being
parted from her for more than a few minutes. He adored
her carriage, her stride, the splash of freckles below her
eyes, her occasional blushes, the way she ducked her head
when feeling especially affectionate or lusty. He even liked
her Germanic insistence and use of the imperative, seeing
these traits as part of Gisela's strength, determination, and
courage. He admired her candid, blunt manner of speech at
times. He studied her as one emotion after another found
reflection in her features. He loved her aroma, nuzzled her
hair, liked to feel her arm hooked with his. At a table he'd
gaze deep into her eyes, seeking to plumb her mysteries
through these windows to the soul.

Gisela became his sum total of existence. Berlin, Hilde,
food, shelter were merely accessories. Mike found her character infinitely absorbing. Although his rational mind argued that Frau Steinbrecher probably differed but little
from several million other attractive, intelligent, educated,
sexually desirable European women, his emotions chanted
her singularity, the unique charm, and overpowering superiority of this woman he'd found one gray day in Leipzig.

He went around in a perpetual state of psychic and sexual arousal. He felt taut and true like a newly tuned guitar
string. The world shimmered. Time danced. He could see
glimmers of nobility in the shabbiest and meanest pedestrian, detect happiness behind the sourest of faces.

As the focus of this adoration, Gisela bloomed like wild
roses. Each day she seemed more beautiful, softer, more
poised. With her flair for the fashionable, she had been
unerring in choosing clothes and accessories that complimented her height, coloring, and easy grace. Within days
she transformed herself from a ragged, timid refugee into an

elegant cosmopolite who looked as if she belonged in Berlin's most sophisticated milieus. Men openly admired her. Once in the lobby of the Komödie at intermission, Mike and Gisela overheard one man ask another, "Who is that striking blonde by the poster?" Gisela drank in the remark like champagne, then said laughingly to Mike: "If only they knew that I'm just an overworked editorial hack from the Communist provinces."

They became insatiable in their love-making, often not falling asleep until two or three in the morning and then venting a rekindled passion soon after waking before noon. At times they treated each other with exquisite tenderness, at times with awe, occasionally with reverence. But more often they were playful, lighthearted, teasing about the agonized sounds that each drew from the other. Sometimes they grew combative, romping on the bed as roughly as animals. For Mike, sex with Gisela became a kind of madness. Like a drug addict, he needed his fix every night, every morning, and often he desired her only a few hours after a passionate encounter had left them both exhausted. "Why don't we return all these clothes and get your money back," said Gisela, laughing, one morning. "All I need with you is a bath towel." That same afternoon they left an Italian film at the Gloria-Palast in the middle of a smoking love scene and hurried back to the hotel to stage their own version.

In his state of euphoria, Mike told everyone he knew that he was in love. He called his daughter, Sally, twice in New York with happy love bulletins and he wrung a promise from his son, Dave, that he would take a short leave and come to Berlin for dinner on the last night before Mike and the Steinbrechers flew to New York. When Mike told Hilde of his love for her mother, the girl merely raised an eyebrow and said, "So what else is new?" A moment later, however, she threw her arms around him, their first embrace not initiated by Mike.

But along with the ebullience and soaring spirits, Mike and Gisela could never forget the fragile state of equilibrium in which their honeymoon city lived. Wherever they went, they either saw the Wall or encountered American, British, and French soldiers, some of the twelve thousand Allied troops garrisoned in the marooned metropolis. Occasionally they saw the Soviet military sedans, always with four Russian officers sitting at attention, that rolled slowly around West Berlin to emphasize Russia's right to maintain a presence there, just as Allied military patrols cruised through East Berlin.

What made the unmarried honeymoon extraordinary was not only the surrounding Wall and the constant reminders of military confrontation, but the fact that along with the gay times, the expansive sense of well-being, and the erotic feast of the lovers, they both recognized that culturally they were far apart. They became aware that these differences had to be handled with tolerance and without judgmental pronouncements if they were to avoid rancorous disputes that might sabotage their love. Mike learned to heed his words lest some offhand remark about East Germany would offend Gisela. The DDR was her home turf and she was quick to counter any statement about it that she considered erroneous or unfair. She was a committed Socialist. She found much in the West to criticize. She thought the incessant competition was wearying and destructive to society. Although the wealth of luxury goods fascinated and lured her, she thought the excess production was a waste of human energy. She deplored the existence of affluence and poverty in so many capitalistic countries. She could not understand how the United States could preach about cherishing human rights while failing to provide free medical care for all its citizens.

Disorder bothered her. Although West Berlin was quite orderly, if brash and pugnacious, the Kurfürstendamm subway station at the hub of the city often presented an untidy appearance late at night. Long-haired hippies in overalls, jeans, beads, and togas lounged around. Winos slumped against the walls sucking on bottles. Fractious, dark-hued Turks in pointed shoes milled about. Black-jacketed youths managed to look menacing. Kids strummed guitars, begged coins, or sang and shouted. Withdrawn young men and women, pale and wasted on drugs, stared vacantly at the few well-dressed subway patrons. To Mike, inured to the gritty chaos and sporadic terror of New York's subways, the Ku'damm U-Bahn scene seemed quite tame. It was, after all, but a single stop in a system remarkable for the cleanliness of its stations and the circumspect behavior of its passengers. Also, Mike rather liked the diversity and the unruliness of the crowd, a relief from the uniform respectability of Germans in public.

Gisela, on the contrary, found the subway scene quite disagreeable. She compared it unfavorably with the decorum on East German trains and trolleys where youngsters customarily yielded their seats to their elders. West Berlin authorities, she contended, should clean up the Kurfürstendamm station and impose a minimal standard of seemly conduct.

And the matter of free speech continued to trouble her. Several days after her disagreement with Mike and Hilde over the Fassbinder film, Gisela was picking her way through the *International Herald Tribune* as part of her daily English lesson. She read several stories aloud to Mike, including one which quoted a Congressman Pilcherman of Illinois as saying to a convention of broadcasters in Chicago that "under the surface the United States is more oppressively racist for black people than apartheid South Africa."

She looked at Mike with a frown. "Is that true?" They were having a late breakfast in their room.

"No. That's political exaggeration. It might have been

true fifty years ago, but not today. We have serious racial conflicts, but we're no South Africa."

"Then why does a government person say so?"

"Well, Pilcherman isn't in the governing administration. He's a legislator, elected by his district. He probably brands us racist to call attention to our black-white problems. And we have them. We're a long way from being an equal society racially."

"If it's not true, why does a newspaper print it?"

"Newspapers print what many people say. They don't necessarily agree with the speaker. That's a free press."

Gisela looked perplexed. "You know that statement will be picked up by the Soviets for propaganda in the Third World."

"I suppose so." Mike busied himself dressing. "That's one of the hazards of democracy. Anybody can quote what we say about ourselves against us."

"So why doesn't the government stop that kind of talk? If it's false, the congressman has no right to hurt his country."

Mike's zest for verbal combat flared. He cautioned himself to proceed with care. "Who's to judge what's true or false?" he asked with forced calm. "You? Me? A board of some kind?"

"Your President McCullough. He represents everybody."

"The President?" Mike was astounded. "How could McCullough possibly monitor what 220 million people say? And who wants that kind of Big Daddy?"

"He could appoint people to do it for him."

"And suppose that appointed agency decided that a certain Professor Otto Kleist, recently moved to America, could not publish or say anything about the increase of carbon dioxide in the atmosphere?"

"Oh, Miguel, you know they'd never do that."

"No, I don't. Censors rule against anybody who displeases them."

"You and I are talking about two entirely different things." She spoke with heavy emphasis.

"No, we're not. It's the same issue—freedom of speech."

"There's no absolute freedom." Gisela, her jaw set, intended to pursue this.

"I agree." He wanted to turn it off. "Look, Gisela, let's knock off this discussion. After you soak up the freedoms on this side for a month or so, then we can try it again."

"I won't change my mind."

"Mmm. Who knows? We both may change a little."

They were edgy with each other as they dressed to go out. They had planned to visit several galleries and the Charlottenburg Palace, then meet Hilde and her friends for lunch. A bit distant walking along the corridor, they entered the automatic elevator without speaking. But Mike couldn't stand even a few minutes of estrangement. He seized and kissed her as the elevator descended. She held him in turn, clinging fiercely.

"I love you," she said.

Never before with him had she uttered the lovers' sacred triad of words. The sound of the syllables transported him and he became acutely conscious of her aroma, the moist pressure of her lips, the beating of her heart. When the elevator stopped at the lobby level, he reached behind her and without taking his lips from hers, he pressed the button for their floor. They never did see Charlottenburg Palace and they barely made the luncheon date with Hilde.

To the lovers, their differences in attitude and background seemed trivial when compared to their fierce hunger for each other and to their many common likes, dislikes, and interests. They were swept up in that dizzy spiral where their mutual esteem accelerated by the hour: his love for her shone from his eyes, further kindling her love for him which shone from her eyes and thus inspired him to greater love for her which in turn—and on and on and round and round and up and up until both Gisela and Mike felt they might burst like skyrockets.

And so the Berlin days rushed to a close. Mike's replacement, an ambitious, fresh-faced young engineer who had studied German in college, arrived on Monday, absorbed a three-hour briefing by Mike and Walter Delaney, and walked through Checkpoint Charlie Tuesday on his way to Leipzig. That night of early January was the last in Berlin for Mike, Gisela, and Hilde. Dave Simmons traveled from Fulda to join them in a farewell dinner before their flight to New York the next day. He was due to arrive at the hotel in early evening and accompany them to Le Bou-Bou, a restaurant on Ku'damm that Hilde liked.

Mike decreed that for this dinner meeting with his son and for their last night in Berlin, the women should wear corsages. While mother and daughter watched television, he would walk over to a florist shop on Marburger Strasse. At the last minute, Gisela decided to go with him.

"You see, for your son, I'm wearing the things his father likes."

She had put on a tailored, brown woolen coat and a flared brown felt hat with a game-bird feather that Mike had bought her.

Arm in arm the lovers kept step as they walked in the brisk, clear night. Overhead the cloudless sky held a sprinkling of early stars. Their breath misted on the chill air. Mike noticed how Gisela's shoulder-length hair swung in cadence with her stride, reminding him of the harmonies of music. Yes, she had entered his life like a new, powerful symphony, perhaps transformed that life, for it occurred to him that, since her arrival, no wall had loomed in his dreams nor had a single phantom or ghoul trashed his nights. Perhaps in defeating the Wall, even by commercial means, he and Gisela had exorcised his demons. He felt terrific, in tune with his woman, with Berlin, with the world. He loved being in love.

"Gisela!" The shout came from a voice they both knew.

"Ulli!" Gisela shook free of Mike's arm and pointed across the street. "What is she doing on this side?"

Ulli Beitz leaned out of the window of a car that had halted opposite them on Augsburger Strasse. Rays of a street lamp etched her familiar face and her jungle of hair.

"Come on over, Gisela!" Ulli waved gaily.

Gisela ran across the street to greet her. Mike followed at a leisurely pace. Ulli, half out of the window, leaned forward to touch her friend. Gisela opened her arms.

At that instant, in a blur of movement, arms from within the car seized both women. Someone yanked Ulli, someone else, Gisela. Her feet flew off the pavement as she was pulled inside with great force. Her scream, a slash of surprise and fear, chocked off at once. The door slammed shut.

The black sedan vaulted forward with a clash of gears. Mike ran after the car, lunged at a rear-door handle in a desperate effort to yank the door open. He missed, went sprawling on the pavement, then tried to right himself in time to read the rear license plate. But the automobile, gaining speed, already was veering right into Ranke Strasse with screeching tires. By the time he scrambled to his feet, the sedan had vanished from sight. Several bystanders gaped at Mike as he stood, dazed, in the middle of the street.

In shock for long seconds, he shook himself, then turned and sprinted toward the corner of Marburger Strasse. He knew there was a telephone in the florist shop. He must phone the police. He tried to think as he ran. What make was the car? A Volga? Yes, a Soviet Volga with diplomatic plates.

14

At noon on Wednesday, January 6, Rolf von Staufen, press officer to the governing mayor, faced a dozen media reporters beneath the red-tiled roof and bell tower of West Berlin's handsome city hall in the Schöneberg district. The building overlooked the market square where several hundred thousand people had roared approval that day in 1963 when President John F. Kennedy, fresh from inspecting the Wall, cried defiantly, *"Ich bin ein Berliner."*

On this frosty January day, von Staufen waited a moment until the replica of Philadelphia's Liberty Bell, a gift from America, had finished pealing its daily noontime homage to the long-suffering ideal of equal human freedom under God.

"The governing mayor today lodged a strenuous protest with the government of the DDR against a gross violation of the 1971 four-power agreements covering operation of this city." Von Staufen coughed discreetly. He was a discreet official, all rosy and plump and unlined like an over-aged baby. "The governing mayor referred, naturally, to the brazen kidnapping on Augsburger Strasse last night of a recent refugee from the Deutsche Demokratische Republik. A respected professional, a doctor of chemistry, this woman was apparently gagged, concealed on the floor of a Soviet Volga sedan, and taken across at the Friedrichstrasse transit point under cover of diplomatic immunity. Known officers of the DDR Ministry of State Security were identified as riding in the kidnap vehicle.

"The governing mayor states that it has been many years since a resident of this city was swept off the streets and abducted to the other side. It is with a heavy heart that he files this protest. He had thought that DDR authorities had abandoned such ruthless tactics under the 1971 agreements. Kidnapping of an innocent civilian smacks of the worst acts of the cold war and stains the good record of cooperation and détente between the two halves of the divided city in recent years.

"The governing mayor calls upon East Berlin officials to release Frau Dr. Gisela Steinbrecher at once and to permit her to travel where she pleases in peaceful pursuit of her aims and wishes."

The reporter for *Der Tagesspiegel* asked if Frau Dr. Steinbrecher was one of the five persons who escaped through Spandau lock on the Second Night of Christmas. Yes, she was, replied the press spokesman.

Answering a reporter for *Die Welt,* von Staufen said that releasing names of others in the escape party would serve no useful purpose and might endanger relatives in East Germany. Of course, he added, the name of Alex Engelmann, captain of the gravel scow, had been made public because DDR officials already knew it.

A correspondent for the Associated Press asked what happened to Frau Steinbrecher after she was taken across the frontier. The press officer said it "was understood" that the SSD had detained her for interrogation.

A young correspondent for Reuters, new to Berlin, asked why no one had stopped the kidnap car at the border.

Hadn't someone alerted Allied officers at Checkpoint Charlie?

"Both West Berlin police and the Allied military personnel at Checkpoint Charlie did receive warning calls," said von Staufen, "but you must remember that the West imposes absolutely no restraints on this side. Anyone may freely leave West Berlin. No one wants to change that policy despite such shameless episodes as that of last night. . . . And of course no one on this side of the border saw Frau Dr. Steinbrecher because she was concealed, we think, on the floor of the car."

Newsmen questioned the mayor's rosy-cheeked aide for another ten minutes to no particular avail and then the woman from RIAS, the American-controlled West Berlin radio station, ended the session.

"As a final question," she asked, "what does the governing mayor propose to do if the DDR rejects or ignores his demand?"

"If and when that occurs," replied von Staufen, "appropriate measures will be considered."

They sat disconsolately in Walter Delaney's spacious living room in the frail afternoon sunlight and tried to subvert the future. They might have been the bereaved, just returned from last rites at graveside. Mike Simmons stirred his fourth cup of coffee that day and watched without seeing as the spoon cut its frothy wake. Hilde Steinbrecher leafed through a copy of *Stern*. She was dry-eyed now, but she had broken into sporadic fits of sobbing. Dave Simmons stretched his long legs and gazed at the wide fireplace and its crackling birch logs.

Sue Delaney, acting on the theory that people who grapple with insoluble problems need constant refueling, went to the kitchen to fill a tray with still more cheese, crackers, cakes, and cookies.

When the wall phone rang, Walter Delaney answered, then gestured to Mike. "For you. The police."

"You take it, Walt. You know my German's not good enough."

Delaney listened, lounging against the wall, smoking nervously, scuffing at a white rag rug. Mike wondered what the police wanted this time. He had left Walt's number at the hotel after talking twice today with the meticulous young officer who had quizzed him at length last night through an interpreter. Right now Mike felt drained, flat, interested in little but sleep. Last night had been an emotional roller coaster. First came the numbing shock, then the burst of frantic activity, alerting the police, Delaney, and the U. S. Mission. He went through an outpouring of rage against the East German regime, then comforted Hilde in her tears only to find himself sobbing as well. Finally, worst of all, late at night, he experienced that desperate sense of loss. The abduction of Gisela shook him physically, snatched his strength, and left him empty and nauseated. At last he managed to fall into a ragged sleep, but a rabble of stinking tramps caroused near the walls of his unconscious, bellowing obscene songs and cursing drunkenly. He awoke after only a short sleep, aware that the ghouls that had spared him for ten long nights had swarmed back to infest his dark hours. It had been a comfort to have Dave nearby. And Hilde, despite her fits of weeping, proved quite helpful. She sensed what ought to be done and did it, never hovering about waiting for others to take the initiative.

"Bad news." Delaney replaced the phone in its wall bracket. "The East German major died in the hospital a few minutes ago."

The news hit Mike like a blow to the stomach. The implication took immediate shape: Gisela's chances of ever leaving the DDR had suddenly plunged toward zero. But instead of raging as he had last night, Mike felt only a deep sense of futility. How to fight? Against whom? With what?

"The guy was fifty-one, named Horst Ludendorff." Delaney took a seat on the sofa beside Hilde. "Unfortunately for us, he'd been a very popular East German bike champion back in the early fifties and he held the DDR's Scharnhorst Order."

Hilde at last broke the silence. "That means they'll put Mother on trial as a something to murder. What's the word?"

"Accessory?" Dave offered.

"Yeah, that's it." Already Hilde was picking up Dave's accent. The two had taken to each other from the start.

Sue Delaney placed the tray of snacks on the long, wooden coffee table, then stood beside Hilde and held her hand for a moment. "And what exactly does this mean for Gisela?" she asked.

"It means a certain trial, so-called," said Delaney, "certain conviction, and probably a long term in prison. Am I right, Hilde?"

"I'm afraid so, Mr. Delaney." Hilde's eyes watered again.

The probable prison sentence pressed on Mike's shoulders like a monstrous, insupportable burden. Then suddenly it occurred to him. My God, she will never get out of East Germany. He would never see her again. A light had been snuffed out, love garroted. He wanted to shout or scream. Instead he tried to breathe deeply and ended with a grotesque yawn.

"The police think that Hilde should be watched carefully," said Delaney. "Another kidnapping, while unlikely, is always a possibility. They're willing to detail a plainclothes man to go around with her."

"Oh, no." Hilde made a face. "I don't want that."

"I understand how you feel," said Delaney. "One thing's sure. You ought to move. A hotel's not a suitable place for you right now."

"You can stay here, dear," said Sue. "We'd love to have you."

"Thanks, Mrs. Delaney, but I'd rather try the Kassels. They already called this morning and invited me."

"The Kassels?" asked Dave.

"The DDR family that came over last year in the American embassy car. There are kids my age to hang out with."

"I guess you should stay with them for a couple of weeks, Hilde," said Mike.

Hilde phoned, reported back that the family welcomed her that very night. "The cousin says I can have his cot and he'll use his sleeping bag on the floor." Her eyes had a sparkle for the first time that day. "I told him I'd switch with him every week."

"So what's our next step?" Dave wanted action.

"Before we step, let's see where we're going," said Delaney. "I don't want to walk off a cliff with my eyes shut."

They all had suggestions. Dave wanted his father to hold a press conference "and nail the bastards with the facts." Mike wondered if Amnesty International could be prodded into mounting a campaign to free Otto Kleist and Gisela. Hilde thought she might write a letter to East German Chairman Volpe, pleading for her mother's release. Sue suggested that the chemistry professors of the Federal Republic be encouraged to sign a petition soliciting Gisela's freedom.

"I think the wisest course right now is to do nothing," said Delaney after a long, wandering exchange. "I'm no expert but I do think I know West Berlin and the politics of the Wall better than anyone in this room. Relations between the two Berlins and the two Germanies are very complex, lots of interlocking services. Mike, you remember Rudolf Lerchbacher, the Deutsche Bank officer you met at the Roma one lunchtime?"

Mike nodded, recalling Delaney's unaccustomed civility.

"As a sample, Rudi has personally handled a lot of loans to Volpe's crew. Hell, East Germany owes about eight billion dollars to Western banks. The two sides talk like enemies, but they know they need each other. That breeds a lot of goddam hypocrisy and double talk." He lit one cigarette from the glowing butt of another. "If Gisela's ever let out—and I think Hilde and Mike have to face the prospect that she may never be—it sure won't be any time soon. If you enlist in the job of trying to spring her, you sign up for a long, long haul."

"So?" Yesterday's shimmering world lay in ruins at Mike's feet. He resented Delaney's dispassionte analysis.

"So I'd advise watchful waiting for a couple of weeks," Delaney replied. "Let's see what the governments do first, then we can decide. Believe me, time is not of the essence here."

They talked for some time, but Hilde was anxious to move to her new temporary home and the Simmonses took her back to the hotel in a cab. Hilde gathered up her belongings, then departed with one of the Kassel boys for the family apartment in the Wilmersdorf district. Dave arranged for a late afternoon flight to Frankfurt en route to Fulda and his duty with the 11th Armored Cavalry. Mike accompanied him to Tegel Airport in a taxi and saw him off on a British Airways plane.

Dave, in a rare gesture, threw an arm around his father's shoulders. "I wish I'd met her, Pop. Words are kind of useless, but I guess you know what I feel for you."

"It's as if we'd just buried her." Mike felt his throat tighten again. "I love her, Dave."

"I know that. I could tell the minute I saw you last night." He gripped Mike's shoulder. "You going to stay here or go back to the States?"

"I couldn't bear to leave now." The thought had not occurred to him. "She's just a couple of miles away over there, you know." He motioned to the east. "I'll stay put. How long, I don't know."

"Fulda's only a hop and skip away." Dave picked up his flight bag. "If you get to feeling low, I want you to take the plane to Frankfurt. I can meet you there."

"Thanks." Mike smiled weakly.

"Promise?" Dave made a fist and tapped his father's arm. "You get the blues, you call me. That's an order."

"Okay, Commander."

Mike was glad to be alone. Riding back from the airport, he lost himself in the anonymity of a bus. Like a wounded animal, he huddled in a rear seat as if it were a cave where he could suffer in solitude. Not that he enjoyed the misery of loneliness and crumbled dreams. Rather his resolve had sunk so low, he did not have the energy to face and deal with people. The long night and day, so like the death, funeral, and burial of a beloved, had depleted him. Now he wanted nothing and hoped for nothing, resigned to face a gray world without tomorrows. Riding toward the city's center, he imagined himself back in the Berlin of May 1945: shattered buildings, gaping bomb and shell craters, ragged, shoeless children, mounds of smoking debris, blocked streets, fallen wires, and blackened, limbless tree trunks.

At the Alsterhof, Herr Kunze, handing Mike a message along with his key, looked heavy with condolence. Everywhere this feeling of death. Walt Delaney had phoned.

Calling Delaney from his room, Mike stared dejectedly at the long, open closet. He must persuade Hilde to take her mother's clothes. He could not bear to see Gisela's new dresses, blouses, slacks, skirts, jackets, and coats hanging there.

"New York called," said Delaney. "Jacoby wants you

back in the office by Monday. He's got a job for you in
Brazil—Recife."

"Did you tell him about Gisela and Hilde?"

"You kidding? I tell him fuck-all outside of business. He
hasn't a glimmer of what you've been up to."

"Walt, I'm not going back. I'm staying here; how long, I
don't know."

Delaney rasped his ragged smoker's cough. "What
should I tell him? That you've gone over to Otis?"

"Just say I need a rest and want a three-months leave of
absence."

"And if he says no dice?"

"Then I guess I'll be fired."

"Come on, Mike. You don't mean that. . . . I'll tell him
you got pneumonia like your predecessor and you need a
couple of months to recuperate."

"No. Just say I want a leave of absence."

"Okay, pal. I'll call you tomorrow."

Mike switched on the television and watched distractedly
the last half of a travelogue through Bonn and along the
Rhine. The evening news led off with the usual quota of international misery, dead Arabs and Jews in Jerusalem, a
border shoot-out between Russia and Chinese patrols, a
jumbo jet crash in Kenya. Then came news from East
Berlin.

"The public prosecutor of East Berlin," said the West
German announcer with a clear articulation that Mike managed to follow, "states that Gisela Steinbrecher of Dresden
will be tried in the Berlin district court on a charge of being
an accessory to murder, according to ADN, the official East
German news agency. He said the Steinbrecher woman and
four others accused of criminal violations of DDR borders
conspired to murder Horst Ludendorff on the Second Night
of Christmas. Ludendorff, who, the prosecutor contended,
was shot and brutally beaten by the five alleged criminals,

died today in a hospital here. ADN said Ludendorff was a civilian engineer, 'a hero of the struggle against war and Fascism,' a holder of the Scharnhorst Order, and a popular bicycle champion of the early fifties. West Berlin authorities said that Ludendorff was not a civilian engineer, but a major in the DDR's National People's Army assigned to engineering duties. They added that he drew a revolver to start the fight aboard the freighter."

Like TV commentators the world over, this one offered his dread tidings in a blandly pleasant, conversational tone as if he were giving instructions from the local garden club. "The prosecutor said the full charges against Frau Steinbrecher included treason, criminal border crossing, and conspiracy to murder.

"In another aspect of the case, ADN quotes DDR Minister of Justice Anton Zumpe as rejecting the 'totally absurd' charge by the mayor of West Berlin that Frau Steinbrecher was kidnapped off the streets of West Berlin last night by DDR security agents riding in a Soviet Volga with diplomatic plates." A still photo of the minister appeared in the background. He wore pince-nez glasses and had the gentle look of those grandfathers who play with little children on playground seesaws. "On the contrary, said Minister of Justice Zumpe, Frau Steinbrecher returned to DDR territory of her own volition and confessed her crime to the authorities. Zumpe will therefore recommend, in event of the Steinbrecher woman's conviction, that the judge take her change of heart into consideration when sentencing the offender."

The phrase "returned to DDR territory of her own volition" echoed hollowly long after the commentator had passed on to the rest of his dreary bulletins on the human condition. Ordinarily Mike would have flared angrily at the official lie, perhaps cursed the minister's benign image on the screen. But tonight he merely gazed hopelessly at the

TV set. He lacked the will to combat, correct, or dispute such a brazen perversion of the truth. The kindly minister had turned the kidnapping inside out like one of those two-way jackets, so that rough, dark leather became a cheerful plaid.

Mike fell asleep without dinner and with the TV set gabbling into the empty night. In his inner world, where terror always camped just beyond the fringe of reason, cloaked phantoms pursued him through fields where bony trees creaked and swayed. Howling winds flung themselves like crippled madmen against a huge, gray wall. Mike woke up twice, each time in the cold sweat of despair.

The chancellor worked late that night in his tidy office in the angular, modern chancellery, dubbed "the savings bank," in West Germany's capital. A bright, scalloped moon etched the city of Bonn, glinted on the flowing Henry Moore sculpture gracing the lawn and bathed the Rhine and the majestic poplars that bordered the swiftly flowing river just below the chancellery. Uniformed guards patrolled the metal fence ringing this power hub of Europe's most prosperous and potent nation. Atop the nearby Steigenberger Hotel a silver Mercedes-Benz logo revolved in the moonlight, symbol of the industrial might on which the chancellor's political influence rested.

While Kurt Rauschnig could look with satisfaction on the condition of the Federal Republic and his own contribution to the health of the nation that had vaulted from ruins to riches in two generations, the world as always was fraught with menace and he had wrestled tonight with two perils to his country's well-being. First was the ugly new confrontation in the forever turbulent, oil-soaked Middle East and second the demand of his powerful but capricious ally, the United States, that West Germany join the U.S.A. in support of the guerrillas harassing the Soviet Union's southern border.

Chancellor Rauschnig had not yet decided on his response to Washington, but he sensed the need for unusual caution. In these times, statesmen must always tiptoe lest a single wayward heavy tread crush the fragile crust of peace and plunge the world into the pit of nuclear war. As a frightened boy, he had lived through the horrors of the bombing raids on Bremen in World War II. He remembered one night in particular when fires raged out of control and splashed the sullen sky with flaming orange streaks that he was sure would consume the world. Now, whenever Rauschnig considered a war of hydrogen missiles, he thought not in abstractions like so many generals and geopoliticians, but in the vivid image of that night in Bremen— the burning of the planet.

With that picture flickering on the outskirts of his mind, he turned again to the major problem of the moment, that ominous business in Berlin: kidnapping, death of a wounded major, the DDR's charge of murder. He read once more through his growing, updated file that included press clips, a new report from his BND intelligence people, and a concise memorandum from his own specialist on border incidents.

All day long, Kurt Rauschnig had grappled with this explosive and menacing event, explosive because of the fragility of East-West relations, menacing because it had been a decade or more since the hard-line comrades over there had dared to kidnap someone off the streets of West Berlin. Did this portend a new era of harassment of the beleaguered city, perhaps the closing of the Autobahns, the delay of trains, and the buzzing of commercial planes in the air corridors?

Early that morning he had marshaled a crisis committee which pondered that question throughout the day. He had talked at length with his permanent representative in East Berlin, had huddled with his foreign minister, who in turn summoned the representative of East Germany and the ambassador of the Soviet Union. The chancellor had conferred with his experts in the ministry of inter-German relations, the opposition leader in the Bundestag, his intelligence chief, several politically astute private advisors, and twice with the governing mayor of West Berlin.

The crisis committee submitted its report early that evening. At last, after ordering his secretaries not to disturb him short of disaster, Rauschnig dined at his desk and devoted the hour to threshing through all aspects of the case.

Now, as the time neared midnight, he had reached his decision and he asked a secretary to put through another call on the scrambled secure channel to West Berlin's Mayor Peter Leonhard at his home in the Grunewald section.

He hoped this talk would not prove difficult. He expected a protest, but on the other hand Peter owed him more than one favor. Rauschnig had persuaded other SPD party leaders to back Leonhard for mayor and he had never faltered when Leonhard pressed him for more federal funds for the always fiscally embarrassed city.

"Peter!" he boomed. "I hate to bother you so late at night, but you know the ramifications of this kidnapping matter."

"No apologies necessary, *Herr Bundeskanzler*. I expected your call."

"Anything new since we talked this afternoon?"

"Not unless it's the American. I think I failed to mention that there was an American businessman mixed up in the Steinbrecher escape."

"Ja, ja. I saw that in the BND report. . . . I thought your statement this noon, as I mentioned before, was excellent, right on target, along the lines we discussed this morning. What's your next move, Peter?" The chancellor came on full volume. He believed in the hearty approach.

"Tomorrow I propose to expose the lie of the DDR Minister of Justice. Zumpe has the gall to say that Frau Steinbrecher returned over there of her own free will." Mayor Leonhard's laugh was a mocking one. "Such audacity! The poor woman was dragged headfirst into that Soviet Volga—and right on Augsburger Strasse in view of a dozen people. We have their names."

The chancellor let silence rule the line. He was noted for his long and ambiguous pauses. "Ordinarily I would applaud that plan of attack, Peter. As you know, I've been preoccupied with this matter all day. I've gathered viewpoints and advice from many sources, including you, and I've come up with quite a different approach. May I give you a bit of my thinking?"

"Naturally."

"We're not at all sure what this kidnapping means for the future. At the worst, reflecting the hardened line over there since the Polish labor upheaval, it may portend a resumption of the whole cold war litany in Berlin. At best, it may forecast no change at all in our current viable, if unsatisfactory, accommodations with the other side. We have a hint, through our sources over there, that the abduction actually may have been a blunder stemming from a feud between two SSD officials. We just don't know. In these circumstances, I believe the wisest course may be to say nothing for a few days."

"I understand. Still, I'm responsible for the safety of our city's streets. If I fail to nail the lie, Berliners will hold me in contempt."

Rauschnig lowered his voice. "There's a chance that if the other side also says nothing, the incident may be forgotten as the days and weeks go by."

"Too many people know of this, Herr Bundeskanzler.

283

On Augsburger Strasse, after all, only two blocks off Ku'damm."

"True. I appreciate your point. Yet it would be irresponsible to let this escalate into a crisis that we might have prevented." Again Rauschnig let silence hover on the line. "I'd hate to see such an escalation in the weeks before my Weimar meeting with the chairman."

"Naturally. That would be most unfortunate." Mayor Leonhard belonged to the high-level political team that would brief the chancellor before his March 18–19 German summit conference with the DDR chairman in the historic city of Weimar in East Germany.

"We can never forget that the other side holds the best cards." They had discussed the dilemma many times: West Berlin's isolation deep within Communist territory, its dependence on a dozen vital services performed by East Germany.

"I realize that." The mayor could feel the pressure. Tiny beads of perspiration covered his forehead like morning dew. "What would you advise under the circumstances?"

"If at all possible, Peter, I wish that you would say nothing tomorrow, and let's see if this thing will fade away like so many incidents before it. After all, when we weigh the interests of one person against the well-being of 62 million people in the Federal Republic . . ."

"Of course." Leonhard thought the exact phrase should be "freedom of one person," but one did not quibble over semantics with the chancellor. "I understand your problem. Sometimes here in Berlin, up against the Wall, we lose perspective."

"Your perspective's a good one, Peter. If it weren't for the Weimar meeting . . ."

"I'll do my best, Herr Bundeskanzler, to defuse the issue. Of course, there will be demands from certain quarters, the Springer press, for instance."

"Yes, sometimes a response cannot be avoided. But, in general, the less said the better. Are we in accord?"

"Agreed. I appreciate your counsel and that you took the time to talk with me personally."

"From you, Peter, right there on the firing line, that's very generous." The chancellor came on heartily once more. "It's a pleasure to work with you."

Mayor Leonhard sighed as he hung up. It was always the case. In whatever system, the freedom of the individual seldom took precedence.

Under the same bright, scalloped moon, not many miles from the mayor's home, another politician picked up another telephone in another home. This one was located ten miles north of East Berlin in a walled and guarded compound in Wandlitz, residence of the supercomrades, or "one hundred percenters," as street slang had it. Top men of the Communist oligarchy lived, if not in a workers' paradise, certainly in a handsome senior bureaucrats' refuge, for they occupied large stone houses overlooking wide lawns and flower gardens that burst into a rainbow of colors in the spring. The supercomrades enjoyed recreational facilities rivaling the West's sleek country clubs, rode in chauffeur-driven, Russian-built limousines, and shopped at exclusive stores stocked with goods rarely seen on the shelves of establishments open to the public.

The hundred percenters had moved to Wandlitz from Pankow, a district of East Berlin now largely given over to the homes of the captains and majors of the Communist bureaucracy. In addition to their suburban residences, the supercomrades enjoyed a vacation retreat, also fenced and guarded, on a lake about thirty miles northeast of Berlin near Eberswalde.

On this night in his Wandlitz home, Chairman Heinrich Volpe had just indulged his wife by sitting with her through a West German cops-and-robbers show on their wide-screen color television set. Frau Volpe much preferred the other side's varied fare to the steady propaganda drizzle on the two East German state-operated channels.

Volpe, who wore steel-rimmed glasses and looked as deceptively unthreatening as a professor of the classics, was out of sorts. Varentsov had called twice from Moscow this week, prodding him to condemn the Polish labor "counter-revolutionaries." Volpe had scant love for the Poles, labor or party, but he had even less for the Russians and their bullying tactics. This one, he hoped to duck. Let the Kremlin crack its own whip.

Also, he disliked this whole messy Steinbrecher business, a seizure dictated less by the interests of the nation than by a petty, annoying rivalry between two section chiefs in the Ministry of State Security. And yet if he disciplined either or both bureaucrats, it would appear that he acted in retaliation for the arrest of a relative. Actually he had met Frau Steinbrecher but once and now thought her an ingrate who got what she deserved for fleeing her native land where she had prospered with honors.

The chairman let his irritation simmer for a moment, then picked up the direct secure line to his Minister of Justice, a key man of the regime.

The clamor of the special phone grated on Anton Zumpe, the gray-haired Minister of Justice, an intellectual of delicate features and refined tastes, a wearer of pince-nez glasses who treasured his private hours in the home located only a short distance from that of the chairman.

Zumpe disliked being disturbed when his wife, Monika, was playing the harpsichord. He doted on the sharp, child-like sounds, so fragile, so tentative, so like a toy music box. When Monika tapped the keyboard ever so lightly, she beckoned her husband into a charming, minuet existence, spheres removed from the dense, didactic party atmosphere in which he spent so much of his life.

Monika stopped playing the moment she heard the harsh, gonglike clatter that distinguished the direct phone to the chairman from the others in the adjoining communications alcove. She put on her faint, ironic smile as Anton stepped quickly to the battery of instruments.

"Excuse the late call, Anton," said Chairman Volpe in his staccato, power-drill manner that belied all apologies. "I've been thinking over your statement today on the Steinbrecher case."

"Ah." Zumpe wondered. Had he, after all, gone too far? He had cleared the matter with the chairman's trusted secretary and been assured that Volpe wanted absolutely no favoritism shown his cousin's sister-in-law. In fact, said the secretary, he rather hoped she'd be made an example. Still . . .

"I thought your statement was excellent," said Volpe, "exactly what needed saying. We just cannot permit a false charge of kidnapping to go unchallenged."

"Thank you, Comrade Chairman." The Justice Minister waited without illusion. The chairman never called merely to pass a compliment.

"Of course, I regret State Security's initial overreaction, shall we say, but that's no concern of yours. . . . What's your next step in the case?"

"I planned to expose Frau Steinbrecher as an adulteress who spirited her own daughter away from a loving father in order to further her sordid romance with an American bourgeois. You've read the SSD file?"

"Yes, I have." The chairman paused. "She certainly deserves public castigation. But are you sure that's a wise move right now? Things have been going quite well with the other side recently."

"I realize that, Comrade Chairman. But I'm considering the internal consequences. Frau Steinbrecher is widely known in the intellectual sector. If we don't make an example of her, we may face a rash of similar attempts."

"Agreed, Anton. Still, I must look at the bigger picture. I don't want a relatively minor incident blown into a crisis in advance of my meeting with the chancellor."

"Yes, naturally. The Weimar meeting must take precedence in our thoughts." The Politburo, to which Zumpe belonged, already had met in several special sessions looking toward the German summit conference in March.

"We must always keep in mind that the other side has, if not many cards, certainly a crucial one." The Politburo had faced the problem many times. Although the DDR held West Berlin a hostage of geography and its services, the nation in turn depended on the vital foreign exchange it received in payments from the Federal Republic. The previous year, East Germany had earned a substantial surplus in West German marks. In addition, the country needed to keep its credit lines open to the West. It currently owed $8 billion to Western banks, including some in pivotal West Germany. Further borrowing in the money market of the Federal Republic appeared inevitable in this day of rocketing energy costs.

"Would you suggest that we postpone or cancel the trial, perhaps let Frau Steinbrecher off with administrative penalties?" Minister Zumpe still felt less than comfortable with the cousin-in-law relationship.

"No, no. Let's by all means go ahead with the trial and sentencing, the usual route. But let's do it without publicity." Volpe's wife now was watching a Munich ballad singer, a young woman with a ripe, sensual voice that stirred memories in the chairman. He glanced at the screen. "Our motto ought to be, 'Say no more than necessary.' Do you agree?"

"Absolutely. We don't want a minor incident to generate a storm that might ruin Weimar."

"You've stated the situation perfectly, Anton. My regards to Monika. Good night."

Minister Zumpe turned back with relief to the living room where his wife began playing a Scarlatti sonata on the harpsichord. The leather plectrums plucked at the strings, drawing forth those exquisite sounds that transported him to a crowded ballroom, gowned and powdered women, dainty dance steps, summery wines, a scene that lay far away from the thick, gray Wall and its dreary cycle of crime and punishment.

15

It came as a shock to Mike one morning some weeks later to realize that he could no longer remember exactly what she looked like. Until then, Gisela customarily slipped into focus soon after he awoke. He could see her tender smile, the splash of freckles, the small, resolute jaw framed by blond hair that curved to her shoulders. To be sure, the picture tended to drift into a pastel haze, somewhat like a painting of the French impressionists, but nevertheless he saw her with a kind of inner clarity.

This morning, try as he would, Mike could not bring Gisela into focus. Half images flitted about, now a flow of hair, now the tilt of her chin, or the subtle line of a breast beneath the orange sweater with the great cowl neck that she'd worn in Leipzig. But even when he concentrated, Mike could not see her as a whole person.

His memory's only distinct picture of her came from that night scene, as from a Fellini movie, when searchlights imprisoned her in the death strip. How ironic that from his memory he could filter only a distant Gisela caught in fear and panic and not the Gisela who ducked her chin and invited him, wordlessly, fetchingly, to snuggle with her beneath a fat Federbett. Today when he summoned the romantic image, he could recall only her aroma, that distinctive compound of breath, body, and bath oil. Gisela herself had dropped from sight.

After the first shock, he began to brood in this old two-room apartment with its depressing woodwork and the small windows that admitted a stained, tired light. Because of the need to economize, he had moved a week ago from the Alsterhof to this second-floor walk-up on Bleibtreu-strasse between Ku'damm and the main railroad line. Mark Jacoby had approved a payless three-months leave of absence from Todd Elevator and the last paycheck arrived ten days ago. Now he would have to draw on his savings for an indefinite period. The old brick apartment building, surfaced with a sooty stucco, was situated in a neighborhood of cobbled sidewalks, cafés, boutiques, antique shops, and one of the Kaiser chain of supermarkets. Its tenants included a cheap pension, a doctor's office, and a dispenser of mud-bath treatments.

Although the building was one of the few to survive the Second World War, it still bore scars of bullets and shell fragments. The bombing of adjacent structures had weakened its framework and occasionally the building shuddered like an old woman. Inky cracks embroidered the ceiling, the plumbing groaned and gasped, and a leaky radiator in the bedroom hissed at peculiar intervals. But the rent was reasonable enough and Mike, gearing himself for Walter Delaney's "long, long haul," calculated that he could sustain himself for some time if he avoided the deluxe restaurants and shops and dipped but rarely into Berlin's expensive night life.

After those first cruelly fevered days following Gisela's kidnapping, he entered a passionless void that now threatened to stretch out interminably. Everything seemed to drop away at once. Dave Simmons went back to the States under detached-duty orders for specialized helicopter training. Hilde, an amazingly resourceful girl who'd already enrolled in school, lived cheerfully, if frenetically, with the Kassel family and the band of teenagers who swarmed about the place. She and Mike slipped into a routine of dining together twice a week and a warm, although still somewhat reserved, rapport grew between them. Delaney traveled around Europe, selling his elevators and reaping fat commissions.

The two opposing Berlins, which had glowered and berated each other the day after the abduction, promptly lapsed into a puzzling, and to Mike, deafening silence. Not another word had been heard from any official, East or West. The press appeared to have joined the fraternity of silence. Only one small story had appeared since the first rash of articles, the *Berliner Morgenpost* reporting that Alex Engelmann, the river freighter's escaped captain, had gone to work for a Rhine barge line.

Mike sloshed about in a depression similar to the one he experienced in mid-December after his duel with SSD interrogators. Again he compared his lot to West Berlin itself. Far from home territory, surrounded by and dependent on strangers, he was as isolated as an island and gripped by old torments and new traumas.

If Gisela had swept into his life like a summer symphony, all exuberant promise and sensuous harmony, she had also disappeared as swiftly, leaving him doubly bereft. Now he heard only echoes of her sweet, vibrant chords in dim hallways, along snowy streets, and through the long, vaulted subway stations.

He began to do the things that lonely men do. He lingered overlong at breakfast. He watched too much television. He struck up conversations with reluctant strangers. One cold night on Augsburger Strasse, not far from the spot where Gisela was seized, a streetwalker slipped out of the shadows and offered herself for fifty marks. Young, slight, vacant-eyed, shivering in a dowdy cloth coat, she stamped her feet as she talked. Mike agreed to terms, walked a few yards with her, then changed his mind. When he turned toward his hotel, shrill German curses indicted America for breach of promise. Another night he went back to the Tano, watched busy sexual athletes score new feats in the nonstop color film, and sat at the bar with a rowdy, busty hostess who hustled him for a *piccolo,* a half pint of cheap champagne, for fifty marks. She offered to spend her day off with him for "no more than it would cost to fly to Rio for the carnival," tugged his ears, slid her hand inside his shirt, and occasionally petted his crotch, the while laughing and taunting him for sexual timidity. When he left, half-drunk, near midnight, she tossed several good-natured obscenities his way and implored him to "come back and fuck me into a coma when you're rich."

Winter settled in, slowing traffic and congealing the city's brisk tempo. Snowfalls, crusting on sidewalks, yards, and parks, soon became smudged with soot and mud so that Berlin took on a mean, mangy look. People peered from frosted windows at the swiftly emptying streets. Dirty icicles hung from eaves like dread locks and the wind knifed through the low-lying city on its way south from the heaving Baltic.

As the cold strengthened its grip, Mike's vigil in Berlin assumed the shapeless aspect of futility. What indeed could he accomplish here? Heavily sweatered beneath his new winter coat, he prowled the frostbitten city. He haunted the Wall, climbing innumerable platforms to gaze down on the frozen strip and the armed, booted East German patrols who trudged along in fur hats, padded jackets, and heavy gloves.

He began to detest aspects of the city's life that he had previously found colorful or amusing: the profusion of tawdry sex shops and bars, the impatience and arrogance of some Germans, the pervasive odor of stale beer, and the legions of fat, sullen dogs who waddled along beside their fat, complacent owners and left their excrement all over the icy sidewalks. Once Mike slipped in a fresh dropping, fell and bruised his elbow. He arose, cursing Berlin for outdoing New York in tonnage of dog shit. And Mike came to dread his nights, for the old mutilated demons had returned in force, ransacking his dreams, scaling prisonlike walls, and leaving him weary and irritable at dawn.

Yet he could not bring himself to leave the freezing city. Whenever the urge surfaced, he thought of Gisela only a few miles away in East Berlin, huddling in a cell somewhere, answering endlessly repeated questions, perhaps suffering through sleepless nights as he had in that frigid SSD room with the single bulb that glared at him like a fierce, one-eyed warden. No, he loved her and he could not tear himself away from this divided city while she remained in either half. He could not let the Wall win a victory over him by default and thus condemn his nights to ceaseless torment. So he hung on, battling depression and hopelessness by such tactics as daily mile runs in the crackling air, listening to symphonies at the Philharmonic Hall and the opera at the Deutsche Oper Berlin, and taking daily German lessons at a school for foreigners near his apartment.

Day after day dragged by without news of any kind of the Spandau escape, kidnapping, and aftermath. Then, late in the afternoon of that same day when he failed to bring Gisela's image into focus, he received a phone call at the apartment. Ingrid, the escape agent, said that she had news for him. She would wait in the back booth at the Tano.

The intimate, three-sided bar stood empty. The sexual-engineering films had not yet begun to roll. A stale, acrid odor of liquor and beer hung in the air as Mike walked past the full-length photographs of nudes and around the corner to the isolated booth in the rear.

Ingrid wore her smoked glasses and the chic gold wrist watch. She greeted him like an old ally and indeed he had come to trust her, despite her clandestine air, as he would a friend.

"Why do we always meet in this joint?" he asked after the felicitations. It seemed a shady place for honest business.

"It does raise doubts, doesn't it?" She lit a cigarette after Mike declined her offer. "But it's really not mysterious. Dahlem bankrolled Sonia, the proprietor who tends the bar, and in return we get this handy, secluded spot whenever we need it."

"So what's the news?" He had no hopes.

"Bad, I'm afraid, Herr Simmons."

"I'm used to the brand. Shoot."

"We have word of Frau Steinbrecher from the other side." She studied him through a veil of smoke. "She was tried, in secret, in East Berlin district court three days ago. The trial lasted only a few hours. Her lawyer, appointed by the court, presented no evidence on her behalf, merely petitioned for leniency because, he said, she had returned of her own volition." Ingrid looked down as she tapped ashes into a tray.

"And?" Already he could feel the hurt like icy fingers in this winter of despair.

"She was convicted on three counts: treason, criminal border crossing, and conspiracy to commit murder. The judge sentenced her several hours later." Ingrid paused again in her halting narrative of reprisal. As if fearing to overload his emotional circuits, she bundled her pain in small parcels. Mike searched for her eyes behind the sunglasses.

"Not a word appeared in any newspaper," she said.

"Nothing on television or radio. All this from our sources, very reliable ones, by the way."

"Come on, Ingrid." This was slow torture. "Get it over with."

"The judge sentenced her"—she touched his arm—"to twenty years in prison."

He had the sensation of falling at great speed. He recalled the time in Buenos Aires when, testing a Todd heavy-duty Clydesdale, he plunged four stories before the brakes caught. Now, as then, instant nausea.

"He lectured her as a once-popular party member for betraying the nation that honored her." Ingrid signaled by her inflection that she detested this chore. "Because of her former position, he said, he would not heed the plea for leniency. Her 'whim' of returning to the DDR did not wipe out her crime. He called her an adulteress and a woman so degraded that she led her own daughter into crime. . . . No mention, however, of Hilde's escape or of you or us."

A dull, gray weariness settled over him. He had expected the worst and now that the worst had come, he felt only numb despair.

"She began serving time yesterday." Ingrid's voice seemed to echo in some distant cave. "We're not sure where."

"Twenty years." A generation of prison life. Gray hair, waxy pallor, perhaps the sad shuffle of an elderly inmate. "Ingrid, I . . ."

"We all sympathize with you. None of us were prepared for a kidnapping." She sounded somewhat petulant as if East Germany had failed to abide by the rules of the game. "It's been many years since the Stasi seized anyone on this side."

"I feel so damn hopeless, Ingrid." The weariness pressed like a heavy weight.

She questioned him about his life, his finances, his plans,

and Mike, relieved to have a listener who cared, poured out his frustrations. He talked for half an hour.

"Herr Dahlem," she said when he finished, "wants you to know that if you're short of funds, he can lend you a few thousand at no interest."

"No, I can manage. But thanks."

"We have means to get a message to Frau Steinbrecher. It might take weeks, but if you have some word you wish to pass . . ."

"Yes, tell her for me that I love her always." His voice seemed to belong to some melancholy stranger. "And not to lose hope. Some means will be . . ." He halted, his mind blank.

"Will be?"

He did not reply and Ingrid covered his hand with hers.

"Some way will be found to help her," he said at last.

On this dauntless pledge that convinced neither of them, they parted.

Back at the apartment, poisoned with pain, he went through the chore of telephoning Hilde at the Kassels'. The girl took it bravely at first, reminding him that they both had anticipated a long prison term, but then she broke into tears and for a long time her sobs were the only sound between them.

"We will figure out some way," he said when Hilde's weeping subsided. But he could not mask his feeling of doom.

"Oh, I know. We must plan something." She tried to rally. "Let's talk tomorrow night at dinner. Okay? . . . And, Mr. Mike, I love you."

The words struck deep within him. "Thank you, Hilde. I love you, too. We're going to face what we must together. Tomorrow night, then."

He broke the news to Sue Delaney and then wrote letters to Sally at Cornell and to Dave at the training base in Flor-

ida. He had just addressed and sealed the letter to Dave
when it happened.

The rage blew up as suddenly and as powerfully as a tor-
nado, sweeping his senses, blackening his mind, and ripping
his melancholy to shreds. He paced the kitchen where he'd
been writing on the creaky wooden table. He smashed his
fist against the swinging kitchen door and sent it banging
back on its hinges.

The bastards! The goddam ideological goons, robbing a
woman of long years of her life for the "crime" of moving
to another country. Just what in God's name was wrong
with the cursed human race that its members could inflict
such idiotic torture on one another? And what about those
officials of the West, the supposed custodians of freedom?
Who spoke up now, or even whispered, of human rights? A
bunch of cowardly hypocrites who prattled of human freedom and dignity, but acted for their own comfort and con-
venience. And as he raged in thought and body, great tides
of energy swept through him, generating a desire for action.
He thrilled at the electric sensation and he vowed to harness
the energy. Somewhere help for Gisela could be found and
somehow he would enlist that help in his battle against the
Wall. To hell with Delaney's watchful waiting. He had
waited too long.

He was pacing the apartment, hands jammed in his pants
pockets, his mind steaming chaotically, when the telephone
rang.

"It's been many weeks, Michael." A rich British accent
with traces of Cockney. "I tracked you down through the
Alsterhof. Dave forgot to tell me you'd moved."

"Spider!" Strange, but among the ideas now boiling was
one that signaled: Call Spider Butler in Helmstedt. He
knows the politics of the Wall, he hates the Wall, and he's a
shrewd operator. "You won't believe it, but I was just

thinking of calling you. I got awful news today, Spider. The bastards condemned Gisela to prison for twenty years."

"I know, Michael. That's why I rang you. I got the word from some chaps who make that kind of news their business."

"So you've kept up with us?"

"Of course. First through Dave and then via that shouting over the Wall by those masters of double talk, our splendid satraps of East and West." Words spilled from the British Frontier Service veteran like a tumbling river.

"Spider, I'm stymied. I need help. Could I come over tomorrow and see you in Helmstedt?"

"Better I come there, Michael. I have a few errands in Berlin anyway. I'll take the morning train and be there in time for lunch." Butler gave the arrival time. "And chin up, Michael. There's a way to beat the Wall and you're the proper man with the proper tools for the job."

Mike met Malcolm Butler in the grimy Bahnhof Zoo rail station near Berlin's central animal park. They walked to the Roma, the Italian restaurant on Marburger Strasse where Mike first visited with Walt Delaney and where he and Hilde now met for their twice-weekly dinners. It felt good striding through the frosty air with this beanpole of a man, all bones, angles, and cheerful, showy talk. The two men had liked each other at once when they met with Dave for dinner in the village of Fladungen. Mike sensed Butler's integrity beneath the showmanship while Butler, he knew, felt a quick kinship, perhaps because of their mutual commitment to defy the Wall.

They found a side booth in the crowded, smoky Roma, ordered wine and lasagna. Mike brought Butler up to date on himself and Gisela since that rainy night at the border.

"But now," he concluded, "I frankly don't know where to turn. Everybody's forgotten the kidnapping already and nobody gives a damn. It might as well have happened back in the Middle Ages."

Butler nodded. "These governments usually follow the same script. If it's a simple escape, neither side says a word. If it's something unusual, they bluster a bit, but then close down like clams. Remember what I said that night at the border, Michael. Except for the East German people, almost everyone is secretly happy with the Wall."

"Yeah, I'm learning that firsthand."

"Actually you can't blame them." Butler sipped at his wine. "Imagine yourself the mayor of Berlin, totally surrounded, dependent on the bloody comrades for this service or that, not excluding garbage disposal, and defended by only twelve thousand Allied troops inside the city. Ivan, with twenty divisions camped in East Germany, has West Berlin by the dark and curly hairs. On the other hand, the DDR desperately needs the hard currency of the West, especially those big, fat Deutsche marks. Then there's the heavy trade between the divided Germanies. And the joint operation of many facilities. So you end up with a lot of mutual dependency."

The waiter brought their lasagna and fetched two new glasses of Italian red wine. "And so," said Butler, "neither side wants to rock the boat too much despite East Germany's growls and dirty little tricks from time to time. Also remember the conference between the chancellor and the chairman in March in Weimar. One more reason to keep an even keel. So the East loses a few passengers now and then. What's that compared to the ease, comfort, and safety of millions who sail this route?"

"I finally figured that out for myself."

Butler leveled his fork at him. "But what you haven't figured out is that you, Michael Simmons, have a powerful weapon that could blast a nice, bloody hole in that Wall, so big our lady of the crossing might walk through it as serenely as Queen Elizabeth herself."

"I do?" Mike's smile was a faint one. He waited. "What is it?"

Butler fixed his eyes on Mike, paused for dramatic effect, then raised his fork like a scepter. "Publicity, my boy! The power of the press! You have one of the great stories of today's Wall. The escapes, shootings, seizures, they happen every week. People have become hardened to them. But your story adds romance, the ancient bond between man and woman." The Spider put aside his theatrics and leaned forward to talk in low, conversational tones. "It just so happens that some reporters from the press and telly have been after me in the last few days. They're all scouting articles or shows about the Wall twenty years after—inside stuff, anecdotes, significance, et cetera."

"Suppose they featured Gisela's story," said Mike. "You think that would build up enough pressure to force her release?"

"It could if you do it right. If you let down your hair and tell the whole story, Michael. Then it might build into something big." Butler looked around at the chattering patrons crowding the tables. "I can see these people lapping up the story of Michael and Gisela and crying for more. . . . Is there any part of this thing you haven't told me?"

"Do you know about Otto Kleist?"

"Kleist?" Butler frowned. "No, who's he?"

Mike told of the chemist's research into growing amounts of carbon dioxide in the atmosphere and of Kleist's house arrest. "When Gisela and I called the Fluid Dynamics Lab in the States," he concluded, "they said they'd prod Amnesty International, but so far I haven't heard anything."

"Wizard." Butler beamed. "Romance and science."

Together they planned approaches to the press. Butler

would tip off newsmen to hidden aspects of the Spandau escape and kidnapping. Mike would make himself available for interviews and would encourage Hilde to do likewise. He would obtain the picture of himself and the two Steinbrecher women that Walt Delaney took the day after the Spandau escape. Hilde would be asked to get more pictures of Gisela from her great-aunt Frieda in Stuttgart.

They parted in midafternoon. Butler had business at British military headquarters in the Olympic Stadium complex before taking an evening train back to Helmstedt.

"Let's stay in constant touch," said the Spider, "as befits the last two enemies of the Wall left in the West. Remember that now and then those DDR sods do release political prisoners to this side. If we're smart, this just might work, Michael."

The first call came two days later from Hester McKinnon, a feature writer for the *International Herald Tribune*. She made a date to interview both Mike and Hilde, and she arrived punctually at four-thirty that evening with a photographer from whom cameras hung like ropes of seaweed. McKinnon, as she preferred to be called, was short, brusque, and mirthless, seven parts ambition to two of perception and one of patience. After listening only briefly to Mike and Hilde, McKinnon decided that the rupture of the Steinbrecher marriage under the strains of East German Communism yielded the juiciest approach. She asked leading questions like a prosecutor.

"You noticed, didn't you, dear, that your parents never talked politics?"

"Oh, but they did." Hilde, at first terrified by McKinnon's blow-torch methods, was now fighting back.

"Mostly trivialities, isn't that right, dear?" McKinnon seldom looked up from her note pad in which she scratched furiously.

"No. I remember a couple of big arguments they had about the system."

"And, of course, you and your mother never breathed a word to your father of your plan to flee?"

"No. By that time . . ."

Under a two-column headline several days later, the story began on the front page and covered considerable space inside. McKinnon saw the Steinbrecher saga as illustrating Communism's corrosive effect on the already fragile state of modern marriage. She did, however, cover all angles of the case, including Dr. Kleist, the border ordeal of mother and daughter, the kidnapping, and Gisela's secret conviction. Two pictures accompanied the article, one of Mike and Hilde by the *Herald Tribune* photographer and the other taken by Walt Delaney the day after the episode at Spandau lock.

Mike anticipated a flurry of inquiries following publication, yet he heard nothing. Aside from phone calls from Sue Delaney and Spider Butler, only one person mentioned the story to Mike. The woman who operated the corner news kiosk and whose steamy breath on winter mornings smelled of garlic and schnapps said she'd seen his picture in the English-language newspaper. "You looked better than those two women from over there," she added as she made change for another customer.

Two, three, four, five days went by without a peep from any source. Again Mike's spirits sagged. He tried to keep up an optimistic front when dining with Hilde, but his discouragement infected her like some contagious disease. He began to grow homesick and he wondered if, when he returned to New York, he should urge Hilde to accompany him.

Then suddenly the dam of silence broke. The phone in the kitchen of the gloomy apartment rang a dozen times in a day. *Bild* of Hamburg, the New York *Times*, the *Frank-*

furter Allgemeine Zeitung, Wall Street Journal, CBS, *Le Monde* of Paris, Stockholm's *Aftonbladet* and the Los Angeles *Times* all sought interviews. A young woman with a voice like sultry summer nights insisted on behalf of Channel Thirteen in New York that Mike fly home to be interviewed by Dick Cavett.

One newspaper interview came off that same night in Mike's apartment with Hilde in attendance. A perspiring, chunky writer-photographer from *Bild,* Axel Caesar Springer's tabloid with millions of German readers, took over the old, creaky flat like an occupying army. Conscious that in a nation of avid newspaper readers, *Bild* far overshadowed all other German journals in circulation if not in tempered judgment, Herr Francke felt obliged to issue orders and decrees as if the place were under martial law. Like McKinnon before him, Francke sized up his story within minutes of arriving. Fortunately his idea of the focus meshed with Mike's. This was to be a tale of international romance, at first triumphant over the Wall and then a victim of that gray monstrosity.

Overriding their objections, Herr Francke ordered Mike and Hilde about for various spurious poses. He snapped them at the old gas stove, Hilde cooking, Mike watching, despite Hilde's protests that she'd never cooked a meal there. He posed them at the kitchen table where Hilde supposedly gave nightly German lessons to her adopted "father." But they both refused when Francke wanted Hilde to sit in "Papa's" lap and weep on his shoulder for her mother.

Once he had finished with the camera, Francke took notes with the speed of a court stenographer. He zipped through the entire escape narrative in ten minutes flat, showed not the least interest in Professor Kleist and little more in the scene at Spandau lock. Instead he zeroed in on Mike's affair with Gisela and sought to bring out the nuances—sentimental, sexual, and cultural—of this across-the-Wall liaison. The reporter quickly took a dim view of Karl Steinbrecher back in Dresden and worked diligently at transforming Hilde's father into a Communist ogre, chained to Marxist ideology and abusing his daughter like a battered child with inane SED rules and precepts. Much as Hilde resisted this picture of a father to whom she was linked by the ambivalences of love, resentment, companionship, anger, and rebellion, she and Mike could see Francke painting the portrait question by question.

When the *Bild* man departed, bulling down the hall like a squadron of tanks, Hilde and Mike sought to weigh the invasion's damages against the probable beneficial results.

"That guy's too much." Mike shook his head. "Who knows what he'll come out with."

"At home the state arranges the facts to suit itself. Here the press seems to do the same thing. After McKinnon and Francke, I wonder if anybody will print the truth as you and I know it, Mr. Mike?"

"Remember *Rashomon?*"

"The Japanese movie? I never saw it, but I've heard about it. I think the theme's that there's no truth, only versions of it."

"Right. Maybe we should think out what we want to say. No sense hurting, rather than helping, your mother."

"I'm not so sure." She gathered her brows in thought. "I guess it doesn't make much difference what the press prints or what the TV shows as long as it puts pressure on the DDR. So maybe if we just tell everything we know, the best we can, that's about all we can do."

"Nicely stated. I agree." Every day he became more impressed with Hilde's good sense and judgment. She could switch in a moment from giddy teenage chatter and giggling into sober, mature reflection on whatever problem confronted them. "I have only one reservation. Let's not tell

anyone about my son Dave's help that night at the border.
So far the Army has spared him."

"What do you suppose the *Wall Street Journal* will want
tomorrow morning? I have to skip school for that."

The *Wall Street Journal,* it turned out, wanted to inspect
the profit and loss statements of professional escape merchants. Or that at least appeared to be the goal of Ted
Ramsey, the thirtyish reporter who flew in from the newspaper's Bonn bureau. Ramsey, who admitted to an MBA
from the Harvard Business School, dressed as sedately as a
corporate executive and held his wavy, prematurely gray
hair in place with a lacquer spray. Mike had the uneasy feeling that a cough or loud laugh might dislodge several
strands of hair and thus shatter the reporter's persona.

"Now how did you pay over that final twenty-thousand
dollars?" asked Ramsey when Mike and Hilde had finished
their narrative.

"In one-thousand-mark bills."

"Where?"

"Outside a neighborhood bar near Spandau lock."

"Is that the going price?"

"No. I think it was cheaper per head because of both
women coming out together."

The *Journal* man wanted to know how many people the
Dahlem network had smuggled out of East Germany at
what total cost, how many employees Dahlem had, whether
abandoning cars was a usual procedure. He had a score of
financial and organizational questions that Mike either
could not or would not answer. At last Mike called Ingrid
who agreed to talk to Ramsey over the phone. When the
journalist left a half hour later, he was irritable and huffy, a
man deprived of his rightful quota of numbers, percentages,
and fiscal footnotes by uncooperative, not to say obstruc-
tionist, individuals.

These first splatters of publicity turned into a downpour.

A half dozen leading European newspapers interviewed Mike and Hilde as did the Washington *Post* and Los Angeles *Times*. The New York *Times* not only printed a comprehensive story in its daily editions, but assigned an American woman novelist living in Paris to write of the case for the newspaper's Sunday magazine. The novelist, Edna Poncet Gambier, spent a week with Mike and Hilde and drew a picture of the Steinbrecher women that quite accurately, Mike thought, caught their personalities, motives, and conflicting tugs of allegiance. Newspapers as distant as the Sydney *Daily Telegraph* in Australia and Rio de Janeiro's *Jornal de Brazil* ran stories.

Almost every major television network in Europe, the United States, and South America devoted time to the Steinbrechers, Mike, and the Wall. A number of stations taped their own interviews and for several weeks Mike's apartment and that of the Kassel family teemed with sweating engineers, producers, gofers, interviewers who sprayed their throats and combed their hair, lighting technicians who cursed inadequate electrical outlets, worried soundmen and cameramen who wore necklaces and shirts unbuttoned to the navel. Cables and wires snaked about, TV crews drank countless bottles of beer, and neighbors complained of the daylong uproar in the Simmons apartment. Each night the two rooms and kitchen looked like the last campgrounds of a retreating army—floors and scarred furniture littered with cigarette butts, papers, cartons, bottles, plastic cups, and forgotten articles of clothing.

The first direct response to this deluge of publicity came not from a government, East or West, but from Todd Elevator, Inc. When Mike answered the phone one evening, he heard the firmly genial voice of Mark Jacoby, vice president and chief of the overseas division, calling from New York.

"You're all over the damn tube and the feature sections," Jacoby said after they had disposed of health and weather.

"NBC gave you and that Steinmetz woman another two minutes last night. Pretty clever, that elevator code, old buddy."

"I thought you'd like that." Mike had completely forgotten his mention of the code.

"But they weren't very happy up on the twelfth floor." Jacoby dropped several notches into his confidential groove. "First, Mike, they were hurt that you didn't let us know in advance of your involvement. The papers caught us off-guard. Then they didn't like bringing Todd into the picture. Frankly, the East Bloc business has become quite a thing for Todd. Between us, we did seventeen million gross last year in Lenin country and we figure to do better this year."

"Terrific."

"Yeah, well, naturally nobody wants to jeopardize our reputation over there. I'm sure, with your Leipzig experience, you can appreciate how easily misunderstandings can arise between the two systems."

"Sure can. The bastards mistook me for a CIA agent and damn near froze my balls off during interrogation one night in East Berlin."

"Yes. We read about that and of course we all admire your cool under pressure."

"Cool, my ass. It was goddam cold." He had tired of the executive fencing. "Come on, Mark. What are you leading up to?"

"I'm afraid it's not the best news, Mike. The twelfth floor has decided to cancel your leave-without-pay and to let you make other arrangements. I'm sure, under the circumstances . . ."

"You mean I'm fired?"

"Listen, old buddy, after all this publicity, they had no choice. Any company trying to land new business with the Russians or their friends just can't afford to alienate them by having a Michael Simmons on the payroll. As one of

Todd's old international hands, you must realize that as much as we do here in New York."

"Yep. An old hand for twenty-five years—and no gold watch." He was steaming now.

"Not even the chairman of the board gets a gold watch at today's gold prices." Jacoby forced a laugh. "Let's try to avoid bitterness, Mike. Believe me, being the courier of bad news is no pleasure trip."

"You tell the twelfth floor for me that I understand Todd's position completely." Mike held his anger in check. "And I'm sure Todd will likewise understand the steps I'm forced to take."

"Meaning what exactly?"

"Listen, a woman I love is being held in prison for a fifth of a century for absolutely no crime at all. Repeat, absolutely no crime." He made a fist as he spoke in slow, measured phrases. "I intend to do everything and anything possible to get her out. When you report back to the twelfth floor, please quote me on that—old buddy."

Some time later when the Associated Press called for its nightly check on the story that now was catching the fancy of news editors around the world, Mike told of his dismissal by a company that coveted Communist business. The next morning the New York *Daily News* carried a headline that mirrored scores of others in print and TV news shows that day:

WALL FIGHTER FIRED

16

By mid-February, as one of the century's coldest winters laid siege to the northern latitudes, the Wall-severed romance of Gisela Steinbrecher and Michael Simmons had captured the emotions of millions of people around the world. The stormier the winds and the deeper the snow, the more people took refuge indoors, and the longer they stayed at home, the more they read, saw, and heard of the luckless lovers. The public's unquenchable thirst for news and gossip about the couple amazed the captains of journalism, electronic and otherwise. Simmons-Steinbrecher stories consistently drew far more attention than those charting the daily progress of inflation, revolution, skiing, energy exhaustion, pollution, basketball, doomsday weaponry, the perfidy of nations, high fashion, urban decay, and human idiocy. A Columbia University journalism professor calculated that Gisela Steinbrecher had become as famous in one month as Jackie O., Muhammad Ali, and Billy Graham in a lifetime.

The thwarted romance reached deep into the world's psyche and touched hidden nerves of empathy. For every person currently in love, there were ten who had seen their own lustrous passion fade into dusty memory. All love was, in a sense, doomed to wither on the vine of daily existence. If tedium, sluggish liver, familiarity, sickness, bad breath, and spiritual poverty did not extinguish romance, then death stood ready in the wings to do the job.

A Stanford University psychologist, summoned on television by NBC to analyze the appeal of the Steinbrecher-Simmons love affair, put it this way: "Every love sooner or later runs into a wall that splits, damages, or kills it. But human hope, as the poet tells us, springs eternal. As members of McLuhan's global village of the electronic age, we all watch as the Berlin Wall divides two beautiful, strong-willed lovers. We hope, of course, that sometime, somehow their fiercely committed hearts will triumph over the Wall. We wish the Wall would crumble, permitting the reunion not only of these two resplendent lovers but that of our own fractured love as well. Yet in the back of our mind, the small voice of reason tells us that the walls to lasting devotion never come down. And so in Gisela and Michael we have the essential tragedy of the human condition: illusion's hope crashing against reality's wall."

Other academics and specialists in the hooded domain of the psyche struck equally somber chords. A Copenhagen psychiatrist, noting Mike's account of Gisela's reactions in West Berlin, said her prison sentence probably "saved" an alliance that would have foundered on cultural differences. An Indian shaman near Taos, New Mexico, predicted the Wall would last for three hundred years because evil spirits were destined to prevail worldwide for another three centuries. A famous seeress in Washington, D.C., foresaw the slow death of DDR Chairman Volpe by malignant brain tumor unless he released Gisela before Easter. A Brazilian astrologer with a global following said the imprisonment of Gisela severed a love partnership that surely would have collapsed anyway because Taurus (Mike) would have dumped Aries (Gisela) after her inevitable infidelity. Aries and Taurus, she proclaimed, were never compatible.

Several noted American demographers took a more practical line. They attributed the great appeal in the United States of the troubled romance between a fifty-three-year-old male and a thirty-eight-year-old female to the continued aging of the U.S. population. As a sociological footnote, not many Americans took umbrage at the adulterous conduct of Gisela and Mike. Aside from a few fundamentalist preachers, the theory, even among adherents of a spotless moral code, seemed to be that if Karl Steinbrecher were cuckolded, as a Communist he deserved it.

While winter shut-ins of the cold northern regions drank in the romantic bulletins like hot toddies, the Third World countries, generally clustered in warmer latitudes, followed the hapless lovers as closely as family. Latins especially clasped Gisela and Michael in fond embrace. South America had known nothing like this rabid interest since the television serial "Simplemente Maria," the drama of a poor servant girl who married into wealth and position, swept mansion and hovel wherever a TV antenna pierced the sad skies like a crucifix. That Gisela and Mike first whispered their adorations in Spanish, the language of passion and evasion, was a fact well known throughout Latin America and served to swell the outpouring of affection for the pair.

As the days passed and the thirsty media lapped like wild creatures at the lagoon of love, Mike watched an image take shape that bore only coincidental resemblance to the facts. It was an image tooled in black and white with none of the grays, ambiguities, doubts, lust, and tangled motives that actually streaked his love affair with Gisela. In the image known to most of the world, Gisela Steinbrecher fled East Germany because of an uncontrollable love, because she wanted to sound the alarm for Otto Kleist's warning, and because she despised the entire DDR and its repressive regime as much as she did her loveless, harsh, doctrinaire Communist husband. Hilde left because she hated her father and pined for freedom. Mike's sole motivation in aiding the escape, according to the world's image, was his fierce love for Gisela. The image, in its greed for simplicity, had no room for Mike's torments of the night, for Gisela's attachments to Socialism, homeland, and university or for her ambivalences, for Hilde's love for the father and friends she left behind. Some versions of the affair differed so widely from reality that Mike had trouble recognizing himself and the Steinbrecher women. He read half of an article from a Mexican magazine, mailed him by an unknown well-wisher, before he realized that the story told of his own agony of waiting.

Mail poured in from seven continents, most of it forwarded by the media, but some addressed merely, "Michael Simmons, West Berlin." One day alone brought more than a hundred letters, including a dozen appeals for funds, two warm notes of sympathy from old MIT classmates, and a brochure advertising an island resort in the Bahamas along with the manager's invitation "to come and stay as our guests when Gisela wins her release."

As Spider Butler had hoped and halfway predicted, the pressure for official action mounted steadily day by day. Mike had expected, at the most, a rash of publicity followed by quick deflation and rapid obsolescence of himself and the Steinbrechers as newsworthy objects. Instead the story spiraled upward and onward. Readers and viewers, insatiable in their appetite, would not let the story die much as editors might weary of it. Initially this interest focused exclusively on Mike, Hilde, and Gisela, but as weeks passed the predicament of Otto Kleist, under house arrest in Weisser Hirsch, the Dresden suburb, attracted more and more attention, especially in the intellectual circles which sculpt so many facets of public opinion. Amnesty International placed Dr. Kleist on its new "ten most wanted" list—those political prisoners whom the human rights society most wanted released from the facilities in which they languished. More than a thousand chemists from many countries signed a petition, beseeching the East German government to free Kleist from house arrest, permit their fellow chemist to publish his findings and travel wherever he wished. In Princeton, New Jersey, Benjamin Garraway, spokesman for the Geophysical Fluid Dynamics Laboratory, said that Frau Steinbrecher's written report, mailed from Berlin before her kidnapping, had proved invaluable in assessing Dr. Kleist's computations indicating that accumulations of carbon dioxide in the atmosphere would prove hazardous much sooner than most scientists predicted. The lab staff, said Garraway, looked forward eagerly to a personal exploration with Otto Kleist of the perils he foresaw. Scientific bodies scattered about the globe called upon the DDR to release Kleist in the spirit of unfettered scientific inquiry, a spirit which, SED zealots claimed, animated research in this other Germany even more than it did in the Federal Republic.

All this attention—an entire class of French first-graders in Toulouse petitioned Chairman Heinrich Volpe to let Gisela rejoin her sweetheart—brought broad and subtle changes into Mike's life. The incessant commotion broke up and dispersed his low-grade depression. He was almost never alone now. If journalists and electronics crews were not tramping about his apartment, he was off dining with reporters, officials, and new acquaintances in cafés and restaurants. People recognized him on the street and he had the odd experience of being greeted by strangers or fixed with bemused, puzzled stares by those who wondered which celebrity he might be.

Much as he fought against it, Mike found himself developing a public personality, a kind of hollow shell in which

314

often-used phrases echoed like political bromides. He began shading the truth because he found that reporters either failed to record nuances that did not fit the established image or because he sensed that people might find the revelation distasteful. As a sample, he quit mentioning Gisela's continued faith in Socialism. Many conservatives, he had learned, lost ardor for the cause when they discovered Gisela's political beliefs. He began to play the bogus role of the free world's gladiator, grappling before the Wall with the fanged beasts of Communism. Sometimes when he heard himself sounding off in rolling clichés, he hooted inwardly, mocking himself. But the public personality, slightly off-kilter like a drunken woman navigating on high heels, continued to grow and harden while the real Michael Simmons, however derisive, shriveled in the background. Only his nights remained unaltered. Demons, marauders, misshapen brutes trudged along walls through the slush of his unconscious, often flailing about with heavy weapons.

Mike learned early in the publicity game that his ready access to the media and instant, wordwide alarms gave him amazing leverage, a kind of power he had never known before. He first used the weapon when he told the Associated Press that Todd Elevator, Inc., had fired him because it feared loss of business in Communist countries. A week later a subdued Mark Jacoby, telephoning from New York, reached Mike at night in his apartment.

"Jesus, what an ungrateful thing to do, Mike," Jacoby complained. "I had no idea you'd repeat our conversation to the press. The media always gives such distorted accounts."

"You didn't listen, Mark. I told you I intended to do everything and anything I could to get Gisela Steinbrecher out of prison. And the press, incidentally, quoted me accurately."

"I think you acted out of a spirit of revenge." Jacoby

sounded put upon. "Airing your dismissal can't possibly help your woman."

"I disagree. It shows everybody just how far and how insidiously the Wall's influence goes. And when enough people get the word, they'll put pressure on the men in power. It may bring action."

"In my book that's wishful thinking. But regardless, I'm authorized to offer you a deal."

"Careful, Mark. Remember I'll use anything you say if it'll help the cause."

"Then this will have to be off-the-record." Jacoby cleared his throat. He might as well have barricaded his door. "Before I relay our proposition, I'll need your promise that you won't mention it to anyone."

"I'm a bad one for secrets these days."

"You'll like our proposal."

"Okay." Curiosity won a brief bout with loathing. "You have my word."

"If you agree not to mention Todd again in your talks with the media, we'll mail you a check for six-months' salary today."

"No thanks, Mark." He found the lure of money surprisingly pale. "Some people would call that a bribe. I'll just say thanks, but no thanks."

"You'll regret it, Mike."

"Nope. To blast open that goddam Wall, I have to level with the press as much as possible and that includes the Todd Elevator angles."

"We can make that a year's salary."

"Say, you guys must be hurting. No, not for any amount. That's it, old buddy."

His honed sense of the power of publicity served Mike in an ominous development two weeks later. He received a surprising phone call from Werner Lanz in Frankfurt. The former brigade leader, atwitter with anxiety, confided that he had information of vital concern to Mike. Could he fly to Berlin the next day for a confidential talk? Of course. Mike said he would have Hilde on hand to act as interpreter.

Mike and Hilde met Lanz the next evening at Tegel Airport. The stocky Leipziger, a bundle of nerves as always, refused all but small talk on the bus ride into the city center. He had a good job in his brother's electrical supply house, thanks, and harbored no regrets about his flight through the Wall. He kept glancing suspiciously at fellow bus passengers and acted like a man under surveillance. He declined to talk in Mike's apartment or anywhere else indoors, insisting despite the freezing weather that they talk outside. So they stomped along in the crackling night air, taking Budapester Strasse where it bordered the Zoo and the Aquarium. Bundled against the cold, they walked swiftly, sidestepping occasionally to avoid patches of ice. Lanz told his story with Hilde translating.

An old friend from Leipzig had arrived that week as part of a small, carefully selected East German delegation attending an electrical appliance manufacturing convention in Frankfurt. When the group returned to the DDR two nights ago, his friend quietly defected and sought refuge in the home of Lanz's brother. Werner had long known that his friend served as a secret agent of the Ministry of State Security and that he had risen to a top SSD post in Leipzig. Lanz had not been prepared, however, for some of the revelations that poured out of his friend when the dam of secrecy broke.

"Right off you should know," said Lanz, "that Wolfgang Dahlem, Ingrid, and Hans, the core of the Dahlem Fluchthelfer group, are all secret informers for the DDR."

"Come on, Werner. That's impossible." Mike had expected anything but this.

"I thought so, too, until I heard all the particulars."

"If that's true, how could you and Hilde and the rest have gotten out?"

"Dahlem has a cozy arrangement with the Stasi. He's allowed to bring out a maximum of twenty people a year without interference, no questions asked, no identities demanded in advance. In return, he reports on anybody and anything over here that the SSD orders."

"That's awfully hard to believe, Werner." Mike felt disoriented, asked to follow a new trail with no signposts.

"Aber ja doch!" Lanz insisted in his high, piping voice. "Ingrid's last name is Watzmann and her code name as a DDR informer is Sparrow. Dahlem is Lark and Hans Orff is Hawk. Ingrid Watzmann came over from Zwickau as a young girl before the Wall. Of the three, she's the most loyal to the DDR."

Mike tried to set his mind to the new course. "Has your friend told all this to the West German authorities?"

Lanz shook his head. "Not yet. He won't go to the police to start his refugee application until next week. The way things work, more time will elapse before the BND intelligence people begin questioning him in detail. Because of Gisela, I knew you would want to know this at once."

"Thanks, Werner." Mike put his gloved hand on Lanz's shoulder.

"How about Erich who guided us out?" asked Hilde.

"No. He had no connection with the Stasi."

"What about the sweet old lady at the Film Theater in Dresden who makes you give the passwords if you want to escape?"

"I don't know about her in particular, Hilde." Lanz quickened his pace. The cold had begun to penetrate. "But none of the people working for Dahlem in the DDR are informers. Only the three here in West Berlin: Dahlem, Ingrid, and Hans. Everyone else is clean. That's why the outfit functions so smoothly."

The night grew colder. Traffic crunched slowly along the snow-packed streets. Stars winked like icy gems in the clear, black sky. In the distance the trio could see East Berlin's bulbous TV tower, brilliantly illuminated, standing in frosty command of the broken city's eastern half. Somewhere over there, Gisela sat behind bars and the thought pierced Mike like a stab of pain. The three walkers turned and began retracing their steps toward the Europa Center.

As they stepped up the pace, Lanz supplied details of Dahlem's long association with the East German Ministry for State Security. With SSD cooperation, Dahlem had twice rigged attempted assassinations of himself and then told West Berlin police that Stasi agents had stalked and tried to kill him. It was Dahlem who supplied confirmation of the treason of Horst Wolgast, the Federal Republic's spy inside East Germany's policy-making bodies. Upon Wolgast's conviction, Dahlem shared credit for the intelligence coup with Carola Probst, a little-known computer specialist at SSD headquarters. Also, according to Lanz's friend, Dahlem had funneled information from West Berlin's city hall, had undertaken surveillance jobs, infiltrated refugee groups, and kept tabs on the whereabouts of troublesome defectors from the DDR.

"As for Gisela," said Lanz, "my friend says there is no question that Dahlem had her under constant watch. On the night of her seizure, Hans Orff, stationed across from your hotel, used a walkie-talkie to alert the kidnap car which was sitting in a parking place just off Augsburger Strasse. The operation had its own code name—Sundown."

"Ironic." Mike felt the bitterness rising.

"Agreed. No sunny side that day."

"Now something that Dahlem asked me begins to make sense," said Mike. "When I hired him to bring Gisela and Hilde out, he asked me what kind of man Sam Wertheimer was. Wertheimer's in the White House, counsel to our Presi-

319

dent McCullough. Wertheimer was over here last fall and
had a look at the Wall like they all do. Apparently Dahlem
made it a point to meet him somehow."

"Oh yes. Dahlem and his two associates pick up any political information they can."

"One thing bugs me, Werner. I can't understand why the
DDR wheels resorted to kidnapping. That seems like tremendous overkill. Gisela had no secrets that I know of."
Mike lowered his head against the gusting wind. "Did your
friend have a line on that?"

"Yes. We talked about it because it's been many years
since the Stasi pulled anything that bold in West Berlin."
Lanz huddled close to Hilde who walked between the two
men. The wind had a sting now. "He had no certain knowledge, but he speculated that the seizure arose from the bad
blood rivalry between two SSD department heads, Heinz
Lungwitz, chief of computer intelligence, and Gerhard
Ehrengruber, chief of interrogation. When Ehrengruber's
examiners questioned you, Mike, they failed to discover
your part in helping Gisela to make her escape try near
Fulda. That was pieced together from computer records by
the Carola Probst I mentioned, obviously a very smart
woman. Ehrengruber, according to my friend's best information and private hunch, felt so undone by Lungwitz's
people that he vowed to get Frau Steinbrecher somehow. So
he prevailed upon the head of the SSD to have her snatched
off the streets of West Berlin."

"A rash act when you consider that the two Berlins had
been getting along fairly well."

Lanz agreed. "My friend says it's rumored inside the SSD
that Chairman Volpe didn't like it, especially because of his
conference with the chancellor next month. My friend
looks for a shake-up in the Ministry for State Security."

"That gives me some hope, Werner. I'm indebted to you
my friend."

Lanz grinned. "We elevator experts never let the doors close between us."

The biting cold at last drove them indoors. They dined before an open fire at Alexander, one of Hilde's favorite restaurants, where they confined themselves to friendly small talk. Mike and Hilde parted from Lanz at the Hotel Am Zoo where the former union politician would spend the night before flying back to Frankfurt.

"Do I have your permission to use this information?" asked Mike. They stood stamping their feet before the hotel entrance.

"Any way you wish. Just leave me and my friend out of it."

Mike felt a rush of affection for this oddly mannered man with his birdlike gestures and his high, squeaky voice. "Werner, I can't thank you enough." He gave him a parting embrace and Werner looked embarrassed. "I think I can use the information to help Gisela."

"That is what we all hope. And so, my friends, *auf wiedersehen*." Lanz walked into the hotel with small, measured steps as if on solitary parade.

"Such a strange man," said Hilde. "But I like him."

"More important, do you trust him?"

"Oh, yes. All the way."

"So do I." Mike smiled ruefully. "But then I trusted Ingrid, too."

They took a taxi to the Kassel apartment. "Hilde, I've decided to face Dahlem and Ingrid right away—tonight. If you haven't heard from me by midnight, I want you to call Walt Delaney and have him take you to the police. Then you tell them everything you heard from Lanz tonight."

"Don't go looking for trouble, Mr. Mike."

"I don't think there's much risk." Mike kissed her as they arrived at the Kassel apartment building. "Not with you as insurance. Here's Dahlem's street and number." He jotted down the address on Fasanenstrasse.

At the Alsterhof he sharpened a plan that had been formulating in his mind during dinner at Alexander. When he called Ingrid, he heard her friendly, businesslike voice giving instructions on an answering machine. He left his name and number, said it was urgent, then turned on the television set. He had barely sorted out the characters in a car-chase melodrama when Ingrid called back.

"I must see you and Herr Dahlem together tonight."

"I'm not sure that can be arranged so quickly." Ingrid's tone was guarded but as pleasant as always. "What's this about?"

"I'm sorry I can't say over the phone—except that it's of vital concern to your business."

"Let me see what I can do, Herr Simmons. I'll call back in a few minutes."

Curiosity surmounts formidable obstacles. Dahlem, it turned out, would see him on short notice after all and Ingrid, after protesting that she never took part in Dahlem's sessions, agreed to be present.

A few minutes later Mike faced Hans in the foyer of apartment 2-A in the building on Fasanenstrasse. The big man with the bull's neck grinned as he passed his hands rapidly over Mike's jacket and trousers.

Wolfgang Dahlem and Ingrid awaited him by the white corduroy couch with its spray of brightly colored cushions. The finely tooled, angular furniture set off the Mexican handicraft including the tufted wall hanging of a yellow jaguar on the prowl.

Ingrid as usual wore her fashionable sunglasses. Dahlem gave the same impression of discretion and class that Mike had noted on their previous meeting. The premier escape merchant wore neatly creased trousers, a beige alpaca sweater, and cordovans with a high gloss. Hans prepared to leave the room.

"Please, I'd prefer that Hans stay with us," said Mike.

"Hans never takes part in our business conferences," said Dahlem in his faultless English.

"This time I think he'd be of great help." Mike was firm.

Dahlem shrugged. "As you wish.' He motioned Mike to the couch. They all sat down, Hans somewhat gingerly like a huge child among unfamiliar adults. Dahlem tapped a cigarette on his manicured thumbnail after Mike declined his offer.

"And so, Mr. Simmons?" Dahlem lit his cigarette and blew a long, lazy billow of smoke.

"I have some valuable information you'll need in your business." Mike put on a troubled look. "But first, Mr. Dahlem, I want to take you up on your generous offer, as relayed by Ingrid, to lend me some money. Frankly, I got myself in a financial jam with the wrong kind of people and I need money in a hurry—tonight." He drew out two savings passbooks, one on the Chemical Bank and the other, the Dime Savings Bank, both in New York. "You can see I have a total of thirty-five thousand dollars on deposit, but you know banks. It would take three or four days to get the money and I need quite a bit right now." Mike tried to look sheepish. "I was a fool . . . a woman, the wrong crowd . . . an old story, I guess."

"Just how much do you need?" Dahlem was wary.

"Forty thousand marks."

"Forty! That's a formidable amount to be asking in the middle of the night, Mr. Simmons. With all the contacts you've made with your recent publicity, I should think you'd have no trouble at all raising the money from your friends."

"Hundreds of acquaintances, but no friends, and this jam I'm in isn't the kind to build confidence in me as a credit risk." Mike put on a mask of anguish. Was he carrying this off?

"Yet you ask me to place such confidence in you."

"That's different, Mr. Dahlem. You went all over my credit and resources before the deal for Gisela and Hilde. You know exactly how much I'm worth. Also, of course, Ingrid said you'd be willing to lend me money. . . . Look, this is only for a few days until these banks can clear the funds to me."

"What's this information of vital concern to my business?"

"I need to clear up this money thing first. Listen, man, I'm in a bad fix. If I don't produce tonight, they'll beat the hell out of me." He was pleased with his acting. He could sense that his voice held just the proper amount of fear.

Dahlem studied him in silence for several minutes. "I haven't got that kind of money here. I only keep a sum for emergencies."

"How much? If I could make a decent down payment tonight . . ."

"Fourteen thousand marks is all I have here."

"Then let me have it, please. I'll sign an IOU and put up these two bank accounts for collateral."

"That won't be necessary." Dahlem nodded toward Hans. "He's our insurance." Hans beamed.

"Then you'll lend it?" Mike injected a note of urgency.

Dahlem did not answer directly. Instead he turned to Ingrid. "Fetch that cash from the safe." He spoke as casually as a man ordering a drink.

Ingrid walked into the adjoining bedroom and closed the door. For the first time Mike realized that she was Dahlem's woman, a quite understandable yet unsuspected arrangement. The three men waited wordlessly. Hans arose and stretched, a flexing of enormous muscles.

Returning, Ingrid handed Dahlem an envelope and the

dean of commercial escape brokers counted out ten one-thousand-mark bills and slightly more than four thousand in smaller denominations. Dahlem slipped the currency back into the envelope and handed it to Mike who tucked it into a pants pocket. They all sat down again.

"And now. This vital concern?" Dahlem's smile was cool, self-assured, even a bit condescending.

"I'm here to lay some ugly facts on the line, Mr. Dahlem, but first you should know that any effort to harm me or take back the money will be useless." Mike spoke with a confidence he did not feel. "Two bodyguards are waiting outside. They'll come up here in an hour if I'm not out by then." Strangely, hearing his own bluff stiffened his courage. "And people who know I'm here are prepared to go to the police if they've not heard from me by midnight."

Dahlem, unsmiling now, fixed Mike with his deep blue eyes. "That's an ominous opening, Mr. Simmons."

"That hard-luck story I just dished out is a phony. The real reason I'm here has to do only incidentally with money." Mike struck. "I have solid information that you helped the SSD kidnap my friend, Gisela."

No one made a sound. Mike saw Hans flex his great hands. Ingrid fingered her clouded glasses. Dahlem sat motionless, his eyes trained on Mike. Smoke rose in a wavering column from his cigarette.

Dahlem broke the silence that seemed endless but probably lasted only a few seconds. "That's the most outrageous statement ever made in this room, Mr. Simmons. It is also, of course, completely false."

"So I thought when I first heard it." Mike kept his eyes on Dahlem. "But not after I learned the facts. You and Ingrid and Hans have been secret informers for the SSD for many years."

"You're a liar," said Dahlem without heat. "Do you real-

325

ize that I could sue you in our courts for—what's the English word, yes—calumny?"

"You could, but you won't because you'd stand exposed as a spy for the East Germans."

"That's all, Simmons." Dahlem arose to his feet and like a huge robot Hans also stood up. "You will leave at once. If you don't, we'll throw you out." He eyed the pocket where Mike had tucked the money.

"If that happens, I'll call a press conference tomorrow morning." Mike paused for effect. He relished this. "To describe your work for the DDR—including Operation Sundown."

Had he not been watching Dahlem so closely, Mike might have missed the motion. The escape boss, in the midst of smoking, halted his cigarette for an instant in midair. Then he quickly inhaled and blew the smoke out in a single, fat doughnut.

Mike pressed his advantage. "For Sundown, we can thank those three clever birds, Lark, Sparrow, and Hawk."

This time there was no mistaking the impact. The code names visibly shook Dahlem. A look of consternation crossed his face and he slowly settled back on the couch. Hans sat down abruptly with an awkward thud. Ingrid shifted on her cushion, recrossing her legs.

Again silence, this time tense and vigilant. Dahlem's blue eyes held Mike in a steady gaze. "Perhaps you'd better tell us exactly what you want," he said at last.

"What I want is to beat the shit out of you." The words came out in a surge of fury. "But that's impractical with Hans Orff sitting there. And I'd like to dump your double-crossing bitch, Ingrid Watzmann, out the window." Use of the last names surprised the escape helpers. Mike hunched forward. "But that wouldn't be a smart move right now either."

He halted and felt the swift, pumping rhythm of his

326

anger. "You helped kidnap the woman I love and send her up for twenty years. . . . Twenty years!" It came out as a hoarse shout. "And then you send your spook, the little Sparrow all decked out in black shades and fake sympathy, to break the news. 'We have means of getting word to Gisela in prison,' she says. I'll bet by Christ you do. . . . And you have the goddam gall to ask me what I want!"

Mike sat back, his chest heaving. Dahlem smoked quietly, then ground out the cigarette. Hans whispered something to Ingrid.

"Is that all?" Dahlem's low tone betrayed no emotion.

"I want the rest of the twenty-five thousand dollars I paid you and I want it by tomorrow noon."

"If I refuse?"

"Tomorrow afternoon I give the media the whole story about Dahlem and Watzmann and Orff, the DDR informers."

"That's it?"

"No. I demand that you go to work at once to spring Gisela from prison. If she's not out in six weeks, the press gets the full story on those three spy birds, Lark, Sparrow, and Hawk. In case you don't know it, I'm hot with the press. They'll use anything I say."

"So I've noticed," said Dahlem drily. "If you get the balance of the twenty-five thousand dollars tomorrow, what prevents you from demanding another twenty-five thousand?"

"Gisela. I know you've got influence and I want you to use it to get her out of prison."

"And if she's released, what prevents you then from making these false allegations public?"

"You think I want to be knocked off?" Mike nodded toward the strongman.

"For that matter, Hans could do a fair job on you right now, put you to sleep for a long time."

Mike forced a laugh. "Do you think I'm stupid? My hired men are waiting across the street." The bluff boosted his pulse rate. He could feel the throb of danger. He glanced at his wrist watch. "If I'm not out in, let's see, another twenty-one minutes, they'll be up here to find out why."

Dahlem lit another cigarette and squinted as the smoke curled past his eyes. He studied Mike as if appraising him for employment. Again silence, a hostile presence.

"Naturally you picked up these lies from Federal Republic officials, either here or in Bonn." The Fluchthelfer was fishing. "So the police will arrive soon, whatever you and I do or do not agree on."

"Oh, no. I got my facts from the other side." The falsehood gave Mike a heady sensation of power. He began to feel that he would pull this off. "I may be a newcomer, but I've learned the Wall leaks like a sieve."

"I don't believe you. Even if true, it's only a matter of time until authorities here learn of this absurd story and order us in for questioning."

"I told you I'm not about to talk. I want Gisela out of prison and I need your influence."

Dahlem stared at Mike as if trying to assess his degree of determination. Mike stared back. A minute passed in silence. Then the escape chief got to his feet, Hans rising with him as if by strings.

"I'll have the rest of the money for you by noon," Dahlem said flatly.

"What about Gisela?"

"I'll make some preliminary calls first thing in the morning."

Mike got up and started toward the foyer. No one bothered with good-byes. "I'll be back at noon tomorrow," he said at the door. Dahlem nodded.

When Mike telephoned the next morning at nine-thirty, the phone rang seven times without an answer. At the apartment house on Fasanenstrasse, the phlegmatic superintendent, scratching at a scab on his bald head, said that the three people in No. 2-A left shortly before six with packed luggage "for a long vacation."

Mike was not surprised. It had been worth the gamble for Gisela. At least he had retrieved a third of the escape fee.

17

Frank McCullough ceased his nervous pacing about the disheveled room and leveled a finger at his friend. "And you know the joke of it?" He promptly answered his own rhetorical question. "The Todd Elevator people never gave me a dime for any campaign, not a single, damn dime."

He paused, frowned, wondered whether he had overstated the case, decided he had not and continued his walking monologue. "But because some philandering Todd executive had the hots for one of those long-legged East German blondes, I get creamed by the press. They made me look like a fool this morning, Sam—a goddam, impotent fool."

"Oh now, Mr. President, that's going too far." Sam Wertheimer knew the signs. Time to rein in his old friend who rode in the clouds when things went smoothly and plunged to the pits when they didn't. "You said that eventually the Wall must come down because free men will not tolerate it forever. That's true enough. Then you said . . ."

"Then Loveland trapped me," cut in McCullough. "I wish ABC would can that faker. The man has it in for me. 'As a free man,' he asks in that sly, silky voice of his, what did I propose to do about it?"

"And your answer was quite reasonable, I thought. You said you'd continue to use the persuasive powers of the U.S. presidency. What's wrong with that?"

"Nothing." McCullough lowered his head as he paced. "By itself, nothing. But then Porter's question and the others that followed, all about whether I would use force to demolish the Wall. I had to dodge and equivocate and fall back on platitudes."

"People understand. They know a President has to choose his words carefully."

"Don't try to kid me, Sam. I saw a videotape of the press conference. I came off mealy-mouthed. The exact word is 'weak.'"

President McCullough dropped into his old leather armchair, a favorite since his days in the Colorado legislature, and gazed out moodily as winter twilight veiled the south lawn of the White House. He and Sam Wertheimer, counsel to the President and his oldest, closest friend, were seated in the third-floor sunroom directly above the rounded balcony and rear entrance to the President's mansion.

The two confidants met here almost every evening to assess the events of the day and let the President unwind in a totally secure atmosphere. McCullough had filled the rooftop room with his own scarred furniture, books, and mementos, giving it the ambiance of a private study high above the scurrying world. Only McCullough, Wertheimer, and an occasional cleaning maid were permitted to enter the sunroom. President McCullough cherished his aerie. He was a man not completely free of anxieties and twinges of inadequacy.

As they sat in silence, Wertheimer could almost hear his friend shed his qualms and worries. Soon, he knew, things would come into focus and they could chat and plan without those wide emotional swings that made life, however intoxicating, such an ordeal for Frank McCullough.

"Strange how this romance of an elevator man and a lady chemist has caught the people's fancy." McCullough could muse now. The darkening room felt comfortable and the world once again was almost manageable.

"It's made people over here think about the Wall again and that's all to the good."

"Good for them, but not for me. The fact is, Sam, that the Wall forces me to be a hypocrite. Publicly I have to view it as an excrescence, but privately—well, you know we've talked about it more than once. Neither of us is exactly unhappy it's there."

"Yeah, like we agreed when I came back from my visit to Berlin last fall. You know I'm one Jew who doesn't worry about another Hitler over there. Still, I'd hate to see those Germanies merge. Can you imagine competing economically against a united Germany with 80 million people working their ass off? Why, they'd own half the world this time without firing a shot."

"Still, I like Rauschnig and I appreciate his problem. What's more, we need him." McCullough drummed on the torn leather of the old armchair. "I just wish this elevator man and his woman would vanish somehow. No way can I get her out of prison and over the Wall without giving Varentsov an arm and a leg to put pressure on the East Germans."

"We can't make the lady vanish, but maybe there's a way to cut her down to size so she'll fade out of the evening news."

"How, for God's sake?" McCullough looked up eagerly.

"Can you hold off your next press conference for a month?"

"Sure. No problem."

"Then if you leave it to me, I think we can defuse this Steinbrecher business."

"How, Sam?"

"Best you don't know, Mr. President, then you won't have to deny or affirm. Just trust me."

"I do that every day."

"There's an angle I can plant with the Gang of Five tomorrow night. Something about the lady's background, let's say."

McCullough smiled. The Gang of Five was a group of the capital's most influential newspaper correspondents with whom Wertheimer had met secretly for dinner once a month for a year. In return for tips on major news stories, the five reporters sometimes floated trial balloons or wrote think pieces that served the President's political interests. Wertheimer dealt his news off-the-record, attributable only to a "high administration source," and all hands regarded the arrangement as cozy and mutually beneficial.

"I hope it works," said McCullough. "That Wall romance is beginning to bug me. Even Helen's mother called her the other night and asked her why I didn't do something to get Gisela Steinbrecher out."

And with thoughts of the President's mother-in-law weighing upon them, the two friends lapsed into silence again. They sat unspeaking while night fell over the Ellipse; a glow marked the dome of the Jefferson Memorial and red lights atop the Washington Monument began blinking their warning to aircraft.

The next night at a newspaperman's home in Georgetown the talk swung to "the Berlin Wall thing" soon after dinner. Sam Wertheimer settled back with an Irish coffee in the book-lined den of the host, Benson of the *Herald*. Someone asked President McCullough's counsel to "think out loud" about the political impact on the President of the campaign to free Gisela Steinbrecher.

"It's my gut feeling," said Jenkins of the *Post*, "that the President's refusal and/or inability to help her get out of prison is beginning to damage him politically. Am I right?"

Wertheimer let his easy smile work its magic before replying. A long, lean Denver attorney with a perpetually tanned, hairless head like a brown egg, he had learned a great deal about the press since these meetings with the Gang of Five began a year ago. He knew that a story written by these five correspondents, rated tops by their peers, might roll onward and outward for days. He had learned that the deeper he dangled the bait, the greater the chance that his five fish would fight for a chance to swallow the hook. Early in the game when he had merely scattered bait on the surface, it had been generally ignored. Now he prepared the hook with care and muddied the waters ever so slightly before dropping his line.

"You people," he complained mildly, "never seem to worry about the substance of an event, but only its political effect on the White House. I'll bet if hydrogen missiles let fly tonight, wiping out half the world, those of you who survived would dash to your typewriters and hammer out pieces about the impact on the President's political ratings."

"That's our business, Sam," said Green of the *Times*.

"It puts the focus in the wrong place," countered Wertheimer. "What we need to know about inflation, for instance, is how to stop it, not its political effect on the President."

"You're ducking the question, Sam," chided Sue Fishelman of the "other" *Times,* the one on the West Coast. "The Steinbrecher case, remember?"

"Yes. Well, on that I'd have to say that of course the President has been hurt somewhat. Any time the White House is shown as less than effective, the man is likely to slide in the polls."

"People up our way can't understand why McCullough doesn't blast the Communists for holding the woman," said Diamond of the *Globe*.

"Sounds simple enough, right?" Wertheimer glanced

about the room. Easy now. Diamond had provided the opening, but the hook must be lowered with skill. "However, there's a special problem to be considered."

"You mean disarmament and the rest of the agenda with the Soviets?" asked the *Herald*'s Benson.

"Well, of course, one always makes assessments along that line." Wertheimer assumed his look of grave concern that hundreds of juries had seen during his summations. "No, this is a much simpler matter, but tough to handle."

"Like what, Sam?" asked Jenkins of the *Post*.

"Look, I wish you people wouldn't crowd me right here. We're heading into a security area."

"Whose?" Green of the *Times* again. "The nation's or the President's?"

Wertheimer sipped at his Irish coffee, frowned, gazed out of the mullioned window. The narrow brick residence dated from pre-Civil War days. The five correspondents exchanged glances.

"Come on, Sam." Sue Fishelman prodded. "You're holding out on us."

"This is delicate." Wertheimer might have been carrying eggs on an icy sidewalk. "Some of our friends abroad are awfully touchy, you know."

"We can handle it under any guidelines you want," said Benson.

"Yes, well . . ." Wertheimer appeared to ponder. "I suppose this really ought to get out, so the American public would understand why the President ducks on Steinbrecher and Simmons."

"Have we ever embarrassed you?" Benson again.

"No. . . . Tell you what, I'll level with you provided you name your source as 'the intelligence community' and you leave us strictly out of it. No hint of the White House."

"Any objections?" Benson looked around at his fellow

reporters. No one spoke. "Okay, we'll lay it to 'intelligence sources'—whatever it is."

Wertheimer thought for a time, then opened his arms, the gesture of a man placing his fate in the hands of others. "The fact is, gentlemen and lady"—he nodded toward Fishelman—"Gisela Steinbrecher is a secret agent of the East German security forces."

The statement carried the shock value that Wertheimer had anticipated.

"But she was kidnapped," protested Jenkins.

"Staged. While it's true Frau Steinbrecher is now in custody, our information is that she's been allotted quite comfortable quarters. In due time, she'll be let out, 'paroled to the West' as it were, and she can go about her intelligence duties as the wife or mistress of a well-placed American business executive who travels extensively."

"Do we have this cold, Sam?" Like Jenkins, Green tried to keep the excitement out of his voice. This was a big one.

"Solid." Wertheimer nodded slowly. "Don't forget, this woman holds one of her country's highest decorations. All this concern over the Wall-split lovers is made to order for East Berlin. They can wait six, eight months, finally 'yield' to the worldwide pressure and then release their good, loyal spy to the West to go about her work." The White House counsel paused. "So you can see why the President wants to lay off the case."

"What about that night at the border?" asked Diamond. "Simmons says she was wounded by machine-gun fire trying to escape."

"Cleverly faked. She inflicted a small cut on her calf herself."

"What's the name of the East German security outfit?" asked Sue Fishelman.

"SSD. Stands for a long German word meaning state protection service, more or less."

"If we know she's a spy," asked Green, "why don't we just say so officially and get the President off the hook?"

Wertheimer shook his head. "No, no. That would escalate matters tremendously and would definitely cause trouble for West Berlin. That city's a hostage, don't forget. Everything involving West Berlin has to be handled with great caution."

"And yet you're telling us," said Green.

"That's different. I'd like to take some of the heat off my friend without causing a diplomatic incident. He's got enough problems right now. But our people ought to have the facts."

"Does the President know you're spilling this to us?" Green had his doubts.

"No, sir. I didn't tell him. I was afraid, frankly, that he'd forbid me to talk."

They discussed, argued, and probed the case for another half hour, went briefly to other topics, then broke up earlier than usual. The five newspaper people, all friendly rivals of morning newspapers, agreed to attribute their story to "reliable intelligence sources" and to hold it until the following day. They also agreed, after Wertheimer drove off in his sky-blue Porsche, that he had dropped, however reluctantly, the best story of the month.

While the American journalists tapped at their typewriters the next day, another government official met with another press six thousand miles and eight time zones away in the city of Moscow.

For Nikolai Varentsov, head of state, secretary general of the Soviet Union's Communist party, top man of the Supreme Soviet's Presidium, this was an unprecedented event, the first open-press conference of his career. A spare, wiry *apparatchik* who had survived three decades of heavy-handed Kremlin intrigue, he wore a beard trimmed like

Lenin's, walked as though in a hurry to catch a plane, and prided himself on his mental agility; all in all, the opposite of the stereotyped, obdurate, ponderous, bearlike Russian leader.

Varentsov met frequently with the editors of *Izvestia, Pravda, Trud,* the news agency TASS, *Gudok,* and other Soviet organs, but these men essentially served as his employees since he could fire them at will and dictate "news" to them with absolute assurance that it would be printed exactly as he wished. For months, now that he had gained the confidence of office, he had yearned to meet the press Western-style, pitting his wits against those of nimble foreign correspondents, confronting the unexpected, taking his chances in the hurly-burly of questioning. In that kind of skirmish, where victory went to the clever and the quick, he was sure he could emerge the winner. Also he knew he would relish the pure theatrics of the scene. As a schoolboy he had acted in a number of plays, had never forgotten the thrill of playing to an audience.

And now opportunity knocked at the medieval portals of the Kremlin, stronghold of tsars and commissars alike, on the ice-glazed banks of the Moskva River. Some fifty Third World journalists, touring Russia as guests of the Soviet government, asked to interview Secretary General Varentsov as a climax to their visit. Press officials automatically said no, but when Varentsov heard of the request, he reversed the decision and invited the touring newsmen and women to appear at his office that evening.

Hailing from such countries as Egypt, Yugoslavia, Thailand, Zaïre, Peru, Nigeria, Turkey, India, and Indonesia, the communicators crowded into Varentsov's place of work, a large office adjacent to the conference room of the Politburo in the walled and towered Kremlin. Flanked by a press officer and three interpreters and filmed by a Kremlin cameraman, Nikolai Varentsov sat at his huge desk beneath a crystal chandelier and portraits of Lenin and Marx. Both bearded gentlemen looked down on their political heir like severe judges about to rebuke a fractious attorney.

Varentsov bantered with his aides as the reporters shed their winter wrappings and settled into chairs. The Soviet strongman fielded the opening questions with ease, seizing on those that suited his purposes and skillfully evading the few that bore an anti-Soviet bias. As he warmed to the give-and-take, his small, black eyes shone with the zest of combat and his whole demeanor invited the junketing writers to throw their sharpest darts his way. He, Nikolai Varentsov, chief of the world's mightiest nation, could deflect or return them all.

Soon the questioning turned to the Wall-sundered romance that so engrossed the world. Did he approve of the imprisonment of Gisela Steinbrecher by East Germany, a satellite of the Soviet Union? A domestic concern of an ally, he replied, and the word was ally, not satellite. Did he think prison an unwarranted punishment for a woman whose chief crime was to love a man of the West? It would be unseemly for him to comment on the judicial procedures of a friendly nation. Had he discussed the case with the DDR chairman? Never. The questions ran on, in time growing less and less polite, more and more critical of the Soviet Union's stance.

"Mr. Secretary General," asked an Egyptian, "do you approve of a nation seizing one of its nationals on the streets of another country?"

"Absolutely not." Varentsov barked his answer immediately after the translation.

"But you apparently condone East Germany's kidnapping of Frau Steinbrecher on the streets of West Berlin," said the Egyptian.

"Not at all." Varentsov looked as austere as did Lenin

surveying the scene from his honored place on the somber, silk wallpaper. "Frau Steinbrecher was not kidnapped. She returned to East Berlin of her own accord."

"Do you have proof of that?" asked a bold newsman from India.

The Soviet press officer, who had never imagined such an impudent challenge of his leader, made as if to remonstrate with the questioner, but Varentsov held up a restraining hand.

"Yes," he said. "We have the statement of the DDR authorities. They are honest men. I believe them."

"But don't governments often lie in their own interests?" asked a bespectacled Nigerian.

"That is an old tradition in the West." Varentsov's broad smile indicated tolerance for the sins of lesser nations. "We still remember President Eisenhower's denial of a U-2 spy flight over our territory. But U.S.S.R. always honors truth. And so do the people's governments of the other Warsaw Pact nations."

"If a Russian woman tried to leave this country illegally to join her lover abroad, would you approve a prison term of twenty years?" The questioner was a female Thai journalist, small, delicate, with a voice of honey.

"Our laws are not that stringent."

"Why don't you persuade the East German chairman to make their laws more humane?" asked the Thai woman.

"The Soviet Union does not interfere in the affairs of sovereign nations," said Varentsov.

"How about Afghanistan?" The prompt question came from a Peruvian newsman.

"Our forces were invited by the Afghan government to come in and help repel the mercenaries of Fascism." For the first time Varentsov betrayed unease.

"How about Poland?" Peru again.

"Go ask the Polish people," snapped the Soviet leader.

340

"They know the difference between helpful, progressive friends and the reactionaries who would bring their economy to a standstill."

"Didn't you personally intervene in East Germany in June 1953?" insisted the man from Peru. "It is said that you commanded a squadron of Soviet tanks in East Berlin on the day of the workers' uprising."

"I acted under orders." Varentsov bit off the words. The insolent clown! Who invited him on this tour? "Also my superior officers did not move that day until they received a written request for help from the DDR authorities. Only then did we act to crush the schemes of the revanchists, agitators, and lackeys of imperialism."

The Soviet chief frowned. Had he, after all, misjudged these writers? He had assumed that they as representatives of the Third World press, hand-picked by Moscow, would be, if not completely friendly, at least neutral. Now the questioners were becoming hostile, inquisitorial. Just who in the foreign ministry had certified the impertinent ones among these people?

"Why don't you persuade the East German chairman to free Frau Steinbrecher?" asked a journalist from Zaïre.

"I do not intervene . . ."

"But that's not intervention," cut in a Yugoslav newsman. "It's just friendly advice from one leader to another."

"I confine my persuasive efforts to foreign affairs." This was getting out of hand. "I do not intrude on purely domestic concerns."

"Domestic!" echoed a Turk. "The romance between the American and the East German has become as international as the high seas."

"You could free that woman if you wanted to," shouted a female voice from the crowd. She spoke in French, a language Varentsov understood. He fumed while the interpreter translated.

"I do not intend to get into this," he said.

"Why not?" asked the Thai writer of the honeyed voice. "You claim the Communist system is so humane. If that's true, why don't you help the poor woman?"

Varentsov thought quickly, weighing his options, while the interpreter reframed the question into Russian. Comrade Varentsov had tired of the game. He had not foreseen such lack of ordinary respect, such malice. He must end this travesty.

"Because I have no pity for people who hire themselves out as espionage agents for a foreign country." There. That should end it.

"Espionage?" asked the Indian journalist with a touch of incredulity. "Who do you mean?"

"The Steinbrecher woman."

There was a rustle in the sedate old room as the Third World newsmen and women leaned forward.

"Are you saying that Frau Steinbrecher is a spy for the West?" asked the Indian.

"Of course she is." The secretary general spoke with a bored air as if noting some widely accepted fact of ancient history. "Intelligence people familiar with her dossier have known that for some time."

"Which Western nation employs her?"

Varentsov hesitated only momentarily. "The Federal Republic of Germany."

"Is the chemist, Otto Kleist, also an espionage agent for the West?" asked the Turk.

"*Nyet*. But he collaborated with the spy Steinbrecher, permitting her to transmit his research to imperialist circles."

"Why have you waited so long to make this accusation?" Despite her doll-like appearance and liquid voice, the Thai journalist pursued the story relentlessly.

"That is no accusation," Varentsov snapped. "That is fact."

"Did she supply the West with military secrets?" The dainty Thai sipped at her reportorial nectar with the fluttery perseverance of a hummingbird.

"Security matter." The secretary general looked properly stern. "No comment."

He whispered something to the press officer who raised his hands and announced that due to urgent business, Comrade Varentsov must terminate the interview. He would take one final question.

"Is the American Simmons also an agent of the CIA?" asked the man from Zaïre.

"No, we do not believe so." Varentsov smiled sadly, much as he had as a schoolboy actor in Chekhov's *Uncle Vanya*. He would end this conference on a tasteful literary note. "The famous American humorist, Mark Twain, wrote a book called *Innocents Abroad*. I'm afraid today's famous American, Michael Simmons, is another innocent abroad. He was taken in by the feminine wiles and professional artifices of a dedicated, highly trained espionage agent."

When he watched himself later on the videotape supplied by the Kremlin's private communications service, the secretary general was well pleased. He had handled impudence with dispatch and, for a sudden inspiration, the spy bit came off quite nicely. He thought his manner was forthright and sincere and his sad smile near the end brushed him with nostalgia.

18

Mike heard the news from Hester McKinnon of the *International Herald Tribune*. She called from Paris two days after Mike's press conference when he disclosed that Wolfgang Dahlem, the most successful and reputable of the professional escape managers, had been a secret informer of the SSD for years along with his top assistants. The trio reportedly had flown to South America.

At the moment Mike was sitting in the gloomy old apartment kitchen with its woodwork stained as dolorous as the winter's sky. He had lunched with Spider Butler and Walt Delaney and now he mulled over their optimistic conjectures. Both men thought that Mike's publicity push had generated terrific pressure, far more than even the Spider had anticipated, and that sooner or later East Germany would have to bow to the worldwide demand, Communist Bloc excluded, for Gisela's release. Delaney predicted she'd get out before the end of the year. Butler wanted to bet ten pounds that she'd come across by June 1. But Mike knew that he had to maintain the momentum by one ruse or another and his friends agreed.

Now, as he took the call from Paris, he felt more

confident than he had in days. If he persevered, held steady here in Berlin with wide access to press and television, he and Hilde would win to freedom the woman they both loved.

"McKinnon of the *Herald Tribune*," the familiar voice began abruptly. "We have a story out of Moscow. Varentsov says that Frau Steinbrecher is a spy for West Germany. What about it?"

"Varentsov said what?"

She repeated, albeit somewhat testily.

"That's ridiculous." He was stunned. "Gisela had no contacts outside East Germany except for me, an aged aunt in Stuttgart, and a couple of friends of mine. How did he happen to say that?"

McKinnon sketched the circumstances. "We also have a wire story out of Washington quoting leading newspapers as saying that 'reliable intelligence sources' state that Steinbrecher actually is an East German secret agent in the employ of the SSD."

"Why, that's just as crazy!" Was someone playing an enormous international prank? "It was the Stasi that kidnapped her in West Berlin. Remember?"

"Yes, but the intelligence people say that scene was faked." Her stress on the word "intelligence" seemed to imply a lack of credentials on Mike's part.

"Listen, Hester, that was no goddam fake. I was there."

She brushed past his avowal. "After holding her a few months in comfortable surroundings, American intelligence says, the DDR will let her return to the West where she can move about the world as your woman, working for the SSD wherever she goes."

"I tell you that's insane." This began to sound like a scene from one of his garish nightmares. "Gisela despises the SSD."

"But, of course, you've only known her less than, let's see . . . about two weeks altogether. Isn't that right?"

"Yes, but Hilde has known her mother for sixteen years, Hester."

"McKinnon, please. How would a child know whether or not her mother had a secret job?"

"Hilde would. She's very perceptive." He was grappling with mist. This was unreal, absurd. "You talked to Hilde yourself."

"It hardly occurred to me to ask whether her mother was a spy."

"How big a story is this?"

"It's taking a lot of space on the wires. Wait, the copy boy just handed me a new lead out of New York." In the background Mike could hear the ticking of teleprinters like dozens of tiny drills. McKinnon rattled a paper. "I'll read you some of it. Quote. 'Gisela Steinbrecher, the imprisoned East German sweetheart of an American elevator executive, was denounced by officials of both East and West today as a spy for the other camp.' Paragraph. 'In Moscow Soviet Leader Nikolai Varentsov publicly branded her a spy for West Germany. In Washington reliable intelligence sources, according to five leading newspapers, called her a longtime secret agent of the SSD, East Germany's security arm.' Paragraph. 'At Harvard University Pierre Armentiers, a leading scholar of East European affairs, said after reviewing the allegations from both capitals that Frau Steinbrecher, a Dresden editor of technical publications, might well be a "mole" or double agent.' . . . Those are the highlights. It goes on."

"Oh, God!" Mike felt huge, unknown forces at work, and he sensed at once probable damage to his cause. How to cope? "The whole thing is fantastic, beyond comprehension."

346

"However," said McKinnon in her blunt way, "you don't have any proof that she isn't an agent, do you?"

"No, but how could anyone . . . Could you prove you're not a spy for the Soviets?" He knew the rejoinder lacked persuasive muscle. "Anybody can make loose charges of espionage."

Hester McKinnon turned out to be the advance scout of forces that came swarming over the telephone lines like an invading horde. Ringing of the phone in the shadowy, old kitchen added its discord to the hissing of the leaky radiator and the sporadic banging of the water pipes. No sooner did Mike put down the phone from one media call than the bell rang for another. Newsmen and women phoned from television networks, newspapers, press agencies, TV and radio stations all over Europe and North America, and from as far away as Johannesburg, Hong Kong, and Buenos Aires. In late afternoon Mike managed to squeeze in a call to Hilde at the Kassel apartment. Furious at the allegations, Hilde came over, handled many of the interviews herself in a voice brimming with indignation, then busied herself making coffee and sandwiches when not on the phone.

As evening wore into night and some of the journalists called back for a second time, Mike began to realize that the testaments of Hilde and himself, however sincere and embattled, counted for little beside those emanating from the power citadels of Moscow and Washington. Trained though they were to treat official sources with skepticism, newsmen nevertheless assumed that somebody in authority had the facts while Mike and Hilde possessed little more than clues to the secret life of Gisela Steinbrecher. Most reporters believed that the truth lay in Washington. A few credited Moscow. Some bought the double-agent theory of Professor Armentiers. But almost no one, Mike decided at last, believed with himself and Hilde that Gisela had no espionage ties whatsoever. A reporter for the London *Daily*

Telegraph expressed the prevailing media mood when he told Mike: "You know the old saying. 'Where there's smoke . . .'"

The news fraternity wanted the proof of innocence—dates, times, places, scenes, character references—that neither Mike nor Hilde could provide. Whatever arguments they might marshal in Gisela's behalf were dismissed as the expected defenses of a lover and a loyal daughter. And as the hours rolled by, Mike came to realize that his revelation two days earlier of the perfidy of the Dahlem trio had been ill-timed, to say the least. Dahlem's link to the SSD only served to confuse a picture already laced with suspicions that a ruthless woman had smashed a family, duped a husband, cast aside her caring daughter, deceived her lover, engaged in the ignoble trade of espionage and then, as an ugly mole, betrayed both her employers with never a care for their opposing philosophies.

Mike and Hilde talked it over during a lull in the night's calls. They sat at the wooden table in the kitchen sipping coffee and eating honey-and-almond cakes. Hilde had become a fond companion. Week by week she matured with less of the brooding and giggles of adolescence and more of her mother's outer grace and inner strength.

"This makes it awfully rough for our job of getting your mother out," said Mike. "The press has made up its mind that Gisela is somebody's secret agent, just whose they're not sure."

"They're horrible. I think they don't believe a word I say, but just write it down to pad their stories."

"They've judged Gisela guilty until proven innocent and there's no way we can prove she's innocent."

"I know it." She scowled. "It's so unfair, Mr. Mike. They pay attention to the men in power and none to ordinary people like us. It's no different than at home."

"Life's unfair, Hilde."

"But it doesn't have to be." The resolute set of her chin reminded Mike of Gisela. Having risked her life to gain the sunny side, Hilde would tolerate no hovering shadows. "We have a right to demand justice."

Later Mike confessed that he had doubts when he first met her mother, but that Gisela's behavior and character purged his mind of suspicions. Hilde, in turn, admitted that she sometimes had wondered whether either her mother or father belonged to the SSD's three-layered organization among the people: the secret main informers, secret informers, and secret collaborators.

"It was only natural to wonder," she said, "since people we knew sometimes got turned in by neighbors. Once we found out that the mother of one of the girls in our group was a secret informer, so I began watching my parents.

"Of course, after Mother and I told each other that we wanted to leave—that was a terrific night—I loved her madly and she became my best friend. After that, the idea of her being any kind of informer was plain silly. As for Father, I decided very early that it was out of the question. He's not the type."

Why Karl Steinbrecher was not of the cut of secret agents, Hilde did not say and Mike did not inquire. Although she had once alluded in derogatory fashion to her father's rigid party stance, Hilde now spoke of her father only obliquely and never critically. He occupied a private place in her life where no others had yet been welcomed.

"I know deep inside me that Mother is her own woman and nobody's agent." Hilde looked toward the small kitchen window where a night wind rattled the pane. "But I can't prove to anyone how I know that."

"I understand." Mike felt at one with the girl. "It's a knowledge made up of a thousand nuances of behavior that we could never identify. We just know it."

Near midnight Mike took Hilde back to the Kassels' in a

cab after a final maddening call from an Italian television
newsman who accused them of misrepresenting the character of Gisela Steinbrecher and exploiting the media for some
malign, if as yet unknown, purpose. Hilde had flared back
with an obscenity, but now, riding through Berlin's cold,
deserted streets, she and Mike were weary and dispirited.
Yesterday's darlings of the press had become today's ma-
nipulators. They had fought for weeks only to be undone by
distant forces they did not comprehend. The prospect of
Gisela's release, which at noonday appeared so brightly
promising, tonight looked shadowed and remote.

A light snow fell as the taxi moved slowly through the
city's icy streets. Signs creaked in the stiff wind from the
north. A midnight hush stilled Berlin's normal clamor.
Mike knew that phantoms as cold as corpses lurked somewhere in the wintry night, ready to shred his dreams and
ravage his sleep. The snowfall lay clean and white on the
city, a shroud for dying hopes.

For Gisela, the news came like a knife thrust. She heard
the word almost as soon as her daughter and Mike did, and
she knew at once that the allegations from Moscow and
Washington crippled her chances of gaining release from
prison.

Her informant, a paunchy, middle-aged man named Gerhard Zweig, spent his days working as a guard in the gray
stone prison in Rummelsburg on the outskirts of East Berlin and patrolling several corridors of the wing where Gisela
had lived for the five weeks since her sentencing. Zweig, a
trusted, veteran guard with flaxen hair, soft mouth, and a
consuming interest in his few "celebrity" prisoners, passed
Gisela's cell every fifteen minutes. Avid for news, music,
and talk shows on his small, portable radio, he often tuned
to RIAS in West Berlin. As soon as the Simmons-
Steinbrecher ruptured love affair became a daily news tar-

get, Zweig began a practice of relaying to Gisela the news items about herself, daughter, and lover.

He did so because it titillated him to chat with a woman who'd become famous throughout the world, but also because Zweig belonged to that vast clan of people who delight in being the first to know. For lonely, isolated inmates of the old prison, Gerhard Zweig was their private postman, town crier, village gossip, and daily newspaper.

On this particular afternoon Zweig leaned against the narrow grilled door of Gisela's cell and called to her.

"I have news for you, Frau Steinbrecher," he said in a low, conspiratorial voice when she stood facing him through the bars. "You're being called a spy in Washington and in Moscow. Some people claim you're a double agent, working for both sides. I heard it on the radio."

"Not so fast, Herr Zweig." Gisela's life no longer encompassed sudden change. Everything had slowed, become muted, lost pace and color. "Tell me what happened, bitte."

Delighted to oblige, the guard rushed through the news, sketching the Russian claim that she spied for West Germany and the American charge that her spying was done for East Germany.

"That's frightful news, Herr Zweig." She could feel the knife twist deep inside her. "But I thank you. If you can, please let me know any other developments." Did this mean that now the dreary years would stretch interminably, hopelessly?

"It will be my pleasure." He continued on his rounds, his footsteps echoing in the empty corridor and his keys jangling at his belt.

Gisela returned to the cell's single chair, a straight-backed wooden chair without arms, and slowly seated herself like a series of heavy weights being lowered into place. While she had trained herself to avoid flights of hope and spells of sinking desperation, this latest news depressed her. She could not help herself. The image of herself as a spy, an image that in other times might have brought a merry, jesting response, today evoked only bitter frustration. As untrue and as cruelly unfair as the allegations were, Gisela could nevertheless understand why the public of both East and West might believe them. Overnight she had become a celebrated idol, and she had observed that sooner or later people smashed the idols that their own imaginations created. Gisela could no more blame people who would now reject her than she could blame Ulli Beitz for beckoning her into the arms of the Stasi kidnappers. At first she hated her best friend for allowing herself to be pressed into a role of traitor, but as the long prison days and nights faded into one another, she realized that Ulli had acted from an instinct for survival and that had their places been reversed, Gisela too might have betrayed her friend.

Now she consciously tried to regain the equilibrium for which she strove. Sitting on the hard chair with her hands folded in the lap of her gray prison smock, she looked about the room where she had spent thirty-seven days since that miserable hour when the judge with the double chin and the greasy forehead had pronounced her a turncoat and adulteress who tutored her daughter in crime and violated the borders of her country. The cell was small but not cramped. She could walk five steps on a side. The four walls, painted a heavy, institutional green, had only two openings—the narrow, barred door and one small window, high on the outside wall and much like the one that Miguel had described from his night at SSD headquarters. The window had not been washed in weeks and through it Gisela could barely distinguish sunny days from cloudy ones. But the window remained closed against the winter cold. Gisela had no complaint about the temperature.

The cell had a toilet, a washstand, a cot with serviceable mattress, sheets, and blanket, the chair, and a small wooden stand for her hairbrush, toothpaste, and other personal articles. The muddy green walls had no pictures, calendars, or hangings of any kind. The concrete floor, also painted green, sloped down to a center drain.

Prison rules permitted inmates to borrow one book at a time from the library and the small stand held Gisela's current choice: *The Sorrows of Young Werther*, Goethe's eighteenth-century novel on which a contemporary East German play, one of Hilde's favorites, was based.

If prison life proved less harsh than Gisela had expected, the dreariness surpassed anything she had imagined. For a woman who cherished elegance, the theater, music, and an active social life, it was somewhat like living on the edge of a malodorous urban dump or perhaps in the long, dank tunnels that carry wires and sewer pipes beneath the streets of a great city. At first she thought the noise would drive her mad. Steel doors clanged, commands, groans, and curses echoed in the drafty corridors like people shouting into a tin box, steampipes rattled, keys jangled, feet tramped, the kitchen and dining hall sounded like boiler rooms, and prison workshops added the clatter of machinery. After several weeks Gisela learned to tune out the din from her conscious mind, but the noise drummed subterraneously, sapping her energy like a chronic toothache or a petulant husband.

The lack of color dismayed her. Nothing was bright, cheerful, or inviting. The corridors, dining hall, kitchen, offices, and visitor center, the only areas she knew, wore the same dull green garb as her cell. The shapeless smocks of the women prisoners were all gray, only a shade off the melancholy uniforms of the guards. For the rest, pipes, tools, fixtures, and kitchenware had the worn, neutral aspect of metal. Gisela felt shorn and deprived as if some disease had damaged her eyesight so that she could distinguish only grays and dull toxic greens. Once a woman at the evening meal opened her fist and showed seatmates a feather. The shred of red plumage, perhaps from a cardinal, caused as much excited comment as might a peacock, with a regal train of many colors, strutting into the drab hall.

In this gray, noisy, lonely world, Gisela found comfort in the steady drip of routine. A self-disciplined woman, reared in the Germanic respect for order, she settled with but brief rebellion into the monotonous cadence of prison life. She awoke at six o'clock to the brutal clanging of the corridor gong, made her spare toilet, marched single file with other female inmates to the dining hall, ate a decent breakfast of hard roll, butter, egg, and coffee and then worked two hours in the brigade charged with washing dishes and cleaning the hall. Although guards discouraged conversation, she managed a few exchanges with her coworkers. Then back to her cell until ten-thirty when she joined a hundred or so other women in the prison yard for walking or running. The walls, surmounted by watchtowers, reached so high that Gisela could see only the sky and the corner of a roof some distance away. The bare yard looked especially stark in winter with the temperatures consistently below freezing. Snow had been shoveled into crusted piles that grew filthier as one cold day followed another. Back to her cell until noon; then the midday meal, adequate if usually tasteless; two hours on the cleaning brigade; the afternoon in her cell; twilight cell inspection; the evening meal, always starring potatoes in one role or another; two more hours of dishwashing and scrubbing; reading in her cell; lights out promptly at ten o'clock. Twice a week she showered in the steamroom in company of three other women under the eyes of a prurient matron.

To this cheerless regimen, Gisela added her own disciplines. Each morning as she awoke, she mentally deducted another day from the thousands she must serve. Returning from morning work, she spent two hours in meditation and yoga, guiding herself by directions she remembered from the West German television series. She had become quite supple and already could assume the Lotus position with ease and touch her forehead to the cement floor while in a sitting posture. She took to meditation like an infant to mother's milk. In seeking to empty her mind, she blanked out that ceaseless chatter which channeled so much psychic energy into a carousel of futility. Gisela's internal jailhouse chatter went round and round those questions that had no answers: Would she be released? When? Would the publicity commotion stirred up by Mike and Hilde accomplish anything? Did Mike love her still? Hilde? Had Ulli Beitz been harmed? Who set her up for the kidnapping? What news would Zweig bring today? What, which, when, drip, drip, dot, dash, in, out, poor me, bastard them, lieber Gott, pain, hurt, Mike, Hilde, Karl, when, if, but, whiz, whir, up, down. Magically, after several weeks of practice, she managed to shut off this pointless dialogue with herself and coast into a mental nook where serenity dwelled. True, the old chatter-natter often intruded, but as the days went by and her meditative skills improved, she experienced long spells of sweet tranquillity and could even envision a distant future when she might savor the bliss of the Buddhas. Of great importance to her mental health in this forbidding environment, the serenity of meditation began to seep through her prison routine, making it easier to put up with the clamor and drabness, the insensitivity of the guards, the stabs of panic, the brooding loneliness, and the long, bleak chain of hours stretching two decades into the future.

"You're a remarkably calm woman," said the indifferent, pallid psychologist and "counselor" whom she saw twice a month for half an hour. "I don't know any other female prisoner quite so self-controlled."

"Oh no, not control, Herr Fiedler, just the opposite. One attains peace by letting go of all controls."

"If you let go completely, you'd be a raving maniac," he said with his anemic smile. He was a man who had surrendered long ago to a system that frowned on the tranquil, interior disciplines of the Orient.

"No, I would drift on a cloud of bliss. You do not understand."

"Obviously not."

The counselor's job supposedly involved helping prisoners with medical, psychological, and administrative problems, but Gisela quickly discovered that his prime task was to persuade her to confess her guilt, indict her coconspirators, and embrace the patent wisdom and humanity of the East German Communist system. At their first meeting he hinted that those who signed statements of repentance could cut their prison terms. When she expressed skepticism, he showed up next time with names of a dozen people convicted of political crimes who had achieved reduced sentences after purging their sins in writing.

"No, thank you, Herr Fiedler. I committed no crime." The meditation was having its soothing effect. "So I have nothing to repent."

"If you change your mind, I'm always available." He arranged his papers, tapped them on the table, squared the corners, then asked: "Would you like to see your husband?"

The question startled her. She had been told she could have no visitors for a year. "I . . ." She faltered, thought of Karl and knew a meeting would be painful. "Yes, thank you, if it can be arranged."

Karl Steinbrecher came the next week, still big, stolid, reliable, and wearing a hip-length woolen coat, gloves, and fur hat. When he took off his outer garments and sat facing her through the screen that separated visitors from inmates, she saw vestiges of the man she had fallen in love with twenty years earlier—the black, curly hair, the cool gray-green eyes, a certain tenderness about the mouth that had once made her weep. Just looking at him evoked the pain of vanished dreams, a pang of nostalgia for the youthful good times. She felt if not love, then a reflection of love's old contours. She might indeed be facing a fond brother unseen for years.

She asked after his health, his work, his stamp collection. He asked about her health, her last time with Hilde, how she fared in prison. Did she know that the "American elevator man" had made her world famous? Yes, she had picked up bits and pieces of the news.

"While I don't like the notoriety," she said, "I understand what he and Hilde are trying to do. My only chance of getting out of here is through pressure from other countries."

Karl gazed at her with those opaque gray-green eyes that had once seemed so mysterious. "No, Gisela, that's not your only chance. Many prisoners have cut their sentences by acknowledging their crime and promising to reform."

"But I didn't commit any crime."

"You broke the law against border crossing."

"That's no crime, Karl." How long had he been a stranger? "The state has no moral right to prevent me from going where I please. And I say that as a good Socialist."

"I disagree, of course. The Wall has enabled us to build a real nation."

"Oh, Karl, please. Let's not go over that tired ground. We said it all ten years ago."

He looked hurt and the expression triggered her old ambivalence. She wanted to mother him and yet resented him for bringing out the mother in her. It occurred to Gisela that not once had she felt motherly toward Miguel, not even that time when he confided his childhood trauma over walled imprisonment and his continuing nightmares. Love, affection, lust, a desire to comfort, friendship, passion, yes. But mother? No.

"I can never understand your desire to leave nor how you

could persuade Hilde, still a child actually, to go with you."

"Karl!" She flared. "I did not try to persuade or influence Hilde in any way. We decided together after that trip to Russia, a kind of spontaneous mutual combustion."

"I'm willing to forgive." He spoke patiently as if indeed he had not heard her. "I love you, Gisela, and I want you back. You could more than cut your years here in half, I'm told, if you'd just sign a statement admitting your crime and promising not to do it again."

Forgive her! . . . Love? Remote, closed-off, shuttered Karl? True, he had always been honorable, reliable, and generous, his measure of the loving husband. And at Christmas, he had been a dear. Politics aside, quite easy and comfortable, Karl.

"I'm sorry, Karl, but I could never go back to Dresden. I have every hope that I'll get out of here someday before too many years pass." Untrue, she told herself. She had no great hopes. "And when I do, I must make a new life."

"I'll be in Dresden if you change your mind," he said quietly. "I'm moving to a smaller apartment next month. The housing office says that without you and Hilde, I don't need all that room."

"Poor Karl. I've caused you so much trouble." She sighed. "If only you understood."

"I think I do."

But he didn't, she knew, any more than she understood the passivity and willingness to conform that made Karl Steinbrecher an uncritical servant of the state, a man who asked of authority only that it never cast its shadow over his physics or his philately. When they parted, she felt a tug of regret, a pining for old, lost love. But they had, she sensed, seen each other for the last time.

And so the days passed, busy days despite the unfailing routine. Through meditation and yoga she found facets of herself never before glimpsed. This voyage of self-discovery

sailed on seas of private peace with occasional little squalls
of excitement. In the third week, she made a friend. Saucy,
irreverent, brown-haired, Anna Mach was also under
lengthy sentence for attempted border crossing without permission. Anna tried to escape at night with two East Berlin
printers who threw a grappling hook over the Wall and
made a line fast to a pipe inside the building where they
worked. Wearing heavy work gloves, the two men went
first, swinging hand over hand down the taut rope. When she
tried to follow them to freedom, Anna lost her grip and fell
some twenty feet to the ground, fracturing an ankle. The
Grepos seized her as she dragged herself away from the
mine field past slanted antivehicle slabs.

Gisela found herself on the same dishwashing detail with
Anna and warmed at once to her bouncy, playful ways, her
irrepressible gusto and her bawdy raillery aimed at the
guards, matrons, and other symbols of authority. Anna refused to be glum merely because she was incarcerated. The
morning she and Gisela met, Anna convulsed her prison
mates by imitating the fat matron who supervised the
kitchen cleanup squad. She waddled about like the woman,
planting her feet in the same plodding fashion, and heaving
her shoulders like a ship at sea.

Gisela and Anna swapped vital statistics in fits and starts
as they bent over a tub or worked together stacking soup
bowls. Anna was twenty-five, formerly a waitress at the
swank Hotel Metropol for tourists in East Berlin, unmarried, twice aborted, a foe of all governments. She and
Gisela began working together, eating side by side, and
walking and running together during exercises in the yard.
At the end of the first week, Anna casually offered herself
as Gisela's lover, an offer of only symbolic value since the
prison afforded no place or time for two women to be together in private. Gisela laughed off the suggestion, but that
night alone on her cot, she felt the first stirring of sexuality

since that glorious burst with Miguel in West Berlin, now as distant as far galaxies. She made love to herself, fantasizing the while of Miguel and their wide bed at the Alsterhof.

She came to enjoy her occasional self-loving after the guards extinguished the lights for the night. When she confided her secret to her friend, Anna welcomed her to the club of "fuck yourselfers," teased her, and relayed several ribald jokes from the prison's great storehouse of obscene humor.

Then, as suddenly as she had appeared, Anna was no more. Guards said she'd been transferred to another wing, but rumor among inmates had Anna shifted to a prison in the north. Gisela missed her sorely, grieved as though she had died. For several days she could not meditate. Images of her frolicking friend kept intruding, images that both warmed and tortured her.

Slowly she settled back into the groove of inner discipline, meditation, yoga, reading, and exercise. She also resumed her former practice of praying. Although a Lutheran like a majority of her countrymen, Gisela in recent years had been only an intermittent churchgoer. Now she prayed daily. She also sensed that if she were to make this lengthy journey inside these gray walls without losing her sanity, she must avoid the emotional extremes. No peaks, no valleys, just day-by-day living in the psychic lowlands. She planned many intellectual projects, reading the complete works of Goethe and Shakespeare, both available in the prison library, working chemical equations in her head, writing poetry, learning about cosmology from texts in the library. Perhaps eventually she might win a transfer from the kitchen detail to the library. But basically, she knew, her salvation lay within herself, in the honing of mental discipline, deepening meditation, questing into the vast unknown reaches of the spirit, banishing self-pity, searching quietly for serenity.

And so the morning after Gerhard Zweig, the gossipy guard, informed her that both Washington and Moscow advertised her as a spy, Gisela awoke without anger and without the previous day's mood of dismayed frustration. What would be, would be. She stretched, long and slowly, studied a crack that zigzagged down the dingy green wall like a graph of her escape hopes, yawned, and deducted another day from her sentence.

Thirty-eight gone; 7,267 more to go.

19

On a blustery night in early March, two months after the kidnapping on Augsburger Strasse, Mike Simmons reached a reluctant but firm decision. Or more accurately, certain feelings, hunches, and intimations coalesced in a pattern he recognized. When the pattern surfaced as a decision, he was sitting at the scarred kitchen table in the old apartment in West Berlin, staring out of the small window that quivered under winds gusting down from the north. Europe's harshest winter in years still held the continent in its grip.

He could do no more. He had lost. They had lost—he, Gisela, and Hilde.

The publicity campaign he had lashed together to force the East German government to free Gisela had broken down, sputtered, and died, destroyed by those still curiously errant missiles from Moscow and Washington. Just what had happened, he might never know. Since the blasts from the superpowers, those reckless behemoths of global intrigue and mendacity, very little had been said officially. True, East Berlin did deny that Gisela Steinbrecher was an East German spy as "intelligence sources" in Washington alleged. True, Bonn denied that she served as a secret agent for West Germany as Nikolai Varentsov charged in Moscow. For the rest, there were only media speculation and uninformed surmises by minor functionaries. After a week of guesswork that included everything from the double-agent supposition to a London commentator's opinion that Michael Simmons, not Gisela Steinbrecher, was the real artisan of espionage, the whole affair dropped out of the news.

Now it had been many days since any reporter had called the Berlin apartment. The fiery Michael-Gisela Wall-ruptured romance, which had captured the hearts of millions, lived on in the media only in dusty newspaper morgues and network film clips. Editors and anchormen lost interest. The affair was tainted. Just as murder casts suspicion on the family of the victim, so Mike and Hilde were judged culpable because of the accusations fired at Gisela. In general, world opinion divided into three broad streams. One: Gisela Steinbrecher was mixed up in some kind of messy spy business and had gulled both Mike and Hilde. Two: Mike and Hilde were accomplices of the lady spy. Three: Mike and Hilde were the loyal lover and daughter putting up the best front possible for a woman they knew to be guilty of selling her soul to a faceless espionage machine or perhaps a pair of them. Many executives and workers in the volatile news industry felt used by the Steinbrecher women, and several editorials complained testily that Mike had exploited the media to make himself into an important personage.

Then the former duke of the German escape merchants further roiled the waters of suspicion by turning up in Paraguay and claiming that Michael Simmons had been on his Fluchthelfer payroll. A West Berlin prosecutor, ignoring that charge, said that if Wolfgang Dahlem, Ingrid Watzmann, and Hans Orff returned to West German soil, they would be arrested and tried as traitors. Dahlem retorted from Asunción that they would not come back because "the supposed American elevator executive had framed" the trio in the world press, thus obviating the chances of a fair trial.

Todd Elevator, Inc., washed its hands of the whole business. The company announced that it had fired Simmons "the moment" it learned of his "outside pursuits," and it left the clear implication that he was in the secret employ of some government or other. Mike might have retorted that the company offered him a year's salary if he would leave Todd Elevator out of his talks with the press. But he said nothing. He had no leverage left. Indeed he doubted that any wire service would bother to carry a report of the bribe offer.

Sally and Dave Simmons both called several times from the United States to offer moral support to their father. Dave thanked him for not drawing the 11th Armored Cavalry into the controversy and encouraged his father to continue the fight. Sally, on the other hand, sounded confused. She clearly wanted to comfort her father, yet she had heard so many conflicting reports that she did not know what to think.

It was not as if he had given up without a fight, Mike told himself. He had tried any number of new angles after those maverick bombs from Washington and Moscow destroyed his amateur publicity campaign. He called the American embassy in East Berlin and as a long shot implored it to intercede on Gisela's behalf despite the charges from Washington. A political officer promised to restudy the case, but a half dozen follow-up calls found him unavailable. Hilde wrote a pleading letter to Chairman Volpe, another to her father, a third to the head of the Technical University in Dresden. Mike flew to Frankfurt and prevailed on Werner Lanz to contact some of his old SED friends who had influence in high echelons. Mike indeed tried anything that came to mind.

One night very late he suddenly remembered Delaney's

friend, Rudolf Lerchbacher, the banker who had floated loans to East Germany. Although awakened from a deep sleep, Delaney swore only perfunctorily when Mike called and he promised to contact the Deutsche Bank official first thing in the morning. Later Delaney reported back to Mike that Lerchbacher had obliged by calling the East German minister of finance and applying what pressure he could.

"But frankly, Mike, Rudi's not at all hopeful," said Delaney. "The finance minister knows the West will continue to extend credit whatever happens to Frau Steinbrecher. No credit, no trade, but both sides want the trade."

"I appreciate your help, Walt, especially in view of the company's attitude toward me back in New York."

"Fuck the company. If I could spring Gisela with my bare hands, I'd do it."

So, in the end, nothing had worked. Day after day passed without word of any kind from East Germany. Gisela Steinbrecher might have been entombed centuries ago for all the official reaction that Mike's efforts stirred.

Now, weighing all factors, Mike concluded this bitter March night that he could do no more for Gisela, his love forlorn. Once he had accommodated himself to that bleak fact, he called Hilde at the Kassel apartment to tell her.

"I understand, Mr. Mike," she said when he finished. "I guess I agree. Trying to do anything else, at least this year, would be a waste of time and energy. So, now? Will you stay here?"

"No. This isn't my town, Hilde. I've been away from home six months now. My money will run out soon. Time I get back to the States and rustle up a new job."

"Don't forget that Mother and I owe you about forty thousand marks—well, twenty-six thousand with what you got back from that crook Dahlem. When I get out of school, I intend to pay it all back."

"I didn't lend that money, Hilde. I gave it." He was

touched. "I don't want you to start your adult life weighed down by a debt."

"Oh, I'll pay." She made it sound as easy as returning a borrowed stepladder. "When do you think you'll go to America?"

"Next Monday. That'll give me time to clear up things here." But the scant "clearing up," he knew, could be done in a day. Was it perhaps that he could not bring himself to leave so hastily the same partitioned city where Gisela survived on hope alone? He felt a sudden ache for her, could picture her ducking her head in a shy overture to love, recalled how she lay like a child, nestled under Ulli's Federbett in the Leipzig apartment, her corn-colored hair flung over the pillow. Where was she at this moment and what was she thinking? Though suddenly manifested, the ache had deep, painful roots.

"I'll miss you, Mr. Mike," said Hilde. "A lot."

"I wish you'd come with me, Hilde." A touch somehow of Gisela. In time the pain might fade. "I think you'd like America."

"No, I've had enough change for one year. I'm beginning to feel at home here now. But I'd love to visit New York during vacation."

"Sold. We'll put it on the calendar. . . . And, Hilde, even if we failed, we did our best."

"But, Mr. Mike, we didn't fail completely." Her voice took a quick lift. "I'm here for good, after all, and we did a lot for Dr. Kleist. I'll bet he gets out sometime."

"Yeah. It looks like the DDR will fold under the pressure. Sooner or later they'll have to cough him up. . . . Okay, see you Wednesday night at the Roma."

"So, you see, we can beat the Wall—and more than once."

Hilde was right, of course. In his absorption with Gisela, Mike tended to forget the ever-growing movement in the non-Communist world to force East Germany to terminate the house arrest of Otto Kleist and permit him to travel to the West. A dozen organizations led by Amnesty International and the International League for Human Rights had rallied supporters in more than a hundred countries. Scientists, academics, professional and artistic people made up the vanguard, but politicians, children, and save-the-earth groups also took part. The media paid modest but continuing attention, presenting Kleist as "clean," with no suspect undercover connections despite his former academic dealings with the dubious Gisela Steinbrecher. But what persuaded many foreign-policy experts that the campaign might succeed eventually was the agitation on Kleist's behalf in Third World countries which East Germany courted so lavishly. A conference of foreign ministers of the nonaligned nations, meeting in Sri Lanka on general concerns, passed a resolution urging East Germany to restore "normal travel rights" to Professor Kleist. Significantly, Cuba also backed the drive to free the Dresden scientist, a certain sign that the bearded maximum leader himself wanted his East German friends to play fair with Kleist.

Only yesterday, so Mike had learned from Walt Delaney, a rumor circulated in European business circles that "the two lawyers" had opened negotiations on Kleist. The two lawyers, Joachim Mertz in West Berlin and Max Reschke in the eastern half of the fractured city, provided the channel for exchange of hundreds of East German political prisoners for millions of West German marks. While many moralists and anti-Communists denounced the practice as Communist blackmail and the sale of human flesh, the strange brokerage continued for the simple reason that each German state wanted what the other had.

Affluent West Germany, flush in marks, wanted to obtain the freedom of political prisoners for a variety of reasons: to forge a reputation as a friend of humanity, assuage its guilt from the Nazi years, reunite German families, appease voters, demonstrate the superiority of the Western system and provide a source of hope for those East Germans who loathed the Wall and their government's repressive measures. Aggressive East Germany, well supplied with the political-prisoner commodity but short on foreign exchange, hungered for the Federal Republic's mark, one of the safest and most resilient of the capitalistic currencies.

Month after month the two attorneys phoned each other across the severed city, crossed at transit points for face-to-face meetings, bargained on behalf of their clients, and ended up by swapping one or more live human bodies for large amounts of cash. Mertz and Reschke negotiated quietly, far from press conferences and microphones, and often managed to effect an exchange with only scant publicity. Now and then the person released was so famous that headlines and TV cameras could not be avoided, but hundreds of prisoners had walked to freedom in the West without so much as a paragraph appearing in the press. Actually, neither of the Germanies took pride in this secret dickering and neither boasted of the bargaining power of its lawyer. Both sides granted that the swapping of human flesh for money was a seamy business, a constant reminder to Communists of the subversive lure of hard Western currencies and to capitalists of their powerlessness to free political prisoners by other means.

As for Mike Simmons, now that his decision to return to the United States had been made, he felt a release of tension despite his lingering melancholy. He put on his overcoat and fur hat and trotted down the stairs of the apartment house on his way to the corner Kneipe for a nightcap.

It would be sad to leave this city where he and Gisela had spent such enraptured hours and where, only a few miles away beyond the snow-coated Wall, she lived alone with only her fading hopes for company. Some distant day when the political climate altered, he might return and do battle once more. But for now, and for long months of the future, he must learn to live without her. Decision had cut the tension, but the pain, with its roots deep within him, remained.

20

On a bright, frosty morning, the day after Mike made his decision to return home, his British friend, Malcolm (Spider) Butler, sat in the "savings bank" chancellery in the West German capital of Bonn and wondered just why he had been summoned to this Rhineland city with its deceptive pastoral ambience.

As he sat in the reception room to Kurt Rauschnig's office, all spidery angles and long legs and good humor, he chatted with one of the chancellor's secretaries, practicing his German like a cricket bowler warming up for the big match. They had disposed of the weather (cold but clear), their health (his fine, hers marred by a sniffle), and conditions of employment (they both bemoaned the unpaid overtime they were forced to labor in the service of the state) when the buzzer sounded on her desk and she led him to the chancellor's door.

Kurt Rauschnig advanced from his wide desk with hand extended. A ripple of warmth accompanied him. While proper and often formal, Rauschnig liked people and was unfailingly cordial unless encountering a hostile adversary.

"Ah, the famous Spider Butler," he said in measured

English with a trace of British accent. "How nice to see you again. I won't soon forget your briefing at the border. How lucky you could come on such short notice."

"*Guten Morgen, Herr Bundeskanzler.*" Butler shook hands, then continued in German. "I appreciate your kindness, but let's speak German here. In this office and this capital, German becomes us."

Rauschnig laughed, waved Butler to a chair, and settled behind his desk. Beyond the German leader, the windows showed the snowy lawn sloping down toward the busy Rhine with its streams of barge traffic and bobbing ice floes. The river rarely froze over, even in harsh winters.

"I'm honored to have the ace of the British Frontier Service in this office," Rauschnig began. "I'm grateful that you could leave your duties in Helmstedt with so little advance warning."

Butler grinned. "I know you're busy, sir, so we can dispense with the formalities, much as I like your gracious words."

"May I call you Spider? The name has a ring to it."

"By all means. I'd take offense if you didn't."

"Then to come to the point, Spider, I need your advice and help and I must trust you to hold everything said here in strict confidence. By that, I mean speaking to no one outside this room."

"You have my word. In my business, we're used to security."

"Fine. Last night, some time before my appointments secretary called you, I had a telephoned report from Joachim Mertz in Berlin. You've heard of him?"

Butler nodded. "Many times. The lawyer who negotiates for the release of prisoners over there."

"Exactly." Rauschnig leaned forward on his desk with folded arms. "Several days ago Herr Mertz opened talks with the East German attorney, Max Reschke, on possible release of Otto Kleist, the Dresden chemist and ecologist.'

"A famous man now." Butler picked lint from his blue uniform.

"Late yesterday they reached agreement. Kleist will come across in return for our payment of one hundred twenty thousand marks. High price, but his is an unusual case. Kleist will cross Friday night, no newsmen to be alerted until the next day."

"That's good news." But how did it involve him or the Service?

"Here's the point for you." Rauschnig smiled. "After the two lawyers concluded the deal, Reschke asked our man: 'And how much would you pay for the woman?'"

"Frau Steinbrecher?"

"Right. Of course Reschke would never initiate such an inquiry on his own without orders from Volpe to sound us out. My guess is that Heinrich Volpe is just as anxious as I am to come to our Weimar meeting next week with no irritating minor disputes. We have enough trouble with the big ones."

The chancellor paused, apparently ordering his thoughts.

"One never knows about the men over there. Last year they acted tough: increased daily charges on visitors from here, ugly warnings to their own people in the wake of the Polish labor strikes. Russian pressures, no doubt. Recently, except for the kidnapping, they've been more conciliatory.

"In the case of the Dresden woman, I think Rudolf Lerchbacher of the Deutsche Bank may have had some impact. He told me last night that the DDR finance minister, responding to Lerchbacher's entreaty, had called to tell him that he, the finance minister, had urged Volpe to release Frau Steinbrecher. But as I say, one never knows for sure when dealing with East Berlin."

The chancellor paused again, turning to look out toward

the long, low barges and tankers plowing up and down the Rhine. Butler waited without comment.

"So. Now the ball is in our court. How much will we pay for Frau Steinbrecher? Indeed, will we pay anything at all?" Rauschnig settled back in his swivel chair. "And that's where I need your help, Spider. You're one of a number of people I'm consulting today on the matter. I understand from the press and television that you're well acquainted with this American, Michael Simmons. What can you tell me about him?"

"Mike Simmons is a fine human being. Of course, we're friends. I like and trust the man," said Butler. "If he's an agent for his or any other government, I'd be the most surprised man on earth. In fact, I'd bet my last shilling he isn't." Butler patted his trouser pocket as if ready to wager the contents. "Simmons is a businessman with a certain touch of innocence I often see in Americans, although not in the sense that Varentsov called him an innocent. Michael is all up front, as the Yanks say. He says what he thinks. He's terribly in love with Gisela Steinbrecher. On top of that, he's a jolly good sort." He opened his palms with a shrug. What more could he say?

When Rauschnig remained silent, Butler took another tack. "While it never got in the press, thank God, I was with Mike the night Frau Steinbrecher tried to come across the frontier near Fulda. And I learned . . ."

"I know," the chancellor cut in. "I also know of the participation of Simmons' son, the American Army lieutenant. We're fortunate that aspect never got published." Rauschnig pressed his fingers together and studied them as if for a clue. "And Gisela Steinbrecher. What about her?"

"While I haven't met the woman, I've heard a lot about her from Mike," said Butler. "I don't think she's an agent for anyone. If so, Mike has been badly deceived. He had his suspicions at the start of their affair, but she proved herself to him. Personally, I don't believe a word of that slop out of Moscow and Washington."

Rauschnig's knowing smile appeared to be one of assent. "Varentsov told an outright lie, no doubt to get himself off the hot seat with those Third World news people. Frau Steinbrecher has never been our agent. As for the Washington charges that she's a DDR spy . . ." He shrugged, a mute dismissal of the allegations. "What we here in Bonn know for certain is that our own intelligence people have not a shred of evidence that she's anything but what she claims to be."

"My guess is that those accusations from Washington were a matter of internal politics. Somebody wanted to help President McCullough out of a sticky place."

The chancellor made no comment on his powerful if erratic ally. Instead he led Butler back into a dissection of Michael Simmons' character and more discussion of Gisela. They talked for another half hour, Rauschnig running past a scheduled appointment, before the chancellor rose and escorted Butler to the door.

"I'd like to do something for Simmons and his woman," he said, "but first I must think of the Federal Republic. We'll see."

"You might want to talk to Walter Delaney, a Todd Elevator executive in Berlin," said Butler. "He's known Simmons for a long time and he also knows Hilde and Gisela Steinbrecher."

"I intend to. I already have his name and number from Herr Lerchbacher." Rauschnig put out his hand. "And again thanks for coming and for your help."

"My pleasure, Herr Bundeskanzler. And do visit us again soon in Helmstedt."

On a raw afternoon, two days later, the two lawyers, Joachim Mertz and Max Reschke, sat in Reschke's smoky,

disordered office on Rosa Luxemburg Strasse, not far from
the tall buildings of Alexanderplatz, showpiece of downtown East Berlin, and a few blocks from the television spire
that pierced the wintry overcast.

Smoke hung in lazy layers in Reschke's office for both
men were nicotine addicts, Mertz with his cigars and
Reschke with his cigarettes. Newspapers, file jackets, clippings, and legal notes overflowed the rolltop desk and
shelves and drifted like heavy snow about the cluttered
room. Reschke actually had to shove aside piles of papers to
accommodate his friend Mertz in a chair near Reschke's
desk.

A stranger meeting both men for the first time would
most certainly mistake their political loyalties. Mertz, from
capitalist West Berlin, was lean, harried, had a nervous
cough, and spoke in jerky, unfinished sentences. Reschke,
from Communist East Berlin with its recurrent shortages of
foodstuffs, was broad and heavy, supporting a comfortable
German beer belly. Gorged with good humor, he spoke with
a drawl and thought the whole world somewhat absurd.

The two men had become friends despite their widely
differing loyalties and political creeds. They reveled in the
gamesmanship of negotiation, haggling as stubbornly as
tradesmen at a bazaar. Yet each knew the other had limits
beyond which his client would not permit him to go. They
respected each other and overlooked the other's eccen-
tricities. Mertz brought little consumer goodies across the
Wall for Reschke, but neither man looked upon this gesture
of friendship as a social bribe to soften Reschke for the kill.
Indeed, Reschke often gave his fellow attorney fragrant cigars from Cuba, East Germany's friendly ally in the Communist orbit.

Because of their frequent meetings and regard for each
other, they had evolved their own style of negotiation, a bit
of banter, a touch of sympathy, a dash of good-humored in-

sult, and a shorthand code for bargaining, all wrapped in
the tradition of German formality. Each was an influential
man, esteemed by the government that employed him, and
each honored the status of the other. Where Americans in a
similar situation would be first-naming each other within
hours, Reschke and Mertz had met for years without laps-
ing from formal standards of address.

"As I told you on the phone, Herr Reschke," said Mertz
after they had chatted and smoked awhile, "I have the
green light to go ahead on the woman."

"A pity."

"Why?"

"I'm afraid you made the trip for nothing." The East
Berlin attorney shook his head. "I regret to say, Herr
Mertz, that the signals have changed on this side. While you
were on the way over on the U-Bahn, I had a call from
Comrade . . . You understand? Alas, Counselor, I can no
longer offer you the woman at any price."

"So I've wasted my . . ."

"Only an hour or two. Why not relax, Herr Mertz?"
Reschke held out a box. "Try my cigars this time? The ones
from Cuba that you like so much."

"Thank you." Mertz smelled the cigar, savoring the bou-
quet, then bit off an end. "Too bad about the woman. I
wonder what you would have asked for her, Herr Reschke?"

"We would have needed a hundred thousand marks,
Herr Mertz."

"Absurd." He coughed, punctuating his disdain.

"She's a big fish, Counselor." Reschke fumbled at the
snarl of papers on his desk. "Look, she even got her picture
in *Al Nadwah* in Mecca."

"We would have offered only ten thousand, you know."

"A joke, my esteemed negotiator, not a serious offer."

"That fellow who tried to make it to Denmark in his
homemade submarine . . . You sold him for ten."

"He wasn't a celebrity."

"Are you charging now by the number of TV appearances?"

"If we charged by looks, Steinbrecher would have cost you a fortune."

"Please, Herr Reschke." Mertz feigned a look of pain.

Reschke held out a lighted match for the West Berliner's cigar. "We might have been persuaded to drop to ninety."

"She's not a major general, but we might have gone to fifteen."

"I must remind you. The woman's not for sale, so it's futile to talk price. Tell me, how is Frau Mertz's health?"

"The usual. Another cold. She stays in bed and takes nose drops." Mertz glanced down. "This ashtray's smoldering. One stray spark . . . They'd hold me for arson."

Reschke tamped out the fire with a pencil and dumped the ashes into a waste basket. "Why did the Western press make such a fuss over the Steinbrecher woman for so long?"

"Simple. A drama of Beauty and the Beast."

"Are you implying that someone's client is a beast, Herr Mertz?"

"I imply nothing, Herr Reschke. . . . Look, as long as you lured me over here on false hopes, why don't we arrive at a price for the Beauty anyway? Then your people and mine will have a definite picture in case the climate . . . And, as you well know, the climate always changes."

"True, Herr Mertz. . . . So, as long as we're here, why not, as you say, reach a figure that might guide us to a quick settlement at a later date, if and when . . . subject always, of course, to the wear and tear of inflation."

"Naturally."

"As I said, we might have taken ninety." The East Berlin lawyer looked pleased to slide back into his familiar bargaining role.

"Ninety!" Mertz laughed in mock disgust. He too relished

the colloquy, a verbal dance as stylized as a ballet. "If she's a spy like Varentsov says, why not get rid . . ."

The East Berliner leaned back in his old swivel chair. It squealed like an anguished cat. "Do you know what happened at the border near Kaltennordheim the night the woman failed in her criminal crossing?"

"No, what happened?"

"The son of the American, a lieutenant in the U. S. 11th Armored Cavalry named David Simmons, fired across the frontier at our troops. An outrageous, completely unprovoked attack."

"I never heard . . ."

"No, Counselor, but you will. The U.S.A. armed forces incited and helped the woman in her foolish criminal venture."

"That sounds like a bluff—or perhaps blackmail."

"Have I ever lied to you? That's plain fact about the son. Go back and check with your BND people."

"Never mind, Herr Reschke. I'll take . . ."

"So, the woman is expensive. We would need at least eighty."

"My client might be willing to go to twenty-five—if, of course, you ever let the poor woman go."

"You're not in our range, Herr Mertz. She was guilty of conspiring to murder an innocent civil engineer."

"You mean an armed major in the People's Army. Let's not be loose with the facts. And she didn't conspire to murder. She was at least fifty meters away when Ludendorff was slugged in a fight." Mertz propped his feet on the wastebasket, smoked quietly, and waited.

"Did it ever occur to you what a wonderful stink we'd cause by a double defection?" Reschke stroked his belly. "They'd give you my job, of course, and I suppose the chancellor would give me yours."

"No thanks." Mertz scratched at a sunken cheek. "Not

for the slave wages they . . . Look at this slovenly excuse for an office. Over here, the state is a Communist slumlord."

"They don't feed you enough over there and they work your ass off. Look at you, skin and bones."

"Seriously, Counselor, how can a man of your humanist traits tolerate a police state? The muzzling, the fear, the informing, the ludicrous . . ."

"Seriously, Counselor, how can you tolerate the exploitation? The cruelty, the inhumanity, the hypocrisy."

"Hypocrisy!" The West Berliner snorted. "A man can't even buy a decent sex magazine over here."

"If this side is so gruesome, how come we produce more champion athletes per capita than any other country in the world?"

"You set your own trap there, Herr Reschke. In a word, steroids. Your female swimmers grow goatees and your male runners sprout hair between the toes like . . ."

"Like?"

"Don't heckle me. When are you going to name a sensible price for the woman?"

"All right, out of my personal regard for you. Seventy."

"Thirty."

"Don't you realize why we would need a decent sum for this woman?"

"Tell me."

"Because your Neanderthal politicians slandered my country, that's why. Accusing us of kidnapping her. Ugh. It turns my stomach, such gross slander."

"More stomach than slander. We have a dozen witnesses to . . ."

"Perjury comes cheap over there."

Mertz tapped off the fine ash of his cigar, inhaled again, and blew a great white cloud like an armored truck laying down a smoke screen. "Truly, Herr Reschke, that story's pathetic. Walked back of her own volition, eh! I'll give you a D-mark for every person outside the hammer-and-sickle bloc who believes that nonsense."

"It's a fact, all the same, Herr Mertz. If this had been real bargaining, I would have required seventy, as I said, for the woman. We would have to be recompensed for the émigrée's skills which would be lost to the nation. We are dealing here with an editor with a Ph.D., schooled and trained at great expense to the state."

"Yes, you never fail to bring that up on every case. However, I should point out that this woman's skills are already lost to the state—for twenty years, God help us!"

"But if she were released, your side would profit by the schooling we paid for. So, seventy would be quite reasonable. And why is it always I who deals in reasonable sums?"

"I haven't heard a reasonable figure all . . . I repeat, thirty."

Reschke waved off another billow of smoke and then lit a cigarette himself. "An onlooker, you know, might note that if we split the difference, we'd arrive at fifty."

"Out of the question. I would, however, have gone to thirty-five."

"Forty-five."

"Any conditions, Counselor?"

"My people mentioned none."

"Forty." Mertz held out his hand.

"Done." Reschke shook it. "Forty thousand marks when and if my clients change their minds."

They notarized the hypothetical deal in scribbles of smoke.

"That would have been a 160,000 package with Professor Kleist." The East Berlin attorney sighed.

"Yes, too bad your people decided not to deal for the woman. It would have made a neat, tidy parcel."

"Yes, it would." Reschke looked sad. He folded his hands on his belly, an act of resignation.

"You've forgotten, Herr Reschke. We've struck a deal, even if our clients haven't."

Reschke brightened, swung out of his chair, went to a shelf and took down the bottle of Scotch that Mertz brought across on his last visit. He poured liquor into two shot glasses, a ritual of many years' standing.

"What time did we say for Kleist?" he asked.

"Eleven o'clock, Friday night."

"I regret it's not a package crossing."

"Yes. I wonder what happened with your people?"

"I have no idea." Reschke smiled at his old adversary. "But if I did, I wouldn't tell you."

"You never do." Mertz's seamed faced folded in what passed for a grin.

"Someday, I might, you know." Reschke's eyes had a twinkle. "I just might take pity on you. . . . Prost!"

"Prost!"

The two lawyers clinked glasses and drank.

21

Mike returned from his favorite neighborhood restaurant feeling oddly restless. He had anticipated a full, leisurely meal, but had left half the venison on his plate and had drunk so little of the red wine that his waiter corked the bottle and put it aside for Mike's next visit.

Here it was, Friday night, only three days before his departure for New York and home, and already the loose ends of his long Berlin sojourn had been tied. There remained only the phone calls to friends, people like the Delaneys or Spider Butler over in Helmstedt, and dinner the last night with Hilde.

With no niggling chores left undone, he could settle down with a book, go to a movie, or perhaps the bar across the street. Yet he felt strangely unsettled. He opened the refrigerator, peered about, closed the door again. He picked a scrap of food off the floor. For no reason, he inspected the kitchen trash basket. He raised the small window, peered out at the night. Icy cold, clear skies, a splash of stars, not much wind.

What was bothering him? Perhaps that phone call yesterday from Sue Delaney. Walt, she had said, had received a call from some high official in Bonn, but he refused to discuss the nature of the conversation with her. He'd given his word, said Walt. However, she'd overheard him mentioning Mike's name. Just a hunch, she said, but she thought there might possibly be some development in Mike's, well, situation. Maybe he should not leave the apartment for long periods. Just her intuition, nothing more.

He closed and locked the window, walked to the living room, and sank into the tattered armchair beneath the floor lamp. He leafed through a copy of *Stern*, found an article purporting to give the final word on Gisela Steinbrecher, heroine or spy. The opening paragraphs held a fact that Mike had not known before. The magazine reported that Hilde said her mother could recite the whole periodic table of elements. He read further, became engrossed in the writer's version of the story that Mike knew so well.

The telephone rang, an unnerving sound, perhaps because it rang so seldom these days. He went to the kitchen and lifted the phone.

"Herr Simmons?"

"Yes."

"My name is Joachim Mertz." He spoke unevenly. The words might be flapping on a line. "I don't know if . . ."

"Of course." Mike went on the alert at once. "Everyone knows you."

"Would you be available for a meeting later?"

"Tonight?"

"Yes. If eleven would suit . . ."

"Eleven's fine. Certainly." Hope shot upward. Gisela? "Where, Herr Mertz?" he asked eagerly.

"You know Friedrichstrasse at Kochstrasse?"

"Checkpoint Charlie?" Had someone worked a miracle for Gisela?

"That's it."

"Sure. I've crossed there a number of times."

"Good. This must remain confidential for another fev
hours, you understand, but the DDR is releasing someon
you know. . . ."

"Frau Steinbrecher!" He felt a powerful lift.

"No, no." Mertz coughed, a ragged, nervous clearing c
the throat. "The other side, unfortunately, refuses to let he
go. It is Professor Kleist who is coming across."

"Oh." Mike's disappointment saturated the line.

"I'm calling on you because of your connections wit
Frau Steinbrecher and with the laboratories in the U.S.A
which await Otto Kleist and his data."

"Of course, I'd be glad to help." Mike tried to pum
some vitality into his voice, hiding the deadness within.

"If you could assist me . . . Go with me while I get th
professor settled in the home of a faculty friend at the Fre
University. I understand Kleist speaks English. It shoul
be . . ."

Mike waited in vain for Mertz to finish his thought. "N
problem. I'd like to meet him and help in any way I can.'

"My government will be in your debt, Herr Simmons. So
I'll meet you in front of the Haus Am Checkpoint Charlie
an old building. . . ."

"I know it. At eleven?"

"You should be there a few minutes. . . . Shall we sa
ten-fifty?"

"Sure. Ten-fifty. I'll be there."

"I am undistinguished in appearance, but I'll be wearing
a black overcoat with fur collar and a blue cap."

"Okay."

As he turned away from the phone, Mike somehow felt
cheated. It was as if Joachim Mertz had tricked him into be-
lieving that Gisela had been freed. No, that was unfair.
How could the lawyer foresee that at the mere mention of
the Mertz name, Mike's spirits would spring upward like a
kite in a spring breeze? No, Mike's own hopes and yearnings

had deluded him, planted the swift expectation that his love would flower once more, floating out of some dismal prison to bloom on the sunny side.

But that was not to be and Mike found himself drifting once more into melancholy. It took a force of will, a physical wrenching, to make him part from his own deep disappointment and turn toward the good news of Otto Kleist's coming release. Hilde was right. They had scored, if not total victory, at least a partial triumph. The worldwide campaign to free Professor Kleist, a campaign they had helped originate, had succeeded. Apparently Chairman Volpe was freeing the Dresden chemist to smooth the path to the German summit meeting in Weimar and to prevent further erosion of East Germany's image as a patron of science.

Slowly adjusting to the prospect of meeting the famous professor, Mike set about preparing himself. He found the last two letters from the Geophysical Lab in Princeton, the stack of Amnesty International press releases, and the thick file folder that held several hundred news clippings that he and Hilde amassed. The good professor would surely want some of these.

More than two hours to go. Mike settled into the old, frayed armchair, finished the *Stern* article, and then began perusing the Kleist material. He had neglected to read much about Kleist and now he discovered some interesting sidelights. An Austrian journal told of the man's significant contributions to the petrochemical industry. A London specialist on the atmosphere, assessing Kleist's theory on the accelerating accumulation of carbon dioxide in the upper air, said his own calculations lent support to the Dresden chemist. *Paris Match* gave an account of Kleist's year in the Sachsenhausen concentration camp at the end of the Nazi era, a confinement Mike had not known of before.

Some minutes after ten, he bundled up sample papers and clippings, put on his overcoat, gloves and fur hat, and walked down to the street. He hailed a cab, rode through the center of Berlin out to the drab commercial area near Checkpoint Charlie.

The night seemed to crackle as he stepped from the cab at the intersection of Friedrichstrasse and Kochstrasse. A light snow had fallen in the afternoon and it dusted cars, trees, and shrubs like fine ash. Beneath the film of snow, patches of sidewalk ice had a brittleness underfoot. He accidentally kicked one chunk that skidded down the walk and struck an iron guard railing like a gong. Though moonless, the night was as clear as those in the Far North. Hundreds of minor stars hugged the familiar constellations etching a velvet sky. Buildings like the corner bank and the nearby Springer headquarters stood out in intricate detail as though sculpted from the block of night.

Two corrugated metal huts just this side of the border housed the Allied soldiers who manned this notorious channel between the two worlds just as their predecessors had done for almost four decades. The first narrow shack in the middle of Friedrichstrasse provided quarters for the British and the French. The one closer to the border housed the Americans. On the right side of the street a low, brown structure gave shelter to the West Berlin police unit which rotated duty twenty-four hours a day. Beyond stood an observation platform for tourists who came to see the Wall near the famous passageway.

Overhead flood lamps, burning through the night, lighted the control point like a movie set and stroked the building that held the bright yellow Haus Am Checkpoint Charlie, the first-floor museum that chronicled a whole generation of the Wall's heroes, villains, victims, idiocies, triumphs, and brutal killings. Such celebrated Wall visitors as John F. Kennedy, Willy Brandt, and Nikita Khrushchev were memorialized here. So were ordinary folk like unsung driver Klaus Brüske who, although dying from bullets fired by

East German border guards, smashed through the early Wall with a truckload of refugees or eighteen-year-old Peter Fechter who bled slowly to death for an hour at the foot of the Wall while the East German Grepos who shot him ignored his cries for help.

Tonight, in the downpour of waxy light, a slim man in a black overcoat with fur-trimmed collar paced up and down in front of the museum. He wore a cap and, like Mike, he carried a folder under his arm. Beyond him Mike could see the concrete watchtower, the red-and-white vehicle barriers, and the metal sheds of East Germany's border control, structures that offered an illusion of impermanence despite two generations of guns, separation, mines, wire, walls, and barricades.

"Herr Mertz?" No one else was about.

"Herr Simmons." His breath climbed the night like smoke. Mertz glanced at his wrist watch. "I see you believe in . . ."

Mike nodded. They shook hands.

Since Joachim Mertz continued to pace, Mike pocketed his folder and fell into stride beside him. They walked several minutes in silence, up to the stand of white birches near the dividing line and back again toward the blue glow of the subway station across Kochstrasse. Save for the military men inside the control huts and the West Berlin police at their post, no one was to be seen. The cold bit through Mike's coat. Street ice glinted in the spectral light.

"I assume you've been in contact with the other side, Herr Mertz?"

"Yes, with my counterpart in East Berlin. We reached agreement on Professor Kleist. The Federal Republic is buying his freedom."

"How much?"

"One hundred twenty thousand marks. They gouge us when they . . ."

"Was there any news of Frau Steinbrecher?"

"Yes. At first they hinted they might sell her, too, bu
when I got instructions to bargain for her, Volpe's peopl
backed away." He shrugged. "They are unpredictable, thos
supercomrades."

"Any chance she may be released soon?"

"Oh, I would think not." He coughed nervously. "The
seldom reverse themselves twice. Point of pride, I . . ."

Old packed snow, blackened by a thousand soles
crunched underfoot below the new dusting. Mertz, witl
Mike at his side, circled the American hut. A sergeant in
side grinned at Mertz and flashed a V signal with hi
fingers. The lawyer was well known here.

A German police officer stepped outside his comman
post. "A phone call for you, Herr Mertz." He held the doo
open. "From over there—Herr Reschke."

"Ach." Mertz hurried into the station. Through a windov
of the one-story structure, Mike could see the lawyer picl
up the phone.

Mike continued to walk, his breath misting in the cold
clear night. Ahead of him, on the East Berlin side, raise
red-and-white automobile barriers stretched skyward lik
huge barber poles. The garish light spilled over the broad
gray watchtower where two soldiers looked out from win
dows at the top. One of them was sighting through binocu
lars, apparently at Mike.

Minutes passed. Mike walked as far as the white dividin
line, turned, and tramped back to Kochstrasse. The col
stung his ears. He clapped his gloves, huddled inside hi
coat. The frigid air pierced despite the lack of wind. H
made two full turns, a matter of ten minutes or so, befor
Joachim Mertz came out of the police station.

"False alarm. Kleist is not coming across tonight," h
said. "He has had the flu and he told my counterpart that h
wishes to wait until tomorrow for the crossing."

"Do you believe that?"

"From anyone else over there, I might not. But Herr Reschke, I believe. We never lie to each other."

"Well, I want out of this cold." Mike motioned with his head. "Let's grab one of those cabs on Kochstrasse and hit a nice, warm bar. I'll buy you a drink."

"Another night, perhaps," said Mertz. His sunken cheeks held a sudden broad smile. "Right now you have more important business. The supercomrades have done what I said they wouldn't. They've reversed themselves again. The lady doctor of chemistry from Dresden is being . . ."

"Gisela!" Mike seized Mertz by the arms. "You mean it? When? . . . Tonight?"

"Yes, yes. They finally decided to let her go with Kleist." He was grinning now. "She's going through the controls this minute on the other side with Herr Reschke."

Mike felt the shock like a jolt of electricity. Then came a rush of joy that all but overwhelmed him. The surge became a broad river of exaltation, mingling power and hope and passion. He had a wild urge to laugh, shout, and cry all at once.

"But why? Why?" He was soaring. "What happened to make them change their minds?"

"Thank the good professor," said Mertz. He stamped his feet on the icy sidewalk. "He's a tough old bird with the courage of eagles. In his final interview today with the Stasi, he warned that the minute he crossed the line to this side he would launch his own media campaign to free Gisela."

"Bless him. . . . But why didn't they just put him back under house arrest and keep 'em both?"

"They couldn't. I paid over the 120,000 marks this morning. Reschke and I have an iron-clad agreement. Once the money passes, no changes can be made by either side."

"Thank God for Otto Kleist. Anything the man wants, he can have from me."

"All this is confidential, you understand, but you should know. Herr Reschke hinted the matter went up to Volpe today for decision. Realizing the storm that a scientist of Kleist's caliber could kick up around the world, Volpe ordered them to let Frau Steinbrecher go." Mertz consulted his watch. "She's due to cross in just three . . ."

Mike broke away from the lawyer. Ignoring the slippery ice, he ran toward the white line that separated the two Berlins at this narrow aperture in the Wall. Just to the right of the birch trees stood the ten-foot-high observation platform. Mike raced up the steps, leaned over the railing, and peered toward the DDR border compound. He focused his sight on the iron gate, last exit from East German controls, through which he had passed several times.

He caught his breath. Was that she? In the distance, just beyond the gate, shadowed from the carnival glare of the floodlights, stood three figures—a civilian, it seemed, flanked by two officers in field gray uniforms. The military men moved aside and the third person stepped forward. A pause. Silence. Then the gate creaked open.

Yes, yes. It was Gisela. She walked out. The gate clanged behind her like a gunshot.

Here she came. In the bizarre, ivory light, she wore a flared felt hat with jaunty feather and tailored brown coat, the same outfit in which she had been kidnapped. Mike brushed at his eyes. Tears had welled up, feeling oddly warm in the night's snapping cold.

She came alone. She walked proudly with a defiant swing, head high, not a backward glance. Lady Stone Breaker, poised, resolute. Oh, dear God.

"Gisela!" He shouted it from the platform.

She looked up. "Miguel!" She began to run, slipped,

regained her footing, and hurried forward. He rushed down the steps and ran toward the white line.

They met on West Berlin terrain beside the clump of four birches, coming together just a few feet inside the line. They held each other tightly. She murmured something after a strangled little cry. He found her lips. She kissed him longingly. They stood quietly, head beside head, luxuriating in the warm presence of a lost lover newly found.

"Hilde?" she whispered.

"She's fine. We'll see her soon."

"Ahmm." Lawyer Mertz cleared his throat. "There will be some papers to . . ."

They separated and Mike introduced Gisela to the attorney. Mike adored the sparkle in her eyes. He had presumed a prison pallor, but no, the cold had put roses in her cheeks. He recalled her blush that first night at the Astoria in Leipzig.

"Welcome to the sunny side once more." Mertz handed her the folder. "Please fill these out at your leisure. This time you must be processed in the regular manner. You're expensive cargo, you know." He smiled thinly. "Last time . . ."

"How much was paid for me?"

"We haven't paid yet, but we will. Forty thousand marks."

"Forty!" She beamed at Mike and her eyes glistened. "So, mi amor, you see how valuable I am?"

"The word is priceless." And the love that he had suppressed recently in the interest of survival came surging up in a great, rich flood.

Mertz told her briefly of Kleist's stand with the Stasi, of his vow to free her. The scientist, he said, would cross tomorrow if his flu had fully subsided.

"Dear, dear Otto," she said. "How much I owe him.

Miguel, we must have a great feast of celebration with Otto and Hilde!"

Mertz escorted them toward the intersection. Allied soldiers and Berlin police inside their control huts waved as they walked past. Two taxis waited on the otherwise deserted Kochstrasse. The lawyer motioned them to the first in line, but Gisela demurred.

"You take it, Herr Mertz. There is something I must do."

Hooking her arm in Mike's, she walked back through the Allied control area and guided him to the observation platform. They mounted the steps and stood by the railing, gazing down at the grotesque plumage of her homeland. Save for the narrow passage of Friedrichstrasse, the Wall stood on either side. Actually the barrier here was a double wall, one about fifteen yards in front of the other. Between lay the lethal paraphernalia to thwart escape: mines, spikes, barbed wire, slabs.

The main Wall loomed high, gray, smooth, gross, snow-crusted, menacing. They faced it without speaking. From the East German watchtower, the guard surveyed them through binoculars. Mike shivered. The cold was piercing and he wondered about the demons and those other walls that plagued his nights. Would they vanish for good now that he and Gisela had triumphed over the Wall of Berlin?

"That's enough." She tugged at his arm. "I had to see it one last time. Now I must put all that out of my life forever."

Mike took off his glove to hold her chilled hand. Quickly it warmed in his grasp. Hand in hand they left the platform and walked to the waiting taxi.

¿Te acuerdas de mí?

MAYA BANKS

Bryony Morgan se había enamorado del millonario hotelero Rafael de Luca cuando éste la había seducido en sus tierras a orillas del mar. Y de repente Rafael había desaparecido, obligándola a viajar a Nueva York en busca de respuestas.

La amnesia selectiva que Rafael sufría desde el accidente de avión lo tenía perplejo. ¿Cómo había podido olvidar a una belleza tan explosiva como Bryony? La única solución era regresar a la isla donde se habían conocido y revivir las inolvidables noches hasta recordarlo… todo.

¿Nos conocemos?

¡YA EN TU PUNTO DE VENTA!